LOVE IN A PICKLE

GREEN VALLEY LIBRARY BOOK #9

L.B. DUNBAR

WWW.SMARTYPANTSROMANCE.COM

COPYRIGHT

Made in the United States of America

Print Edition
ISBN: 978-1-949202-76-2

Content Edits: Melissa Shank
Editor: Jenny Sims/Editing4Indies
Proofread: Karen Fischer
Proofread: Judy Zweifel
Proofread 2.0: Rebecca Kimmel

DEDICATION

For second chances and foster parents.

*Gratitude to M.E. Carter for her extensive support in helping me with
information about foster care.*
*Any errors in this fictional work about the foster care process or system are
my own, and I apologize in advance.*

CHAPTER 1

ALL BETS ARE OFF . . . AND SO ARE MY CLOTHES.

[Scotia]

March

A heaviness presses over me but not as weighty as my head feels.

Lord have mercy did I drink too much last night.

My brain weighs fifty-million tons, as does my pasty, swollen tongue behind teeth that feel as fuzzy as a cat's tail. I roll said tongue over dry lips, smacking them in my dehydrated state.

You sure were thirsty last night. My stomach roils, and I discover something equally heavy resting over my side, just above my hip. I squirm under the weight, pressing back into something long and thick and protruding into my backside.

"Karl," I mutter. "Get off me."

My hand reaches for the arm over my midsection, the movement taking all my strength until I touch something else long, thick, and slightly coarse and curly. My palm skims the length of a solid forearm, allowing the tight curls of hair to prickle my skin.

Karl? I'm slow to register the silliness of my thoughts. My husband has been dead for nearly seven years.

"Who's Karl?" a rugged, rumbly voice asks, and two things surprise me at once—the depth of the tenor and the unfamiliarity of it. I twist, knocking my shoulder into a brick wall of male chest, not putting a dent in his position but making my clavicle ricochet and my head pound harder.

"Who are you?" I squeak, wondering how in tarnation a man got in my hotel bed.

"You answer me first," he mumbles still sleep-rough and with his eyes closed.

"He's my husband."

I never knew how fast a big-bodied man could move, but the speed with which this man scrambles from behind me is record-breaking. He stands at the end of the king-size bed staring back at me a long moment, eyes blinking until I come into focus to him. The reality of who he is becomes clear to me.

"You have a husband?" he chokes, swiping a hand the size of a dinner plate over thick midnight-colored locks. Despite several swift wipes, his hair refuses to stay in place, and I wonder what it would feel like to run my fingers through those reckless waves.

Silence settles between us. He's waiting on an answer from me.

"*Had.* My husband is dead."

He blinks, eyes dark as rich coffee searching mine. The sympathy in them tightens my chest. "I'm sorry."

"He was murdered." It was a case of mistaken identity. I don't know why I offer this information to a complete stranger, but there it is. My husband, Karl Simmons, was wrongfully killed.

Is there a rightfully killed?

Shaking my head, I dismiss both my crazy question and my sorrowful memory. Karl and I might not have had the best marriage, but we had an understanding. I didn't want to discuss him.

The stranger nods, and I take a second to assess him. Broad shoulders

2

under a tight white tee. Black dress pants minus a belt. A well-trimmed beard that looks as if it would be unruly like his hair within another day.

"You're Chester Chesterfield," I blurt.

The corner of his lip tweaks upward, crooked and sarcastic. "That's right. Thanks for remembering."

How could I forget? Chester Chesterfield was the esteemed guest and keynote speaker at the Tennessee Entrepreneur Conference yesterday evening, where the honor for outstanding female-led small-business owner of the year was awarded. I was a nominee, but I didn't win. *I'm not bitter. Nope. Not at all.*

Chester Chesterfield, however, is a prize in and of himself. Rumored to be a tycoon in petroleum oil— not to be confused with petroleum jelly, the moisturizing kind—he spoke about the benefits and necessity of locally owned small businesses as important to a community and to Tennessee as a whole. Easy for him to say, though, as he's worth millions from a business I can't imagine remains small.

"I'm Scotia Simmons," I tell him as if he might not remember me. Then again, he was in my bed, so I hope he knows my name at least. My eyes travel to his belt region, noting once again the lack of one.

"Did we . . .?" I clutch the bedsheet I'd already been grasping higher up my chest, realizing how very naked I am underneath the soft material. Minus all but my underwear, I'm nearly as bare as the day I was born.

He shakes his head, and relief washes over me. *Thank goodness.*

Then another thought occurs. "Why didn't we?" I mean, he's Chester Chesterfield, known rogue lover at this event.

Last night started when I met up with a few other female entrepreneurs, and the first round of drinks included a discussion on the famous one-night lover.

"Who will be his lucky conquest this year?" One woman snickered.

"Oh, Leslie, you only wish it could be you," another snarked.

"If only he was a repeat offender." The last one sighed, and the other two turned to her wanting details.

My eyes found him sitting quietly by himself at the bar. The large, solitary man gave off a vibe of untouchable but incredibly sad. Not pathetic, just sad. He was dark everywhere—hair, eyes, facial expression—and I was curious. I didn't know if any of the ladies' remarks were true, but somehow, Chester Chesterfield became my mission for the night.

Get laid.

What would uninhibited passion feel like? Would two sweaty bodies combining in raw desire be a fulfilling connection, or would I be disappointed again by a man?

Recalling the stiff length pressed into my backside only moments ago, I should know satisfaction would be guaranteed. I also should have immediately known it was not Karl, not in girth or firmness or enthusiasm. Karl rarely got it up for me. Ironic, considering where he was when his death occurred, but that's neither here nor there for right now.

I'm staring at Chester as all these thoughts race through my head, and I'm waiting on an answer.

"Your art of seduction needs some polishing." His teasing voice is gravel while his body is a boulder.

"Meaning?" I snap, but I wince. My head throbs too much for sass. *My art* is just fine. I work out six days a week. It takes dedication to be this physically fit at almost forty-eight. I wear pretty lacy things under my clothing to empower me. Then again, I can't fully recall how we ended up in this bed after three strong gin and tonics. Perhaps, my verbal finesse faltered somewhere.

"Puking on a man's shoes isn't sexy."

"I didn't." I huff in disbelief while appalled with myself when I realize I did. I recall lots of flirty banter and eye contact in the bar. We made it up the elevator and down the hall to my room. Then that's where I get fuzzy. "Where's my dress?"

Becoming hyperaware of my nakedness under the sheet, I glare back at him as his left brow rises higher and a spark comes to those swirling brown eyes—eyes that drew me to him.

"No," I whisper, awareness slowly dawning on me. *I made a mess on my dress.*

"It's hanging over the rod in the shower."

"You washed out my dress?" I'm surprised at the sweet gesture while biting back my mortification. *I threw up on my own dress!* Well, there's your lack of seduction skills, Scotia.

He shrugs, looking away from me, and I take in his profile. Burly and buff, I want to curl myself around that barrel chest and feel his heartbeat next to mine. I wonder if said chest has hair on it like his arm—prickly, springy, and sexy as . . . *oh my.* Last night, he wore a tuxedo with his hair slicked back. This morning, that tight T-shirt shows off muscles I want to explore, and his hair is wild. My curiosity wonders if more enticing hairs trickle from his belly to below his beltline. I shiver with the thought and the desire to discover him. My eyes stroll his form, returning to the glorious riot on his head. I surmise it can only be contained for so long.

What else is uncontained on him?

"But we didn't . . . you know . . .?" I'd whistle what I mean if I could whistle. Then again, whistling is vulgar behavior.

I think puking on your own dress might surpass a little tweet from wet lips.

What did I say to him last night? I remember we were discussing something but don't recall the subject.

I said, "I beg your pardon."

He said, "You don't need to beg."

Our eyes met, and I sensed his statement went deeper than proper conversation. Did I beg him? Did I tell him how desperately I wanted to rub my body against his? I wouldn't know how to ask for what I wanted any more than I'd know how to beg a man to take me.

Then he asked me to tell him three things. He probably meant tell him three things *about me*, but instead, I said, *"You. Me. A bed."*

It's the boldest thing I've ever done, yet here I lie—naked, alone, and unsexed.

Doesn't anyone want to sleep with me? I'm successful. I'm wealthy. I'm physically fit. I'm perfect.

I fling myself backward, the heaviness in my head thumping as I hit the pillow and stare up at the ceiling.

"Maybe it's your approach, darlin'." He chuckles, and I realize I've asked my question aloud.

I just wanted him to sleep with me.

One night.

It's been so long.

My head lifts, noting he's still standing at the foot of the bed with his hands in his pockets, gazing down at his feet. I drop my head back one more time and close my eyes. He rustles around the room, and I roll to my side, opening my eyes to stare toward the window. The sun beams through the sheer curtains. We never closed the room-darkening ones, and I see it's going to be a glorious spring day here in Nashville. Soon, I'll need to make the trek back to Green Valley, my hometown, but I'd give anything to remain in this bed and curl into myself.

I catalogue the sounds of movement at the edge of the bed. A shoe tapping on the floor as though he's struggling to place his foot in it. The clink of a belt. He wore a tuxedo jacket and a bow tie. Where are those things? I don't look. I just stare at the window.

My heart aches, which seems silly, considering we didn't even have sex. I realize that's the clincher. At one point during the night when he looked at me, I really thought he saw me differently than others do. Of course, the remainder of the evening is a bit fuzzy, but his eyes will haunt my dreams and my fantasies as I'll be back to self-pleasuring after this mortifying moment.

The women said he wasn't selective. I wasn't too old. Too graying. Too anything. He'd do me, they'd teased.

"Who said such a thing?"

I still as if I'd been moving, which I wasn't. I'm even holding my breath.

"Umm . . ." *Did I say all that out loud again?*

"Was it those bitches you were sitting with? Is that who said such a thing 'bout me?"

Glancing at him over my shoulder, I meet his eyes, which toss axes back at me. I don't have the strength to spar with him, although fighting is one of my finest skills. I can pick and poke at the best of them, making certain I always have the last word. But not today.

"They told me you weren't discriminatory, and I would be good enough for you."

6

He huffs, shaking his head, and I notice he holds his tux jacket over his forearm. The belt and tie drape his arm as well. His fingers curl into a fist at the edge of his belongings, and for a second, I wonder if he liked holding me last night. Did he enjoy having his arm over me? Did he even know he did it?

"What does it matter?"

"Forget it," I snort-huff. It's an unattractive sound, but I don't care. I don't care because he wasn't attracted to me after all, and I'll likely never see Chester Chesterfield again. I twist my body away from him, returning my gaze to the gauzy curtains.

"No, I want to know. Who cares what those ninny know-it-alls think?"

My head rolls to peer at him over my shoulder once again. "It isn't that I care what they think. It's that I cared to have sex with you, and you didn't *care* to have sex with me." It's been such a long time, and I put myself out there, propositioning him in some manner to get him back to my room. Now, I'm just embarrassed while missing the full memory of my behavior.

"Who said that?" he huffs.

"Who said what?"

"Who said I didn't want to have sex with you?"

"Well, you . . ." I blink at him. He said we didn't have sex. *Isn't that what he meant?*

"I have another question. Why sex with me? And I want a real answer. Be real with me."

I continue to stare at him before taking a deep breath and answering, "Because I haven't had sex in over a decade, okay? Not with a real man. A man who wants me. One virile and passionate and solid in the . . . you know . . ." I wave a hand toward the general direction of his . . . you know.

"Say the word."

"Pardon me?" I blink at him, but he holds firm, daring me to say one word.

I'm not saying that word.

We glare at one another for what feels like an eternity. The weight of those eyes is as heavy as his arm over my waist had been, but there's something deeper in those midnight orbs. A vulnerability that mirrors my own.

Fine, I'll say the word.

"Dick. There. Satisfied? I wanted your dick."

He shakes his head as he softly chuckles. This will definitely go down as the worst seduction ever. I close my eyes, mortified. I have no idea what he looks like underneath those tuxedo pants. He could be a pencil, sharpened down to just above the eraser for all I know, but his stature suggests otherwise. He'd be as solid as the tree trunk necessary to make a dozen pencils.

Admittedly, the discussion with those ladies at the bar got out of hand, and then I wanted him in my hand. I wanted to know what it would feel like to hold and be held. To caress and be caressed. To be penetrated by a man who was not Karl. Chester seemed like the perfect specimen.

Suddenly, I hear the drop of a belt to the floor and feel the strain of the bed near my feet. My eyes open, and I watch as he tugs his T-shirt over his head by the back of his collar, removing the white material like a curtain for the opening act. On display before me is a broad chest smattered with dark hair and a thick trail leading lower. He tosses the T-shirt on the floor. His feet shift, kicking off his shoes, which make a soft thud near the foot of the bed. When he begins to crawl up the bed and over me, I can't think.

"What man doesn't want you, darlin'?"

Huh? *Oh.* I mentioned that, didn't I? But words escape me as he hovers over me.

His brawny body blocks out the sun like a thunderous cloud, and I want him to rain down on me. He lingers over me but doesn't lower. I want to spread my legs for him, but he has them trapped between his. My body hums for a connection with him. He remains on all fours, a predator over his prey, and I'm ready to scream *devour me.* I'm so turned on, and he hasn't even touched me. There's a feral appeal to him. His nostrils flare, and he licks his lips. My heart races, and my breasts heave under the sheet hardly covering me.

"You sure about this, darlin'?" He attempts to whisper, but that rugged sleepy tone returns, and the timbre rumbles over my skin like the rush of a rainstorm.

Yes.

No.

I shouldn't do this.

But who am I kidding? I'm Scotia Simmons. I want to do this, and I always do what I want. Despite the throbbing in my head, I hold my chin higher and answer him.

"Definitely."

CHAPTER 2

GOT NO GAME

[Chet]

March

"Uncle Chet," seven-year-old Louie calls out in greeting as I enter the playroom, which was once a family room. The view overlooks the Smoky Mountain range and Green Valley down below. The boys gathered on the floor are building an intricate and elaborate system of roads and tunnels for their Matchbox cars.

"Where did you find these?" The plastic orange track intended to hold small metal cars seems like an antique, although I never had such toys when I was a child.

"Mrs. Pickle found them," Dewey explains without looking up. He's concentrating on stacking boxes under the track to raise the angle. Dewey is eleven and has a structurally creative mind. His ingenuity and vision hints that one day he's going to design roads and build bridges that will blow the minds of what we already know. He's also a Harry Potter look-alike with round glasses and bangs a little too long.

"Who's Mrs. Pickle?" I ask, thinking the name sounds like a cartoon character and not one five boys would be interested in.

"Mrs. Pickle," Louie drones as though he can't believe I don't know who she is. *Am I supposed to know her?* "She's only the best book reader ever." Louie peeks around me and hollers, "No offense, Maura!" I glance behind me and find Maura Hawes standing in the opening to the large sunshine-filled room.

Maura would be considered a beautiful woman to most men, but for me, it's not about how she looks. She takes on the care of the three boys under my guardianship. I was gifted custody of the boys and considered it a huge honor under the circumstances. I had no qualms about taking them in —it's what Harper and Davis wanted—but I quickly realized the care and structure needed to raise three boys was more than I could handle on my own. I was honestly concerned I'd screw them all up.

Louie had technically been a baby while Hugh and Dewey were still so young. Harper had been a natural at motherhood, and she'd been good for Davis. He matured a bit when they fell in love, and he embraced father-hood. But me? It freaked me out. What did I know about being a dad? Without decent parents as role models, I didn't think I was cut out for parenthood. I didn't want to fuck it up with someone else's kids. Being the fun uncle was a better fit for me.

That's where Maura and her knowledgeable ways with kids came in. I found her when she was considering a leave from foster parenting. I needed her, and as it turns out, she needed me, too. Her beauty lies in the love she's shown these children and the additional boys we've taken on in this home. With her blonde hair, blue eyes, and contagious laughter, some man is missing out on her. Our relationship has never crossed that line because in a sense, I'm her boss. We keep things professional, but the work is personal to us both.

"No offense, buddy," Maura replies, her voice sarcastic. The boys love her, so there are no hurt feelings over Louie's praise of someone other than their caretaker reading stories.

"What makes Mrs. Pickle so great?" I ask Louie, who helps his brother build the looping track. Louie's hair is shorter than his older brother's as he prefers it closely cropped to his head, but his eyes are no less inquisitive about all things.

"She makes all these great voices. It's awesome," Louie states, enthusiastic in almost everything he says or does. I exhale, trying not to consider how much his mother would have loved this kid. Loved all her children as they grew.

"What a strange name. Mrs. Pickle," I mock. The image of an elderly woman with gray hair curled tight like an old-fashioned perm, wearing a floral dress that looks like an antiquated housecoat and gnawing on a dill pickle comes to mind. In my head, she bites into it like she hates dick.

"She is strange," Hunter adds. Dropped at our door when he was only a baby, he's now six-years old. There must have been some confusion as to the purpose of this house. That's our best guess. To this day, we don't know who found us or why they chose us, but Maura is a licensed foster parent with foster-to-adopt status. In hindsight, Maura is relieved she never left foster parenting. One look at Hunter, and she couldn't turn him away. With the state's permission, Maura adopted him, and it led to the idea of Harper House—this house—becoming a group home for boys. In order to keep Maura in my service and welcome Hunter into our fold, I became a certified foster parent as well. It's a little surprising I'm now on the other side of the system.

"What's strange about her?" I ask, continuing a conversation I really have no interest in.

"She smells like a pickle."

"She does not," Louie defends of the best book reader, and Hunter glares at Louie.

"Does too," Hunter insists.

"Alright, boys," Maura interjects. "Ten more minutes and then clean up and supper now that Uncle Chet is here." Maura gives me a chiding look. My morning resulted in 'unplanned' activities.

Although I'm not a blood relative to any of them, all the boys call me Uncle Chet. Davis was the closest thing I'd ever had to a sibling when I was young, so I'm family in name. As his three boys have always called me uncle, it's just been easier to let any boy living here do the same.

Typically, I'm here every other weekend. Maura deserves respite, and she's required to receive time off by the foster system. I try to help when I can on other days, but my permanent residence isn't close, and I run several businesses in multiple locations. Today is an unscheduled stop.

With a collective groan from the group, Dewey looks up again. "We can't pick this up. We aren't finished." From his serious tone and shocked expression, you'd think we just requested he commit a crime. However, the boys know Maura does not like for them to leave toys lying around. Everything has its place, and it's the reason she's in charge. If it were me, the entire house might look like a giant playland, and it typically does on my weekends. I have no business raising kids, so I don't. Maura does all the hard work.

"Boys, we mind what Maura says," I remind them, watching Dewey's crestfallen face. "But maybe she can make an exception today since I'm here." My visit here today was unplanned, but the past twenty-four hours have been a bit surreal and being here grounds me. This is my church as I no longer believe in God. If there was one, he wouldn't have taken from me all that he has.

"By the way, you clean up nicely," Maura teases, knowing I had to trim back my typically bushy beard and tame my wild hair to attend a *thing*. I actually allowed a haircut. I rub a hand over the space at my nape, which feels a little bald, but I don't respond to her compliment.

"Where's Hughie?" I ask, doing a head count of the boys in the large room. We currently house five, including Hughie, Dewey, and Louie. Hunter was adopted by Maura, and ten-year-old Campbell is a distant relation to her. The state asked her to keep the boy when his parents died a few years back as kinship placement.

Harper was a nut when she named her three boys. Thank goodness Davis's last name wasn't Duck. It was Maverik.

Harper and Davis Maverik.

I swallow at the thought of them.

"Hugh," Maura corrects behind me. The fourteen-year-old no longer wants the -e sound at the end of his name. *I'm not twelve anymore*, he said when he officially became a teen. He currently argues Hughie is too cute

14

for a growing man. As an eighth grader, he's practicing his new name before high school.

"Uncle Chet," Hugh says in greeting as he exits the study room located at the side of the giant playroom. I turn to find a boy who looks exactly like his mother. With sandy brown hair and bright blue eyes, he's her miniature in masculine form, and my throat clogs again.

"Where have you been, kid?" I tease him, understanding he's starting to separate himself from the other boys as the eldest and only teenager in the house.

"Homework," he groans. He's a smart kid but also turning into a bit of a scrapper at school like his father had once been. His big heart is getting him into big trouble as he defends the underdogs of the schoolyard. He's a modern-day mini-Robin Hood. A part of his aggression comes from hormones and an underlying anger he can't define. I'd be pissed too if I'd lost such loving parents. Then again, I never knew my own.

The call for supper comes from a sweet and sultry voice in the front hall. Maura hired a kitchen assistant a year back, and Savannah is beautiful with silky smooth jet-black hair and bright blue eyes, but she's too young for me. I'm a forty-six-year-old man who likes to keep things uncomplicated, and her youth is a complication I'm not interested in tapping. Not to mention, Maura is very selective about who enters the home, and Savannah works hard as part-time kitchen help.

"I think you might be drooling a bit," Hugh teases me, reaching for my lip. He likes to pretend I have a crush on the cook. I think he's projecting his own youthful desires, but he's too young for her. I grab him by the back of the neck, giving it a squeeze. My touch is not hard, as I'd never use force on these boys. I've had my own experience with a firm hand, so I'd never replicate it on another.

"I don't know what you're talking about," I retort as the other boys rush around us to line up near the bathroom outside the great room to wash their hands before entering the dining room.

"Sure, you don't," he chides.

"One day," I jest, knowing his fourteen-year-old self really is on the edge of being a young man with too much sex on the brain already.

"One day?" He snorts. "I'm there now."

"Oh, yeah? Got a *girl*friend," I jest as though I'm the same age as his friends.

He shrugs. "I'm keeping my options open," he replies, tugging free of me and joining the back of the line for the restroom.

This kid. He's going to be a heartbreaker one day, but not too soon, I hope. I don't want him growing up too fast, and I definitely don't want him doing things like his father and I used to do. Random hookups stopped short the second Davis saw Harper. Me, I'm still keeping up the practice.

And that woman this morning . . .

Tell me three things, I teased her before we ever made it to her room.

You. Me. A bed.

It hadn't seemed real.

There was just something about her when we met last night. She was sharp, snarky even, with socialite written all over her. But she was also willing and wanting. She had a vulnerability to her that made my brain disconnect and my body take over. One-night stands keep emotion out of the heart, and I'd been burned too bad in the past to let anything near mine again. Not all of us can be lucky bastards like Davis, who found the love of a good woman in Harper.

Again, I consider the woman under me this morning. Her exotic gray eyes held wisdom with a strong dose of hurt buried deep within. She looked upon me with hesitation, as if at any minute I might pull back and she might lose me even in the heated moment. She clung to me, desperate for my touch, my kiss, and my dick, and I can't explain my response. It's as if I wanted to give her everything and more. I wanted to assure her I had staying power if she'd ask.

But Scotia Simmons would never ask me to be with her. Not long term.

Overly confident in one breath, then slightly cautious in another, she was a puzzling contradiction until my body entered hers. Then we were on the same page. I never struggle to leave a bed, but I wasn't eager to rush off from hers this morning. However, lingering is not my modus operandi, and there came a point when it was just time to walk away. That point was after giving her three orgasms and getting a big one of my own.

"Hi, Chet," Savannah quietly says, catching me off guard with my thoughts on the powerful release I had this morning. I lift a hand to wave but accidentally smack Hugh in the back of the head. He turns bright red and curses under his breath. I notice he's straightened and smoothed down his shirt. Savannah continues to the dining room with a serving plate, not noticing either of us in her mission to serve dinner. Hugh turns back to me, exaggeratedly rubbing at his hair, mortified.

"Smooth, Romeo," he mutters to himself. *Does* he have a crush on Savannah? I grip the back of his neck again, gently shoving him. The momentary awkwardness breaks, and he laughs. "We need to work on your game."

"My game?" I snort. I don't need game. I got plenty this morning. "How do you know who Romeo is, anyway?"

"I told you, homework," he groans. Ah, the tale of fated lovers, starry-eyed and star-crossed. *It ends in doom, kid*, I want to tell him, but I don't.

I think back once more to this morning's hotel room activities.

I want someone to belong to me.

A woman like Scotia would never be interested in me. Not if she knew the truth about me. Shoving my dick into her might have been the wrong thing to do, but she felt so good. Her fingers in my hair, tugging gently on the ends. Her mouth sucking at my neck. Her nails scraping over my hairy chest.

You like that, I teased.

I like you, she said, not holding back. Her words were a heady concoction, and I was drunk on her this morning. I wish I could have another sip, but it's best to let things remain where they were.

A hotel. One morning. And her.

CHAPTER 3

THEM'S FIGHTING WORDS

[Chet]

August – five months later

It's hotter than Hades as I stand outside the Viking MMA studio late one afternoon. I'm waiting on the boys. After Hugh got in a fight at the end of the school year, I made a deal to allow him to learn to fight responsibly, and Viking offered classes for boys. Of course, all the boys wanted in, and I eventually caved. Hugh wasn't happy about the additional attendees, and I understood he was looking for ways to distinguish himself from the other kids since he's entering high school soon. Showing favoritism to one boy over the others is difficult, though, as I try to be fair to all. I don't want to deny any of them any advantage I can offer.

I'm standing on the sidewalk, leaning against the minivan belonging to the house, when I hear a group of women as they tumble out of the space next door. They practically bump into me like it's not obvious a large man is standing on the sidewalk.

"Did you see her thighs?" one says, stubbing her nose at me over her shoulder at my nearness without actually looking at me. Some people just have no boundaries.

I was here first, lady.

"I just don't know how she can wrap those ham hocks around such a skinny pole."

My eyes glance up at the name of the storefront next door to the MMA studio. Stripped—specializing in the art of pole dancing and more. Returning my gaze to the women who clearly aren't professional strippers or pole dancers, I note their clothing of black stretchy pants and oversized T-shirts on most of them, not to mention a few wrinkles and some gray hairs among them. *Nope, not your typical strippers.*

"And the other needs to shower more frequently," the woman states again, wrinkling her nose and exaggerating a pinch to it. Her head tips to the side, sensing I'm still present, but she continues. "Hoo-ey, she smells like the pigs she's raising."

One more head tilt, an over-the-shoulder glance, and then she's waving her hand as though I stink, too. I might. It's hot.

I hate hearing women put down other women. It reminds me too much of someone I used to know. And these ladies, all red-faced, sweat-laden —*is that a 1980s headband on one of them?*—sure aren't anything to brag about. However, the one with her back to me, doing all the yakking, has a fine ass in her tight pants, and her racerback tank shows off a muscular back and toned arms.

"Hazel, I can't believe you talked me into doing this," the fine-ass woman continues.

"I can't believe how well you did," the woman I assume is Hazel responds. "You're a natural."

"Bless your heart, I hope not," Fine-Ass admonishes. "I wouldn't be caught dead wrapped around a pole like that in public."

"But you just did wrap around one," a third woman in the party reminds her, referring to the pole dancing class they must have just finished.

"Must be your years since widowhood. Are you doing something we don't know about?" Hazel leans in as though she's asking for a secret. "Riding poles we don't know?"

I snort.

Fine-Ass glances over her shoulder again, looking down her nose at me. "Do you mind?" Her sugar-sweet Southern drawl rubs on me like sandpaper on rough wood.

"Not at all," I snide, crossing my arms and spreading my legs wide to balance me better against the van. *I'm not moving.*

"Hay-zel," Fine-Ass drones, turning back to her friend and lifting her fingers for her throat to grasp for pearls she isn't wearing. "You watch your mouth."

"There's nothing wrong with a little side dish," the third woman states, leaning in as though she's offering a secret but still speaking loud enough for the entire block to hear her. "Since Junior's death, I've had to get it where I could *get*. I didn't always want to follow Vilma's rules for self-stimulation."

Okay, TMI. I should not be hearing this. I'm not a good judge of age, but these women are like forty-*something*. Shouldn't they be talking about knitting, cats, or some shit like that?

"Well, I'm not dancing on poles or any other phallic symbol," the first clarifies, stiffening her shoulders, and I can't help but wonder if a good pole ride is what she needs. She continues, "And I'm assuming neither is Rebecca Sue. Did you see the brows on her? She needs a good esthetician. Her lip could use a wax as well, but once you start that, there's no going back."

Jesus. Some women just do not have the good sense to keep their mouths shut.

"Well, at least she was giving it her best effort," the third woman states, attempting to soften the endless insults.

"Mabel, you are too kind, but just because J-Lo and Shakira pulled off pole dancing during the Super Bowl a few years back doesn't mean every forty- to fifty-year-old woman should run out and try it," Fine-Ass chides. "Some women are best keeping their clothes on and their feet planted on the good earth."

Aren't these women roughly the age Fine-Ass is harping on?

Jee-zus. She definitely needs to be stripped down and have her toes curled. A good *pole*-ing might do wonders for her. Suddenly, the door to the MMA studio opens, and the boys rush out like scattering ants. I press off the side of the van, bumping into Fine-Ass. She flinches, steps aside, and swipes at her arm as though she's flicking dirt off her skin. *Whatever*.

The other two women shift only minimally as I open the side door for the boys. Keeping my back to the biddies, I shield the boys from their venom with my big body.

"Uncle Chet, did you see us?"

"I took down Hugh."

"Campbell almost broke my nose."

"I broke my glasses again." I look down at Dewey. He's going through eyeglasses like changes of underwear.

"We need to get you some sports eyewear, kid," I say, watching the boys scramble in. For some reason, I glance over again at the women ripping apart other women to find the ringleader observing me. She's focused solely on me. Her eyes scan my body, sizing up my height, taking in my broad shoulders, and noting my too-thick beard. Her nose wrinkles as though she smells something bad.

Yeah, that's right. I'm all man, and that means I sweat. God, her attitude reminds me so much of someone I don't like to think about—looking down her nose at others and being catty toward other women. 'Course, I didn't recognize these things in that woman until after. After I fell in love with her. After I built a house for her. After I wanted to marry her.

As the boys finish filing into the van, I really look at Fine-Ass, and something about her strikes me as familiar. Seeing her face full on, I notice a white stripe of hair pulled back in her ponytail, visible as my eyes squint.

Scotia?

Despite all the other things that distinguish Scotia Simmons in my memory, there's a unique physical characteristic that marks her as different—her hair. Amid the fading blackness is a white strip along the right side of her face.

"It's called poliosis," she said when I couldn't take my eyes off the bright contrast.

"You had polio?" I questioned, concerned she'd once been sick.

"No, poliosis. It's a lack of pigment in the hair. It's like a birthmark. It makes me special."

That comment made her special all right.

"Ah," I said like a dumbass. Since I'd known an overconfident woman or two in the past, I couldn't seem to stop myself from asking, "Does the carpet match the curtains?"

"Of course, my carpets match my curtains. I'll have you know my home was professionally decorated by Sonya Stevens."

I had no idea who that was, nor did I care. She hadn't understood my taunt.

"I meant . . ." I let my wandering eyes explain myself, giving her body an obvious perusal from her curtain top to the covered rug at the top of her thighs.

"I beg your pardon," she snapped.

"You don't have to beg."

Our eyes connected then. My meaning clear. Hers cautious. I instantly felt bad for taking my surly attitude out on her. My presence at the conference was at fault, not her. I'd gone too far and apologized for being crass. Then I'd offered to buy her a drink.

After she finished the first gin and tonic a little too quickly, a gentle hand came to rest on my arm.

"Did you mean it?" she questioned, lowering her voice while her tone screamed of vulnerability. "I wouldn't have to beg." Her eyes closed like she couldn't believe she'd asked me for clarification. I didn't question her hesitation. Her hand began to retract, and I reached for her fingers before she pulled completely away.

"Whatever you want, darlin'."

There is no denying the woman presently before me is Scotia Simmons. There just isn't enough coincidence in life to place two different women with the same white streak in my presence.

Does she live here in Green Valley? When I met her in Nashville, I hadn't considered where she lived. I can't remember the fine details about her from the event. I don't recall what business she owned. It wasn't what we discussed when she approached me at the bar. It wasn't my concern when she was under me and I entered her repeatedly. We didn't really talk past her request that I sleep with her.

You. Me. A bed.

She wanted my dick. It was that simple and just as complicated.

I gave in to her because she was beautiful and sweet.

And now I hear all this.

She is all salt and vinegar. I hate women like this and realize I've been holding on to the wrong impression of who Scotia is. That tends to happen to me—thinking a woman is one way and finding out later that she's completely different than I thought.

Watching Scotia's nose wrinkle as though something on the sidewalk stinks, I don't feel the need to identify myself. Her narrowed eyes and disgusted face remind me again of someone I don't like to remember.

I turn away from her and slam the door behind the last boy after he enters the van. After circling the front of the vehicle instead of the back—I don't want to step anywhere near the shit these women are slinging—I enter the large, eight-seater van.

If we add any more boys to the home, we won't all fit in this thing.

Adjusting the rearview mirror, I catch another glance of the women on the walk. Scotia is still staring at the vehicle, but it doesn't matter. She isn't the same woman I had under me. The one who whispered how good I felt, how she'd never been so complete, and how she couldn't get enough. That woman was full of sweet praise and sugary compliments while all that fills the woman behind me is vitriol and vinegar.

I don't need that kind of woman in my life.

"All buckled?" I call out to the boys. When I get the *all clear*, I shift my eyes forward and decide not to look back.

* * *

Later that night, I return to The Fugitive, my bar and motel off The Tail of the Dragon, located just over the Tennessee border inside North Carolina. The place is one of a variety of businesses I own. The popular spot marks the southern end of the famous and dangerous strip of road motorcycle enthusiasts love. In the heat of the summer months, my bike gets me here best, and I need the ride today.

My head requires putting on right after this afternoon. I was so disappointed in what I'd seen and heard on the street in Green Valley, but I don't know why it bothered me. Maybe because I'd been holding on to fantasies of Scotia in my head, while in reality, she was quite different. She was exactly like Hennessy Miller, and I should have known better. A woman like Henny didn't look past the nose on her face. She didn't read *into* a person.

Then again, that's the kicker. I thought Scotia had a good read on me that morning.

She had no recollection of me on the sidewalk today, though.

Eventually, I saunter into The Fugitive. The place is a typical biker hotspot with dark wood paneling, a broad bar with a scattering of tables in the main area, and a separate pool room off to the right. The detached motel stands to the side of the bar in a classic two-story, L-shaped layout. Some might consider the place seedy, but we keep clean rooms which offer updated furniture, a flat-screen television, and a handy lovers' kit including protection, lubrication, and a couple of mints. That last bit was not on the list of improvements this motel needed when I bought it a while back.

"We ain't Vegas," I snarked when one of my former housekeepers came up with the suggestion, but somehow, the sex care packages stuck. The production of them eventually became another one of the businesses I own.

And of course, there's a Stop-and-Pump gas station located here. I own that, too.

"What's up?" Todd Ryder calls out to me from behind the bar. He's been my best friend for years. Whatever I need, he's the man. At The Fugitive, he's the bartender, manager, and bouncer.

"Whiskey," I call out, and Todd pours one for each of us. I slam back the drink as Todd watches me.

"Jesus, what happened to you?" We don't usually share our shit. We don't need to discuss feelings or the things we do behind closed doors, but Todd and I know a bit of each other's history. I should mention the woman I haven't been able to get out of my head. The woman who looked at me like I could be her hero back in March. The woman whose body responded to mine in ways I couldn't have predicted. Her hunger. Her willingness. It was all she wanted that morning, but I don't mention any of this to Todd.

Admittedly, I don't spend much time in Green Valley. Mainly keeping to myself, I don't make anyone else's business my own, so I had no idea Scotia lived in the area. I recall her eyes from earlier, assessing me and finding me unworthy in my sweat-laden T-shirt with an unruly beard and hair bushy from the humidity.

She didn't like what she saw.

I didn't like what I heard.

She was not the same woman I shared a night with last spring.

And I can't explain why I'm upset by the interaction.

"Got a new kid," I mutter, dismissing my real thoughts. Todd knows about Harper House, but I don't need the rest of the place knowing my affiliation with it. "We can't seem to identify him. Is he a runaway, or was he kidnapped and then ran away? He's locked up tighter than a Bible-thumping virgin."

On my most recent visit, prior to today, one of the boys mentioned someone named Malik while we were hanging out in the giant playroom.

"Who's Malik?" I turned my head to Maura, who lowered hers.

"We were playing with paint guns in the woods, and he got hit by accident," Hugh explained.

"What have I told you about those paint guns?" I admonished, turning on my nephew. More importantly, who is this other boy?

"The boys found him in the woods," Maura answered, and I stared back at her. "We don't know where he's from."

"Maura," I moaned. Could we even take on another mouth to feed? Not to mention, does the kid have parents who miss him? She knew the drill and surmised the questions running through my head.

"I called the authorities and our caseworker. They agreed to let him stay here while we figure it out."

"Why doesn't the kid just tell you where he's from?" I asked her. Maura explained he isn't speaking.

"We're lucky we got a name," Maura told me, and my tipped brow questioned how she got that information.

"Mrs. Pickle," she answered.

Mrs. Pickle. Who the hell is this woman?

Maura occasionally uses volunteers to give herself a break during the week and offer additional support to the boys, so I don't question her. *Variety in the village,* she calls it. With her bevy of experiences, especially with older kids who come with baggage, she knows how to vet people before letting them enter the house. She's a natural caregiver, protector, and provider of love. I wish I'd had a foster mother like her.

I don't recall a thing about my mother. She'd disappeared so deep into alcohol she'd forgotten she had a son. I was placed in the foster system at eight. After years of bad luck and moving from one house to another, I finally met Davis. We'd been thick as thieves and more bonded than blood, despite what anyone said about family. I wanted the same ties and stability for our crew. No boy gets left behind—*ever.* It's another reason we need to learn more about Malik

"Where's the boy?" I asked, and Hugh jutted his chin toward the stair-case leading upstairs.

"You okay with this?" I asked Maura. Could she handle one more child?

This ups the count to six.

Although we accept some donations, Harper House is mainly privately funded. We also receive a small stipend from the state for any kids we keep before other foster placement is secured for them. Additional children among our five has been rare. I don't worry about those things as Maura's in charge and knows the foster care system better than I do. She follows all the state and federal regulations, but she's also one of the system's favorites because she has an excellent track record with kids.

"You know I'd never turn someone away," she whispered, and the beauty within her radiated outward. Her heart is too large.

"Okay, but the proper channels," I reminded her, but she didn't need reminding. Somehow, these occasional stray boys end up with us, but I want them to be legitimate strays and not some angry pissant kid looking for a place to hang out at for a while. We have enough mouths to feed, and bodies to clothe, and brains to inspire. We don't need trouble with the local sheriff's department.

"We're all good so far," she assured me.

Only, we are still no closer to learning where Malik came from or what he was doing in the woods. Maura could homeschool—in addition to being a foster parent, she's also a former teacher—but it's a lot to teach all the boys given their various ages, so they attend the local school. She's been able to discern that Malik can read, write, and do arithmetic through our mystery volunteer, Mrs. Pickle. He just won't speak to anyone. He's stolen a few things in the house but nothing of consequence. It's all been survival things like snack food, water bottles, and blankets. The fear is he'll run from us before we find out who he is.

"That sucks," Todd says, interjecting on my thoughts. Todd's always been good about supporting the boys where he can. He remembers when his brother nearly landed in trouble with the wrong crowd, and just like me, he doesn't want that to happen to any of these impressionable kids. For the most part, I don't involve the guys who roll through my place in my mission. I have enough businesses financially supporting Harper House directly, and that works for me. The bar and motel are my nest egg. My retirement lies in these investments, although I'm not certain I'll ever retire from riding my bike, hanging out in my bar, and occasionally sleeping with a woman.

Life is easiest lived in this manner.

"And not a word from the kid?" Todd questions. We've done our best to guess his age and figure he's around eight or nine. He hasn't ever answered direct questions other than once giving his name to Mrs. Pickle, written on a piece of paper.

Mrs. Fucking Pickle. I'm getting tired of hearing about this woman. I had to ask Maura to remind me again what was so special about her.

"Clothes. Books. School supplies. And that's just a start." Maura *berated me when I questioned not only a volunteer but also her contributions. Apparently, she's some rich old woman with nothing else to do with her money.* "And Dewey's convinced she's the best book reader on the planet next to Miss Naomi at the library. Louie is smitten with her, and Malik lights up when she's around."

"You sure something else isn't on your mind?" Todd asks. I hold out my glass for another hit, and he gives me a second healthy pour. My mind immediately travels back to the scene on the sidewalk earlier. I don't know why I can't let it go.

Perhaps the insulting words have tarnished my memory.

I want someone to belong to me.

Then again, I need to remind myself Scotia was a one-night-only opportunity. Or rather one morning. She wasn't meant to be anything more to me. I once knew a woman like her, wanting a ride on the Chesterfield Express. That woman wanted money and status.

The problem is this feeling I had that Scotia was different. Deep down, I'd thought . . . *It doesn't matter what I thought.* I didn't need nor want a snooty woman. I'd had one once. I wouldn't go there again.

"Yeah. Just been stupid, that's all. Used my dick to make a decision instead of my head."

Unfortunately, I haven't been with anyone else since that encounter months ago, and I don't know why I've been holding out.

Todd chuckles and taps his glass to mine. "Been there, done that, my friend," he mutters before lifting his shot glass to his lips.

I could have looked Scotia up after the event last spring. I could have gone through the conference brochure, contacted someone on the board, and found her phone number. But even though I'd wondered what happened to her after that morning, I didn't.

I don't know why I didn't.

Seeing her on the sidewalk paints a different picture of her than I remembered—one of a woman with succulent breasts, a firm ass, and a sweet mouth.

That mouth was not so sweet after all. All salt. All vinegar.

Lord knows, I'm not perfect myself, but I try not to be a dick to my fellow man. I'm doing what I can for my friends. I run several legitimate businesses. I don't fuck women over, and something tells me, my little tryst with Scotia did her no harm.

Still, I've never been a good judge of character when it comes to women. Case in point—the last woman I gave in to was not who I thought she was.

Why don't I ever learn?

29

CHAPTER 4

HALLOWEEN ROUND TABLE

[Scotia]

October

Admittedly, autumn is not the height of pickle season, but a good fried pickle works anytime, anywhere. Especially when our newest account is a chain of bars in North Carolina, and I'm in a dither when something goes wrong with the order.

"What do you mean it didn't arrive?" I bark into the phone. When my husband was killed—God rest his spirit—I inherited money I didn't know the penny-pinching pediatrician had set aside for a rainy day. That rainy day arrived when he died, and I decided to enter my fried pickles in a contest.

And I won.

Take that, Diane Donner-Sylvester.

My former best friend thought her daughter was always all that. Banana Cake Queen, my yoga-toned backside. She wanted to live vicariously through her prize-winning, baker daughter and look where it got her—on the run from police with a motorcycle man named Repo.

Me, on the other hand . . . I won that contest. *Me!* And I've been nick-named the Fried Pickle Princess by *Roadside Rumblings*, a television program hosted by a famous foodie. I'd like to be considered a queen because princess has a coquettish and juvenile connotation, but royalty is royalty, and I won't give up my newfound status. By marrying a Simmons, I shed the history of growing up a Winters—the product of religious fanatic parents in a small armpit of the mountains. I didn't disapprove of my upbringing—Daddy loved me best—but I didn't want to be poor my entire life. When I met and married Karl Simmons, sealing my future to protect his, I fell into a different type of royalty—small-town society.

Don't get me wrong. Diane had been a good friend as far as friends go when you're a member of the Green Valley upper crust. We had a love-hate relationship. I loved to hate her and vice versa, and nothing fed our competitive spirit more than the comparison of our daughters.

Her daughter was a beauty queen.

Mine was valedictorian.

Her daughter was a master baker.

Mine went to medical school.

Whereas my girl, Darlene, dodged a bullet by *not* ending up with one of those Winston boys—her sight originally set on Beau—Diane's daughter seemed to feel it was a badge of honor to become one of them and eventually married that oddball Cletus.

In my opinion, intelligence outwitted beauty. Clearly, my daughter won.

However, over the past few years, I have come to an understanding with Diane's daughter, Jennifer Winston. She's lost her mother, and I'm missing my daughter something fierce. Being that I was one of her mother's best friends, despite our competitiveness, I've grown fond of the younger woman who has a kind spirit and trusting nature.

"I trust you today, Mrs. Simmons, but I'll be checking in on that trust tomorrow." Bless her heart, she's too cute for her own good some days. And with age comes reflection, and I'm coming to appreciate that kindness trumps smarts. Perhaps, Jennifer Winston wins after all.

"I want a delivery update stat," I bark into the phone to my assistant, Gideon. He's my fifth assistant in as many years, and he's lasted the longest.

Hanging up, I toss the device on my desk where it instantly rings. "Yes," I snap.

"Hey, Scotia, just reminding you of our plans tonight." My sister Beverly's chipper voice grates over my current nerves. Apparently, finding true love can make you happy.

"Look, Beverly, I'm having a situation here, so I don't—"

"Great, Naomi will be there at five."

"Beverly, I don't— Hello? *Hello?*" The line is dead. I pull the phone away from my ear, glaring down at the screen.

"Did you just hang up on me?" I growl at the technology in my palm, cursing my sister. Despite Beverly being only two years younger than me, we weren't close as children. She always sought my approval, but I didn't eagerly give it. We were just too different. She wanted happily ever after, and I wanted status. It's been almost thirty years since we were teenagers, and we've slowly begun to rebuild our sisterhood. Especially after the showdown with her no-good *ex*-husband, Howard, last fall.

Age brings wisdom on who should be important in your life.

Our relationship rehab includes mandatory once-a-month meetups, and this month is our youngest sister Naomi's turn to decide on a location, which means she will be driving us.

I glance at the clock on my phone and see I have forty-two minutes to get my pickle order processed properly before the sister cavalry arrives and forces me to go with them to wherever we're going.

* * *

"Once upon a time," Naomi begins.

"This isn't a fairy tale," I quickly interject as we sit in some biker bar almost forty-five minutes away from Green Valley. My youngest sister's nose scrunches in displeasure at my interruption. With hair that is a mix of white and silver, she wears it in a long, intricate braid over her shoulder and looks like a magical witch more than a fairy.

"I love a good fairy tale," Beverly adds, which I ignore while watching Naomi sympathize with our middle sister. Once upon a time, none of us Winters sisters had anything close to a fairy tale in matters related to romance. Then Nathan Ryder and Jedd Flemming appeared, and my sisters each fell down their respective rabbit holes of bliss.

"We need an idea for the Halloween party," Naomi reminds me.

"Remind me again why we are going together," I mutter into my wine glass. My lips purse at what I consider a terrible idea, even though I promised to go along with it. Naomi recommended we attend the annual Green Valley community center Halloween party at the end of the month. That is, we attend collectively, as in the three of us together, as in sisters in coordinating costumes like we are still children.

"A fairy-tale theme works. We could be three fairies, like from *Sleeping Beauty*. Fauna, Flora, and Merryweather," Beverly offers, and my nose wrinkles this time, not caring for the suggestion. My sister has snow-white hair cut short to her chin in a tumble of loose waves. She's tall and wiry thin and more similar in appearance to a wise elf than some fluffy fairy in a pastel dress.

"We are not fairies." I scoff, recalling us as children in princess nightgowns.

I take a moment to allow my gaze to roam the layout of the bar. A clientele of bikers and tourists surround us. The Fugitive was Naomi's idea. My sister's new husband has connections here. Nathan's older brother and his best friend run the place. I have nothing against Nathan Ryder, other than taking my sister's virginity—*once upon a time*—and causing a family ruckus because of it, but that's old news and happened twenty-something years ago. Time passes on what we can no longer rectify.

"What about symbols? Like the Deathly Hallows? A triangle, a circle, and a wand." Naomi's lips curl upward on the last word, and her eyes dash across the bar to Nathan sitting on a stool talking to his older brother playing bartender.

"How very *Harry Potter*," Beverly beams.

"I'm not going as a square," I grumble.

"Not a square. I just said a triangle, a circle, and a wand," Naomi repeats and bites the corner of her lip as though she's holding back a secret.

She and Beverly exchange a glance, and I'm reminded again of when the three of us were children. Naomi and Beverly, while six years apart, were closer to one another than Beverly and me.

You're our promise, Scotia, Daddy used to say to me, making me feel special and unique from my siblings.

Our mother wanted more children, fulfilling God's mission to procreate, but I believe the *act* of procreation was an excuse to get Daddy to conduct some husbandly business. I used the same excuse on Karl until we had Darlene. One child was all God would provide to us.

"No shapes, then," Beverly states, trying to pacify Naomi and me. Ever the peacemaker that one, which is ironic, considering her past.

"We could go as three witches," Naomi suggests next. She looks like a witch with her silver and white hair in riotous waves. Our Irish bloodline cursed her and Beverly with premature white hair. I was blessed from birth with this unusual pigment defect, giving me a permanent white strip of hair on the right side of my head. Some people say I look like Stacy London, the *What Not to Wear* fashionista, who I consider beautiful. Others have called the colorless locks the mark of the devil. Some days, I equally take that comment as a compliment.

"Like *Hocus Pocus*, the movie?" Beverly excitedly questions.

"No hocus pocus," I interject, shaking my head. My youngest sister is a tree-hugger with religious practices I consider strange and bordering on witchcraft. She's a Wiccan.

"We could be like the legendary Irish sisters: the maid, the matron, and the crone."

"And who is who?" I question, eyeing my youngest sister.

"I'd have to be the maid," Naomi says, nodding once.

Right, the eternal celestial virgin. I don't say it aloud, but Naomi's watching me and replies.

"There's nothing wrong with holding out for the man of your dreams." Naomi defends herself and her honor in remaining a virgin until she was almost forty. Well, *almost* a virgin, as she'd done the deed once—but only once—back when she was young and ironically at this bar.

"But there is an issue when the man of your dreams holds out against you," Beverly adds, and my chest squeezes at my sister's words. Her husband rarely had sex with her, preferring the beds of other women.

I suffered on both counts. I'd saved myself for my husband, who then held out for most of our marriage, preferring the beds of others as well.

"I could be the matron." Beverly clarifies, "As I've been married." Beverly's ex-husband was a worthless philanderer who didn't deserve her kind heart or youthful innocence.

"So I'm the crone?" I shriek a little louder than necessary. Turning my head, I notice others in our proximity have heard me. "What are you looking at?" I snap at a man dressed in head-to-toe leather. Twisting away from him before he can respond, I lift my wine glass for another sip. The flute is narrow, and I bet I've only received half a standard pour at the price of an entire bottle. The Fugitive isn't a winery but a biker bar. Their drink specials include whiskey or domestic beer.

"Think of us as representing the Emerald Island in the Green Valley," Nathan's brother teased when he took our drink orders. I don't believe Todd Ryder could find Ireland on a map, and we aren't in the valley but up and over the mountain in North Carolina. I can't believe I let my sister convince us to travel that treacherous highway. The same road that claimed our brother and could lead us home, if home still existed.

Green Valley is your home, I reminded myself as we passed Cedar Gap's old turnoff, where our house and church once stood. When I married Karl Simmons, I swallowed the proverbial Kool-Aid of Valley society and shunned my upbringing as if it had never occurred. I never wanted anyone to think I didn't deserve my position among the Green Valley elite.

"How about the three Fates of Greek mythology?" Naomi suggests, hoping to refocus our attention and defuse the ugly glare weighing on us from the biker at the nearby table.

"Isn't that almost the same as the three sisters?" Beverly asks. Her hands fidget with a paper napkin.

"Why don't we just go as the Three Little Pigs? The idea is just as ridiculous."

Beverly clamps her lips, refusing to engage in conflict as we try to restore our sisterly relationship which was once strained and distant.

"Because the big bad wolf is already one of us," Naomi says, twisting her lips, sizing up how I will react to the implication. I'm the hotheaded, quick-to-judge, eager-to-huff-and-puff one among us.

"I thought I was your wolf." A deep masculine voice interjects from behind me, and I spin to face Nathan, Naomi's husband. He's a jovial guy despite his large stature and leather jacket. His smile and the dimple hardly hidden under perfectly manicured salt-and-pepper scruff give his biker appearance a softer look. He appears mischievous in a good way as though he's a guy who just wants to have fun. He addresses Naomi when he asks, "Need anything, sweetheart?"

Next to Naomi, the slump of Beverly's shoulder is almost like a full-body sigh of awe. *When did my sister become the romantic?* Beverly suffered a failed marriage like me, yet I don't consider mine a complete failure. Karl and I had some success, including his medical practice and our daughter. My marital secrets will go to the grave with me. Thinking of gravestones, cemeteries, and death—

"So, Halloween?" I circle back as Naomi shakes her head at her fine husband.

"We could be the sisters of Native American legends. Winter squash, maize, and beans," Beverly suggests. Of course, she'd mention agriculture as she's a farmer.

"I am *not* dressing up as some vegetable raised on a pole," I definitively state.

"You could be a pole dancer," a rugged male voice suggests nearby, and all three of us turn to stare at the man dressed in leather at the next table. His white mustache reminds me of a sinister stalker. He looks like the poster child for motorcycle Santa minus a stocking cap. In its place is a red bandana over his thick skull.

"I beg your pardon," I drawl in that voice I reserve for gum under my shoe, scum of the earth, and those I believe have wronged me.

"Begging is what you'd do with me, honey." He winks at me, and my breath hitches, like a hiccup. Sitting taller in the backside-aching seat, I widen my eyes at the innuendo.

"I'd do no such thing," I state to the stranger as my gaze roves over his body, and I decide I'd rather drink raw sewage than solicit him for anything. "I beg for nothing."

For the flash of a second, I recall when I did plead with a man for something.

He told me I didn't need to beg him, though.

"You just *begged* my pardon," the man counters.

A deep chuckle hums behind me, but my eyes remain on the vulgar man who has no business interrupting our private conversation. Biker dude twists at the waist, providing himself a better view of my seated position, and he blatantly scans my body.

"Then again, I suppose with that tight ass, you don't need to beg. You need the pole removed from it."

My mouth falls open.

I take pride in my body, which is nearing fifty. My daily gym routine includes alternating yoga classes and circuit training, but I wasn't going to accept this *questionable* gentleman's compliment of my assets when he was insulting me in the next breath. Heat rushes my skin, and the flame of my tongue ignites, prepared to put this biker in his place.

"Bless your heart, but the only pole that needs to be taken down a notch is yours." My eyes roam over his leather-clad body before I add, "Then again, *it* probably shouldn't get any shorter." My implication of one partic-ular body part of his is evident.

The man's chair slides back, loudly scraping against the wood flooring as his body shifts, and I sit taller, bracing for his verbal assault while his body language suggests physical harm.

"All right, Herbie, that's enough. Don't make me call your old lady." The distinct male voice behind me sends a ripple up my spine while my entire body trembles with agitation, which includes wanting to fling more condemning words at the insulting biker. However, the rugged voice at my back forces my attention away from the biker. I spin and look up.

And up, and up, *and up.*

A solid man with thick arms crossed over a barrel chest glares at the opposite table, holding his protective stance directly behind my chair. I'd forgotten his presence for a second, or perhaps it emboldened me to speak as I did to the neighboring table. Ready to question the man behind me who was defending my honor, my mouth freezes at the sight of him. My tongue thickens, and I literally cannot find the words to address this male specimen who looks like a grizzly bear with his bushy beard and sex-roughened hair, both the color of midnight. His eyes are deep and equally dark, but I can't get a good look at them from this angle. Something about his stature screams not to mess with him. In some ways, he reminds me of Vernon Grady from Grady's Seed and Soil, but this is not Vernon. This man is . . . someone else.

Someone familiar.

But that can't be.

I'm imagining things because I just thought of him, and that night and the *not*-begging beg.

I'm imagining a man who never called me. I hadn't expected him to. That wasn't part of our arrangement. Still, I'd wanted to hear from him again. I wondered if he ever thought of me as I thought of him often.

His soulful, sad eyes. His powerful hands and tongue. His tender but hard kisses.

"Hey . . . Big Poppy," Naomi stammers, addressing the man whose glare does not leave the pole dancing requester at the other table.

"Naomi." His voice softens. "Brought some friends tonight?" His eyes drop to Beverly, and my heart races. *Why is he looking at her?* Beverly is taken as is Naomi. They both have a man. Then again, why do I care? This man is not my type. With his thick limbs and tall stature, a too-tight Henley and rips in his jeans, not to mention unruly hair and that beard, he is not a man of interest. If I had an interest in men, which I currently do not. I'm happily living the life of a single, productive businesswoman, taking full advantage of the freedom of my widowhood. Even to me, the thought feels crass, but I admit I don't miss Karl. We were partners, not lovers. We had an image to uphold, and we upheld it, but at the end of the day, our life was exhausting.

Glaring at my sister before turning my attention back to the grizzly creature, I come eye to belt buckle with his . . . *belt buckle.* I gaze up at him once more. His beard. His hair. He looks as if he could be . . . *but that would be impossible.* This man looks a little unruly, wild, and dangerous.

Swallowing thickly, my blush deepens, and I turn away again, facing my sisters. Naomi's eyes land on mine, and her brows furrow in question.

"Scotia?"

A heavy silence falls around us for a second, and then the man at my back speaks.

"Excuse me." Without looking, I feel the loss of him as he walks away. Then I take a deep breath as though I hadn't been able to breathe in his presence, and the scent of something crisp and fresh fills my nostrils.

Warm. Grassy. Lemony. Neat.

My heart gallops faster. My breathing grows shallow.

"What did you say his name was?" I shakily address Naomi, whose eyes narrow.

"Big Poppy. It's a little strange to call him that, but I don't know his real name. Everyone refers to him as Big Poppy. Are you okay?"

Spinning in my seat, I grip the back of the wooden chair. My gaze follows the movement of the large man as his body circles behind the bar, and he slaps Todd Ryder on the back. I can't pull my eyes away from him.

Something's familiar about him.

But it can't be who I think it is.

Something's recognizable in his size.

But he would never be here.

Something's intoxicating about his scent.

My eyes squint, tugging at my memory.

The pleasant scent. The size of him. The beard and hair are the confusing part. The man in my memory didn't have such fullness to either, but the way he saunters more than strolls triggers me. He pauses at the entrance to the pool hall and turns back to the bar, his stature resting in profile. With his hands cupping the edge of the wall, marking the entry to the pool room, he glances over his shoulder at me, and the unfamiliar registers as all too familiar. His position reminds me of a hotel wall and a man ready to leave my room. In under a minute, this man disappears, just like the man from that night.

Or rather, early morning.

"Sweet Jesus," I mutter in disbelief. "It can't be."

I stand without thinking. My hand grips the back of the chair to steady me at first, willing me to still, but my heart thunders, propelling my legs forward.

"Scotia?" Beverly calls out, her voice sounding far away. Ignoring my sister, I take a step forward, my eyes catching on an image of blackbirds on the wall.

"Three crows, I see. Good luck to me."

"You want to be three crows?" Naomi questions, and I wonder if my sister's hocus-pocus beliefs include reading minds.

I want good luck. *I want someone to belong to me*, I recall telling him. Memories of tangled sheets, deep kisses, and racing hearts flood me as I cross the bar, enter the pool hall, and note an emergency door in the back corner. The loud crash of it closing vibrates around the room.

Tell me three things, he said.

You. Me. A bed. I'd never been so bold.

Well, he replied, *good things happen in threes*.

CHAPTER 5

BUS RULES

[Chet]

"Chester?"

I ignore the soft call of my formal name in the darkness of the night. The tone is that of a woman I recall in fantasy but who doesn't exist in reality. This voice is the woman who settled under me, giving in to me and pleading with me not to stop what I'd started with her body.

This is not the tone of a woman standing on a sidewalk tearing others down.

I round my home located behind The Fugitive and stand against the side, catching my breath for a second. My heart thumps because Scotia is in my bar—*my bar, my space*—and she was mouthing off to Herbie, of all people. Harmless as a hedgehog, he's still a biker and a man with friends in the wrong places.

Jesus, she has no boundaries.

Waiting out the silence in the woods, I determine she's returned inside the bar, unwilling to venture into the dark around it. She *shouldn't* wander around my place.

No longer hearing sounds other than those familiar in the night, I enter my home.

Ten seconds later, a knock comes to the door.

My heart races again as I swing open the door and find Scotia standing at the base of the steps. There isn't much space on the narrow stairs inside the door, and I tower over her as she looks up at me with questioning gray eyes. Without thinking, I step back, and she takes the three steep steps upward. I walk farther into my home, keeping several feet of distance between us.

She called out a name I rarely hear. Maybe I misheard it echoing in the night air. Maybe I've been wishing someone had said it again in a voice soft with yearning.

Does she remember Chester Chesterfield? Does she think about last March?

Her gaze wanders around the tight space, taking in the dinette table with booth seats and the kitchenette area complete with miniature appliances. My large body blocks her vision of the back, which includes a bathroom and a bed.

"Do you live here?" she questions without the formality of a greeting or re-introduction. Her tone returns to the haughty woman on the street, and instantly, my hackles rise. I shouldn't have opened the door, and I damn well should not have let her into my home.

You should have never slept with her.

But she's so pretty despite the sneer of her mouth. Those dark locks with that distinguishing white strip, those silvery eyes like polished metal, and those kissable red lips that were all over my body once.

"You shouldn't be wandering around in the dark," I snap, noting the blackness outside the windows.

"You were," she reminds me. This is my land, though, and I'm familiar with it, which reminds me . . .

"You shouldn't enter the home of a stranger."

Her head tips at my warning, chin held higher.

"But we aren't strangers. You're Chester Chesterfield." For some reason, I don't confirm her statement. We stare at one another. Her eyes soften and the hesitation I recall from that morning appears in them. I give her a long moment to assess me—taking in my eyes, looking at my beard, roaming down my belly, and stopping at my zipper. If nothing triggers her memory that she's familiar with this body, I don't need to remind her who I am, especially as I shy away from being recognized, identified, or publicized as Chester Chesterfield.

"Name's Big Poppy," I say. Chester Chesterfield feels like another lifetime and the persona of a man I don't really know how to be. At first, I'd strived for all I have as him. Riches. Wealth. Property. I had one reason for that drive, and then that reason didn't want Chester Chesterfield. So I dumped him. Unfortunately, my legal name is on my assets, and on rare occasions, Chester Chesterfield returns.

"Big. Poppy," she repeats slowly, feeling out the name on her tongue. Davis gave me the name once we stole our first motorcycles. Riding my bike is the one thing that hasn't changed, even when I've tried to eradicate everything else from my past. My bike is a part of my soul, and my buddies are like family, so the name stuck.

Her head shakes in either disbelief or confusion. "And you live *here*?" Censure rests in her tone, and I recall her voice from a few weeks back.

"Are you judging me?"

"It's a bus," she states, gazing over everything once again as if she still can't believe it.

"You're observant," I snark, pride pinching as she recognizes the vehicle but not me. She didn't see *me* under the thick beard and reckless hair. I'm the same guy who looked into her vulnerable eyes and gave her what she asked of me. Yet she stands before me, not seeing me.

It's definitely for the best, I decide.

She is bitter and briny.

So why does her opinion bother me?

"No, I mean, it's a *school* bus."

"Brilliant again," I mutter. Her genius declaration states the obvious. My home is a *school* bus—a bus converted into a tiny house. With floors that look like hardwood and vertical pine boards on the walls, the space includes a built-in loveseat, booth seating, and modern conveniences for a micro-kitchen. The entire width of the back is one giant bed. The irony in this tiny house is I'm a big man. The other irony is, I learned my lesson. I don't need large material assets to be the man I want to be.

Her eyes narrow on me, and she shakes her head as if she's come to some sort of understanding with herself. "Yes, of course. You couldn't be who I thought you were."

"You thought I was this Chester dude?" I question, wondering why I'm egging her on and not kicking her ass out. Or telling her the truth.

Because you kind of liked her ass when you had it in your hands, holding her in place to dive deeper into her.

Because deep down, you don't want her to be a judgmental Judy. You want the woman who was sweet on you for one morning.

And you want her to want you as you are.

"Yes, Chester Chesterfield." Her voice turns dreamy on the name.

"And you know him how?"

"Are you kidding me?" She pauses, glaring at me before turning to stare out the side windows. Then her demeanor shifts. She stands taller, glancing around the space once again. Her nose wrinkles as though she smells something rotten. "So that's how you want to play it?"

"What do you really know about him?" I question next, not letting it go that she claims to know him—me—when she clearly doesn't.

With her head held upright and her neck elongated, I expect another voice shift, and I'm not disappointed when she goes into haughty-heiress mode. "He's a respected and esteemed citizen of Tennessee worth millions of dollars, which he generously donates to causes all over the state."

He sounds like a tool, I want to retort. It also sounds as though she's reading a LinkedIn profile, and I almost laugh.

What causes? How many millions? What do you mean respected and esteemed?

Could you see past all that and still want to be with me?

My guess is she knows all the answers to my first line of questions, and it's all the more reason not to bother with the second. I don't need some greedy woman after my millions nor do I need her finding out my biggest cause. She probably eats children for breakfast. She'd definitely hate the ones I help. The underprivileged. The forgotten. The left behind. She's the type who considers those kids beneath her. Not salt of the earth, just salty.

They represent who I once was.

So screw her.

"He sounds like an asshole," I say, arms still crossed over my chest as I narrow my gaze at her.

"He isn't," she defends, sounding like Louie when he argues with Hunter. Her arms fall to her sides, fingers fisting. Her brows pinch, puzzled. "Or at least, I didn't think he was. He was tender and sweet. Noble. . . and generous."

Somehow, I don't think we're talking about donations anymore but something else. Consummation. The Chester in her head gave her orgasms —generously—and he tried to be kind and delicate, sensing that was what she needed.

"I'm going to be so deep inside you, you'll feel me for weeks."

Did she? Did what we did haunt her like it haunted me?

She can't see past the Chester in her head, though, to realize I'm actually standing before her.

Her head tilts as she takes in my attire and my appearance once again. "I liked him." She wrinkles her nose as if to say, *You, not so much.*

My dick recognizes the softening of her tone, but it will not be allowed out to play with her. Her sidewalk show and her school bus disdain are reminders that she is not the same person I had passionate sex with months ago. Her true colors are showing, and they aren't as pretty as her face.

"Sounds like a putz," I say because that's what I am, or he is, or we are . . . whatever . . . by letting this woman get to me.

"He's not a putz."

"Right, because he's a millionaire who's *kind and generous*," I mock. Because who would give away most of his millions to support others in need? Don't know a guy like that. Nope. Not at all.

Her eyes roam my body once more, tripping down my chest and landing on my thick thighs, which I flex in my jeans. She flinches. Does she remember those legs between her own? Does she recall the power in them to move her at will? Does she want to tangle her legs with them again?

Her stuck-up attitude tells me probably not.

47

"You didn't call." Her gaze lowers to the floor and her voice drops so quiet I'm not certain I've heard her correctly.

"You mean that Chester fella didn't call." Hurt instantly crosses her face and then a mask falls into place. She doesn't want me. She doesn't know me. She wants a part of him, but he isn't going down that path again.

Any woman I allow close to me will know all of me and accept every slice and sliver or she wouldn't get near my heart. And as this woman isn't going to get that close, I don't have to worry.

"I see I've made a grave mistake," she says, stiffening her shoulders and her voice as she lifts her head. "I apologize." If shutters could slam shut on her expression, they just did. Her apology carries not one drop of sincerity, and without further words, she turns and walks to the door I left open. Her feet stomp down the bus steps, and then I hear the thud of them on the earth outside.

Because I'm not a total ass, I quietly follow her, making certain she re-enters the bar. She shouldn't be wandering around in the dark, even if only a hundred feet rests from my door to the building. Scotia Simmons could be a cold fish, and even a bear wouldn't mess with her, but I still want her to be safe.

I want to take care of her which is the most asinine thought I've ever had.

CHAPTER 6

MEN-STRUATION IS WOMEN'S FRUSTRATION

[Scotia]

A few days later, I'm still reeling from my encounter with one Big Poppy, who looked like Chester Chesterfield. They just could not be the same person.

Chester was cleanly trimmed with slicked-back hair and wore a tuxedo.

Big Poppy's beard was obnoxious and his locks unruly. He wore dark jeans with a hole in the knee like a wayward teenager, and his shirt was a size too small for his large stature. On display were thick arms that could wrap around me and tug me upward as he thrust into me, filling me, moving me like a plaything.

Of course, Big Poppy did not do those things with me.

So full, I cried to Chester Chesterfield. He's the one who made me feel as though I'd never been so complete. He's the one who kissed me like he needed me to breathe. He's the one who touched me like I was a tender flower. I felt every part of him inside me, and I wondered even more how I'd put up with Karl all those years.

You know why you did it, I remind myself.

Why had I asked that man about calling me? That had not been the plan. We were one night. Or rather one morning. Still, he'd been on my mind. Had I been on his?

The way he reacted he didn't want to be recognized by me. He didn't want to recall what we'd done. He was so different, and I'd misjudged him. As in, he was not who I thought he was.

He was not Chester Chesterfield.

Chester would never live in a converted bus—*a school bus!*—even under the disguise of pretty, modern, real estate terms like 'tiny house'. Honestly, who comes up with these names to glorify things?

A pickle is a pickle.

Then again, there is a difference. Genuine dill. Kosher dill. Sweet. Bread and butter. Gherkin.

This all reminds me I need to speak with Gideon and follow up on the delivery mishap from the other day, and I dismiss my aimless thoughts of Big Poppy or Chester. I'm on my way to take my SUV in for an oil change. I'm not feeling so great, though, so this is the last thing I want to do today.

Womanly issues, Karl politely called it.

Some days, it sucks being female and getting older. To put that in pretty terms, I'm menstruating in a peri-menopausal way. *Oh, who am I kidding?* There's no fluffy way to state what's happening to my body as I near fifty. I'm only forty-eight, but still, my female organs can just quit. They've already served their purpose, and that objective set sail a long, long time ago. Even though the doctor recently told me I could still conceive, I'm done. I almost fell off the exam table with that news.

Besides you need a man to fill the cruise ship.

"Dear God," I mutter as I drive to Winston Auto. I've lost my mind, comparing my body to a giant sea vessel. Is this another sign of peri-menopause nonsense? The time before the actual time. I just want this business over, especially as the cramps seem to have grown more painful in the past year and the flow heavier, and there's just no way to decorate that description.

I'm hit with a whammy of a spasm as I pull up to the auto shop, deciding I need a bathroom stat and something strong enough to rid me of the unnerving pain. I really should have rescheduled.

After I enter the service dock as directed, I park. I turn off the ignition, leave the fob in the cup holder, and open the door. I step out the driver's side.

And freeze.

Unbearable pain grips me, and my body expels something I don't even want to consider. I shiver with chills and tremble uncontrollably. Gripping the open door's edge and reaching for the headrest of the driver's seat, I bend forward and just know without looking that something is trickling down my leg—something red and obvious.

And I'm mortified.

"What can I do for you today, Mrs. Simmons?"

My eyes close. *Please don't let it be that awful Shelly Sullivan.* She's so strange, and the past few times I've been here, we've had words.

Then again, she is female, and I don't want one of those Winston boys assisting me. Swallowing all my pride, knowing I can't step away from this vehicle without giving away what's happened to me, I do something I've never ever done before.

"Please help me." My voice cracks as tears I didn't know existed trickle down my face.

Her quiet pause tells me she's caught off guard by my distress, or perhaps it's the awkwardness of my position. Maybe it's just that she really doesn't like me, and I've never cared so much about another's opinion as I do at this moment. I shake off my concern and slip my hand to the seat of my SUV.

"Just get me some paper towels," I snap, ducking my head inside my vehicle. I don't even want to see the evidence on my own leg, and as I'm wearing a skirt, I'm certain things appear unsightly.

"What's going on here?" a gruff male voice asks.

Oh God. No. Just no on every level of no.

Big Poppy.

I refuse to look up. Instead, I close my eyes as more tears drip from under my lids. Nothing could be more embarrassing than my current state, and the fact I recognize the rugged voice somewhere behind me takes this humiliation to a new stratosphere.

"Scotia?" The tenderness in his questioning tone brings heavier tears as my body continues to tremble with chills and panic. I'm afraid to move, and there's no way I can lift my head and walk as if something isn't trickling down my leg, giving away the fact I'm only human, a female, and nearing fifty.

"Please go away," I whisper, my voice quaking. That ninny Shelly still hasn't moved to retrieve any paper towels, and I'm trying to remember if I have napkins in the glove box. *Can I even reach the compartment?* I sense motion behind me, hear some shuffling, and then a wad of rough paper towel swipes up my leg to the back of my knee.

Oh God, could this get any worse?

"You don't need to . . . Just hand it . . . I can . . ."

More swiping. More scratching on my skin.

"Can you move?" he asks.

"I need my purse," I mutter. I need more than a change of feminine products, but it's at least a start until I can get home. I'll need to call Naomi and hope she isn't working, as Beverly doesn't drive. "And the glove compartment."

"What's in the glove box?" he asks, but I can't speak. As if mentioning my unmentionables would be more undignified than my current position. However, I keep a spare pair of underwear in the compartment.

"Just something . . ." My voice croaks. A hand rests on my lower back, and instead of flinching, I absorb his comfort. I could use a hot pad and a warm soak in a tub, which is out of the question. What I really need is a stiff drink and the past ten minutes of my life erased.

"I'll get it, darlin'." His deep voice is close behind me, and while I don't care for the endearment, the term is rather sweet and soothing coming from him. I slip to the side enough to press my body against the open driver's door, but he's too large to reach around me and across the front seat.

"Stay right here," he says. I almost snap, *where do you think I'll go*, but I don't. I bite the inside of my cheek hard to keep myself in check.

Big Poppy rounds my sensible crossover SUV and opens the passenger door for my purse and to access the glove compartment. I don't look directly at him but watch his thick fingers find what I need and hold the fabric off the tip of his finger for a second. Thin. Red. Lacy. It's not the most practical pair for my situation, and I'd forgotten which one was in the compartment. *Mama always said never to leave home without a spare pair of underwear.* What can I say? I like pretty panties and matching bras. I needed to feel sexy somehow when my husband wasn't interested in me, but sexiness is the last thing on my mind. Big Poppy crumples the pair into his fist and slips it into his pants pocket before shutting the passenger door and rounding my SUV again.

"Okay, darlin'," he says again as if warning me of something. The alert becomes clear when I'm suddenly tucked underneath a thick arm and curled into his chest.

"What are you doing?" I snap without much sass. I'm in no state to be arguing. He ignores my irritation anyway and my arms wrap around his waist, instantly hanging onto him. I still can't look him in the face. In fact, I don't want to meet anyone's gaze, especially that twit Shelly, who remains near my open driver's door. My eyes close as if no one can see me as Big Poppy guides me through the waiting area and suddenly it hits me.

I'm in the most embarrassing position of my life and this man is being kind to me.

Eventually, we stop before a restroom door.

"I'll wait here," he says, pressing open the door and nudging me forward.

"I'm going to call my sister." There's no way I'm waiting out the time for an oil change. I can come back for my car later, tomorrow, or never, as I won't be able to show my face in this garage again. And I will never be able to look at Big Poppy again.

"I said, I'll wait here." His voice roughens, emphasizing he wants no argument from me, and a new shiver ripples up my spine. I step into the restroom and clean up as best as I can. My skirt is ruined in the back, so I remove my cardigan to wrap the material around my waist. The drooping sweater isn't enough of a disguise, but I could at least get home without exposing myself to more attention. My hands tremble as I wash up, having disposed of everything, including my previous underwear. I left my coat in my car, but I won't return for it. I call my sister instead, explaining my situation. Thankfully, she can come pick me up.

"Just come to the bathroom because I'm not stepping out of here." I'd rather sleep on the nasty tile floor than ever walk out of this room to witnesses.

As I click off the phone with Naomi, a soft knock sounds on the door, and then it opens a crack. Apparently, I forgot to lock it.

"Scotia, you doing okay?" His deep voice startles me.

"Yes. You may go now." I don't know why I say such a thing in such a tone. After dismissing him, I lean against the sink with my back to the door. My eyes flick to the mirror where I see only a partial reflection of him.

"I can drive you home," he kindly suggests.

"Don't be silly. I'm sure you have an appointment." I straighten my back and hold my head up. *Mask in place, Scotia.*

"I'm here to have my car winterized, but I can come back another day."

"I don't want to put you out." I fluff my hair as though what happened is no big deal. As if I'm not uncomfortably standing in a public bathroom with a sweater around my waist covering the large stain. As if the most humiliating moment of my life hadn't just occurred before this man.

"Dammit, darlin'. I'm trying to help."

"Well, I don't want your help," I bark, although I clearly was in a position of need a few minutes ago, and he did assist me to the restroom. I shift so I get a better glimpse of him reflected in the mirror. His thick hand holds the edge of the door. His broad bicep on display. His brows furrow beneath the shaggy droop of unruly hair.

"I called my sister. Naomi's coming for me." I lean forward and pretend to check my lipstick. *Mask in place, Scotia.* I can hardly focus on my mouth and ignore my trembling finger as I swipe at the corners.

Big Poppy huffs. He knows my sister, although she doesn't know much about him. During the entire ride back to Green Valley after our night at The Fugitive, I grilled her about her association with him. I wanted to know everything, and she offered nothing more than he was the owner of the bar, motel, and gas station, and best friend to her husband's older brother, Todd. I had already learned he lived in a bus, but I questioned why he didn't have a room in his own motel. Not that a person wants to live in a motel room any more than a school bus, but—

"Scotia," he growls.

"Thank you. That is all." *It was really sweet of you to help me*, I should add, but I don't say the rest of my thoughts. I don't offer him the kindness he deserves after being kind to me. I have dismissed him again. *Mask in place, Scotia.* I've never had to work so hard to keep myself under control. I'm so embarrassed by all that has happened, which means it's best to pretend nothing happened. I cannot regulate what my body does. It's happened before. It would most likely happen again in another month.

Yay for peri-menopause, says no one ever.

The door to the restroom closes, signaling Big Poppy's finished with me, and I slump against the sink, covering my face with a hand. Internally, I scold myself. *Mask in place, Scotia!*

Then I stand taller, forcing myself to look into my own eyes, and return the invisible shield I always wear to stay in disguise. *Mask in place, Scotia.*

Over the years, the pep talk has been the same. *You've got this. You know how to pretend nothing happened. Nothing hurts you. No one can see what's inside you.*

The façade falls back into place. I've had decades of practice keeping everyone out, but there's a crack in my protective covering. A sliver I plan to seal shut as soon as I forget about Chester Chesterfield and Big Poppy, and the kindness they've each shown me. I also need to rid thoughts of how similar the two of them look despite one in a tux and the other in flannel. Their striking appearance is only the surface level. The chip in my mask is from the kind actions displayed despite a trimmed beard or an unruly one. It's the man beneath the beard—whoever he may be—who has me flustered and regretting, perhaps for the first time, that I hadn't been a little kinder in return.

CHAPTER 7

MRS. PICKLE

[Chet]

Getting what I'd seen a few days ago out of my head was difficult. Scotia trembling as she was, red running down the inside of her leg, and tears in her voice. My first thought upon recognizing her was she was dying, but then I immediately realized that was ridiculous.

When she used her sharp tongue with me when all I was trying to do was help her, I wanted to strangle her myself.

Days later, I'm still pissed.

Once again, I am reminded of that woman on the sidewalk, tearing down others. I recall her disgruntled words about my bus-home a week ago. And now, I can add her ungraciousness to the list. Her attitude sucks. She's judgmental *and* unappreciative.

And once again, I'm wondering why I care.

I know her type. Hennessy Miller was like that. *Henny*. A beauty queen in my eyes. The girl of my dreams. We were sweethearts once upon a time. Only I wasn't good enough for her daddy's approval—a kid in foster care, a guy who was trailer trash, a man without means—doesn't make the cut for a princess. I set out to prove my worth, and I did.

I want to marry you.

I built this home for you.

Thoughts of Henny peak like the mountaintop as I pull up to Harper House—the house she didn't want after she told me she didn't want me.

I should have burned this place to the ground, but the idea makes my blood run cold. Instead, I call to mind the new purpose of this home and the unfortunate tragedy that started its purpose.

I shove open the door of my Dodge Charger, telling myself I'm just in a sour mood. *Again.* I haven't seen Scotia for months, and now, I've seen her twice in one week. I need her to stop haunting me. She isn't the person I thought she was. She isn't the person I experienced back in March in a hotel room. And she's too similar to another woman who broke me.

As I enter the playroom of Harper House, I find my pissy mood isn't over.

"And then . . ." A tender, feminine voice drifts to the edge of the room, the tone shifting as she transfers to another character. I'm dumbstruck for thirty seconds. I don't even hear what she reads. Instead, I see red.

"We weren't expecting you today," Maura says with surprise, sneaking up next to me. I had business at my office in Knoxville. Her comment snaps me out of my focus on the woman reading to the boys. "She's good, right?"

"What the fuck is she doing here?" Maura's blue eyes blink as she glances up at me. I've never used such a rough tone or direct language with her. She knows I appreciate her. I couldn't do what I've done without her, and I'd never want to lose her, but this is just too much.

"She's—" I don't let her finish before I step fully into the room. Dewey turns his head to greet me.

"Uncle Chet!" he calls out and waves his hand for me to come closer. He smiles under his dark-rimmed glasses, eager for me to share this moment with him, but I want another story.

"What are you doing here?" I growl at her, staring at the woman who looked down her nose at me for the last time.

"I—" Her voice squeaks as she looks up, noticing my presence for the first time. The boys shift. Louie goes up on his knees, drawing closer to where she sits in a chair holding a book. Our current tenant, Malik, the boy who doesn't speak, crawls on his knees behind the furniture, disappearing from view.

"I asked you a question," I bellow louder. Louie covers his ears.

"You're frightening the children," she states as though I'm the monster. As if I'm the bad guy for giving them a home and trying to keep them safe from women who will take advantage of their kindness one day. I'm the bad guy providing them with a haven of warm shelter and education with the hope they'll grow to be smart and generous without being a fool like me.

"*You're* frightening the children," I snap back at her, although that isn't the scene before me. Louie tucks himself under her protective arm, and Dewey stares daggers at me. Hugh comes out of the adjoining study room.

"What's going on, Uncle Chet?"

"Chet?" she questions, her brows creasing, her mind processing.

Hugh looks from me to Scotia. "Do you know Uncle Chet?" he questions, and Louie's little head looks up at her with all the love of a child enthralled by beauty and tenderness. Her hand absentmindedly strokes up and down his spine, and the motion annoys me.

"You aren't allowed to touch him." There are guidelines to being a volunteer here.

"Hey," Hugh interjects with all his fourteen-year-old masculinity.

"I beg your pardon," she defends, stilling her hand on Louie's back and tightening her hold on him.

I had a comeback for those words in that tone one night, but this isn't the same scene. This is the home of boys put in my care, and I will not let her tarnish them with her snide comments, hurtful words, and demeaning sneers. She's all salt, brine and vinegar, and she will not be like that here.

My heart hammers. Blood pumps. My ears fill with thumping sounds.

"She's been vetted and approved," Maura states at my side, and I turn on her, a woman I trust with everything. My home. The lives of my boys. The future of the foster kids we've taken in.

"How could you let her in here?" I glare at the woman I consider a devoted friend and partner. Maura stares back at me as though I've lost my mind, and I suppose I have a bit.

"She volunteered and went through the necessary requirements." Trained. Certified. Qualified. It was a process. It took time. I know the channels.

How did I not know Scotia Simmons was a volunteer here?

"Why?" I turn on Scotia. "Why here? Are you stalking me?" Does she want Chester Chesterfield so badly that she was willing to pry into him until she dug so deep, she learned his history? His pathetic rags-to-riches sob story. I own this house as the one good deed I've done in my life, but it's furnished with heartache from the tragedy that started it. Does she know about Harper and Davis? Will she judge them too? How deep did she shovel? Does she want dick that badly? Or maybe it's the money?

I'm spiraling out of control with my thoughts and my anger.

Before she can answer, I speak again. "You are not welcome here."

"Chet!" Maura shrieks beside me, and I turn on her.

"I do not approve of this. Of all the things, over all the years, this is the one thing I'm saying no to."

I turn back to Scotia. "Get out."

She stares at me, mouth agape, and I prepare myself for the venom this woman can spew. I've heard it on the street, heard it in my bar, and heard it in my own house.

"Don't speak," I warn her. Her lips clamp shut. "I don't know what you're playing at, but you cannot be here. Do not return." My body vibrates with the threat to her and fear for the boys. She'll expose them. She'll use them for some nefarious advantage I can't put my finger on, and she'll hurt their innocent hearts.

Holding my ground, I watch as she turns to Louie under her arm. "It's okay, darling." Her soft voice reminds me of Harper speaking to her child. Louie was only a baby when his mother passed. Scotia gives him another squeeze and leans forward to kiss his forehead.

The audacity. She can't touch him. She shouldn't offer him affection. She can't be kind to him.

My blood races faster. My heart pounds triple time.

She closes the book on her lap and slowly stands, setting it on the cushion. Leaning around the chair, she holds out a hand for Malik. "It's okay, precious. He won't hurt you. He's a good man."

Her words slam into me like a Mack truck.

She can't mean what she says. She doesn't *know* me. She doesn't know any of my many sides. However, she's completely correct. I'd never harm any of the children coming through our doors. My mission has always been to offer safety and unconditional love.

I continue to watch as Scotia reaches for the poor kid I've frightened enough he's hiding, and I realize I've set us back with my outburst. He'll never approach me. He might never open up to anyone. He might even run away from here.

Dammit. My shoulders fall. I didn't intend to scare the kid.

"Okay, precious," she whispers in defeat. Her own shoulders sag when he doesn't respond to her.

He only trusts Mrs. Pickle, I want to yell at her.

My eyes narrow as Scotia stands and glares at me with the glare of all glares. I already know she can be salty and vitriolic, but I've also seen her vulnerable and sweet. There's so much more to her than her briny tongue, and I'm slow to recognize what's been happening before me.

She'd been reading to the boys.

Boys who look heartsick and puzzled on her behalf.

She used endearments, soft touches, and encouragement.

He's a good man.

No, she cannot mean it. She's after something, but I don't know what it is, and she can't have it. Not with them.

"Chester," she sneers my name, her recognition of me clear. "Or should I call you Chet?"

She hasn't earned the right to call me by the nickname, and she hasn't learned we are one and the same but very different. Chet Chester Chesterfield Big Poppy—I am a complex man.

Chet wants her out of here.

Big Poppy thinks she has some serious nerve.

Chester remembers a morning spent enraptured with her.

All three parts of me agree that she needs to leave, but I do another sweep of the room. Malik remains hidden while Louie looks horrified.

Dewey and Hunter question me with puzzled eyes. Hugh places his hands on his hips, giving me a look, like *What is your problem?* Campbell just shakes his head.

How am I in the wrong here?

My mouth opens to ask the question and then snaps shut when Scotia moves. She bows her head at Maura, who smiles sympathetically at our intruder. An unreadable expression fills Scotia's face. Her shoulders straighten. Her head lifts higher. I witness once again her building a wall around herself, and then she walks out of the room with the grace of a queen and without a single word.

When the front door to the house closes with a soft click and not the slam I'm expecting, I return my sight to the playroom floor, taking in a stunned Dewey and quiet Hunter. Campbell has lowered his head, and Hugh folds his arms over his chest, glaring back at me as fiercely as Scotia can. He almost pulls it off but then I remember his age, and I want to laugh until I look at Louie.

Tears fill his soft eyes, and his lower lip trembles.

"She's not a good woman," I say in my defense, my voice weakening as I wonder how they don't see her judgement, ridicule, and spite. Too quickly, I feel the uncertainty of my words. With them, she was the sweet voice of a woman reading beloved characters. With them, she was a tender touch and soft encouragement. With them, she was clearly someone they all adored.

Louie continues to look up at me, broken and questioning.

"But she's Mrs. Pickle." His small voice quivers, and I stare back at him, my brows forming a tight crease of concern.

"She's . . ." *What?*

CHAPTER 8

HOLD THE PICKLES

[Chet]

Finding Scotia was easier than I thought. The hardest part was sucking up my own pride to go to her. Days after kicking her out of Harper House, Louie still hadn't spoken to me. Dewey could hardly look me in the eye, but Hugh did, with a constant glare of disdain.

"They'll get over it," Maura said but even her heart wasn't in the suggestion. She felt schooled that I'd called out her judgment in allowing someone the likes of Scotia Simmons near the boys. And I felt equally bereft that I might have misunderstood the situation.

"You're missing the fact that I'm raising five boys, now six, without a partner. Savannah is part-time. Scotia has been a welcome addition to give me support with their homework and the personal attention each boy rightfully deserves," Maura argued, which made me feel as if I haven't been available enough for the boys.

In A Pickle is located on the edge of the business district in Green Valley. After the ladies' night at The Fugitive, I learned Todd's brother is married to Scotia's sister, and it didn't take much to discover more about Scotia, at least on a surface level. Widowed years ago, she used her inheritance to start her own small business focused on fried pickles and pickle-related paraphernalia. This was noted when I opened the door to the small store and read a sign that said: *A pickle is a cucumber with experience* quoted by someone I don't recognize.

"May I help you?" The young man entering the front was a decent-looking guy, too nice-looking, which made me feel all creepy for noticing, but he was almost pretty. His dark hair was so gelled in place a tsunami wouldn't move it. In a dress shirt rolled to his elbows, bright green pants, and fancy leather shoes, he looked like a pickle product. It was weird.

"I'm looking for Mrs. . . . Simmons," I state, stumbling over calling her Mrs. Pickle like the boys.

"Do you have an appointment?"

"I have an apology." I stare at Pretty Boy, who artfully lifts one brow. He looks like he should be modeling cologne, not working at a pickle place.

"I'll see if she's available." He looks me up and down, and then adds, "On second thought, she's available." He shakes his head as if he knows something I don't and leads me toward the back of the location. He cuts us short at a staircase, and I follow him up.

As we enter her office, I hear her speaking into her phone from where she's seated in a swivel chair with her back to her desk and the door. "You would not believe the hair on that woman. It's as big as her mouth some days."

Pretty Boy clears his throat, and she spins, eyes narrowing at him for the interruption until she sees me.

"Hazel, I've got to go." Without additional commentary, she hangs up and drops her phone on the desk before her. It's a large piece of furniture, almost too big for the frame of the woman behind it, but not so large as to cover her sneer at her assistant before speaking to me.

"Mr. Chesterfield, to what do I owe this visit?" She side-eyes Pretty Guy and addresses him. "Make yourself useful and find something to do." She flicks her hand at him as though she's shooing away a bug, and I shake my head, wondering if being here is a huge mistake.

Louie's sad eyes come to mind.

Dammit.

Once her lap boy leaves, she directs me to take a seat on the other side of that big desk. I feel like I'm in the principal's office or at the bank asking for a loan, the first of which I did many times, and the second of which I only did once. I don't sit, and she stares up at me over the imposing furniture, crossing her arms on top of it. Like a hawk narrowing in on prey, she's waiting me out.

"I apologize. The boys would like you to return."

Still squinting at me, she says, "That's it?"

"Not sure what else to say?"

"From the moment we've met, it's been one lie after another with you, and this is all you have to say to me?"

"Lie to you?" I chortle. "How did I lie?"

"You are Chester Chesterfield, the renowned Chester Chesterfield with a fortune in oil and a multitude of philanthropy behind your name."

"That's not a lie. I am him."

"But you're claiming to be Big Poppy, biker bar/motel owner, and living in a school bus."

"Those things are also true." I lean forward, bracing my hands on the back of the chair where she suggested I sit.

"Then which one is it? Mr. Chesterfield or Big Poppy?"

"I'm both. And people closest to me call me Chet." The name is reserved for those I consider most important, like Maura and the boys.

"You cannot be two people, Mr. Chesterfield. Or three."

"Why not? You are." A short huff comes from her, and her shoulders visibly flinch. Her fingers tighten together.

"You have no idea what you're talking about," she states. I take her in for a minute. Her midnight hair looks a little closer to charcoal ash with that white strip near the right side of her face. Her exotic gray eyes border on black when she's hell-bent and sparkle silver when she's not. Her seated position is a pose. She looks regal once again, haughty actually, and I almost laugh. She's uptight and taking herself too seriously, but damn, is she pretty.

"I know exactly what I'm talking about, *Mrs. Pickle.* See, I met this woman more than six months ago, and she begged me to have sex with her—"

"I did no such thing," she interjects.

"Never said it was you," I say, pausing to let the possibility sink in. "But let me rephrase. The exact words were 'Doesn't anyone want to have sex with me?' And here's the thing, I did. See, there was this moment when she looked at me with caution but also desire, and my insides got all mixed up. She was sweet, unbuttoned, and eager for my touch. She wanted me, responded to me, and man, she just felt good." Scotia's cheeks pinken, but I continue. "She told me she had three desires—her, me, and a bed—and I wanted to give her anything she asked for. Or rather, begged." I huff, reminding her of how we started. "I couldn't resist trying to please her for some damn reason, and then I found it strange when she pleased me."

"I pleased you?" Her head snaps upward. Her voice is a whisper, swallowing around the words. A faint smile curls her lips, but she rolls them together to fight it.

"But then I see this woman on the street a few months back, and she is ripping apart other women, tearing them down for their lack of pole dancing skills."

"I did not—"

Funny, I didn't say it was her. "And then I find her in my bar, and she's cussing out one of my biker patrons."

"He started—"

"But the real kicker is when she attacked me in my home."

"I did not attack you!" she shrieks.

"You insulted my house."

"It's a bus!" she bellows.

"We've established that, but I live there. It's my home, and I'll be damned if I'm going to let a woman full of *piss* and vinegar come into my house and patronize the place where I live, even if she is the prettiest thing I've ever seen."

Scotia blinks up at me. "You think I'm pretty?" Her voice cracks as her knuckles turn white.

"That's all you got out of what I said?" I'm flabbergasted. What is *with* this woman? Does she not hear herself? Does she not know what she says about others? Is everything always about her?

"I'm sorry."

I stand straighter, surprised by her words. "What are you sorry for?"

"You're right. I shouldn't have misjudged your bus. It's a lovely bus."

"It's my home," I say through gritted teeth.

"Yes, fine. Your tiny house is pleasing."

We stare at one another for a long minute.

"Explain to me how you got to the boys." I need to know she didn't dig into Chester Chesterfield's private affairs. That her being there isn't about *him* but to truly help the boys.

"My sister Naomi works at the Green Valley Public Library. She knew I was looking for volunteer work, and Maura had inquired about assistance with homework and activities, like reading to the boys."

I continue to stare at her. It's a simple enough explanation, but something still feels off. Then other thoughts occur. She's a desirable woman in bed. She's a salty socialite. She's a foster home volunteer. "You're just as complicated as I am, *Mrs. Pickle.*"

Silence falls between us again, and her eyes turn hungry just as they did that morning. I need to learn all her signs. *Is she turned on?*

"But what I really can't figure out is why such a powerful woman . . ." —I pause and look around the office—" . . . needs to ask a man to fuck her?"

I take another glance around the room noting something that looks strangely like a pickle on a stick. It looks like a golden dick. *What the hell?* "Then again, is that why you have Pretty Boy around?" Maybe she's into younger men. He's polished and shiny and perhaps more her type.

"Pretty Boy?" she questions, and I nod toward the door. Her mouth gapes wide before she speaks. "Why I never . . . Gideon is my assistant."

"He assist you in all means?" I tip up a brow, questioning his purpose. And wondering myself why I'd care if he dipped his dill into her.

She glares at me. The silence that falls between us is thicker than a pickle and just as crisp.

Shoulders back, she states, "I'm a widow. I don't date."

"Don't need to date to have sex," I tell her.

"I'm not like that," she says.

"You were with me," I remind her.

"You were different."

"Why?" Herein lies the million-dollar question. *Why me?* "And don't tell me it was some girly-gossip, peer pressure thing. Why did you really approach me at the bar?"

"You have sorrowful, soulful eyes, and I wanted them to look at me, like maybe you might see me differently, see me for who I am."

I . . . *what?* This softens my tense stance but not my retort.

"Lady, I have no idea who you are." I mean, she's playing two sides of a fence herself, but I don't really know who she is or why she's like this. Why was she sweet inside a hotel room with me, but salt and sass on a sidewalk?

Her shoulders stiffen, and somehow, I recognize this signal. She's going into mean-girl mode, and I clutch harder at the chairback I'm gripping. I'm not going to like whatever she says next.

"I'm the Fried Pickle Princess. In A Pickle is my wedge of heaven, and it's time for me to get back to business." Her hands unclasp, and she lays them flat on the desktop. Slowly, she stands. Something in her demeanor has shifted. She looks at me, but her eyes are different. "I accept your weak apology because I miss the boys and I'd like to see them again."

"Weak apology," I mumble under my breath. She has no idea the strength it took to come here and grovel on behalf of those kids, yet it's still not good enough for her. I know her type. Nothing will ever be good enough for Scotia. And she owes me.

"Where's my apology?" I question as I pace around the chair before me and stand in front of her desk, pressing the tips of my fingers on the surface. I mirror her position, raising my own barbed wire fence against her.

"For wh—" She stops herself short, hopefully recalling the other day when she brushed me aside despite trying to help her at the auto shop. Her gaze lowers for the surface of her desk, and I'd like to think she's chagrined, but a live fish has a better chance against a hungry grizzly bear than I do of getting her to admit she was ungrateful.

Taking a deep breath, I move onto another topic. "Funny that the pickle princess is so desperate for dick. That why you surround yourself with a phallic-looking vegetable?"

"Technically, pickles are a fruit because of the seeds on the inside of the meat, but your reasoning for my interest is offensive."

Her eyes dilate as though she's taken a hit of something sweet, something strong, something sending her into an abyss, and I wonder again if she's getting turned on because, for some reason, I am.

"Shocker. Scotia is offended by something." My heart hammers. My blood pumps faster. My dick rises, matching the phallic symbols around us. She leans against her desk, mimicking my stance, and I notice the hint of cleavage in the opening of her blouse. I've had those breasts in my mouth. I've nipped those nipples. I've had her begging me for more.

"I'll have you know my interest in pickles is because my late husband hated them."

"He hated pickles?" My eyes leap up to hers, tugging away from those tempting tits.

"He hated phallic symbols."

He . . . "What?"

"He . . . Never you mind. Just leave. You said your piece. Now get out and let me return to work."

There is no way I'm leaving yet. I have *got* to know more here. Besides, my own phallus is ripe and ready for peppering.

"To work with penis imposters."

"Yes. No. With the pickles—"

"Which you like to coat in special sauce?" I make a motion with my hand, jerking up and down an imaginary cylinder object, and man, that is a bad move because I want her hands on my cylinder, working me up.

"Well, no, not exactly . . ." Her chest heaves, and that blouse opens a bit, spreading the material to give me a better view of her breasts.

"Because you like to play with dick," I tease.

"I beg your pardon," she retorts, turning bright red and leaning further toward me.

"Remember, you don't have to beg with me, darlin'." I pause to let the words sink in until her widened eyes display her recollection of our first meeting. "If I offered to let you work with mine again, would you deny me?"

"I . . ." Her breath catches. That swell of breast appears. I'm so hard I'm ready to burst, and I need a taste of those lips, hanging open and softly panting.

"Desk sex?" I say, lowering my voice in suggestion.

"I never . . ."

I lean across the desk, curl my fingers into her silky blouse, and gently drag her to me. My mouth crashes against hers, lashing her with my tongue. She quickly responds, matching the eagerness of this kiss until she's on the move, climbing up on the desk to her knees and scooting over the surface to press up against me. Her arms circle my neck, and I tug her to my chest with my fingers hooked in her blouse.

"You're a vile man," she says against my lips, but her bark has lost all its bite.

"But you want me," I counter, assured by the eagerness of her mouth on mine.

"God yes," she whimpers. She wants me badly—phallus parts and all. Her fingers delve into my hair as mine scrunch up the material of her shirt. A button pops off her blouse, exposing those luscious breasts to my hands, and I flatten my palm over her racing heart. I like laying my skin against hers. She feels real to me when I touch her.

My other hand slips around to her ass, cupping a firm globe and tugging her tighter to me. She's still on her knees, leaning over to kiss me. Continuing to kiss her, I step back, so she can swing her legs over the edge of the desk. Something falls to the floor, scattering over the carpet.

"Really want to do this here?" I say to her, slipping my hand to her knee, and then working it under her skirt. More skin. More touch. The hand on her chest slips to the back of her neck, bringing her mouth back to mine while my fingers massage up her thigh. I can't get enough of her.

"Yes," she whimpers again, without removing her lips from mine. Her fingers fist in the front of my shirt, holding me to her while her other hand is buried in my hair, cupping my head.

I tug at the scrap of fabric under her skirt, discovering the material flimsy like the pair I found in her glove compartment. This woman likes pretty, lacy underthings. I easily brush the soaked strip aside to get my fingers where I want them to go. My thick fingertip circles her briefly before I thrust my index finger inside her.

Her mouth breaks from mine as her head tips back, and her fingers loosen on my shirt. She's still holding me, but she's falling into me, loving my touch.

"Like that, darlin'?" I whisper to her neck, sucking at her skin while my finger strokes in and out of her wet heat.

"I like everything you do to me," she says breathlessly, and I grin, recalling our first time. She let me do so much to her that morning, and I'm ready for a repeat. Adding a second finger to the first, she cries out at the stretch, taking me deeper. Her head tips upward, and her eyes seek mine.

"I like you best like this," she says, and my grin twists to a crooked curl.

"I like *you* best like this." My mouth covers hers again for another rough kiss before my thumb finds the trigger spot to push her over the edge.

"Chester," she whispers, pulling back but staring directly into my eyes. "I want you inside me again."

"Coming soon, darlin'. Going to finish this first." My fingers move faster, pleasuring deeper, and she quickly breaks, opening her mouth but holding back the cry since we are in her office. As she settles, I work my buckle and zipper with one hand, shoving my pants down my hips enough to set me free. Then I'm hiking up her skirt and scooting her to the edge of the desk. Her arm slips around my neck, and I line up with her entrance.

"Condom," she states, breathless and desperate.

"I'm a little old to carry them in my wallet," I retort, returning my mouth to her neck and holding myself just outside her, pressing the tip through her sensitive folds ready to accept me into her.

"Top drawer, right-hand side."

I freeze.

I pull back to look at her. She's all sex kitten with half-mast eyes and puffy lips, but I'm wondering how often she does *this* if she keeps a box of condoms in her desk. I thought sex was a rarity for her. Maybe Pretty Boy gets her off after all.

Still breathing heavily, her body stills as well. Her legs dangle off the desk on either side of mine, and her eyes give me that look—the one where she's concerned she'll lose me, the one where she's afraid I'll pull back. And I can't seem to help my retreat because I need to know what this is all about.

"This was my husband's old desk. They were his."

"How old are they?"

"Over seven years," she says, her voice cooling a bit as her hand slips from my shoulder to my chest. Her palm flattens against my heaving pecs, and I'm certain she can feel the hammering under my skin.

"And you still have them?" I snort as if it isn't an issue, but it kind of is to me.

"I was hoping one day I'd finally get to use them."

What? "What?"

"Never mind," she says, pushing at me to step back, but I'm not letting this go. What does she mean she'd finally get to use her own husband's condoms?

"Explain this to me," I say, releasing my phallic part and tugging up one side of my pants as I sense us both shutting down a bit. My balls are going to ache bad if I don't get inside her, but I have to hear this.

"I . . . I can't." Avoiding looking at me, she tugs at her skirt to lower it and then fumbles with her blouse, realizing a button is missing. Clutching at the loose material with a fist, she slips off the desk and shimmies her hips. One-handed, she smooths down the remainder of her skirt.

"Scotia, what do you mean?" This isn't making any sense. How did she not use the condoms with her husband? Only a brief glance meets my eyes, and I see the security wall begin to slide around her.

Sighing, she walks around the desk, leaving me to fumble with my pants, righting my zipper and buckling my belt while I'm still mostly hard behind it. I gaze back at her, and it's as if I see the armor curling around her and locking into place like a giant shield.

"Mr. Chesterfield, this is old news. My husband was killed in a case of mistaken identity exiting a motel room after spending time with his lover."

"Your husband had an affair?" The words insensitively tumble forward before I can catch them, but I stare at her, taking in her body. She's in excellent shape with an amazing figure. Great tits. Perfect ass. Who cheats on that? Unless he couldn't take her mouth. Maybe she wasn't sweet with him in the bedroom like she's been with me. Was she verbally rough on him? Did she school him? Scold him? Scowl like she's doing at me right now?

"Yes, thank you for so eloquently rewording it. He had an affair." Her voice turns haughty like it can, and the final link of armor slams into place. She's closed herself in and not letting me through the barrier.

"Don't do that," I demand.

"Don't do what?"

"Don't lock up like that."

"There's no reason to let you in." She tips her head, opening a drawer of her desk. To my surprise, she pulls out the old box of condoms and sets them before me. "Perhaps you're right. I shouldn't have kept these. He had a small penis, and they'd never fit yours."

I choke out a bitter laugh. She can't be serious. Staring at her, I wonder who the hell she is and what the hell she's hiding inside. Where did the vibrant woman of minutes ago disappear to? A better question is, why?

"What if I come back with my own?" I snark, hoping to restore a little humor to this awkward situation. Her eyes leap up to mine.

"Mr. Chesterfield, we both know you won't be back in my office. What we had was one time."

"What about this?" I point at the disarray on her desk. My heart starts to beat triple time again. This cannot be happening.

"This was a—"

"Don't," I growl, holding up a hand. I've heard the words before, and bile stirs in the pit of my belly. "Don't need to tell me twice."

You and I were never going to be, Chester. It was a mistake to think you could come back for me.

Turning for the door, I see myself out, passing Pretty Boy on the way to the front door and wondering if maybe he could fill out those condoms for the phallus princess.

Maybe has a small penis like her small heart.

CHAPTER 9

HALLOWEEN SURPRISES

[Scotia]

"Happy Halloween," I call out to the boys when I enter the Harper House after my week banishment. I'm a few days early for Halloween, but I've brought each of the boys a treat in a plastic orange jack-o'-lantern.

"You spoil them," Maura says, greeting me with a smile and taking a few buckets from my hands.

"Every child deserves to be spoiled." I believe that. I spoiled my own child, maybe a little too much, but she was the only one I had when I'd hoped to have many. I miss my Darlene, but she's busy following in her father's doctor-footsteps, saving the world one patient at a time as Karl did. A Simmons through and through, there's almost no trace of me in my grown daughter.

"Well, the boys will love this," Maura says as I follow her into the great room where they play. It's a beautiful room with two-story windows that overlook the mountain-scape, and on a sunny day, it's a glorious space to be in.

"I've missed them," I mutter. Maura catches my eye, knowing why I haven't been present. She must also know that Chester apologized, although I don't know if he included the fine details of his apology—an orgasm on my desk. Of course, there could have been more on that ancient piece of furniture, left over from my husband's years as a prominent pediatrician, if I hadn't killed the moment by mentioning the condom box.

"Why didn't you ever tell me Chester Chesterfield was the benefactor of this place?" I ask Maura, who levels her eyes at me.

"Would it have made a difference?"

I consider my response carefully. "No, but it still would have been nice not to be blindsided by him."

"I think he's the one a little blind lately." She winks at me and then calls out, "Boys, we have a visitor!" Her voice carries in the vaulted ceiling of the room. We both hear the scampering of feet, and for a second, I worry they won't be as excited to see me as I am to see them.

"Mrs. Pickle!" Hunter cries out, and Louie almost plows him down, trying to get to me first. I'm circled in an embrace at my waist, which nearly knocks me over, but Maura catches me from behind.

"You're back," Louie says, his sweet voice coming to me as he lifts his head but doesn't release his arms from around me.

"Yes, I am." I smile down at him. This child stole my heart the first moment I met him almost a year ago. Their story is so tragic, yet they've been given everything. They want for nothing, except their parents, I suppose. Maura is the only parent most of these boys have known to give them love, and Chester fits the bill as well.

"How's Malik?" I ask Maura, still stroking my hand over Louie's hair. I had to answer a strict questionnaire, pass sexual predator training (meaning I'm not one), and pass child protective services training (meaning I recognize signs of abuse) all to become a volunteer at this home. Maura keeps tight records on those who pass through the doors of Harper House. One thing I'd been told in my training was to withhold physical contact, but Maura assured me an occasional hug or an affectionate touch did not make me a sexual deviant or warrant pedophile concerns. I hope to never tell her how I know all about pedophile stigma and the types of people mislabeled with it.

"He's missed you," Maura says, her eyes drifting to the chair where I sat when Chester kicked me out. Malik sits behind it, staring out the large window. "He goes there every day after his schooling."

There still isn't any word on who Malik is or where he's from. He seems to have appeared from nowhere, and he's frightened of something. As Maura's a registered homeschool instructor, she doesn't send him to school. She worried about emotional or behavioral issues connected with putting him in school temporarily. Malik's caseworker agreed with the homeschool option until more is known about him, as long as he proves he's learning, which he does very efficiently and eagerly. He's bright, following Maura's instructions and more, but he still doesn't speak to anyone, not even the other boys.

I lean forward to press a kiss to the top of Louie's head and hand him a pumpkin bucket. "For Halloween, a few days early," I tell him. Maura helps me distribute the remainder of the treat bags, and then I lower myself beside Malik.

"Malik, precious." I speak softly to him, and he turns to me, eyes widening. Offering him the biggest, most genuine smile in return, I say, "I have something for you."

Holding out the container, I watch him glance at the gift. His dark eyes are nearly saucers.

"It's okay. You can take it." The package holds more candy than a sweet store, a T-shirt with a pickle carved like a jack-o'-lantern and the words: *Keeping it in the Family* because cucumbers are related to the gourd family of which pumpkins are a member. We sell another shirt with a pickle in sunglasses and his thumb up, saying: *Gherkin It*, but that didn't seem appropriate for a child. There's also a book inside every bucket, one I specifically picked for each child with the help of Naomi's recommendations. As a local librarian, she's well versed in children's reading interests.

"How have you been?" I ask him, but his response is only a shrug. "Maura says you're doing well with your schoolwork."

Malik's big eyes examine each item in the bucket, lovingly holding them up before setting each aside. He isn't looking at me, but instead fighting a grin at the T-shirt I've given him. Next, he reaches for the book, *Artemis Fowl*.

"I hope you like it," I say as his hand skims down the front cover, and he flips it to the back. "It's yours to keep."

His head pops up, and he stares at me, his eyes questioning mine. I have my own set of inquiries. Who are you, precious boy? Where did you come from? Did somebody hurt you? Because I can't imagine running away from anywhere unless you were hurt in some manner. Deputy Fredrick Boone has been out to investigate, but as Malik wouldn't go to him, Maura had to snap a picture of Malik from her phone and share the image so the authorities could conduct their search. Malik's case is a reverse situation. A child has been found, but we don't know where he's lost from.

"Should we read it together?" I offer, and Malik flips his position so he can sit with his back to the windows. I scoot myself to the wall, keeping my legs bent and angled awkwardly to my side because of my skirt. I open the book.

"Chapter one," I begin when a loud voice immediately interrupts us.

"It looks like Halloween puked in here," Chester says, scanning the room littered with boys, candy wrappers, and unpacked plastic pumpkins.

"Mrs. Pickle is back," Louie excitedly tells his uncle.

"She brought me my own copy of *The Red Pyramid*," Dewey announces him.

Hunter is already wearing his T-shirt over his other clothing along with a pair of sunglasses with pickle-shaped lenses. "How do I look?" he asks.

"Pickle-icious," Campbell answers, and the boys break into laughter. Malik softly grins next to me and curls against my arm, tilting his head as if he can hide behind my small bicep. Chester meets my eyes and stiffly nods.

"Mrs. Pickle," he states, and I dip my chin to him in return. *So this is how it will be? Formal instead of familiar?* Of course, I didn't expect anything else. Expectation is the work of the devil. When you expect something, you are sure to be disappointed. That's been a motto all my life. I've worked for all I have—Darlene and my business. I worked *with* Karl, but not in the way people would think. The devotion to our marriage took that word to a level different from an average couple.

Chester busies himself with the other boys, and I admire how he treats them as equals. I don't know the full story, other than three are siblings. Maura is a mother figure to all the boys, but the three Maverik children do not call her mom.

"They had their own mother. He doesn't want them to forget her," Maura once told me, never offering me their mother's name or the private patron to this facility. This large house is really more a private home with a collection of loving people living here, but it is also state-certified as a licensed foster home. I don't understand all the particulars, but it never mattered. I'd been searching for a place to volunteer in child-related services when Maura found me through Naomi.

Chester lowers his large body to the floor, sitting eye level with the boys and listening to their exploits. Watching him, I see him as a different person once again. He's been Chester the successful businessman, and Big Poppy the gruff biker, but this new side is another contrast. Uncle Chet is compassionate and caring toward his nephews. He's watching them, interested in what they are saying, and adding his own thoughts to their conversations. He isn't just present; he's involved. When he catches me observing him, I lower my head once more.

My attention returns to Malik. "It's okay, precious. Remember I told you he is a good man." I don't actually know how good Chester has been to the boys, but I have a sense Uncle Chet adds another dimension to a complex and kind human being adored by these children. "You don't need to fear him," I tell the boy huddling at my elbow. Malik meets my eyes and nods. He taps the book, so I begin reading.

Despite soulful eyes pressing on me from across the room, I don't look up. Instead, I concentrate as best I can on the adventures within the story in my hands.

"Chet, it's time for dinner," Savannah eventually announces, and I realize I've lost track of time. My head lifts to the dark windows, and I curse inside as I hate driving down these mountain switchbacks at night. My older eyes trick me. Smiling down at Malik, I direct him to wash up as requested and notice Chester watching the young woman standing at the edge of the room. Savannah is some sort of kitchen help, mainly with cooking support, as Maura is a busy housemother of five, now six, boys.

I note how she addressed Chester moments ago. *Chet. Only people closest to me call me Chet.*

Just how close are Savannah and Chet?

Savannah is a pretty thing, possibly in her early thirties, quiet and sweet, and holding the interest of one man in this house. Chester can't take his eyes off her, and Hugh says something to his uncle. The teenager laughs, and Chester's eyes find mine across the room. Then he reaches out for Hugh's ankle as the teen walks away. The boy trips to the floor, and Uncle Chet holds him in a headlock, rubbing his knuckles in the boy's hair. Ruckus ensues.

Louie and Hunter run to the rescue of the eldest house member while Campbell and Dewey can't be bothered. Savannah observes all this with a tiny smile on her lips, and I wonder if she's just as intrigued by the man wrestling with the boys on the floor. They'd make a stunning couple, even though he's more than a decade older than her. Both have dark hair and deep-set eyes with tall statures. She's thin to his solid frame. My imagination drifts to her under him, similar to how he was once over me.

I don't like that image.

"Mrs. Pickle, stay for dinner?" Savannah addresses me, although both adult women know my real name. I roll to my hands, positioned on all fours, and then use the edge of the chair partially hiding me to help me stand.

"Oh, I best be going," I say. I give another hesitant glance to the darkness beyond the window. *Why did I stay so long tonight?*

"We have plenty," she says, pointing over her shoulder toward the dining room.

"She said she needed to go," Chester interjects, flipping a final child tenderly over his shoulder and righting him to his feet. The loving uncle swats at Louie's backside, who runs off to wash his hands. Hugh remains on the floor, catching his breath with his hair standing on end.

"Why can't she stay, Uncle Chet?" Hugh interjects, becoming my defender as he did the day I was kicked out.

"She said she had to go," Chester counters again, scrambling my thoughts. I didn't say that, not exactly, and his dismissal of me encourages me to counterattack.

"On second thought, I'd love to stay for supper."

CHAPTER 10

A SLICE OF HONESTY

[Chet]

Of course, Scotia stays for dinner and then hangs out afterward, helping Savannah clean up and reading Louie a final bedtime story. Once I do my rounds to say good night to all, I head down the stairs and find Scotia putting on her coat in the large front entryway. I've decided to stay the night in a guest room kept for me off the kitchen.

Savannah addresses Scotia as she stands near our guest. "Thank you for your help tonight."

"It was my pleasure," Scotia replies. As I hit the bottom step and land on the entryway's tile flooring, Savannah looks up at me.

"I'm finished in the kitchen, so I'll be heading out."

"Sure. Have a good night."

"I guess I'll be going as well," Scotia states.

"You're still here?" I mock and instantly regret the words. I step closer to where she stands near the front door. Scotia reaches into her pocket for a pair of gloves. Watching her slide them on, I replay the night's interactions.

Louie admires her more than I'm comfortable with. Malik is like a shadow to her. She asked Hugh and Campbell about the MMA classes. Dewey enjoyed conversation with her about some popular book I know nothing about, and Hunter teased her about her hair. She smiled at him—a genuine, reached-her-eyes smile—and those orbs sparkled like polished silver.

"Why *are* you here, Scotia? Why are you volunteering at this home?"

"I already told you. I was looking for volunteer work and—"

I raise two fingers and cover her lips, stopping her babble. "I want the real answer, Scotia. Be real here." My voice softens as I slide my fingers down her chin. They twitch to continue the path along her neck and around to the nape, but I'm still raw from our sudden end the other day in her office, and she's been distant with me all night.

She shrugs. "My husband was a pediatrician. He loved children." She smiles weakly. "I thought this was a good way to continue his mission."

Does she think of her late husband often? Her actions honor him, but I remember learning he had an affair. I also recall how she retains a box of *his* condoms. Can she not let him go even after he broke their marital vows?

"You really loved him, didn't you?" It seems a silly question to ask. Of course, she loved her husband, but something in her eyes has me questioning her marriage all the same. "Do you miss him? Your late husband?"

"Karl was my best friend," she says, her eyes avoiding mine. "But I hated him." Her eyes close. "God forgive me." Her hand lifts to cover her mouth and mine tips up her chin, forcing her to open her eyes and look at me in the dim light of the entryway. The sweet vulnerability has returned to them for a second.

"Being married to him was exhausting," she says, and for a glimmer of a second, I see she's being very real with me. "And I don't know why I tell you these things," she mumbles more to herself than me.

I nod, realizing I don't need more details about him tonight. I still want to know why she chose Harper House for her volunteer work, though.

"Nathan told me you have one child." It's not a question, but I'm hoping she'll tell me more. My fingers slip from her chin to her cheek, curling loose hairs around her ear. My eyes focus on the white strip.

"Yes. A daughter named Darlene. She's a doctor like her daddy. He would have been so proud to know she follows in his footsteps." She pauses until my eyes pull away from the pigment-less strip and meet hers. "He wanted a boy. Someone to carry on his family name. Simmons. They were lawyers and doctors and advanced education professionals. I never finished college. I got my M-R-S, instead."

I don't know the Simmons name, and it takes me a minute to realize M-R-S means she became a missus. I softly chuckle as my fingers absent-mindedly continue stroking her hair.

"Nothing to be ashamed of, darlin'. I barely finished high school, and I'm still a success. So are you," I remind her.

"When Karl passed, I . . . well, lots of things happened, and then I started my business in pickles." She quietly laughs to herself as though she holds a bitter joke inside, and I want to know the secret. "When I was nominated for small-business entrepreneur of the year for a female-led company, the one thing holding me back from winning was the fact I didn't have any community service."

My fingers stroking her hair over her ear still, and my eyes meet hers again. My skin bristles. *Is this why she's here?* To beef up her resume? Words climb my throat, ready to tell her once again to get out. Her eyes try to hold mine, and she interjects before I speak.

"I wanted to help where I could. Help some child fulfill his dream because . . . well, I have my reasons," she huffs, stiffening her shoulders. I wish there'd been someone who wanted to help me fulfill my dreams when I was a kid. No one read to me when I was little, brought me Halloween treats or gave me kind kisses on the head. All I got were slaps and insults until I started working for Frank Sepco. He's the person who really turned my life around, but I was a late bloomer. I'd been twenty when that happened.

"What do you know about the boys?" Thinking of Davis and Harper, I swallow against a lump in my throat. Our voices have remained low despite the fact we are the only two standing in the entryway. The darkness here somberly surrounds us, keeping us cocooned close to one another.

"Enough. They all call you Uncle Chet, but you're not related to any of them by blood. Hugh, Dewey, and Louie are siblings who lost their parents. Hunter was left on the doorstep and adopted by Maura while Campbell was a kinship placement, meaning the state asked Maura to take him in as she's a distant relative to him."

"You know enough," I say. "I won't let anything hurt them, blood or not. If you're volunteering here to plump up your resume, you'll need to quit. I won't let you list this place somewhere to soothe your soul. You won't get a reference from us." Harper House is privately owned and operated. We follow strict guidelines. We exist for the boys. We will not be fluffing her feathers.

"I'd never expose them like that," she defends, holding her head higher, and my hand slips to the side of her throat. "You've done so much for them. You really are a good man."

My hand pulls back from her, feeling unsteady with the compliment.

"Why do you do it?" she questions, and I step back, unprepared to share *all* my secrets with her. She watches me retreat, eyes softening while she struggles to shut herself off. I'm not certain who needs to protect who here.

"Do you really think I'm an evil witch?"

"I don't think you're a witch, Scotia." I sigh, struggling with my thoughts. "You're an entitled woman who is easily bored with things, started a business to say fuck you to your late husband, and then took on this place to clear your conscience."

She flinches, hurt stinging her cheeks, and I instantly feel guilty. What I said might have been too harsh, too real, but I don't think I'm completely wrong. She'd grow bored with me after a while, using me as a phallic plaything. And she'll get bored of these boys with their ruckus and roughhousing.

When she peers back at me, the shutters are shored up, and she's shut down on me.

"I'm sorry. That might have been too much."

"You wanted to be real," she whispers. "I see where I stand."

"Where do you want to stand?" I question before I consider what I might be asking. Could she stand by a man like me? Take on these boys and love them as I do?

"Seeing as you have me all figured out, Mr. Chesterfield, I don't suppose it matters."

Although I've stepped back from her, we're still only inches apart. Her chest begins to heave in her winter jacket, and I feel her breath reaching me with her sharp exhale after her statement. I reach for the white strip in her hair, twirling the locks around one thick finger and spiraling down the length.

"I hate when you call me Mr. Chesterfield," I say, feeling like it's a derogative dig, or maybe she's trying to remind me she thought I was someone else, and I'm standing here proving I'm not him. I'm not some rich dude with millions in oil, but just some guy doing the best he can. She'd be disappointed to learn the truth.

"I hate you like this," she whispers. My eyes flick to hers. She told me she liked me the other day on her desk. She told me she liked me in a hotel bed. There's disappointment in her voice tonight, and something pressed on my chest. I'm breaking the illusion she has of me. She liked my dick, but me? Not so much. Maybe it's for the best. Why do I care how she feels about me?

My eyes remain on that swatch of hair. I start at the top again, wind it around my finger, and slide down to the ends.

"And I suppose I've kept you from enjoying your evening with someone."

I stop my motions and stare at her. My nostrils flare. "Careful. You're as green as your pickles."

"I am not jealous," she stammers, fighting words never so *un*true from a woman.

"It's okay, darlin'. It's a good color on you." Her mouth pops open, but I don't let her have the last word. My mouth covers hers. She stills a second, surprised perhaps, but then she gives in to me. She falls against the front door, and I press my large body against hers. I brace my forearm against the closure near her head, while my other hand wraps around the back of her neck. This isn't meant to build, to tumble us down to the entry room floor. This is only a kiss to tell her where she stands with me.

Against a front door.

In Harper House.

With my body over hers.

And my lips attached to her.

85

Not anyone else. There's only Scotia, and I can't explain why she's under my skin and often in my thoughts.

"Again, I'm sorry I kicked you out," I whisper against her lips, hoping this time she doesn't consider my apology weak.

"I'm glad to be back. I missed the boys." She smiles slowly, her mouth still against mine.

"Is that all you missed?"

Her smile grows, and she kisses me back one more time before leaning away from me, head lightly tapping the door at her back.

I struggle to fight a smile mirroring hers.

"I kind of like you like this," I tease, and then I reach around her for the doorknob. If she doesn't leave, we might end up on this entryway floor after all.

* * *

Since I spent the night at the house, I wake early to have breakfast with the boys before they start their day.

"Uncle Chet, you ask any girls out lately?" Hugh asks, and I choke on my cereal, thinking he saw me kissing Scotia last night in the front hall.

"Ask who out?"

"Anyone," he states.

"I think you should ask out Mrs. Pickle," Louie interjects, and my head lifts. "Whatever 'ask out' means?"

"He means make out. He should kiss her," Campbell explains, and I almost drop my spoon. He's ten. How does he know these things?

"Kissing? Ewww," Louie moans.

"He means date. As in, Uncle Chet should ask Mrs. Pickle out on a date. Take her to dinner. Maybe a movie." Dewey's been the one offering an explanation, and I stare at him. When did he get date-wise? I pause that question and move to a different one.

"Why would I date Mrs. Pickle?"

"Yeah, she looks like a skunk," Hunter says.

"She does not," Louie defends.

"Boys," I interject.

"Because then you could marry her, and we could be a family." Dewey's words stun me. They also make me feel a little sick to my stomach. Does he not feel like we're a family? He has me, although I'm no prize. He has Maura. Does he miss his parents? Of course, he misses them. Davis and Harper were amazing together and amazing with their children. They were a perfect family.

As Dewey's eyes lower to the table, I don't have time to address my concern when Campbell speaks again.

"She doesn't smell like pickles," Campbell adds, shifting the conversation away from the sad head dive it was about to take. "She smells pretty."

She does smell nice—fresh, expensive, fruity even but understated.

"She does too smell like pickles," Hunter insists, then giggles.

"Does not," Louie argues next, but I can't take my eyes off Dewey.

"Of course, you probably shouldn't ask her to marry you unless you love her and make sure she loves you back. It's hard when you love someone when they don't love you in return." My spoon clatters to the bowl as I stare at the middle Maverik boy. What does he know of unrequited love? Who has hurt him already?

"Who said anything about love?" Campbell questions. "We're talking about kissing."

"We aren't talking about kissing," I stammer, sensing that one day I am going to have to have a talk with each and every one of them about kissing, and women, and protection—for both their peckers and their hearts.

"You're talking about love because you're all in *luu*-uve with Clementine," Hugh teases of the middle brother.

"Am not," Dewey defends, his face heating to fire-engine red.

"Are too," Hugh teases back.

"Who's Clementine?" I interject, picking up my spoon, but no one listens to me.

"You're just jealous," Dewey retorts.

"Oh, right. Like I'd be jealous over a mini-Professor McGonagall." Hugh snorts.

"It's Professor Trelawney, and she does not look like her," Dewey stammers in defense, the red of his cheeks turning purple in anger.

"*Okay*, what's this?" I hold up my spoon, tipping it toward Dewey.

"You like a girl at school?" I can't handle a second boy becoming girl-obsessed like Hugh.

My thoughts flip back to last night and the kiss in the entryway with Scotia. She turns me upside down and all around, and I feel like I'm chasing my tail with her. One minute sweet. One minute bitter. Yet, I might have a crush on her like my boy Dewey has on some girl.

"She's just a friend," Dewey says, but the heat in his cheeks tells me there is more in his heart toward this girl.

"They're *Harry Potter* nerds," Hugh drones.

"We are not," Dewey whines, pushing his glasses up the bridge of his nose and reminding me of the fictional character.

"Hugh, don't pick on your brother like that," I warn. *One day your brother might be all you have*, I want to add. Davis was that brother to me, and then he was gone.

"Even you call him that," Hugh retorts, nodding at me, and I swallow back the scolding as he isn't wrong. I don't understand Dewey and his mind. I marvel at his smarts, but I don't try to comprehend his intelligence because I just can't. Sometimes, his nerdiness befuddles me.

Dewey's wide, soft eyes look up at me. Minus the glasses, he's Davis in miniature. He doesn't ask me if it's true. His eyes give away his hurt. Suddenly, I'm helpless, wishing to defend myself, but I can't. My heart rips in two.

Dewey lowers his spoon to the table. "May I be excused?" he asks, keeping up his manners while probably wanting to disappear under the table. I know I want to.

"Dew," I say softly, but he slips from the seat, running up to his room.

Dammit. This is why I can't be in charge of children.

CHAPTER 11

COSTUMES START A CUSTOM

[Scotia]

As Halloween nears, I acquiesce to both my sisters' decisions on costumes. I'm still wondering why we need to coordinate, but I bite my tongue, which is difficult some days. I'm working on it.

My sister Naomi being a Wiccan means all kinds of things I don't understand, like tree-hugging and celestial loving under moon cycles and inner-goddess stuff. I'm still the church-going Christian our religious parents raised us to be. Beverly is sort-of hit or miss with church attendance. As sisters, we've agreed to respectfully disagree on religious matters.

For Naomi, her autumn traditions revolve around Samhain, a Gaelic celebration on the American Halloween. Her practice includes a bonfire to honor the dead, which Beverly has decided to host on her property this year. To my surprise, my once reclusive sister wants to throw a party, and I'm thinking Jedd has everything to do with it.

"I'm not dancing around some gigantic firepit, prancing barefoot and praying to the moon," I state as the three of us meet at Daisy's Nut House, a favorite local eatery specializing in donuts. We're here for a final discussion of the upcoming holiday.

"You don't have to dance. I just thought it would be a nice way for the three of us to celebrate Jebediah," Naomi says. She was closest to our brother when we were younger. I do not want to discuss him—*may he rest in peace*—and Lord knows I mean it as he was reckless and wild as a child.

"I can't dance around a fire anyway," Beverly says, her voice soft as she references her permanent limp and use of arm-cuff crutches to support her weight. Physically, she's come a long way in a year with the help of her fiancé, Jedd Flemming, but Beverly isn't going to whip around a roaring tower of flames any more than me.

"Fine, I'll just dance later," Naomi admits, saddened we aren't more willing participants in her fiery jig.

"Why are you hosting this bonfire again?" I question Beverly.

"Jedd and I thought it would be fun for adults after the community center party."

The community center is the focal point of Green Valley society with a year-round farmers' market, the annual Halloween party, and the Friday night jam sessions where one of our own had her start before she became a famous country singer.

"Well, I'm not wearing a mouse costume to the community party," I say. Naomi's last vote in the costume debate was to dress like the "Three Blind Mice," wearing all black with mouse ears and sunglasses. Then Beverly found us official costumes. The concept is simple enough, but I don't like the symbolism of the getups—we were three women blinded by love. My sisters are both missing the fact that they are no longer blind but all-seeing. I'm the only one who is still a visually impaired fool in matters of the heart and body.

I have no idea where Chester and I stand, or if we are standing at all.

His kiss the other night was pretty powerful, as they all have been.

"I'm sorry I kicked you out."

"I'm glad to be back. I missed the boys."

"Is that all you missed?"

How do I tell him I think about him daily? I think about that morning on the regular. We've been up and down this month like a rollercoaster.

One minute he's sugar kindness. The next he's brine with extra salt. When he kisses me, though, he's the refreshing fragrance of dill and I lose my head.

Had he missed me? It's a question I'd never ask.

"I think we should save the mice costumes for the party at The Fugitive and wear our celestial bodies T-shirts to the tamer gathering at the community center. It's going to be chilly later that night, anyway."

Naomi found us shirts—the Sun, the moon, and the Earth—for the three of us to wear. We can form an eclipse depending on how we stand next to one another.

"What party at The Fugitive?" That's the bar Chester owns as Big Poppy, or whatever he goes by depending on where he is.

"The Fugitive is hosting a Halloween party on Saturday," Naomi explains. I stare at my sister, unaware of this party and very aware I was not invited. The sting in my heart does not go unnoticed.

"Won't it be dangerous?" The only way to get there is drive The Tail of the Dragon and the fact it's essentially a biker bar, attending a party at The Fugitive does not sound like a smart idea, even if we've already been there once.

"We'll stay the night," Naomi offers, and both my sisters blush in varying degrees. For Naomi, The Fugitive is where everything began for her and Nathan. For Beverly, she's living with Jedd, so the admission she's sleeping with her fiancé is not a secret. I'm the one alone, outside their happy little love-bliss nests.

"I wasn't invited," I say, turning up my nose at being excluded. *Mask in place, Scotia.* "Sounds stupid," I immediately add, hoping to disguise my hurt. A bunch of bikers getting drunk and raising a ruckus while dressed in costumes—I can't picture it. And for some reason, I don't want to because all I see is a beautiful biker woman dressed in some glorious historically correct medieval outfit dancing with a roguish Big Poppy Chester Chesterfield Chet as they fall into the mating traditions associated with Halloween. It's the number one holiday for random hookups, a fun fact shared with me by my assistant, Gideon.

"Oh, your invitation is a given as Beverly and I were both included,"

Naomi states, not necessarily reassuring me that the invite did include me directly.

"I have plans," I lie, knowing it will likely be like any other night for me. I'll work late, then eat dinner standing by my kitchen sink. Maybe read something dirty and fall into bed turned on and dreaming of one lumber-jack-looking biker named Big Poppy. Maybe that night, the fantasy will be a partially tux-clad millionaire named Mr. Chesterfield. Or perhaps, the evening will include images of an easygoing bearded guy named Chet on a living room floor.

"We can't be the two blind mice," Beverly states. "It's not a thing."

"Then go as Mickey and Minnie Mouse," I retort.

"We aren't a couple," Naomi clarifies, as if I don't know this about my siblings.

"What is Nathan going as?" I question, wondering why there is so much emphasis on us dressing up and not the men in *their* lives doing the same.

"Nathan says he's going to be a mouse catcher and carry around a net."

Mouse catcher? Is that a thing?

"Jedd's going to be a mouse-trap. He claims his mechanical arm will give off the look well enough." Jedd is comfortable working with only one arm, but he's also known to wear a prosthesis, which looks like something bionic, on his amputated arm.

"And who's going to match me?" I question, noting I'm the fifth wheel in this collection.

"We'll need to find someone who will be a giant wedge of cheese," Naomi states as if that's a possibility and won't look ridiculous on a grown man.

"Yes, you need a good wedge," Beverly says. We fall into slow silence while Beverly twists her lips. Her mischievous eyes dance, Naomi snorts, and I can't seem to help myself. I chuckle a little at my sister's ribbing.

Yes, I'd love a thick wedging.

CHAPTER 12

BONFIRE CONFESSIONS

[Chet]

"I think my nephew has a crush on your daughter," I say to Nathan as we stand around the bonfire on Beverly and Jedd's property. It's the night of the local community center's annual Halloween party, which I attended earlier this evening at the insistence of the boys. In hopes to see Scotia, I agreed to go with the collection of pirates, Harry Potter lookalikes, and one too-cool-for-a-costume fourteen-year-old.

That's where I noticed a fuzzy-haired blonde with large glasses hanging out with Dewey most of the evening. They are on the school's robotics team together, but there is something more than teammates in Dewey's eyes when he looks at Clementine Ryder.

Another thing I noticed at the party was Scotia's avoidance of the boys and me, but I don't mention it to Nathan.

"I didn't know Dewey Maverik was your nephew," Naomi says. "I don't suppose I should mention we have a pet hedgehog named Dewey Decimal, should I?" As she's a local librarian, I've heard Miss Naomi's name a time or two, but Maura does the library runs. It's funny how small our world is in Green Valley. The librarian Dewey adores is now the stepmother to the girl he has a crush on.

"I didn't realize your Clementine was Dewey's love interest."

"They won't be dating anytime soon," Nathan warns while tucking Naomi under his arm.

"You just shush. They're too young to date, but nothing's wrong with a little crush. They have similar interests, and it just leads to a natural inclination to like each other."

"Then how do you explain us?" Nathan teases his wife, who is pretty dissimilar to him.

"Opposites attract."

I shake my head, thinking of her sister Scotia. The pull of positive and negative forces must be the explanation for my attraction to her because no matter how hard I tell myself to look away, I'm drawn to her like a high-powered magnet. Her marked hair. Her vulnerable eyes. Even her sharp tongue.

Something lures me to her. My eyes followed her earlier at the community center party, but she never looked up at me once. Is she ashamed of who I am as Big Poppy? It wouldn't be the first time I didn't meet a woman's approval in a social setting. Henny never took our relationship public. I was her dirty little secret—trailer trash, serviceman, good in bed —to a reckless girl with a rebellious spirit.

Thoughts comparing Henny to Scotia put me in a foul mood. Adding in the fact Scotia didn't acknowledge the boys, and that snub was just unacceptable to me. The boys adore her, and she told me she was happy to be back at Harper House.

"I'm glad to be back. I missed the boys."

"Is that all you missed?"

She'd stared up at me, eyes hesitating. She's afraid to open up to me, and I can't exactly blame her after our back-and-forth with misunderstandings about Mrs. Pickle and her purpose at Harper House. Then again, she's been equally disillusioned between Chester, Big Poppy, and me.

Still, I crave one of her honest comments.

I like you best like this.

However, now, I'm just pissed off. She disappeared from the party shortly after our arrival, and I've been stewing ever since. She was wearing a T-shirt with a giant sun on it. Maybe she ran off with some swanky astronaut wanting to circle her sun and make her the center of his universe. I gag with the adolescent thought.

There aren't any children at this party. This is adults-only, including Beverly and Jedd, obviously. Nathan and Naomi are here. Jedd invited a veteran friend named Tower Hudson who is living in his old farmstead with Jedd's younger brother. They're turning the place into a veteran's refuge. Vernon Grady from Grady Seed & Soil is here with his wife, Abigail, who's a drunken mess, and Vernon's sister, Wilhemina, is with them. I'm introduced to Jedd's sister, whom I've never met before. We're an odd collection of old friends bringing together new ones.

Not too long after introductions, a posse of women joins us, and it's like witnessing the mean girls arriving at high school. The way they walk. The way they talk. Before they even near the blazing fire, I recognize Scotia Simmons and her friends from the sidewalk last summer.

"I still cannot believe she tried to imitate Julianne MacIntyre's coleslaw. I mean, you just do not do such a thing. That slaw is like a national treasure," one biddy states.

"Sacrilegious, indeed, sister," the other agrees.

There isn't enough beer for me to handle their kind of showdown in my piss-poor mood, so I chug the rest of mine and excuse myself from Nathan. I head to a cooler packed full of refreshments a few yards from the bonfire. As I remain in the shadows away from the roaring flames, Scotia eventually approaches me.

"Hi," she says, all Halloween-candy sweet, but I'm not having it. She ignored me at the party earlier and then arrived with these biddies. Opposites will not attract this evening. "I saw you at the community center. Did the boys have a good time?"

"As if you care," I clip, and instantly, Scotia stands taller. She covered her T-shirt from earlier with an old barn jacket, but she's still wearing tight jeans and rubber boots up to her kneecaps.

"Excuse me?"

"Yeah, I saw you at the party, and you didn't look up once at the boys."

Scotia turns her head, looking over her shoulder at the group of friends gathered around the towering fire. Twisting back to me, she narrows her eyes.

"You're the one who told me I couldn't use Harper House to . . . how did you word it? 'Plump up my resume'. I took that to mean I needed to be disaffiliated from it, so I was doing what you asked. I thought I was being careful and respectful. I didn't come anywhere near the boys and left early on the off chance one of *them* noticed me. I didn't want to blow your cover, *Big Poppy*."

"I—" I did say all that to her, and it was thoughtful that she was respecting my wishes. I don't want her parading around her volunteer work like the boys are some charity case.

She spins away from me, but I'm quick to catch her elbow. "I'm sorry." The words aren't enough. "It's not as if you aren't keeping secrets yourself, *Mrs. Pickle*."

She exhales heavily before lowering her head. "I thought it would be a fun name for the boys," she defends. That isn't what I meant. There's something deeper inside Scotia Simmons, something buried down at the base of her. She's hiding herself. Mrs. Pickle is only a thin layer. However, the boys do like the name. It's as if they have their own private Mrs. Doubtfire.

"And it's not like you approached me either," she hisses, snapping her head back up to glare at me. Those silvery eyes gleam like polished daggers.

"I'm not the one embarrassed by you," I defend thinking of how often she's dismissed me as Big Poppy. My home. My bar. My help at the auto shop.

"Embarrassed?" Despite the darkness around us, her eyes spark in shock as her brows lift. "Who said I'm embarrassed by you?"

"I see you with your gossipy friends." I nod in their direction. "You tell them you banged me?"

Her arm tugs in my grasp, and if I wasn't holding her, I'm certain she'd slap me.

"I don't like you like this," she mutters through clenched teeth.

Yeah, well, I don't like me like this either. And I don't know why I'm acting this way. Maybe because I want us to be seen together. I want her to introduce me to her friends. Then again, I don't need their approval. I definitely don't need friends like them.

"They wouldn't approve of me anyway," I state.

"You don't know that," Scotia insists, glaring at me.

"I've heard how you talk about people with those women, and they most definitely would not approve of Big Poppy."

"I—"

"And before you think you can just introduce me as Chester Chesterfield, let me tell you it ain't gonna happen. He doesn't come out often, and I prefer it that way. I don't need to be torn apart like you and your friends were tearing down women on the street or some lady for replicating a coleslaw, for shit's sake."

"I didn't do that," she defends, settling her arm still in my grasp.

"You did," I snap. "Putting others down is so second nature to you, I bet you don't even realize you're doing it."

Her brows lift and then her eyes narrow. "What does it matter how or who I talk about?"

"It's just plain mean, Scotia." Her mouth falls open. Then clamps shut. Silence falls between us. I've said what I said. It's the truth.

"It's just chatter among friends," she weakly argues.

"It's mean," I repeat, hoping I've struck a nerve with her.

Her head lifts, struggling to still her expression. She's working on shutting down on me. "Well, plenty of people speak ill of me, and I give zero fucks about it." Her haughty voice returns, mixing with the harsh profanity, and I'd laugh if I wasn't still wound up.

"It's mean, darlin'." My tone softens. My hand slides up her arm and rests on her shoulder.

"I'm old enough to do what I want when I want with who I want." Her eyes still spark. Her tone terse. But something heavy weights in her voice. She's losing a bit of her salty snap.

"Is that what's happening here? You do me to prove something. Fortysomething and not giving fucks. Is that your thing?"

Her mouth falls open again, then clamps shut. With her shoulder under my hold, she steps closer to me. "I didn't just *do* you." Her eyes blaze like polished chrome. Damn, she's so pretty when she's on fire but I'm not looking to be burned by her.

"What are we doing, then?"

She doesn't answer and her silence says everything.

"Yeah, me neither," I state to the emptiness around us. *I don't know what we're doing with one another either.*

Scotia shrugs to loosen my hold on her and slips out from under my touch. "And for your information, I did not discuss you with my friends, and it has nothing to do with being embarrassed by you. It's because . . . because . . . I don't wish to share. I want someone who belongs to me."

Instantly, I'm reminded of our first morning.

And with that, she stalks off for the bonfire, and I'm the one left stumped.

* * *

Later that night, I learn that Scotia's friends are the Hester sisters, and they're twins. Hazel Cumberstone is the older one by four solid minutes, and she's bossy as hell as if she were four years older than her twin, Mabel Murphy. Mabel's a widow, and through the course of the night, I discover her husband was in the military. I also notice she can't keep her eyes off Tower Hudson. She's quieter than her sister, cutting off the other or correcting her rude comments, softening the blow of insults and verbal injuries. Her behavior is a reminder not to judge a book by its cover, and I seem to be guilty of judging.

I've been unfair to Scotia.

"I'm sorry," I say, eventually approaching her as she stands near the bonfire. The heat of the flames and the dancing of the blaze are messing with my head, and so are thoughts of this woman. I clip a part of her coat and tug. "Come back here a bit, will ya?"

She quietly follows me, and I don't miss her sullen expression. I also realize it's my fault.

"I'm just in a mood." It's not much of an excuse. I seem to be up and down on a wave of emotion this evening.

"You've been back here quite a bit tonight," she states, keeping her arms around her midsection as she looks off at the bonfire, burning brightly. We're a good ways back from the flame, and I want to open her coat and touch her skin.

"The flames get to me," I explain, giving her some of the truth.

"My sister loves fire. It's a part of her religion."

"Oh yeah, what's that?"

"She's a Wiccan. The American Halloween coincides with her ancient celebration of the dead. Tonight is called Samhain."

Celebration of the dead. My eyes focus on the orange-yellow blaze moving over a pile of small tree trunks. "Fire doesn't equate to a celebration for me," I say under my breath, until I notice Scotia's watching me, waiting for more. "Forget I said that."

"You know you can talk to me," she says, softening her tone and loosening her arms as she turns to face me. I remain silent, struggling whether to open up to her or not. For some reason, I talk.

"My best friend and his wife died in a house fire." I can't pull my eyes from the flames, watching them flit and waver. Try as I might, I can't get rid of the image I have in my head of them burning alive in a bed. Scotia's hand lands on my forearm, but I can't feel her touch through all my layers of clothing. I can't feel her skin, and I need to feel her.

"I'm so sorry, Chester."

"Yeah, not as sorry as their three boys." I tip up my chin, dismissing my own heartache.

"Hugh, Dewey, and Louie? It was their parents? Were the boys in the fire?" Her voice dips lower, coaxing the remainder of the story from me.

"They were home, yes. But Hugh woke Dewey from their shared bedroom and took Louie from his crib in the nursery. Hugh was all of seven. He'd been well trained. They had a fire escape plan. Get out of the house and meet at a tree near the street. He waited and waited. By the time the flames thoroughly engulfed the house, Harper and Davis hadn't come out."

"Harper?" she whispers, but I ignore the obvious answer—I'd named the house after the boy's mother, so they'd never forget her. She asks another question instead. "How did it happen?"

"It was ruled inconclusive. The investigation found evidence of candles in their bedroom and a diffuser in an electrical outlet. I can't comprehend how either small item could have started such a blaze. A fire from such a thing should have been detected." I recall the investigator on the scene telling me it happens. Poor building materials. Perhaps a blaze burning hot and fast. People can easily be trapped. "They'd been sleeping when it happened. How do you not wake up from the scent of smoke?"

I sniff the air. The smell of the bonfire reaches my nostrils from yards away and the scent burns. I suddenly feel nauseous. "It woke a seven-year-old kid, but not Davis and his wife? I'll never understand." My voice lowers, my head shaking. To this day, I still don't believe it.

"Why didn't Hugh call 911?"

"He was only seven. He didn't have a cell phone."

"What about neighbors?" she softly prods.

"The boys' home was in the woods, and they were separated from others by quite a distance. Eventually, one night-owl neighbor noticed the flames." Davis's house comes to mind. He was so proud of his home.

"My first real home," he said, bringing to mind for both of us that we'd grown up in other people's houses and then shit trailers and apartments. I'd built a house for someone, but I've never lived in it.

"It wasn't at Harper House?" she questions, noticing my mention of a separate home.

"No, that house is mine. Theirs was burned beyond repair."

Scotia's breath hitches. "Those poor babies," she whispers, her gaze shifting to the wobbling flames of the bonfire. "Your poor friends."

Seven years later, and I'm still questioning how a simple candle, or a small diffuser, could burn down a house and kill two adults sleeping in bed, but I'll never have answers. Harper didn't have an enemy in the world, but Davis did. We both did. When they met at The Fugitive, he was concerned his dirt would find her, but she convinced him it would never matter. She loved him. And Davis loved her, and those boys.

"So Harper House . . ." Scotia pauses, and I close my eyes for a second. I don't look at her when my lids open again. My vision aims at the flaming pyramid, but it blurs before me.

"I named the house after their mother, so they'd never forget her."

"You *gave* them your house. That's why you live in a bus." Her tone drops. The wheels are spinning in her head. *Not the damn bus again.* "You're a hero."

"Hugh's a hero. I'll never measure up to that kid." I'll never measure up to any of them. Not my best friend, who took me under his protection at the last foster home I lived in. Not his beautiful wife, who loved him no matter what his past held. Their son, who fights for a good cause. Their other son, who's so smart I can't keep up, or the infant child Hugh saved, who has the biggest heart. I'm not worthy of any of them.

I toss my beer bottle in the recycling bin near the cooler, listening to the crash of glass on glass and stalk off into the darkness, needing to pull myself away from the nasty memories.

CHAPTER 13

SOMETHING HOTTER THAN FLAMES

[Scotia]

I give Chester a five-second head start before I follow him. My heart bleeds for him after hearing the story he's told me. This big, beautiful man —his heartbreak is so huge.

We move away from the crackle and snap of the fire and into silent darkness. The loud crunch of my wellies on gravel echoes in the night. My sister's farm has been restored now that she owns it outright and shares the land with Jedd. He's built a horse barn on the property, and Chester stalks in the direction of the structure.

I want him to talk to me, but he continues to walk faster without looking back. With his long legs, he's put quite a distance between us. He detours into the barn as I'd suspected. Once I enter, he seems to have disappeared inside the dark building. Despite a dim light illuminating the passageway, I've lost him.

"I know you're in here," I call out as if we're children playing a game of hide-and-seek. Perhaps we are, as it seems we share bits and pieces of ourselves with one another, hiding truths, and then seeking full disclosure.

We're . . . curious . . . about each other, or at least, I am about him. I want to know more about him. And I'm not letting him walk away after the bomb he just dropped.

I pause before a horse stall. The heavy breath of Lucky One steams into the cold passageway. Jedd breeds and trains horses for the rodeo. It's a process I don't pretend to understand, not being much of an animal lover myself, but it makes him happy. Jedd's happiness makes Beverly ecstatic, which is something she rightfully deserves after all she's been through.

I think about Chester. His best friend, Davis, and his wife, Harper, lost their lives in a house fire, leaving behind three beautiful boys. Chester is now their guardian and an excellent provider for them. For a moment, I wonder why he doesn't live with them. Why does he live in a bus just over the border instead of the valley? I suppose the locale might have something to do with his ownership of The Fugitive, but then again, his Chesterfield Oil offices are said to be in Knoxville. There's a hefty distance between the locations with Green Valley in the middle.

I'd reach up to pet the horse, but I'm afraid he'll bite me. Jedd likes to call him a mean sonofabitch, yet surprisingly, the animal has a soft spot for Beverly. While Beverly loves animals, Naomi loves the woods, which reminds me of her Samhain ritual later tonight. I'm doing my part to keep up the sisterhood rejuvenation plan, and after what I've learned about Chester's friends, I take a moment to recognize I'm blessed that my sisters are still with me. I've missed them. We're very different people as adults, and in many ways, it should make us more incompatible than ever, but there's something about blood I can't deny. My sisters are the truest people I have in my life next to my daughter, who I haven't spoken to in a week.

After a few minutes, I decide I'm not going to find Chester in the dimly lit barn and give up on the hope of him speaking further to me. I turn toward the entrance and pause when I see him blocking my exit.

"Why did you follow me?" His low, gruff tone startles me, and we stare at one another for a minute.

"Because I don't want you hurting. That was a lot you shared, and I just want to be sure you're—"

I'm cut off from more words as he closes the distance between us in three broad steps and crushes his mouth to mine. His hands firmly cup my face. He kisses me as though he can't get close enough. Our mouths nip and suck, devouring one another, reminding me how I've never been thoroughly kissed. Never like this.

While his beard is scratching my chin and his mustache brushes my lips, his mouth is heaven, and then his tongue seeks mine. I'm lost in the flutters racing up my middle and the pressure of his tongue swirling with my own. His fingers slip downward, clutching at the edges of my jacket, and my hands lift for his biceps, curling as best as they can over his firm muscle. We're wearing too much clothing as far as I'm concerned, but it's cold in this barn.

"I need to touch your skin." His hand works its way under my hair and into the scarf around my neck. His fingers wiggle to get under my sweater, but the contact isn't enough.

"I want to have you right here," he mutters against my mouth. The desperation in his powerful kiss tells me everything. He wants to forget. I recognize the feeling. It's what I wanted with him on that first morning. Then again, what I wanted was to make a new memory. I gently push at him until he steps back, breathing as heavy as the horse in the stall behind me. Then I reach for his arm and tug him by his jacket into an empty stall across the passageway.

Once inside, Chester slams the sliding door shut, and I'm pressed face-first to the wall. At shoulder height, my hands catch the metal bars on the upper portion of the wooden wall to prevent my cheeks from slamming into the grid.

"I want you like this," he says. His fingers tug at the scarf around my neck, freeing my skin so his lips can meet my nape.

"Like this?" I squeak as open-mouth kisses suck at my flesh and move toward my ear.

"Ever done it like this before?"

It's not like I never faced away from Karl. There were times he didn't want to look me in the eye when we consummated our marital duties, but I'd never done it like this—in the heat of passion, pressed into a wall, outside in a barn. It's as close to animalistic as I imagine one can get.

"Not exactly," I mutter, closing my eyes at the half-truth. Hands fumble at my jeans and the button is undone. The zipper comes next as I clutch the bars near my face. Thick fingers slip under my panties and find the place where I love his touch. I melt into him as his finger dives into me.

"Sweet Jesus, you're already wet."

I don't think I'll ever dry up when it comes to this man. Just the thought of him makes me damp, and it's darn embarrassing to consider how often I think of him.

"Let me in, darlin'." He means my pants, but I long for him to mean my heart. It wouldn't take much to enter that beating organ, but we aren't talking about emotions right now. This is purely physical, and I'd like to get lost in him as much as he wants to be lost in me.

I lower one hand to my jeans, leaving the other hand wrapped tightly around the metal bars near my face. I'm afraid if I let go, I'll fall over. Sensing my one-handed struggle to push down my pants, Chester is there with a sharp tug on each side. The denim falls to my knees, baring my backside to him. I can't spread as well as I'd like, the jeans being a barrier, but Chester doesn't seem to mind. Within seconds, his belt is undone. His jeans are at his hips, and the warm tip of his hard shaft presses through damp folds eager to welcome him into me.

"Condom," I strain, and I hear the grunt along with a pause as he fumbles behind me. Apparently, he's not too old to carry one in his pocket tonight, and I briefly wonder if he was hoping we'd get to this point this evening.

"There's more to this condom thing," he grumbles behind me. "And you're going to tell me, but another time." I close my eyes, hoping to never tell him the truth of my conditioning. When he's sheathed and returned to my entrance, all other thoughts are dismissed.

"Hang on, darlin'," he warns, slamming into me before he's even finished his caution. I rise on my toes and squeak at the rapid intrusion. His hands grip my hips, tugging me back down over him, and he stills, allowing me a minute to get comfortable with this position. Everything with him is so different, like the perfect blend of crispy coating and slivered pickle in my fried delicacy. Chester is prize-winning and delicious.

He slips to my entrance, teasing me with an exit from my body. Then he rams upward once more. My breath hitches again, but I'm better prepared, using the bars clutched in my palms as leverage. He taps me some place special inside and I groan. I press back, drawing him into me, keeping him deep. He pulls away and then returns. *Sweet Jesus.* Back and forth, we move as he fills me. We rock, and my hips buck forward, nearing the stall wall. Just when I think I'll collide with the wood, he tugs me back to him, tapping me in that spot I've never felt before. I love the sensation. I love the fullness, but I need a little more.

"Get there, darlin'," he commands, straining with the command, but I'm not there yet. It's a familiar position I don't want to recall. Karl hardly satisfied me.

"I can't," I whimper, and Chester grunts behind me.

"You can." His hand slips forward across my lower belly until his fingers fumble with a bundle of nerves certain to break me.

It's never felt . . . *I've never* . . . This is too much.

"Chester," I groan. Moving on my own—faster, harder—I draw him deeper. I'm going to break, and his responding movements demand I do. With hands on the bars, I press myself backward, forcing my backside against him as I bite my cheek, holding in the scream I want to release. Small pinpricks of light dance before my eyes as I explode around him.

"Atta girl," he mutters, as if I'm one of the horses in these stalls and I'm as wild as they are. He surges forward, and my hips hit the wood wall covering my lower half. He stills, and instantly, I feel him jolting inside me, pulsating with pleasure. His head rests against the back of mine, his warm breath coating my nape. We breathe in tandem with heavy puffs and sharp huffs.

Too quickly, he pulls out of me and stands to his full height, but his arms encircle my waist, and I'm glad for the support because I'm worried if I release the bars from my grip, I'll fall. As he holds my back to his front and presses his lips to the back of my head, I realize it might be too late. Metal posts in my grasp or not, I'm definitely falling for him.

"Call me Chet," he whispers, and a smile breaks out on my face.

CHAPTER 14

SHE WHO DANCES WITH FIRE

[Scotia]

"Call me Chet." I can't seem to help the tingles rushing through my body at what this means.

He considers me someone close to him.

Unfortunately, we don't return to the bonfire holding hands or gushing over one another after our animalistic mating. He tells me to exit the barn first, and I'm left with a sinking sensation that what we've done didn't mean as much to him as it did to me.

I realize I've just had sex with Big Poppy despite what he says I can call him. I've slept with two out of three of his sides. I have no idea what it would take to complete the triangle of him or if my heart even could take more from this complex man.

Shortly after our reappearance, the party starts to break up. It's almost midnight, so us sisters remain while the guests depart. Chet says his goodnights, and Nathan and Jedd follow him to the main house. Hazel and Mabel drove me to the party, and I tell them I'll find a way home later.

The sensation of his roughness as he entered me lingers, but so does the emptiness of his departure from my body. There's a hollowness in my chest, and I don't like the feeling. Chet seems even more distant after what we did, and my sudden melancholy mood plays into the ritual Naomi has planned.

"Tonight, we celebrate those who have passed." As a solitary Wiccan, my sister typically celebrates alone on this night, but in our continued efforts to reconnect our sisterhood, Beverly talked me into being present.

"I don't want to be invoking any spirits."

"We aren't invoking. We're remembering those who have left this life. Jebediah. Mother and Daddy. You could think of Karl."

Our brother is dead. He's been gone almost two decades. In my opinion, we don't need to bring him back, but let his restless heart rest. Jebediah's death was an accident, but Naomi took his passing the hardest of all of us and has struggled to let it go.

Karl is another spirit I don't wish to resurrect. He did what he could as a local pediatrician, caring for the physical and mental health of children for decades. He loved kids, which is surprising when you consider we only had one child. However, our marriage was what it was, and it's over.

"Don't you want to talk about him?" Beverly interjects as we stand around the lowering flames.

"Talk about Karl? Never." *Call me callous*. But Karl is the last person on my mind most days. It's been over seven years. I'm grateful for the birth of our child and the finances he left me. I've valued his family name. I'm even appreciative of the years of friendship, but when it comes to our marriage, it's something I don't wish to discuss.

"Not even a little bit?" Beverly pushes. My sisters both know that Karl was having an affair. It was the only explanation I gave them. He was killed outside a motel, which didn't make sense to them. *What was Karl doing in a motel?* He was mistaken for Kip Sylvester. *Karl Simmons. Kip Sylvester.* The men did not match in stature, but I suppose it was an honest mistake, as honest a mistake as one can make when committing a murder.

"Do you want to talk about Howard?" I snap back at my sister. Her philandering husband made quite a name for himself with his womanizing ways. It isn't something we've discussed at great length between us sisters, although there has been plenty of gossip over the years.

"If it would help, I can share how I felt about his adultery." The ease with which Beverly speaks, offering we compare notes on wayward husbands does not settle well with me. Is it really adultery if you and your spouse agree? Is it breaking our vows if discretion was the only request? Is it infidelity if you are only being true to yourself? These were all questions I'd tried to put to rest over the years.

Karl tried to be considerate. While he wasn't faithful to our marriage vows, he was faithful to me. *What do you want to do, Scotia?* How do you tell your husband you want him to love you like a man loves a woman? He just couldn't do it. Not how I wanted, at least.

"No, I do not need to hear about your reaction to Howard's affairs," I state, staring at the fire before me until I hear Naomi gasp. I turn to Beverly and see her stricken face. Sighing, I rearrange my words before I next speak.

"Why drudge up all that past, Beverly? You can't change it. You don't need to go back. You have Jedd now. Life should be moving forward. One foot in front of the other."

Beverly holds her head a little higher. My sister struggles to walk due to an accident and needs arm-cuff crutches for balance and support, but I'm not insulting her ability to move. We all need to move on from the past.

"Let's dance," I mutter.

"Why are you here if you're going to be like this?" Beverly interjects, reading my mood.

"Because . . ." *Because I want to belong somewhere.*

"Sissy?" Beverly calls out my childhood nickname, a name I despise, and pulls me from my thoughts.

"I'm here because you are my sisters, and you asked me to join," I say, mustering the strength to speak with honesty. I mean what I've said. I want to be involved in their lives because, at the end of the day, family is all we have. Karl was my family. Darlene as well, but she's pulled back, making her own way in the world. I've been very lonely for the past few years.

I think about Chet and what he told me earlier this evening. His best friend sounded very important to him, and obviously, Davis and Harper had enough faith in Chet to leave their three sons to him. Family is what we make of it, be it blood or not. In my case, I want to reconnect with my sisters. In Chet's, his family is a group of boys relying on him, plus Maura and Savannah.

"Then let's begin." Naomi suggests we simply dance around the flames. "It can be very freeing. Just let that negative energy release."

This sounds easier said than done. I'd like to be free of so many things —mainly a secret that wasn't mine—but I keep it tucked away. It's the first thing I would let go of if I could. Would it be wrong to share the truth with my sisters? What harm would it bring to be honest?

"Let the rhythm of the fire guide you." Naomi interrupts my thoughts. With my arms swinging like elephant trunks, I feel ridiculous. At first, I only walk, following her lead. She starts to skip and twist in an intricate dance that seems practiced and perfected, but I can't seem to loosen up. As I watch my sister before me, her dance appears freeing, elegant even. To be so lighthearted. To be so confident. Confidence is sometimes a façade and takes practice to own. Naomi, however, is not faking her strength. She's comfortable in her own skin, as she is. I'd love to be that open and strong.

I glance behind me at our middle sister. Beverly cannot possibly maneuver the way Naomi does, and it feels almost insensitive to encourage her to follow our youngest sister's lead. However, Beverly gives it her all, moving in measured steps around the flames. I wish I had her strength, her courage. She's braver than I'd given her credit for in the past.

Out of the corner of my eyes, I see we have an audience tucked into the darkness. Nathan watches in wonder as his wife moves around the softening fire, but Jedd struggles. His hand fists near his pocket as he watches Beverly. With the tip of my head, I signal him. He doesn't want to intrude, but he can't stand to watch her stumble. He'll give her space, but if he can offer his body for her to lean on, he's there for her.

Both my sisters are fortunate to have a partner. A true love match.

We circle the flames once more before Beverly stops and Jedd's at her side. He slips his leg between hers as if entwining them like a three-legged creature. Slowly, he canters them around the fire. Nathan moves closer but keeps his distance, allowing his wife her moment.

I halt when I see one more figure lurking in the shadows. Breaking from the circle, I step toward the darkness.

"Chet," I whisper, surprised he's still here. Earlier, he said goodbye to everyone, including me. He looks left as if he's been caught doing something he shouldn't be doing, and I step closer to him, slipping into the shadows away from the warm fire. "What are you still doing here?"

"Jedd invited me to the house for another beer, and Nathan spilled about what you women were doing. Curiosity got the best of me."

"I'm not much of a spiritual dancer," I admit, sheepish about my lacking ability, waning confidence, and pitiful courage.

"I'm not much of a dancer, period," Chet states. We both watch as Jedd escorts Beverly around the bonfire, and Nathan intercepts Naomi, joining her in her intricate dance.

"You mentioned tonight is a celebration of the dead. You thinking about your man?" Chet's lips twist after asking as if hesitant to ask and equally uncertain he wants an answer.

"Karl was my husband, and I won't speak ill of him tonight, but our marriage wasn't what one would consider equitable." Unfortunately, Karl's been on my mind too much tonight, and I'd like to let him go a bit. I suppose that's a part of Naomi's ritual. Releasing the spirit, the memories, and setting them free.

"Ever gonna tell me more about him and his phallic symbol prejudice?" Chet chuckles softly.

"Nope." I smile myself. Why does Chet even care, and why did I offer that little bit of Karl to him anyway?

"Maybe someday," Chet teases, and again, I wonder why it matters. This man turns me upside down. "For now, want to dance?"

"Here?" I stammer, glancing around the shadowy darkness surrounding us. "You just said you weren't much of a dancer."

Chet looks around as if searching for something. "No one here to see," he teases. "We can make this *our* secret."

Our secret? Not his. Not mine. Us together. But I've been a keeper of secrets for a long time and I'm not certain I have room in my heart for more.

"And we wouldn't want people to see us, would we?" I retort, recalling our earlier conversation.

"Don't pretend you'd want people to know what we've done." His rough voice drops, and I bite my cheek.

"Well, I wouldn't be announcing it in the Piggly Wiggly," I snark, but I'm not ashamed I had sex with him. Maybe he's embarrassed? Maybe he doesn't want to be seen with me? We seem to have come full circle to earlier this evening.

"If I keep you a secret, it's because I want someone only for me," I admit again, lowering my eyes as the truth seems easier to say in the dark. Chet steps closer to me, cupping my jaw tenderly in his big paw.

"Give me that secret, darlin'. What do you mean?"

"I wish I could explain it." *Which I can, but I won't because the revelation would be too much.* "I don't know what we're doing, but I like you."

I swallow at the heavy truth clogging my throat as I admit more than I should. He's complex and complicated but there's something I really like about him, and it's not just the way my body reacts to his touch. He isn't afraid to call me out. And I find I'm sensitive to his thoughts of me. I don't want him to think I'm . . . mean.

I'm honest and straightforward, but I also have my reasons for being that way. *Mask in place, Scotia. Speak before spoken about.* If I reject others, they can't reject me first.

"I like you when you're truthful with me," he whispers, curling his finger over my ear to brush back the loose hair near my face. "When you're *real.*"

"What are we doing with each other?" I whisper. It's an honest question. Are we just hooking up, filling a need in each other? Or could we be something more to one another?

"For now, we're dancing." He's a large man, but he takes my hand, pulling me into him. I raise my arm to set my other hand on his shoulder. We don't dance as much as we sway. He holds me close, and I rest my body against his. It's nice to be held.

"I like you best like this," I murmur, thinking he can't possibly hear me as my cheek lays near his thumping heart.

"I like you best, darlin'." He leaves the statement without a modifier, making me fill in the blanks with hope.

CHAPTER 15

A GAME OF CAT AND MOUSE

[Scotia]

The next night, I find myself at The Fugitive.

"Heard you're having a party," I said to Chet the night before. "My invitation got lost in the mail."

"The party is all Todd's thing. But after your first visit to The Fugitive, I didn't think you'd want to come back," he stated, reminding me of my behavior toward his patron and shock at his home.

"I'd like a second chance for first impressions," I whispered. He didn't answer, only kissed me. It was soft and sweet and too short, but we were standing in the shadows of the barn by then. The bonfire dance was over, and the night was ending.

We sisters arrive in tandem, and it's obvious the crowd does not know what to make of three grown-ass middle-aged women dressed in tight, gray clothing with dark sunglasses. Beverly found us these onesie-style costumes, complete with mouse ears on a hood and a long tail near the backside.

"Are we getting robbed?" one biker jokes before lifting his mug of beer.

"I think we're being punked," another states, leaning back in his chair, getting comfortable like he's about to watch a show.

"Maybe they're strippers," a smoke-roughened voice calls out from a corner, and I'm ready to take my tail and turn around when Nathan saunters up to Naomi, and announces, "This little mouse belongs to me."

Jedd isn't far behind, wrapping his arm around Beverly and stating, "And this mouse is mine."

My heart drops as there's no one to claim me, and for some stupid reason, tears prickle my eyes until a hand takes mine, and I turn my head.

"And I'm *wedging* bets on this one." Todd Ryder wears a bright yellow, cheese-wedge shape on his head like a Wisconsin fan, and I laugh despite the desire to cry.

"You are too kind, sir," I drawl. He lifts my fingers to kiss my knuckles. The gesture is sweet and unnecessary, but I'm also so grateful for Nathan's older brother being here, humoring me. He's a nice-looking man, broader and stockier than his brother, earning him a biker name of Toad when he's anything but one. With solid silver hair and a sprinkling of facial hair plus beautiful blue eyes, he's lovely, but his cheesy-ness doesn't cut it for this mouse. Still, he's charming, and I'm thankful he escorts me to a table where the others are seated.

I don't want to look around for Chet . . . *Big Poppy* . . . but my eyes drift.

"Who're you looking for, sweetheart?" Todd asks me, and I snap my attention back to the table. He winks.

"Just taking in the scenery," I say, holding his gaze a second. His eyes really are a brilliant blue, but I'm not getting lost in them as I desire midnight orbs that are clearly not present.

After my quick scan, I see we really do look ridiculous in our costumes. The body-hugging material is all sexy mouse among some cool cats. The attire isn't something my curvy, prefers-loose-fitting, makes-her-own-clothing sister typically wears. I remember last Halloween when she made an exception to her clothing selection for a Jack Skellington costume. That's a story in and of itself. On the other hand, Beverly's always been angular, so something formfitting actually hangs a bit loose on her body. My physique is in between theirs with a more athletic build, but I'm not comfortable with the curve-hugging shape of this light fleece material nor the mouse-ear hood on my head.

"What's this?" The loud, rugged tone has me turning my head to find Chet standing behind me. In a waffle-fabric Henley and dark jeans, I'm assuming his costume is night-off lumberjack.

"Big Poppy, take a seat," Jedd offers like they are old friends. Somehow, they are, but I don't remember the particulars.

"Seems the table's full," he states, noting the six chairs around the circular wood. His eyes narrow when he lands on me, and Todd quickly stands.

"Take my seat, boss," my cheese-man suggests, tugging the wedge off his head and pushing it into Big Poppy's chest. Big Poppy snorts, grabbing the foam hat in his hands.

"I'm not wearing this damn fool thing," he states and then does a double take at the attire of the women at the table. Repeating himself, he snides, "What's this?"

"We were told it was a Halloween party," Naomi defends, her eyes shifting to Nathan.

"It is," Big Poppy states. I scan the room again, realizing the only people dressed in costume are women in devil outfits or skimpy dirndls as if it's an Oktoberfest. One man wears fake eyeglasses with a false mustache attached, and another has a pirate hat on his head with a patch covering his eye, but for the most part, the rest look like bikers. I don't think it's an act.

"We thought that meant costumes," Beverly clarifies. Her voice is quiet while Jedd wraps an arm around her and says something in her ear to make her blush.

Pushing back the hood with ears from my head does nothing to conceal that we are the only people wearing true disguises, and I feel ridiculous.

"As your costume must be a barkeep, get me a drink. I'll take a chocolate martini neat." I slap my hand on the tabletop for emphasis. I'm not certain if I'm allowed to recognize Chet as Big Poppy or anyone for that manner. Do we pretend we don't know one another as anything more than casual acquaintances? Or can I announce to this bar that I slept with him and I'd really like to sleep with him again?

"I'm not a fucking beer wench, and we don't sell martinis. This isn't the Omni Hotel," Big Poppy states, glaring down at me, reminding us both of the hotel where we met.

Uh-oh. Big Poppy is grumpy again.

"It's Halloween. You must have something chocolaty sweet," I say, noting his tall stature towering behind me.

"We've got whiskey and more whiskey. That's our sweet," he states, looking at me. With those dark eyes lasered in on me, I want to twist in this seat, climb his body, and hate-kiss the crap out of those pouty lips. He's oil and vinegar tonight and I want that sweet dill I know he can be.

My fingers clutch at the back of the chair, and I push myself out of the seat to stand. "Perhaps Todd can help me figure out something," I say. I hardly take one step around Big Poppy before his hand wraps around my upper arm to halt me.

"Todd won't be wedging his cheese anywhere near you," he grunts. Somewhere nearby, I hear, "Oh my."

"I'm not looking for cheese. I want something smooth and velvety chocolate against my tongue." I lick the front of my teeth and twist out of Big Poppy's clutches. Sauntering to the bar, I catch Todd's eyes.

"Whatcha need, sweetheart?" He teases me with another wink, and I sense Big Poppy's presence behind me.

"She doesn't need anything," the gruff voice at my back mutters.

"I'd like a chocolate martini," I say, my voice louder than necessary. I glance right, and a man on a barstool looks me up and down. I give him a fake smile. He grins back seductively, and mine becomes more genuine. It's nice to be smiled at in an appreciative manner. He's nice-looking, too, despite his dark clothing and leather vest.

"We don't make chocolate froufrou drinks," Big Poppy says, standing close behind me. The heat of his chest radiates toward my spine, but I ignore his nearness.

"Let me see what I can do," Todd offers, dismissing his boss and turning for the wall of alcohol opposite the bar top.

"You are pushing my buttons, lady," Big Poppy whispers at my ear.

Without conscious thought, I press my tush backward, hoping to land close to my intended target despite him being taller than me. *I'll give him a button to push.* A firm hand comes to my hip, stilling me.

"That button?" I drawl, gazing over my shoulder and up at him. He bites the corner of his lip, trying to keep up the glare but failing just a bit.

"Do not flirt with other men in my bar," he mutters. "And don't count on Todd to fill any need you have, either."

I'm not flirting with anyone, but his demand has me wondering . . . *is he jealous?*

A glass taps on the bar top, and I turn my attention back to Todd to find something light brown with a thick white foam and a drizzle of chocolate over the top. Reaching for the glass, I lift, sip, and lick my lips.

"Delicious," I purr, making eye contact with the man to my right after I take my first drink.

"You sure you're a mouse, lady? Because you look like a pleased pu—"

"You watch your mouth, Striker," Big Poppy warns before he finishes, and the man on the barstool chuckles softly before returning his attention to the television behind the bar.

I take another sip of the chocolatey concoction Todd made and shift as best as I can, placing the bar at my back and a giant of a man at my front.

"What are you playing at tonight, Scotia?"

"What are you playing at, *Big Poppy*?" I don't know my place here, and I'm not comfortable without control.

"You look ridiculous," he states as his eyes drift down the length of the zipper, from neck to crotch and back up. I'd be lying if I said it hurt a little that his body scan was not appraising but appalled. Then his eyes meet mine, and the heat in them is molten steel. My insides do a little dance.

"She looks pretty good to me," the man named Striker interjects. "I'd chase her." His throat rumbles, *rawring* in my direction. My body shivers. *Is he flirting with me?* Attempting to meet his eyes, I see he's egging on Big Poppy, but I don't fully understand why.

I use my best Southern drawl to say, "Thank you, darlin'." Then, take another sip of my liquid chocolate heaven. *Oh my, that is delicious.*

Big Poppy sets a hand on the bar. His large arm acts as a barrier between Striker and me. His big body leans forward, crowding my space even more.

"I've got you trapped," he warns me.

"What if I don't want to be caught?" I say, dropping my eyes and noticing he's still holding the foam cheese hat in his hand. He tosses the headpiece behind the bar where Todd catches it and chuckles. It's a lie, though. I don't want him to toy with me. I want him to catch me. Instead, he presses off the bar top and glares at me. Holding his gaze, I take one more chocolate sip, toying with him.

"Good thing I'm not interested in chasing," he states. His meaning becomes clear. Despite our tender moments last night, he isn't playing tonight.

He glances up, nods at Todd, and then takes a step to the side. "Behave," he mutters as he pats Striker on his shoulder, passing him before he disappears into the pool room where I know there's a door leading outside. He's not interested in cat and mouse tonight, and my heart plummets to my belly.

"Sometimes, big cats are too dumb to realize they're running in the wrong direction," Striker states beside me, tipping up an eyebrow and nodding in Big Poppy's retreating direction.

"Seeing as I don't like to be toyed with, I guess it's for the best," I state half-heartedly. I've been ensnared by one Chester Chesterfield. I've fallen for his alter ego, Chet, who adores six boys in a house once his. But I don't need to get caught up in Big Poppy and whatever game he's playing with me.

"Don't you worry, sweetheart. You're his kind of catnip," Todd interjects from behind the bar, but I have no idea what that means.

Striker's eyes roam me once again from my high-heeled shoes to the white stripe in my hair.

"No, pussycat, I bet you capture hearts all over the place." He shifts on his seat. "Want to capture me, kitty?"

"She's with Big Poppy," Todd intercedes, and my head swivels in surprise. I most certainly am not with the grumpy, gruff man who just exited the room without a look back.

"Don't see him standing here," Striker notes, and I admit he's correct.

"Want to dance?" he asks me. He's another lion playing with a mouse, so it's a good thing I know how to move and protect myself. I'm becoming steel with the rejection from Big Poppy/Chester Chesterfield/Chet, once again.

* * *

I dance with Striker for several songs before a man named Bones cuts in for two more dances. I'm actually having . . . fun. It's been a long time since I've been so carefree. I've let my hair down, as the saying goes, or rather, removed my mouse ears.

Bones and I rock right, kick left, and then release one another, spinning out so we're side by side. Without missing a beat, we turn back to each other, hands reconnecting, and we shift left, right, left. It's been forever since I've danced like this. Bones releases my right hand and twirls me away from him. I spin outward and collide with a hard wall of man chest.

I hiccup as I look up and meet narrowed eyes as dark as ink.

"Dance over," Big Poppy says, directing his gaze to the man behind my back, still holding my fingers.

"The song ain't over yet," Bones clarifies in a soft Tennessean drawl. He's not as tall as Big Poppy, not as dark, nor as crisp and fresh scented, but he's attractive in his own right.

"It is now," Big Poppy states, still glaring over my head as he crosses his arms over his chest. His eyes don't leave the man behind me.

"Excuse me, but I think I can speak for myself, and I'm not finished dancing." My focus remains on Big Poppy's face. He's so good-looking in a lumbersexual, manual-labor kind of way. My insides flutter when I look at him, even though he's everything I haven't been attracted to in the past. He looks unrefined, a bit wild, and on the edge of breaking the man still holding my fingers. Everything about him screams *all male* and his imposing presence says *I'm all his*. Everything about this moment is in contrast to his earlier stance of not chasing. Maybe it's because he's already claimed me.

Then again, my interpretation of the scene could be inhibited by the three chocolatey wonders Todd's made me this evening. The lines between

Chester Chesterfield, Chet, and Big Poppy are blurring in my head as my body loosens up, and my tongue feels thick. I might be a teeny-weeny bit tipsy.

"Tell him the dance is over," he commands, lowering his gaze to me. Those eyes demand I follow his orders. However, I rarely do as I'm told.

"I don't think so," I say, spinning to face my dance partner, but as soon as my hand connects with his shoulder, my waist is encircled, and I'm tugged backward.

"Party's over," Big Poppy mutters near my ear. My real ear, not the mouse substitutes, which I've kept lowered since walking up to the bar. Naomi and Nathan disappeared a while ago, presumably for the motel. Beverly and Jedd left two songs back, possibly for the same location. I don't want to consider where Big Poppy has been for the past half an hour. I've been left alone in this strange place, and I'm enjoying myself despite my being without a date.

Screw Chet Chester Chesterfield Big Poppy.

However, Bones releases me and steps back, holding up both his arms in surrender. His eyes remain on the man behind me as if the two men are having a conversation without words.

"She was safe with me," Bones states as though clarifying something unsaid, and I don't like his tone or how this silent discussion is literally over my head.

"Excuse me again, gentlemen, but this mouse can determine what's best for her." And what's best for her . . . *er, me* . . . is letting the man at my back know he's interrupting a perfectly fun evening. I spin to face him, ready to speak.

"Don't," he barks so sharply I flinch. He catches my hand in his and walks around me, pulling me behind him. Nearly dragging me through the pool room, we near the emergency exit and step into the brisk coolness of a late October night.

"What the heck?" I snap once the metal door slams at my back. Big Poppy halts, and I smack into his broad shoulder blades. "What in the devil are you—"

"Hop on," he commands, keeping his back to me. I have no idea what he means. Craning his neck to look over his shoulder, he repeats himself. "Hop on."

"I don't know—" Big Poppy squats a bit and wraps his palms around the back of my thighs.

"Hang on," he warns, and I'm suddenly rising into the air, against his body. I squeal as I'm lifted by the back of my legs, and my arms circle his neck. He stumbles backward for a moment.

"I'm too heavy for you," I squeak, praying he doesn't fall backward and crush me as I'm attached to him like a barnacle on a wooden ship.

He chokes out his reply. "Loosen up a bit."

Realizing I'm cutting off his airway, I slacken my hold at his throat, and he hitches me upward. My body jostles against his, forcing my thighs to spread and tighten at his waist while the heat of his body seeps into mine. He secures his large palms on the underside of my thighs and starts walking to his bus.

"Just what are you doing?" I grumble. This has to be the most ridiculous position I've ever been in.

"Giving you a piggyback ride. You'll sink in those heels in this mud."

Gazing over his shoulder, down at the dark soil, I note the moisture from days of autumn rain. It's rather thoughtful that he's carrying me, but he hasn't answered my question.

"Are we headed to your bus?"

"I'm taking you home," he mutters.

"Oh," I state, unable to mask my disappointment. I was actually having a good time tonight, and for a moment, I think of my old friend Diane Donner. She once went to a biker bar and had herself a good time being there. There's nothing wrong with being over forty, flirty and fun.

Gosh, I don't know what's happening to me lately.

Big Poppy drops his hold on my thighs once we reach the opening to the bus, and I slither down his large body, landing on an outdoor mat at the base of the metal stairs leading up to the entrance. He reaches around me, pressing on the folding door, which opens inward. When he places a hand at my lower back, it seems I don't have a choice—I'm going inside. This is confirmed when two big hands grab my hips and lift me onto the first step. As I climb the three stairs, I take a better look at the entry than I did the first time I was here. The driver's seat is the first thing I notice. It's a warm brown leather captain's chair and looks comfortable but crisp as though it hasn't been used often.

Immediately turning to my left, I take in the faux hardwood flooring and the shiplap paneling on the walls. The space is decorated in light browns and soft grays—masculine but somehow pretty. It's very tidy for such a compact size.

Big Poppy follows behind me and stops near the driver's seat to tug off a boot. Hopping from one foot to another to remove the second one, I expect the bus to rock and wobble. I recall school buses being bouncy and unstable. For such a large man, it's surprising he has so much balance and equally surprising is that the bus doesn't shift from side to side with his moving mass. When he looks up at me, I hiccup.

"What are you doing?" I question as the second boot drops with a thud. *Hiccup.* "I thought you said you were taking me home."

"Do you want to go home?" He stands taller, his eyes softening a bit.

"No," I whisper. *Hiccup.*

"I meant, I was bringing you to *my* home."

"Oh," I answer again, my insides doing little cartwheels of relief. "Am I still supposed to call you Big Poppy here?"

With a crooked smile, he shakes his head. "Chet works."

Chet.

He watches me, and the intensity of his gaze has me looking away and scanning the remainder of the space. I spin to take in the full layout, realizing I'd missed the back of the bus on my first visit.

"Is this the bedroom?" *Hiccup.* After taking a few short steps, I find myself at the end of a raised platform with a thick mattress that fills the entire width of the back of the bus. Helping myself, I climb up and flip to my back, swishing my arms and legs spread eagle, making a mattress angel. It's silly, actually, but I'm riding the high of a few too many chocolate drinks and the attention of a few good-looking men. Accepting I'd never see those biker dudes again, I gave in to one night of letting loose. My legs open and close, open and close, until warm palms land on my inner thighs in the open-wide position, halting my exercise.

I tip up my head as my heels are removed from my feet. My heart races. My core pulses. I hiccup again.

"Do not be sick on my bed."

"I'm not going to get sick on your bed." *Hiccup.* Then I recall my track record with this man. Vomiting on the night we met. Having my period mishap on another day. Almost having sex with him on my desk. Giving in to sex in a barn. I've been a hot mess more times than not in his presence.

And I don't understand what I'm doing here.

There's a subtle shift to the mattress, and I glance up to find Chet crawling over me. My legs spread apart. His knees come between my thighs. I'm instantly thrown back to that morning we shared together. He'd asked me if I was certain I wanted to do what we did, and I'd never been so sure of something in my life. This moment is no different. I want him, even though he ruined my night.

Hiccup.

"Scotia Simmons, why are you such a mess?"

"I am not a mess," I stammer. *Hiccup.* I'm one of the most put-together people I know. Just ask me, and I'll tell you how put together I am. *Mask in place, Scotia.* But as I lie on his mattress, reality slowly seeps in. I'm coming unraveled, one loose thread at a time, and it's all because of him. "Why are you so grumpy?"

Chet shakes his head, ignoring my question, as he balances on all fours over me. He stares down at me, the intensity of those dark eyes making me feel naked under him despite my silly costume. I'd like to be naked under him but not with him looking at me like this—looking at me as though he sees beneath my skin. He knows how ugly I feel inside.

"You gonna puke on my bed?" While my stomach suddenly feels unsettled, it has nothing to do with the alcohol I consumed.

"I am not going to *puke* on your precious bed," I snap.

Suddenly, I wonder how many other women he's brought here. *Am I one of many?* "You know, you could improve your seduction skills." It's a reminder of what he said to me on that first morning.

"I'm not trying to seduce you, Scotia." He slips to my side, perching himself up on an elbow and looking down at me.

"You're not?" My voice drops as I peer at him, and disappointment fills my stomach again.

"Nope." He continues to stare at me, and my skin begins to itch a bit. I'm suddenly overheating in my fleecy mouse onesie, and remembering my costume makes me wonder if this is why he's not seducing me. *Who would want to seduce a mouse?* The costume does not fit my personality one bit. I'm the cat. I need to be on top at all times.

"Because I'm not sexy," I quip, and Chet snorts.

"Oh, you're sexy, darlin'." He throws himself on his back and stares up at his ceiling.

"Then I don't understand?" I snap, feeling all kinds of foolish.

"You're a danger to yourself, and Nathan asked me to look after you for the night."

"Like a babysitter?" I huff, taking a second for the endearment to rattle over my heart. "I do not need a babysitter. I can take care of myself." I've been doing it forever. I always look out for me first. I'll figure out a way home on my own. To prove my point, I sit up, ready to leave his bedroom, or bed, or whatever this portion of his crazy bus-house is, but a thick arm hooks my waist, and I still.

"I don't need you doing *Nathan* any favors," I quip, growing irritated myself.

"How much you have to drink tonight?" he questions instead of replying to me.

I hold up three fingers, wiggling them. He sighs.

"If you want me to drive that road in the dark, I'll take you home myself." There's more to his words as we both know he means The Tail of the Dragon and the twisty-turning highway that could be dangerous in the best of light and deadly in the dark of night. "But I want you to stay."

His softened tone loosens my tense shoulders. I slump a little in my seated position.

"My brother died on that road," I say, keeping my voice quiet. Why those words slip from me, I do not know. Chet remains silent. "He was coming here to The Fugitive. Naomi had called him." I take a deep breath before continuing. "She was here to celebrate her twenty-first birthday.

She'd been with Nathan. That's how they met." I smile weakly. "Jebediah had been drinking, and he crashed into the boulders."

I stay quiet a second, recalling the phone call from my parents informing me of his death. I hadn't been living at home. By then, I'd been in my beautiful house in Green Valley, raising my adorable Darlene and conspiring with Karl. He'd begun his practice, and with the perfect life built around him, his secrets were safe. I was safe. I had married into society and proved myself over and over again to be worthy of a Simmons. It had been exhausting.

"I'm sorry about your brother," Chet says beside me, and I shrug as if the loss doesn't still hurt. I wasn't particularly close to my reckless brother, but he was still my brother. I hadn't always been a good eldest sister.

Giving in to the arm around me, I lie back on the bed but curl onto my side, placing my back to Chet.

He rolls toward me. "That might have been the most real-you you've given me, Scotia." His deep gruff voice quiets a little. I tuck my hands under my cheek and stare at the wall opposite me. The space is enclosed, intimate as I'd thought earlier, and the world spins just a little bit. It's not the alcohol, but something else inside me, like my axis is tipping off-kilter. I need to right myself, but I don't know how, and I don't want to move. That's where the alcohol takes over, I decide. I'm relaxed and slipping into the comfort of this bed and the man at my back.

His hand comes to my side and travels up the curve of my hip. He stops and retreats, skating down the slope of my hip to the dip of my waist. He halts again. His hand moves upward, reaching for the neckline of my costume, and thick fingers connect with the zipper.

"I thought you said you weren't trying to seduce me," I mutter, a pleasing grin curling my lips.

"I just want to feel your skin." My heart leaps to my throat, and the pulse between my thighs beats double time. *He only wants to touch me?* It's such a foreign thought after years of Karl's distance. Karl was not cruel. He just wasn't comforting. At least, not in the manner in which the heated palm slips into the costume now unzipped to my waist. Thick fingers spread over my belly as if he wants to touch as much of me as he can. The tail of the costume is trapped behind me, and the hood has ears on it, but with his heavy hand on my stomach inside the onesie, I don't feel so ridiculous. I'm not certain what to feel.

"Tell me something else that's real about Scotia Simmons."

"I've never felt how I feel when I'm with you."

The sharp intake of his breath, and the weight of silence behind me after what I've said tells me my admission might have been a little too much truth.

"That is to say, you annoy me," I teasingly remark, and he softly chuckles behind me.

"I don't like you when you're like this," he jests, and my eyes close under the warmth of his hand over my belly.

I like you, I wish to tell him as I said last night, but I've already said too much.

"Why do you live in a bus again?" I question instead, hoping to ignore the unspoken.

He sighs. "Why does it matter where I live?"

"I'm just trying to understand you. You're a millionaire, and you live in a converted school bus in the woods behind a biker bar in the middle of nowhere."

"This isn't nowhere. It's North Carolina. I own these woods, and I like my converted school bus. Stop being a judgmental Judy." His tone turns defensive.

"I'm not judgmental. You could own a mansion in the hills. You could have a sports car or an airplane."

"I don't want an airplane. I do own a sports car, and this year I'm on target to make over a billion."

"Fine, you make over a *billion* in oil."

"Who told you that?" His voice lifts in wonder.

"*Fortune 500*." I read up on Chester Chesterfield, knowing I'd meet the Tennessee-famous entrepreneur who went from rags to riches. There wasn't much info on the rags part of his story, though, only the riches in oil.

"*Fine*. I'm proud of Stop-and-Pump," he admits. Now, I'm stumped.

"Stop-and-Pump?" I snort, shifting on the mattress to look at him over my shoulder. "Those are gas stations with convenience stores attached."

"Yes, and I own them."

I flip completely onto my opposite side to face him. "You own service stations?"

He falls onto his back. "Got something against service stations?"

"No, but how does it make you a billion unless you own the entire company?" I snark, pausing a beat as he stares at me with a gleam in those dark eyes. "You own the entire company, don't you?" I hold my breath waiting on his answer.

"Yes. That's the company that makes me a billion dollars."

"But I thought—"

"Again, something wrong with owning gas stations?" he defends, his eyes narrowing.

"No, but the article said oil." Chesterfield Oil is one of the largest companies on the East Coast, specializing in oil production and related services.

"Where do you think gasoline comes from, darlin'?"

I know the answer, but when I read oil, I assumed . . . and I assumed incorrectly.

"If my money is all you're interested in, then just tell me now, and we can stop whatever this is," he adds, tucking a hand behind his head and staring up at the ceiling once more.

"Is this something?" I question, dropping my voice because I honestly don't know what I'm doing with him. We're nothing alike, but something's drawing us together. I can't be the only one who feels it, even if it's only physical. As he hasn't answered me, I add softy, "It isn't about the money for me."

He sighs. "Look, I have everything I need. I own The Fugitive and the motel. That's what matters most to me. And Harper House."

Ah yes. The home for boys adds another layer to an already complex man.

"Okay, fine, you live in a . . . *tiny house* as a billionaire," I say. Then, I recall why he doesn't live in a regular house. He gave it to three boys not his own, so they could have a large house filled with love and everything *they* need.

Something else comes to mind and I realize we're all over the map, but

I have to ask this question. "Why did you sleep with me that first time? Besides my asking, why did you do it?"

He stares back at me, holding his gaze with mine. "In your office, you told me I had sorrowful, soulful eyes, and that's what attracted me to you in the first place. I saw something in your eyes that reminded me of myself, and I wanted to chase away that sadness. I knew you could spark, darlin', and I wanted to see those kinds of flames."

Biting at my lower lip, I didn't know how to respond. *He . . . wow.* I lean forward and kiss him, quick and stolen, before I roll to my other side, fighting the biggest grin, like the cat who's caught the mouse. Blindly, I reach behind me for his hand, returning it to my belly. Covering it with my own, the coarse hairs on the back of his tickle my palm. Immediately, he shifts to press closer to me, and his hand relaxes against my skin, remaining in place of his own accord. He nuzzles his nose into my neck, and I settle into him at my back.

"I retract what I said earlier," he whispers. "I like you like this."

And I like him, a lot more than is safe for my heart.

CHAPTER 16

ANOTHER MORNING AFTER

[Chet]

This woman can really get under my skin. While I'd been anticipating her arrival in the bar, I wasn't prepared for her mouse costume and how it would hug her body, letting everyone know how fit she is. I also wasn't prepared to find her cozy at a table for six with Todd next to her. He's my best friend and he'd never dip into what's mine, but I saw red.

Then Striker had to push me when I was already making a statement by encroaching on her space while she stood at the bar.

Mine, my stance had said, but then she had to run her mouth, and as much as I wanted to shut it by kissing her silly in front of my bar, I didn't know how she wanted me to play it. Is she some socialite slumming it? Because if she is, I want nothing of that. I've been there before. Or would she allow me to claim her? Announcing our relationship to others?

Without knowing which way to go, I'd left, needing time to cool off before I did something stupid like sling her over my shoulder and carry her out of the place.

I hadn't cooled off enough, because I practically did the same thing a half an hour later.

I'm not surprised when I wake alone in the morning. However, I am surprised when Scotia steps out of my bathroom and stands at the foot of the bed. Both our eyes leap to the same thing—my morning wood standing erect, tenting the sheet that's draped loosely over my body. During the night, I'd peeled off my clothing down to my skivvies. Scotia remained in that damn costume that hugged her curves and left nothing to the imagination.

She's standing at the foot of my bed, eyes wide and hungry on the appendage peaked at attention, and then she does the damnedest thing. She lowers the zipper of her costume and slides it down her body. Stripped before me is a sultry woman in a nude bra and matching lace panties. I have to give it to her. She likes pretty underthings, and even in the dull color, she's a vision.

"Whatcha doing, darlin'?" My voice cracks like a prepubescent teen.

"No talking," she says, her voice quiet as she climbs back up the platform near my feet and crawls over me like a starving predator. The way she looks at me gets me every time. She's so hungry, and I want to believe it's more than sex. She's starving for attention. I don't want her to be another Henny—status-thirsty, money-loving, and sex-desperate. After last night's conversation about the service stations and my near-billion, I'm still a little doubtful. This morning is probably not a good idea.

However, my dick has other thoughts, especially when she tosses two dark packages next to me on the mattress and then curls her hand around my thick shaft holding up the sheet. Her eyes focus on where she's cupping my dick so reverently, stroking up the length, and squeezing the crown.

"Darlin'," I practically whimper. Her touch is just right yet not enough.

"I didn't really get a good look at you the first time," she says, her voice quiet as she inspects me with the palm of her hand, squeezing and tugging the stiff length, ready to blow. "May I?"

Her head pops up, and those silver eyes polished to perfection question me. For all her confidence, there's an innocence to her. She wants me. I have no doubt of her desire, but she doubts herself, and I can't get a read on it. I also can't deny her when that vulnerable look lands on me.

Like I told her last night, her eyes drew me in. I see something in her. I see something of myself in her as well. Her heart is lonely. Who hurt her, and why? How?

With her shield down and the shutters open, the real Scotia shines even if a little tarnished. She's more beautiful than she knows when her words are genuine sugar instead of all salt.

I slide the sheet down, taking my boxers with it, lowering both to my thighs. I'm wearing old, loose plaid underwear because I'm at the end of my stack. I need to do laundry, but that's the last thing on my mind when her firm hand wraps around my bare shaft. Heat. Pressure. Bliss. My eyes roll back a second as she caresses me, taking her time to slide up and down the hot skin pulled taut.

"Scotia," I groan. Her touch is a tickle, light and teasing, when I want fast and hard. She gives me just a bit of what I need, squeezing harder, tugging tighter. The tip leaks, and she uses her thumb to spread the liquid. Her head lowers, and I'm engulfed in more heat, wet and wild. Her tongue circles the shaft before her lips pucker at the crown. My hips buck, and Scotia pulls back.

"Sorry," I mutter, feeling as if I've frightened her, but my body can't help its response to her exploration of me. Surely, she's familiar with male anatomy. My thoughts flip to that damn box of condoms in her office, and my head rolls to the two packages on my bed.

"Where'd you get those?" I huff.

"Your bathroom," she says, her voice smoky and sleep laden. Her hand continues to stroke me, now moistened from her mouth, making the glide slippery. I don't ask any more questions, and her head lowers again, drawing me deep within her mouth. She sucks and swirls, drawing out the pleasure until I'm ready to break, but I don't want to do it like this.

I press at her shoulders, and the look in her eyes stabs me. It's not a devilish glance but one of . . . fear.

"You didn't like that?" she whispers, her eyes lowering to her hand wrapped around the base of my throbbing appendage—a part desperate for more of her.

"I loved it, but I'm about to blow, and I want inside you."

Her breath hitches, and she reaches for a condom. Now, I'm as modern as they come, and I understand all the precautions behind precautions, but Scotia seems *overly* condom concerned. What's her obsession with them?

"You're pretty worried about them condoms," I state, wondering if I should have something to be worried about. It doesn't make sense that the woman anxious about sucking me correctly would have something I could catch, but I still want to know her thought process.

"I'm not on the pill." The statement surprises me. "I've never been."

For the second time, Scotia hesitates. Her hand uncurls from my thickness, but I'm quick to catch her wrist. I hate awkward conversations, but I want to understand her. I want to know what's going on in that pretty head of hers.

"Why not?" It's intrusive, but I'd still like to know.

Scotia swallows, and I watch the roll of her throat, wanting to lick along her skin on that slender neck.

"When I was . . . married, we always used condoms. There didn't seem to be a point to being on the pill, and if I was to get pregnant, well, then . . ." She shrugs. I already know she only has one child.

"You aren't looking to get pregnant now, are you?" I confirm, giving an anxious chuckle, uncertain how I feel about this topic in my mid-forties.

"Don't be preposterous," she huffs. "I'm forty-eight, and while I've been told I could still get pregnant, it'd be the last thing I'd want at this stage of my life." Like the flip of a switch, she has returned to haughty Scotia.

"Don't get your knickers in a twist, darlin'. I'm just trying to understand you." *Trying to figure you out, pickle princess.* And your husband's dislike of phallic symbols, especially after the weirdness of you keeping that old box of condoms.

She's quiet for a second, but I have an issue that needs tending, and I'd like her to take care of it. Something else niggles inside me, though, and I realize once more, I want to take care of her. Scotia seems like a woman in need of some positive reinforcement. Like assuring her I think she's sexy and she doesn't need to be so perfect. Like telling her it's okay to have secrets just don't ever lie to me. Like I'm not shying away from her when I question her. I want her. I want us to be together.

But I don't say any of those things. "Condom," I mutter instead. "Put it on me."

Scotia's quick to do the honor of sheathing me. Her fingers hastily roll the rubber down my shaft. *Holy hell*, it shouldn't be such a turn-on, but the second she finishes, her hand strokes upward, and I'm almost seeing stars again. She scoots her body closer to my stiff appendage, straddling my thighs until she's at my hips.

"Let me—" I'm not fast enough with my suggestion and she impales herself on me. She'd pushed aside the thin lacy covering at her heat and drew me into her body with one swift motion. My head tips up. I was about to offer I touch her a bit, but the ease with which I've slid into her tells me she was more than ready for this. She stills, and I glance up at her face. Her expression has shifted. She's pleased with herself, like a proud kitten getting a favorite toy. *Is she playing with me?* Then her hips flex, and all thought goes out the window.

Her palms rest on my chest, fingers curling into the hair covering my pecs. After a glimpse of her pretty boy assistant, I'd guessed Scotia to like the clean-cut, manscaped, hairless types, but the way her fingertips are raking through the thick mass on my chest tells me she likes the coarse covering. Her pleasure-filled expression turns to ecstasy as she moans while she drags her fingers down my body. Her hips rock back and forth, coasting over me within her.

"Like that, darlin'?" I croak, aware that I like it more than I should. She purrs in response, and I realize *I like her*. Which is just weird because we don't make sense. We have nothing in common. Then she sits up, straightening her body over mine, shifting my position within her, and I realize we do fit rather nicely, at least like this. Her hips start to undulate in sharp, short rolls, causing her to pulse around me, and friction builds as her clit rubs over my pubic bone.

Her eyes close, and her head turns to the side. She's lost in the rhythm she's creating with my body, feeling me connected to her. Watching this strong-willed woman take from me what she needs is doing strange things inside my chest. My palms lazily caress her bare thighs, stroking upward before tickling my fingertips down to her knees. I repeat the path while she rocks faster, increasing the pleasurable tension. She reaches for her chest, pressing one palm above her breast while the other curls around her neck and scoops up her long hair from her neck. She's an erotic vision, and my hips buck upward. Her eyes flip open, and her sight lands on my face.

"Do that again," she whispers. A quiet command mixed with her cautious asking makes me want to give her anything. I repeat the quick thrust, and she gasps. Her hands fall back to my chest, palms flat as we fall into a dance of her short shifts and my sharp surges. Her head tilts back like a wild animal, and her mouth falls open as an elongated groan fills the space around us. She's falling apart over me. The look of passion on her face—I put that there—and the thought does something to my heart.

Tight and deep within her, I feel every clench, every clutch. It's too much, and I increase my thrusts, tapping into her once, twice, three times until I'm over the edge myself. I grasp at her hips and hold her still over me, keeping her in place to take all I give. And for a second, I wish I was bare and spilling into her.

We take a minute to enjoy the aftershocks of mini-twitches and final drops before she presses off my chest, and my hands glide down her hips.

I'm worn, but my head rolls on the pillow to face the second package on the bed. "I'm gonna need a moment before a repeat."

She laughs, and I turn my head to glance up at her. She looks different. Relaxed. Satisfied. Happy. Still seated over me, still with my dick inside her, her laughter ripples up my body, and I slowly smile. I haven't heard her laugh before.

"Think it's funny I'm an old man and need a few minutes to recuperate?" I tease, quickly jackknifing upward. My hands grab her firm backside, keeping her in place as I soften. Her hands cup my cheeks, and those silver-polished eyes undo me a bit.

"I think you're a beautiful man," she whispers. Her gaze lower to my lips, and her head begins to tip forward until a sharp rap on the hard exterior of the bus surprises us. Sensing Scotia's need to retreat, I slide both hands up her back and press against her shoulder blades to keep her in place.

"Big Poppy, you in there?" Jedd Flemming hollers, knocking on the door at my back. As a converted school bus, there's still an emergency exit at the head of my bed.

"Whatchu want?" I call back, a little too loud for the closeness of Scotia, and she flinches in my arms. I stroke up and down her back, attempting to settle her. Her hands on my cheeks slid to my shoulders but now cover her face as if Jedd can see her. He can't actually as the bus's outer shell is raised feet above ground level.

"If Scotia's with you, it's time for her to get a move on. The girls need to get back to Green Valley."

I shake my head and press a quick kiss to Scotia's shoulder.

"Okay. Give her a minute." My voice is still loud, but necessary for it to travel out of the sealed-up structure.

"Had all night," he bellows in return, and then I hear deep laughter. *Damn him.* If Jedd weren't another business investment, I'd be riding his ass for this interruption. Then again, as I glance at Scotia, I realize I might owe Jedd in the end.

"Hey," I whisper to her, reaching for her wrists and tugging them down to see her face.

"Why do I feel like a teenager caught in the back of a minivan?"

"That ever happen to you?"

"No comment," she admits, and I can't help but grin. Miss Buttoned-up Business Suit might have a bit of a wild streak in her past. *Wonder what else she's hiding about herself?*

"Ever get caught having sex in the back of the bus?" I tease.

"Never," she shrieks until she puts two and two together. Her hands cup the sides of my neck, and I like her touch returned to me.

"Have you ever been caught in the back of the bus with a woman?" she hesitantly asks.

"Never been on this bus with a woman before, so that's a firm negative," I clarify for her, and a soft smile curls her lips. Her silvery eyes sparkle.

"I like you like this," she whispers, stroking her fingers over my beard. She's sweet after sex and I'd like to bring out more of the saccharine bits than the acidic spice in her. I'll take that vinegar in her for what it is, and her dash of salt on occasion as well, but I want more sugar.

I like her like this.

CHAPTER 17

WINTER SURPRISE

[Chet]

November

"Henny?"

Finding Hennessy Miller at Harper House was the last thing I expected when I opened the front door on this early November evening. Before me on the stoop stood the woman of my dreams twenty-five years ago. Same blonde hair. Same bright blue eyes. Same sheepish smile that made my insides flip once upon a time.

I'd been hoping to see Scotia tonight as I hadn't seen her most of the week. Maura told me our volunteer needed the day off, and I wondered why. Although Maura seemed to know, she hadn't offered any hints to me.

"Hello, Chester." Henny's smile widens. "I took a chance you might be here."

"Come in," I offer, remembering my manners as the blast of wintry air hits me. I step back so she can enter the grand foyer of the house. Our eyes focus on one another for a long minute, and a million questions scramble through my mind.

"I can't believe I remembered where this place was," she says, breaking contact and looking around the two-story cathedral ceiling of the entryway—of the house I built for her. She'd never seen the interior before. She refused to enter the house. "It's beautiful."

"I don't suppose you were just in the neighborhood." This house up on the mountain isn't anywhere near where Henny grew up. As Knoxville royalty, her father owned a hydroelectrics company using the Little Tennessee River as an energy source. Living in one of the surrounding valleys was the last thing she wanted, which I didn't learn until too late. She eventually moved to Nashville.

"Come in," I repeat myself, still in shock as I hold out a hand, waving in the direction of the great room. "Want to take your coat off?"

She slips off her winter jacket, and I take it from her, placing it over the back of a chair once we enter the large living room. She observes the intricate K'Nex structure being built in the center of the floor, and the collection of boys constructing it.

"Mrs. Pickle, come here," Louie calls out without looking up and then falters with disappointment when he sees our guest is not his favorite book reader. *I feel the same, kid.* Scotia and I need to talk and iron out where we're at with one another.

"You're not Mrs. Pickle," Hunter states, following up Louie's observation.

"Hello," Campbell says quietly, watching Henny like he doesn't trust her.

"You're married," Henny quietly states. *Is that disappointment in her tone?*

"I—"

"Did I hear the doorbell?" Savannah inquires as she enters the large room.

"Savannah, this is Hennessy Miller." I don't know how I should label Henny. Do I explain she was once the love of my life? That she ripped out my heart and reminded me I was no better than my upbringing? Henny saves me from further clarification by holding out a hand to shake with Savannah.

"She's very pretty, Chester," Henny states, addressing me as if Savannah isn't standing before her. The compliment makes Savannah sound like a specimen to be assessed, and it reminds me of the old Henny. The gossipy, sugar-sweet woman disguising comments and insults in candy-coating. It reminds me of someone else who I haven't heard from, and I don't like the comparison. "You're a lucky man."

"Uhm . . ." Savannah pauses, glancing up at me.

"She isn't my wife," I clarify, finding my voice.

"I'm going to go check on dinner," Savannah quickly states, dismissing herself.

"Are you here to build with us?" Hunter asks Henny as Savannah exits the room. "You can take Uncle Chet's place."

"Uncle Chet?" Henny questions, glancing at the child with an arched eyebrow before addressing him. "I'm not here to build, no."

Hennessy knows my history. As a foster child, I didn't have any blood relatives. I had Davis, and eventually, Harper accepted me because she loved him. Henny never knew Harper, and it's a good thing because Harper was loyal, and she would have never approved of Hennessy. Davis didn't like Henny, and I almost lost my friendship because of my fool hearted blindness when it came to this woman.

"Why are you here, Hen?" I guide her to a set of chairs on the edge of the room. My heart pumps a little faster because I don't want her asking more about the boys, learning about them, or misjudging their circumstance.

"I shouldn't be here," she suddenly says, taking in the boys before gazing back at the entryway.

"But you are."

"I just wanted to see you."

I don't know how to respond to that, so I don't.

"How is Davis?" My friend's name on her lips does not sit well with me. We fought so much over him. He and I fought so much over her.

"You have nothing to prove," he told me over and over again, but I disagreed. I wanted the woman and I needed to better myself to get her.

"He died seven years ago."

"Oh, I'm so sorry." She reaches for my forearm, and the touch reminds me of a thousand soft caresses when we were young. We did a lot of touching. Back then, sparks flew. She was an outlet, electric and dangerous, while I was the key warned never to be placed inside her. Her rebellious streak attracted me, and I loved that she chose me to love her.

But she hadn't loved me.

Her current touch is not the same thrilling sensation from my youth. Instead, something prickles up my skin in warning. Being dumped by the love of your life will change a man.

"So what are you doing here?" I ask, slowly retracting my arm from under her hand and curious about this impromptu visit twenty-plus years later.

"I wanted to see what happened with our house." She smiles, glancing up and around the room again.

"*My* house, you mean," I correct as it never became *ours*. She sheepishly looks over at me, and her smile weakens. Those lips were so sweet, so eager, so delicious once upon a time. The memory is wicked. What she did to me was cruel, yet who do I have to blame? I thought I knew her. I thought I could give her what she wanted. I thought she wanted me. I had been wrong.

"Yes, your house. Of course. And your nephews?" she inquires, curious about the Uncle Chet comment.

"Do you have children of your own?" I ask, not interested in explaining Harper House.

"Yes, two." She hesitates without giving further explanation. Her jaw tightens as if holding her smile in place, and I sense there's something she isn't telling me. I learned long ago I was never as good at reading Henny as I thought, but she still surprises me with her next comment. "We should have a drink sometime. Catch up, maybe?"

"What about Jeffrey?" I state, recalling *her husband* as I grip the armrest, holding myself still at the shift in conversation. After all this time, she wants to . . . catch up? What do I even say to her? *I went on to make the millions you wanted. I went on to make something of myself. I'm involved with someone, sort of, I think. And now you want to catch up?*

There comes a time when too much time has passed for connection, reconciliation, or even explanation.

"My husband passed away a year ago," she clarifies, shifting her eyes away from me and back to the boys on the living room floor.

"I'm sorry to hear that." I am sorry for her loss. Jeffrey Heiner had the prestige she wanted—the family name, the history behind it, and the money. *Never forget the money.* "What are you doing in the area?"

"Just visiting," she states, remaining strangely vague. It's a conversation of quipped questions and short answers like an awkward interview, but I remind myself Henny came to me. "So a drink sometime?"

Before I realize what I'm saying, I answer. "I'd like that, Hen."

"Great. It's a date. I'll give you my number." Reaching around herself for her bag, she produces a phone and asks me for my phone number. Then she texts me hers.

She looks at the boys one more time, lingering over each one, and a strange sensation fills my gut. Is she wondering what it would have been like? Wondering how many children we would have had? What they would have looked like with the combination of my dark waves and her blue eyes? I envisioned Hennessy as a mother. Just thought it would be the natural progression between us, perhaps. We'd marry. We'd have children. I'd take care of our family—the family I never had as a kid.

Her gaze shifts, glancing up and around the great room, noting the large couch, the two armchairs where we sit and the two-story fireplace. A flat-screen television hangs above the mantel for movie nights, and a shelving unit holds bins of toys and stacks of board games. The large three-paned window overlooks the mountain range, difficult to make out in the dark landscape but there nonetheless. I built the home I thought she'd want.

I never asked for this, she'd said.

"It's so great to find you're still here, Chester. You look good." Her smile deepens. Her lips look larger, different than I remember, and it throws me off. Something warns me not to trust her, but I ignore the nagging hint. The thing about me with Hennessy—I'm stupid around her. I always was and, apparently, still am.

"You, too." My shoulders tense, and my grin falsely grows. The more I look at her, the more there's something off about her appearance. Her eyes are pulled a little too tight at the corners. Her nose looks thinner.

I stand to end this impromptu visit, and Henny follows my lead. I pick up her coat and walk her to the front door. Holding open her winter jacket for her, she slips her arms into it.

"Such a gentleman," she teases over her shoulder, and a thousand things flash before me. Frank Sepco taught me to be a gentleman. Hold the door for a woman. Take her hand. Bring her flowers.

Life lessons on women from a service station gentleman, he teased.

"Things change," I mutter. Was I not a gentle man when we were younger? I wasn't polished, but I wasn't rough either. I was good to her. I'd assumed Henny would spiff me up once we were married. She'd teach me how to be better. Instead, she hardened me when she ripped out my heart.

"Yet some things stay the same. I never forgot you, Chester." The sound of my name on her lips feels wrong. I'm reminded she never called me Chet. She doesn't know me as him, and she'd definitely disapprove of Big Poppy. "I'm so glad you're still here."

Her hand comes to my chest, and she pushes onto her toes, pressing a kiss to the corner of my lips before I know what's happening. I'm stunned, as stiff as the banister near the stairs. My brain is slow to register the most important question that I don't want to ask myself. *What does she want from me?* Because there must be something after all this time.

"Be careful on that drive," I say as I open the front door in order not to catch her eyes, which are searching for mine. The night is cold, and the scent of snow lingers in the air. A dark, sporty car sits in the driveway.

"I look forward to seeing you soon," Henny says, and her hand pats my chest once more. She was always touchy, and it distracted me in my youth.

How could something so beautiful touch my filth? I'd marveled at the thought when I was young, but Henny touched me in more ways than one.

I watch Henny with curiosity as she walks across the drive, slides into her car, and reverses into the night. When I close the door, I press my large back to it and tip my head against the panel, closing my eyes.

"Was someone here?" Maura asks, coming out of her office off the entry.

"Hennessy Miller," I state. Hennessy Miller *Heiner.*

"What the hell did she want?" Maura questions, nearly as surprised as me, and I glance at her. Maura and I have known one another for years, so we know each other's pasts. We've never been attracted to one another, giving us a true male-female friendship. In many ways, Maura reminds me of a female Davis, and I'm grateful to have someone like her in my life.

"Drinks." It's so unbelievable. "Her husband is dead." Is she looking for sympathy? Does she want more from me? Does she want comfort in the form of something I'll never give her again? My money. My dick. My heart. I'm instantly disappointed in myself.

Way to judge someone, Chet.

Maybe she meant what she said. She only wants to have a drink and catch up.

"Drinks?" Maura repeats, uncertainty filling her tone, along with a side of *I-don't-believe-it*. I stare at my nephews' caregiver. *Yeah, I probably shouldn't believe it either.*

"I don't know what she wants." I'm answering the unasked question, confused myself by Henny's sudden presence and how surreal it was to have her in the house I built for her.

I don't think I should see the inside. I'll only fall in love with it, and it can't be mine.

You're in love with me, not him. You're *mine.*

"Maybe this is a sign it's time for you to date," Maura states, and I blink back to the present.

"Henny?"

"Anyone but," Maura harshly huffs. "Find a nice woman. Settle down a bit. Have stable companionship." Maura has no idea about the instability of my relationships. The one-night stands. The distance I keep from women. The craziest thing I've done in years is Scotia Simmons. Thoughts of her collide with memories of Henny. The two women are night and day in appearance but not quite so different in personality. It's one reason I've had my doubts about Scotia. My body doesn't distrust a thing about her, but I don't understand Scotia's motive to be with me. The way she looks at me. The way she touches me. I don't understand. *Why me?* And that question stems from what Henny did to me because she'd had a motive, and I'd been fool enough to fall for everything.

"Who says I don't have all the companionship I need?" I joke.

Maura shakes her head, giving me a knowing look. "Wouldn't someone steady and stable be nice?"

The question throws me off guard, and I wonder if she's speaking about herself. In the six years she's been with me and the boys, she hasn't dated once that I know of.

"Dinner's ready," Savannah announces, entering the front entry where Maura and I have remained, and I'm grateful for the intrusion on this awkward conversation.

My thoughts rush to Scotia. She's stable. She runs her own business. She has a solid family in her sisters. But she's still a contradiction to me. What does a woman of independent means want with a man like me?

I wouldn't share you because I'd want to keep you for myself.

The words almost erase the strange sensation prickling my skin after Henny's exit. Scotia doesn't hold back—not in words or opinions—but she also doesn't hold back when we touch. She sparks like an unlit match, crackling to life, and I want to keep feeding that flame. I want to know how brightly she'll burn. How hot she will heat. How intense can she be.

Maybe I should ask Scotia out on a date.

However, I'm too old to date. Dating is some kind of youthful mating ritual, testing the waters of compatibility and leading toward a commitment I can't offer someone. I already have too many responsibilities as it is and don't need the complication of a woman just because she smiles prettily at me.

But you do like when Scotia smiles at you. Her eyes light up. Her lips curl as though she knows a secret.

The boys scramble to the bathroom to wash up, scattering my thoughts, and Maura does a quick survey of heads.

"Has anyone seen Malik?" she asks the collective group.

"Maybe he's upstairs?" Hugh suggests.

"I didn't see him in the guest room," Dewey volunteers as he had to pass the bedroom to come downstairs for dinner.

"I'll check," I say, taking my time to search the upper rooms. I only grow slightly uneasy as I scan the lower floor. But by the time I reach the dining room, with one empty chair among the rows of boys, I've moved from unease to anxious.

"I couldn't find him."

Maura glances up at me, her expression matching the concern in my chest. "I'll call the authorities."

CHAPTER 18

ARRESTED IN TRUTH

[Scotia]

"Mrs. Simmons, this is Deputy Sheriff Hughes." The second my phone rang, I pounced on it, answering breathlessly without greeting.

"Yes," I cut him off.

"We've arrested a young man who had your business card on him." On a typical day, I wouldn't admit to knowing any young man with a business card, but Malik isn't typical. Deputy Sheriff Hughes didn't say the boy was Malik, but I'm already collecting my bag, knowing it can't be anyone else.

He's been missing for two days.

"I'll be right there." I hang up without further explanation. When Maura called me two nights ago to tell me Malik was missing, I was at my office. I haven't left it, hoping he'd come here. Since the moment I met the boy at Harper House, I've had an affinity for him. I don't know how to explain it. That lost look. That silent, sharp mind. Something about him just spoke to me, and I want to gather him in my arms and tell him the world isn't always such a cruel place. I just wish he would open up to me.

I race for my SUV parked behind the building and swiftly make it to the sheriff's department.

Rushing through the front doors of the station, I nearly yell, "Where is he?"

"Where's who?" Flo McClure states from the reception desk. The evening hour seems a little late for her to be working, but I don't pay her any mind.

"The boy. Aaron Hughes called me about him."

"You mean Deputy Sheriff Hughes," Flo corrects me for calling Aaron by his given name and not his title. *Bless his heart.* His parents were at their wits' end with him and likely felt relieved when he slipped right into this position at the local sheriff's department. Flo takes her time to make the call back to him, asking him if he has a boy in interrogation.

"Interrogation?" I question. "He's a child."

"Kids still commit crimes."

"What could he possibly have done?" I don't need Flo to answer me as the deputy saunters into the reception area.

"Mrs. Simmons, if you'll follow me." I'm led toward his desk with no sign of the boy.

"Where is Malik?"

"That the boy's name? He isn't speaking to me, but I found your business card on his person."

I'd given Malik the card in case he ever wanted to speak to me. It was probably against protocol for Harper House, but I wanted him to know he could reach out to me when he was ready to talk.

"Yes. His name is Malik."

"Any idea where he's from?"

"Isn't that supposed to be your job?" I remind him. It's been up to the sheriff's department to further investigate Malik's unexplained appearance, although Aaron is not the one assigned to his case. Deputy Boone is the investigating officer. Apparently, Officer Boone isn't present this evening.

"He one of those homeless kids up on the hill?"

"He is not homeless. He lives in a private residence that's a certified foster home. They're approved by the state and well provided for." I hope I've said that correctly. I don't want anything to happen to separate any of the children from Maura or Chet. I should have called them, but my first concern had been getting to Malik.

"You seem to know quite a bit about the place," Aaron states as if *I'm* under investigation.

"That's none of your concern," I admonish. "Or rather, it should be your concern. You should be investigating where this child came from and why he's missing. What happened to him? Does he have parents? A family? Are they missing him, or did he run away from them? Was he kidnapped or harmed? And how long has he been out there alone in the world, Aaron?" I feel myself growing hysterical with worry, and I clutch the pearls at my throat.

"It's Deputy Sheriff, Mrs. Simmons." *That's all he has to say to me?*

"What's the boy's offense?"

"Caught him stealing food outside the Piggly Wiggly."

My mouth falls open while my chest clenches. *Poor thing.* "How was he stealing food *outside* the store?" It's too cold for produce and products outside the building.

"He was in the dumpster."

I stiffen in my seat. "Let me get this straight. He was in the dumpster, scrounging for food, and that warranted an arrest?"

"Well, he's not really under arrest."

"But did you cuff him? Toss him in your vehicle? Turn the lights on and drive him here?"

"Maybe not the lights part—"

"Did you handcuff him?" I'm aghast.

"He could have been dangerous."

"He's all but nine years old." I take a deep breath, placing my palm on my chest as my heart hammers within.

"What's going on here?" Deputy Sheriff Chris Williams steps up to where I'm seated, and I turn on him.

"Chris, how could you let this happen?" For a moment, he stares at me, shocked at my accusation. Chris Williams is the son of an acquaintance of mine, Debbie Williams, who is a local second grade teacher. His daddy is a decent man, having looked out for his only boy by using his pull with Sheriff James to help get Chris into the department when he was of age.

"What's going on here?" Chris directs again to his fellow deputy, and then blanches at the explanation Aaron gives about cuffing a nine-year old. Chris scrubs at his forehead, pinching the skin a bit before his eyes meet mine.

"Mrs. Simmons—"

"Now don't you Mrs. Simmons me, Chris. Your mama would be ashamed of this situation. She *is* a schoolteacher. What do you think she'd say?"

"Yes ma'am, I agree, and—"

"And I don't reckon your daddy would approve either," I continue.

"No ma'am, he definitely wouldn't, but—"

"No buts Chris. Where is my boy?" I'm almost shrieking. Malik must be so frightened and obviously hungry if he was digging in the trash.

"Hughes, get the kid." As Aaron hoists his lazy body out of his chair, Chris leans toward me.

"Mrs. Simmons, I apologize for all this. Hughes is brand new and . . . excitable. Let's just say the department has a budget. We don't always get the most qualified applicants given what we can pay. Sometimes it's impossible to know a person's character until they're in the field, but that's really no excuse. I'll take this to my grave and deny I said this to you, but we have to do with what we have. Hughes is a warm body on these late-night shifts. It's either he fills the spot or no one does. It just is what it is."

Chris's words do nothing to appease my ire, but I try to understand.

A gruff voice from the front area demands to speak to the sheriff at the same time Malik rounds the corner off a hallway under the firm hand of Aaron.

"Malik!" I squeal, and the boy runs to me. He smells six-ways to Sunday, but I draw him to me, pressing his little head to my chest.

"You had no right to frighten him," I scold Aaron, narrowing my eyes at him.

"Traffic duty the rest of this month," Chris adds, his voice more assertive than I've ever heard.

"You arrested *a child*. You scared him half to death, and he's obviously hungry and afraid. Where's your compassion?"

Aaron mutters, "I wouldn't say scared to death—".

"Not another word from you," Chris interjects, his irritation and annoyance with his co-worker apparent. Perhaps Chris is growing into his own. He might make a fine sheriff one day after all.

"What do I need to sign? I'm taking him home with me."

"Now, Mrs. Simmons, I can't just turn him over to you. I need to follow protocol and find out who's responsible for him," Chris turns back to me.

"I'm responsible for him," the gruff voice returns, and I spin to face the front area of the department. Chet stands tall on the opposite side of Flo's reception counter.

"Mr. Chesterfield?" Chris questions. "Great to see you again." Chris's face softens and I'm hopeful he's familiar with Malik's case.

"You can call Veronica Mason with the Department of Child Services if you need further evidence of the child's current placement," Chester informs Chris.

"Flo, get Miss Mason on the phone," Chris directs, sounding important in his own right. At this point, though, I just want to take Malik out of here. I'm stroking his head, smoothing back his oily hair and wrinkling my nose again at the stench coming off him.

While we wait for Chris to get the confirmation he needs, Chet is ushered around reception and crosses to Aaron's desk. Thankfully, Aaron hasn't spoken again.

"What are you doing here?" Chet asks me, keeping his voice low.

"They called me."

"How?" His gruff voice turns gruffer as he glances around the room.

"I gave Malik my business card for sticky situations just like this one."

Chet glares at me. "We'll deal with that later," he warns, keeping his eyes on me.

Chris finally returns with some paperwork for Chet to sign and gives us permission to leave.

"Stay out of those dumpsters, kid," Aaron chides under his breath, and I'd like to skin his hide for acting like this innocent child is a criminal.

* * *

We decide to leave my car at the sheriff's department and ride together in Chet's truck back to Harper House.

"Thank you for coming tonight," I address him, keeping my voice quiet as Malik falls against my side.

"Where else would I be?" he quips. I don't have the faintest idea what he does with his time. Between running a business that he doesn't talk about and owning a bar where he seems to spend most of his time, I don't know much about his daily life. I also know he hasn't called me.

He shifts on his seat and swipes a hand through his hair. "I've been staying at the house. Spending my days searching everywhere I could think a kid might run."

I glance down at Malik, knowing he can hear us and wishing he would answer the million-dollar question. *Why did he leave Harper House? And where has he been these past two days? Better yet, where is he from?*

When we return to the house, Maura immediately sweeps Malik up in her arms and whispers sweet things to him.

"You need a shower, little man," she teases him eventually and guides him up the stairs to the bathroom. I want to follow. I'm afraid to let him out of my sight, but it's not my place, and I've never felt so helpless.

"How about a drink?" Chet mutters, and I nod, following him into an office off the front hall.

"This is Maura's private stash," Chet says after reaching into her desk for a key and opening a locked upper cabinet to retrieve a bottle of whiskey and two tumblers. He pours a thick sliver for each of us. After offering me a glass, he takes a seat at Maura's desk, which faces the front window, and I take a seat in an accent chair.

"Why are you so drawn to this kid, darlin'?" Chet asks, and I stare into the amber liquid in the tumbler in my hands.

"I don't know exactly." I wish I had a specific answer to give him, but I don't. Am I misguided? Am I trying to replace a loss from over twenty-six years ago? Another child, lost before his time to be born. We learned he was a son. *Mask in place, Scotia.* "There are so many troubled children out there. Karl's mission was to keep them healthy, both physically and mentally."

Using Karl as my excuse explains things best. The task of my husband wasn't always easy, though, because of who he was inside and the position he was in.

"Why don't you have more children, Scotia?"

"That's intrusive," I bite. It's been a difficult question to answer over the years, and my standard answer normally revolves around God and Darlene. *The dear Lord only sought to bless me with one baby, and she was perfect.* But it wasn't the whole truth.

"Just answer the damn question." Goodness, this man can bust my bonnet. His sharp tone startles me.

Mask in place, I want to warn myself, but the shield is stifling me, and I just want to breathe. This man has opened me up in more ways than one, and my heart is on the line with him. But there's something else happening to me. I feel raw and edgy inside.

Perhaps it's Malik's disappearance and the potential of losing him forever.

Perhaps it's the man sitting before me, glaring at me, and if I don't risk myself, I might never gain him either.

I can't close off my emotions tonight. I'm tired of heavy secrets, living half a life, and protecting an empty heart desperate for love.

"Karl always used condoms." Chet has heard me say this before. "He was promiscuous but discreet. He knew the importance of protection both for himself and for me, not that we often . . . you know. He didn't want to ever risk infecting me, which was sweet until you consider the truth. My husband was fucking around."

"Jesus, how could you be so blasé that he cheated on you with other women and returned to your bed?" Chet takes a long drink of his whiskey, emptying the glass, and I'm a bit startled by the offense in his tone on my behalf. I lick my lips before the remainder of my confession slips free.

"Because he wasn't with women."

Chet is startled into silence, which is what I expect. He's processing what I've said as he stares at me from Maura's desk chair. What do you say to such a confession? I shift in my seat, taking another sip of the strong alcohol before I speak.

"My husband was gay." I answer the question he isn't asking to be clarified. "We were married for almost twenty-three years when he died, and I knew his sexual orientation most of our marriage. I was his cover story. We had an agreement. We were each other's best friend, and it was awful." I let out a deep breath, releasing years of pressure within that exhale. "Twenty, thirty years ago, you couldn't be a pediatrician and a homosexual. It just couldn't be done. The stereotypes. The stigma. He wasn't into little boys. He liked grown men, but his desires and his profession conflicted."

I take another deep breath, feeling myself on a roll with this admission.

"Do you have any idea how hard it is to accept that the man you love can never fully love you like you want? Like you feel you deserve? It wasn't in his nature. He wasn't truly bisexual, but he occasionally gave me what I needed, and God, did I have needs. You have no idea how lonely I've been."

A tear slides along my cheek. The confession rolls off my shoulders like a weighted blanket finally falling free. I'm not certain why I'm crying, though.

"Does anyone know this about him?"

"You're the first person I've ever told." I'd never told a single soul. My sisters had a hint that my marriage wasn't all it was intended to be, but they don't know the full truth. Not one person knew Karl's orientation outside the men he fucked and the few he loved along the way. "I swore I'd take it to my grave, but I've just told you."

Chet sits forward in the chair he occupies, and it occurs to me what I've done. I've just bared my soul and given away my biggest secret to a man filled with secrets.

"I shouldn't have said anything," I mutter, suddenly regretting my admission despite the freeing release I feel at finally—*finally*—sharing the information with someone. *Mask in pl—*

"You shouldn't have told *me*." Chet seeks confirmation.

"Yes." In the dim light of Maura's office, I don't look up at him. I take another sip of the throat-burning whiskey instead.

"Why not?" Chet asks, his voice rising a bit.

"Because I—"

"You don't trust me. Is that it?" he interjects, cutting me off before I can explain. He has a habit of doing this to me.

"No, it's just—"

"What?" he practically shouts, and I turn my head toward the partially closed door.

"I don't want you to judge me," I argue back, keeping my own voice lowered.

"Are you serious? How could I judge you for your *husband's* sexuality?"

"Well, you're so nosy about children and condoms, and I just—" Before I finish, Chet is out of the office chair. His large body moves so quickly the piece of furniture rocks back and forth with his release. He reaches forward for my glass, placing it on a small side table. Then he's kneeling on one knee before me, brushing a thick thumb over my cheek to wipe away another errant tear. He shakes his head.

"What am I going to do with you, Scotia Simmons?"

I shrug. *Am I that hopeless to him?*

"What did you get out of it?" he asks, after staring at me for a long minute.

"I became a part of Green Valley society. The wife of a respected doctor from a wealthy family in the community." Listening to myself, I hear the words as they might sound to him—shallow, heartless, cold.

"Money and status are really important to you, aren't they?"

When you come from nothing, it certainly is, but that's not something else I plan to share with him tonight. Let him think I've been entitled all my life. I don't care. I don't need his judgement. *Mask in place, Scotia!*

"Don't do that," he warns, shaking his head again.

"What?" I snap.

"That wall-building thing. You're shutting me out."

"Why do you even want in?" I question, feeling defensive and vulnerable in the same breath.

"Don't have any idea, just like you can't answer about that kid—" Chet begins, nodding toward the door, implying Malik. "But there's just something about you." His thumb continues to caress my cheek, and I turn my face into the tenderness.

"You must think I'm pathetic," I state.

"Nah."

"Hopeless," I mutter.

"More like I have hope for you yet." His lips slowly crook upward, and another tear drips from my eye. He leans forward and gives me the softest of kisses. It's featherlight, and I open for more when a soft knock on the door interrupts us.

"I'm sorry to interrupt, but I wanted to say good night."

Chet's hands instantly drop from my face, and he pulls back as though he's been caught doing something he shouldn't be doing.

"Sure . . . good night." My head swivels back and forth between Savannah and him, noting he's suddenly tongue-tied with a touch of pink in his cheeks.

What is this?

Is he embarrassed he got caught kissing me?

What in the hell is he doing with me, then?

I can't go through this again. With all I just confessed to him, I can't have a man who wants to be invisible. A man who only shares half himself with me and hides the rest. I don't want half a man. I want a whole heart, *dammit*.

Once Savannah spins away from the door, I shove at Chet, knocking him off-balance from his one knee.

"What the fuck?" he mutters, but I'm already standing. I need to get out of this house, but I rode with Chet.

"Savannah! Wait?" I call out, hoping to get a ride to town with the other woman.

I can't do love in the modern era. I'm not a casual-sex kind of person. I'd had casual sex with my husband our entire marriage, and that was a rare, *rare* occasion. I want something real. I want someone who belongs to me. Someone who wants *me* . . . and only me.

CHAPTER 19

WHEN THE STUDENT SCHOOLS THE MASTER

[Scotia]

"Mama?"

"Darlene, baby." I'm breathless from both lunging for my phone in my office and relief in hearing my daughter's voice as I haven't heard from her in two weeks.

"I'm sorry it's been a bit," she immediately apologizes.

"I know you're busy," I assure her. As a new doctor, her schedule is ridiculous. My baby girl works hard. Her father would be so proud of her.

"That's one reason I'm calling now. I don't have much time. I've been *very* busy, but I wanted to tell you that Henry invited me to go with him to his family's home for Thanksgiving." The excitement in her voice should thrill me, but I can't ignore the disappointment I feel. Darlene is my only immediate family.

"Which one is Henry?" I tease. I want my daughter to be an independent woman of means and strong-willed in manner. I'm proud of her for selectively dating. I'm equally thankful she did not settle on that Beau

Winston. She needs to play the field, unlike me, and experience a variety of men before picking one.

I was raised to believe the man in a woman's life determined her worth. *You need a man,* my mother stated. Her voice haunts me. *When you're married . . . When you have children . . . Your worth is in your home.*

Darlene's laughter pulls me back to the conversation. "Henry's the medical student I told you about last time, Mama. I really like him." Her admiration is evident in her voice, and I'm happy for her. "But I do feel bad. If you want me to come home, I can."

While I appreciate her saying what she's said, her tone drastically shifts with her offer. She doesn't want to come home.

"Don't you worry about me. I'll spend time with Aunt Naomi or Aunt Beverly," I counter even though that's the last thing I'll be doing. I'm not going to invite myself to either of my sisters' homes. They each have new memories to make with their new beaus on the upcoming holiday.

"Are you sure?"

"I'll be just fine," I lie, gritting my teeth to force the practiced smile I've used most of my life. The forced energy works as my words sound more agreeable than I feel. "You just go have a good time with your Henry."

I'm not lying with this encouragement. I want her to enjoy herself with men—safely, of course. There's no reason to limit herself as I did.

"I hate to run already, Mama, but I've got to go. I'm on call."

"Of course, baby. Be safe," I say as a reminder to protect herself against the men in her life and the sick people she heals.

"I'll call you on Thanksgiving," she tells me, and I want to remind her that's two weeks away, but I don't.

I grit my teeth and smile weakly to myself. "Thank you, honey. I'll talk to you then."

"Love you, Mama," she says, and while I'm still telling her I love her, the phone goes dead.

I lower the phone to my desk while my body sinks into my desk chair. After spending two endless days in my office, work is the last place I want to be. The emotion of finding Malik and telling Chet about Karl yesterday has me unfocused today, but pickle products don't sell themselves.

November isn't prime pickle season, but we're branching out from our original fried pickle recipe to include a variety of spice levels and a cookbook. We also have a new apparel line for our retail store. We ran a contest for new slogans, and the favorite was *Just Dill with It*. We plan to launch our newest endeavors in the next few days to celebrate National Pickle Day on November fourteenth. *It's a big dill*—another one of our sayings.

I stare at the apparel images before me on my computer, lost in my head. Will the real deal ever happen for me? Am I just too old to consider falling in love? Was Karl my once-in-a-lifetime, even if it wasn't the lifetime I thought I'd have? I can't answer my own questions, and it frustrates me. I'm even more frustrated that I opened up to a man I hardly know. One who, despite being filled with all kinds of contradictions, I'm highly attracted to. Just the thought of him does something to my insides and my panties.

But I've been telling myself not to think of him after our encounter last night. His reaction as he was caught kissing me is still unsettling. It's Karl all over again. *Secrecy.* I want someone who claims me as his because he wants me and does it proudly, not simply to protect himself, not to hide himself. Besides, my husband and I didn't kiss, and it's one thing I've liked so much with Chet. But I can't be with a man who doesn't see my value is more than keeping his secrets.

I didn't want to hide Chet, I wanted to keep him for me, and there's a difference in that logic. I want someone for me, that's mine alone—not shared, not compromised, not a secret. *Someone* who is mine.

Maybe I should date? Maybe I need to experiment more? Maybe I need to be more open like I suggest my daughter be? But first, I need to figure out what's wrong with me—as in, *why aren't men attracted to me?*

"So I have some final thoughts on the pickle party," Gideon states, rushing into my office. He has had some good ideas, making him more valuable than my past few assistants. One of those ideas includes a party to celebrate fried pickles on our five-year anniversary at Genie's Country Western Bar. Getting Genie Lee to agree to a celebration at her place caused me to swallow a bit of my pride, but she finally acquiesced in the name of good business practice.

"Why in tarnation would I allow you to throw a party in my establish-

ment? You don't even like me, and I can never forget what you said about my daughter. Woman of loose morals. Hmph!" Genie huffed at me when I approached her with my plan. I knew it would be an uphill battle, and I had the event barn at Donner Lodge as a backup, thanks to Jennifer Winston's kind offer, but I really wanted Genie's.

Where else should fried pickles be celebrated other than at a bar?

When I glance up at Gideon, I bite my cheek so as not to bark at him for interrupting me. He isn't really disturbing anything. My gaze falls on the pickle trophy I won, kicking off this new journey in my life. The vertical pickle immediately reminds me of a penis.

"Mrs. Simmons?" My name pulls my attention to my assistant.

"Gideon, sit down for a second." At my command, he suddenly drops into one of the chairs across from my desk. Swallowing, I fold my hands over the wooden surface and try to meet his eyes. On second thought, I don't think I can look directly at him as I ask my question, so I return my gaze to the phallic trophy.

"Gideon, I have a serious question, and I'd like an honest answer. Not employee to employer, but from a man to a woman."

My gaze hesitantly shifts to him, and his Adam's apple bobs along his throat.

"What's wrong with me . . . as a woman?"

His mouth falls open and quickly shuts. I hold my pose, squeezing my hands together. *I will not snap at him*, I remind myself. I asked for honesty.

"Please answer freely. I can handle it." The statement is meant to assure him I assume what he'll say will be critical. He continues to stare at me, not offering anything. "Perhaps I should guide you, but don't let me sway your answers. Tell me something good about me."

"You have amazing hair." The comment startles me, and I instantly reach for the white strip. Like a magnet, people can't seem to help but notice it when first looking at me, and I've always hated it. As I aged, I decided to embrace the unique feature. With Chet's new habit of wrapping the strands around his finger, I'm rather pleased with this part of me.

"Thank you, Gideon. Now for something not great about me."

Gideon grits his teeth in a manner his lips pull back over them. His neck muscles stand out with the action. "Sometimes, you are kind of mean."

"Mean?" I interject. The word in Gideon's high-pitched tone merges into Chet's deep tenor.

Mean. I'm all too familiar with the term but haven't paid too much attention to how it relates to my behavior until Chet mentioned the same word to me.

"Well, just kind of. I mean, nothing I can't handle. You're just . . ."

"Mean," I repeat.

"Rough around the edges," he attempts to soften the critique.

"*Mean*, you mean." I nod, commiserating with his initial assessment.

"Well, just a little." He lifts his hand, pinching his index finger and thumb within an inch of each other. Then he spreads them a little farther apart.

"What do I do that's so *mean*?" I ask, still hopeful for his honesty.

"Well . . . uhm . . . the thing is . . . sometimes . . ."

"Just spit it out," I snap. His eyes widen, and I realize I've given myself my own verbal example. "Okay, yes, fine. I see." I drop my voice on each word.

Gideon watches me, visibly nervous.

"Gideon, how would you recommend someone stop being mean, especially if say, someone else didn't find it attractive?"

"Are there people attracted to mean people?" he questions, brows arching, and I stare back at him. In romance novels, women are always attracted to mean men. The swanky alpha. The blunt a-hole. He can insult her, punish her, even do some despicable things to her, which, for all intents and purposes, are abusive, yet he's always forgiven. A woman, however, who makes a few comments about another person is considered a bitch, and it's not a compliment.

I dismiss his responding question. "I consider myself honest," I defend, and Gideon sits up a little straighter.

"Sometimes, people don't need quite so much . . . honesty," he states, scrunching up his nose.

"Give me an example," I ask my assistant.

"Say a woman has a little hair on her lip, which I absolutely agree is not attractive. I mean, girl, get that squirrel tail off your face." Gideon waves his hand as if he's Hazel Cumberstone eagerly agreeing with my assessment. "How*ever*, no one wants to be reminded of their imperfections." His eyes flit to the white patch in my hair, and I bristle as I take his meaning. I had plenty said about me as a child. The mark of the devil was my favorite—*says me, never*. My father disagreed with people's cruel assessment, saying the distinguishing mark meant I was chosen by God for something special in this life.

"As men," Gideon continues, "we can be particularly sensitive. I don't want to be told my hair is thinning, or I look paunchy, or I have whiskers in my ears."

"But what if you do? Shouldn't someone tell you?" I'm an eager student awaiting his answer, which he hesitates on for a second.

"No. Even if I ask, you should probably lie to me."

"But if I ask someone if they like my new shoes or if I look good in my suit, I don't want them to lie to me." Karl was always honest when I asked. When I thought I'd gained some weight, he agreed I had.

"Well, Mrs. Simmons, I think you're an exception to that rule then." He smiles to soften his truth. Perhaps I am exceptional, but maybe I shouldn't be pointing out to others where they aren't.

"What do you recommend instead?"

Gideon stares back at me like I've asked the impossible. I lean forward, prompting him to tell me the secret.

"Maybe you could try to be nicer," he suggests. My expression must suggest that's not specific enough, so he continues. "Compliment someone instead. If you notice their hairy lip, compliment their lipstick instead. If you think they need to pluck their eyebrows, tell them how pretty their eyes are."

"I don't want to lie, though," I admit, as most of my life has been a giant lie.

"Mrs. Simmons, have you ever heard that saying 'if you can't think of something nice to say, then don't say anything at all'?"

"Often," I remark.

"There's a newer saying. If you can't think of anything nice to say, you aren't thinking hard enough."

"Are you insulting my intelligence?" I clip.

"With all due respect, this is what I'm talking about." He pauses, circling a finger in the air as he points at me. "Maybe you need to consider that new suggestion. Think before you react." He nods several times, agreeing with his own assessment.

I take a deep breath and a moment to consider what he's said. If he had been anyone else in Green Valley, telling me I need to improve my delivery, or perhaps keep disparaging comments to myself, I'd have had choice words for him. But this is Gideon, and while my assistant, he is also new to the community. He doesn't have preconceived notions about me, so I'm appreciative of his lessons as an impartial mentor.

"I like your shirt," I say, and he slowly smiles. His face brightens, and I'm a little stunned. My assistant is a pretty man. Not one I'm attracted to and way too young for me, but pretty nonetheless. His shirt today is hideous. Still, I can see the effect of telling him how much I like his shirt and recognize it's considerably different than suggesting he never be seen in it again. He stands, tipping his shoulder upward, giving off a little flare of excitement.

"Thank you. If that's all for now, I'll get back to party planning."

"Of course, yes. Make yourself useful." I pause, grateful for his assistance in securing Genie's for our party. Her bar is a popular place in town, and the joint business venture could be profitable for both of us. "As you always are," I add, attempting kindness again. He takes a step around the chair where he sat and shakes his head.

"That was a lie, but I'll pretend it's a compliment." He winks.

"You know me so well," I mock.

"I do, and that's why there's hope for you yet," he states, just as Chet did.

Is there hope? I want to believe so.

* * *

Deciding I'm useless for the day, I head to my weekly manicure at The Beauty Mark. As I enter the salon, I'm immediately surprised to see a little boy in the waiting seats.

"Malik?" I question the child, and his head pops up. Instantly, I note that he's younger than Malik by a few years but looks exactly like him. *How strange.*

"I'm so sorry. I thought—"

"May I help you?" The sharp tongue of a woman startles me, and I turn to meet a face overdone with plastic surgery. Puffy lips. Too-smooth forehead. Taut eye corners giving her a continuously surprised appearance. Her blonde highlights are brassy, but I practice in my head what Gideon has taught me.

I like your . . . I scan her up and down. Her shoes are decent.

"Is this your son?" I pause taking another glance at the child. "He looks exactly like a little boy I know named—"

"We don't speak to strangers, do we, honey?" She hesitates on the endearment, careful not to address the child by name. Her eyes try to hold his, but his brown eyes are wide as he peers up at his mother. It's almost frightening how much those eyes could be a match for Malik's.

"I didn't mean—"

"No offense taken," she cuts me off and reaches for the child, hastily pulling him by the arm from his seat, but his head twists in my direction, keeping his eyes on me. As I remain standing, waiting for the nail technician to call me forward, I can't take my eyes off him either.

"How much do I owe you?" the woman asks of Tabatha, the hair tech.

"That's thirty dollars."

"Thirty? You hardly did anything," the woman scoffs. Tabatha blanches, looking up at her customer. "This is a second-rate establishment. You shouldn't be charging such exorbitant prices."

Second-rate? Exorbitant? Thirty dollars is not unreasonable, and this is not a second-rate place. It's the best in the valley.

"That's robbery," she states, rustling through her bag before handing over crumbled bills. "I have nothing extra for a tip."

Stepping forward, I'm unable to stop myself. "You must be new to Green Valley?" I question, forcing my best smile. I know the regulars in The Beauty Mark, and I've never seen her before.

"We're renting a cabin nearby," she admits and then cringes as if she's said too much. "Not that it's any of your business."

It isn't my business, but I'm not about to let her insult Tabatha. Even though I've insulted the hair tech a time or two myself, newcomers are not open to opinion.

"Tabatha, put this woman's tip on my session today." I tip my head to the outlander. "Welcome to Green Valley," I snip, holding back all the other things I want to comment on like her tight forehead, Botox lips, and firm eye corners. Keeping my thoughts in my head, I smile as prettily as I can muster to this stranger, and I grit out, "And I like your shoes."

And all the while, her child stares at me with eyes like Malik, causing an eerie chill to ripple up my spine.

* * *

The next day, I catch my breath when Chet enters Harper House. His hair is clipped short on the sides while the top remains longer but not as long as it's been. His beard is trimmed tight to his jaw, accenting the edge of it. He smells exceptionally citrusy and warm today, and my mouth waters.

"My, you clean up nicely," I tease, unable to help myself as I'm reminded of our first meeting.

"That's because he went on a date," Hugh announces after exiting the study room, and all the cheer in my compliment deflates. My head whips from Hugh to Chet, who nervously scratches at the beard under his chin.

"It wasn't a date. It was only drinks."

"Isn't that a euphemism for date?" Hugh questions as he stands inside the great room while the other boys work on an intricate *Star Wars* Lego project, including a variety of vehicles and extensive instructions.

"Where'd you learn that word?" Chet asks, keeping his eyes on his nephew.

"Homework," Hugh states.

"What's a uff-ism?" Louie asks, not looking up from his building project.

"It's when you call something common by another name," Dewey interjects.

"Like when people say dick for penis?" Louie asks. My face heats while Chet chastises his nephew by groaning his name.

"Not exactly," Dewey explains. "I believe Hugh used it correctly. Uncle Chet is substituting drinks with a woman for the term date."

"Whatcha drink?" Louie asks, not even looking up from his project.

"Water," Chet remarks, and Hugh scowls at his uncle. I don't care if he drank the entire Little Tennessee River. I want to know more details.

"Well, that sounds wonderful." *That sounds awful. More teeth gritting. More forced smiling.*

"Was your date with that lady who came to visit?" Louie adds, and I'm about to inquire who said woman is when Hunter interjects.

"The one whose face looked like a Barbie doll?" He pulls at the sides of his face, tightening the skin at his eyes and his lips.

"She didn't look plastic," Chet defends, and I want to question the child about surgeries and Botox, but I bite my cheek.

See, I can be nice.

And it's killing me.

"I'm sure she's beautiful," I reply, still chewing the inside of my mouth.

"She is." Chet catches himself on the admission, eyes wide as they leap up to meet mine. He quickly looks away with guilt written on his face, and I'm crestfallen. Nice or not, he's not attracted to me, or at least, not enough. He hasn't asked me out on a date—not for drinks, not even for coffee. We've never shared a meal of any sort besides a feast of our bodies. My skin crawls a little with the thought. I've been very unladylike with this man . . . and he's gone on a date with another woman.

"She's an old friend," he clarifies as if that explains everything. I chew the inside of my cheek even harder. If I had a nickel for every time I heard that statement from Karl, I'd own land in Hawaii.

"How fortunate," I mutter, working hard to suppress how I really feel.

"I needed to go to the office today. We met after work."

"Oh, you work?" I blurt, wishing I could retrieve the words as soon as I've said them. He's never mentioned details of his business beyond his net worth. I don't know what he does on a daily basis, where exactly his office is located, or how often he enters it.

"Yes, I work," he retorts. "That place I make all my millions." The edge to his voice is unsettling.

"I don't care about your millions," I mutter, and his brow lifts, questioning me. I try to remember what Gideon said—*think before you react.* "I simply meant I didn't realize you were still hands-on with your business."

"I'm very hands-on in all manners." His dark eyes narrow. I wonder if he means outside of business, say, with the likes of me, or does he mean he was handsy with *his date*?

"A woman enjoys a man with large hands," I mutter through clenched teeth.

"What does that mean?" Chet asks, his voice rising as do his brows.

Large hands equate to other large body parts, but I certainly cannot mention *that* in front of the boys. "Nothing," I grumble. "I hope you enjoyed your date."

I snap shut the book I haven't finished reading to Malik and abruptly stand. Suddenly, I'm too warm despite the coolness near the large window. I lean down to run a tender hand over Malik's cheek. Then I step over to Louie and Hunter and press a kiss to each of their heads. Hunter hates it, but Louie smiles up at me.

"Scotia." Chet follows me as I hurry to the front hall to retrieve my winter jacket and bag. His hand grips my upper arm, stilling me from the frantic movements of rushing to put on my coat.

"No, really, Chet. I hope you had a nice time." I grin through the gritted teeth smile I've perfected over decades. *Mask in place, Scotia.* It almost hurts to restore the barrier.

He shakes his head. "It was only drinks. What is this?" he questions slowly as if asking why I'm upset, but that can't be what he's asking. To question if I was upset would mean he has feelings for me, concern for my feelings, which he doesn't. "She's only a friend."

"And what am I?" The question tumbles forward before I think. His silence gives me the answer I expected.

I'm nothing to him.

CHAPTER 20

STRANGER VISITS

[Chet]

"Hey, boss, someone's here to see you," Todd calls out to me when I arrive at The Fugitive.

Between my drinks with Henny and then the showdown with Scotia, last night was total shit. I'd had a shit day consulting with my board, who was approached by a potential buyer. I could sell my company tomorrow and make enough money to last me the rest of my life. I could retire and spend the remainder of my time with the boys and this bar and motel. But do I want to sit still at forty-six? I haven't sat still in so long I'd go crazy if I tried, so the thought of turning my company over to someone else does not sound appealing to me. The last thing I can tackle is another shitstorm.

"Who?" I snap, knowing my agitation isn't with Todd.

"Put her in the bus," he clarifies, not answering my question but smirking at me.

"*Her*?" I pause. "You what?" I clip. He has some balls, that one, even if he is my best friend.

"Figured you didn't want the mouse to get away." He winks.

"Mouse?" I question, glaring at him. His smirk turns into a guffaw, and he winks at Striker sitting at the bar.

"I certainly wouldn't let her get away, but then again, she already slipped by me," the biker-regular teases.

"What the hell?" I retort, not understanding these guys and not in the mood for riddles.

"I'd be willing to trap that one," Bones adds beside Striker, and my blood boils even though I don't know who they are referencing.

"I am not in the mood for this," I grumble, and Striker interjects.

"I'm in the mood. Send her to me."

"Shut it," Todd warns. Whoever he's protecting, she's someone important. "She's Big Poppy's."

"Uh . . ." I don't have anyone belonging to me, and that's the way it needs to stay. Women just mess with your mind and your heart, confuse your body and drain your soul. I stalk toward the exit through the pool room, having parked in front of the bar as I typically do.

"You can thank me in the morning," Todd calls after me, and I flip him the bird. *Just what I need, more headache.*

As I near the bus, I see the lights are on, but I can't get a read on who is inside my home. It pisses me off that Todd so casually let someone in, and I press at the front door with a little more force than necessary.

"Alright, just what the—" I freeze when I see Scotia sitting on the loveseat that doubles as an extra-large lounger for me alone. She sits at the edge of the cushion, elbows on her knees. Her head pops up at the rush of my body entering my space. "What are you doing here?"

"I don't know," she whispers. Her eyes question me, as if wanting me to tell her why she's in my home. My shoulders sag, and I hang my head.

Between her aggravation the other night and her reaction over Hennessy, I don't know what to say to her. She's been all salt and vinegar, and I need sweet right now.

"Darlin', it's been kind of a rough few days, and I can't play games with you right now." I exhale heavily after admitting the truth. I'm just tired. My mind has been all over the place after drinks with Henny. I've been trying to figure out what my ex-lover wants from me after all these years, and what the woman before me wants from me now.

What am I? I didn't have an answer. There are so many things I could want Scotia to be to me, but I'm not willing to tell her. I'm *afraid* to tell her what I want.

She doesn't remark on my plea not to play games, but she also doesn't move. She's dressed in jeans and that barn jacket again, which surprises me. It's different from the business suits I've typically seen her wear. She's also wearing knee-high boots and a scarf at her neck. The entire ensemble makes her softer, less intense, and reminds me of a woman under a hotel sheet one morning, looking vulnerable and scared.

"Feel like a beer?"

She wrinkles her nose before she lies. "Sure."

I step around her to the small fridge and remove two bottles. Before cracking them open, I turn back to her. Wondering if she'd be up for something, I ask, "You warm enough in that outfit?"

Her brows crease in question.

"Follow me somewhere?" I continue.

"Sure," she says again, her forehead furrowed. Her quiet one-word answers are unnerving. What is she doing here? What does *she* want from me? Who am I to her? The questions are too much, and my brain needs a break.

I place both beers in one hand and tug the coverlet off my bed, tossing it over my shoulder. Opening a cabinet, I remove a second blanket and lug it over the first. I tilt my head for Scotia to follow me and we exit my home. Once outside, I lead her to the back of the bus.

"I'll help you up," I tell her as I nod toward the metal ladder hanging down from the roof. It doesn't reach the ground. I shove each beer bottle in a back pocket and grip her waist. She lets out a little squeal as I hoist her upward. She reaches out for the rungs, and I hold her until her feet land on the bottom step. "Up you go."

She slowly climbs upward without question, and I follow her. On the top of the bus is a platform, flat and hanging over the rounded roofline just a little bit. The deck isn't terribly wide but is still big enough for two to lie down on. Not that I've ever brought someone up here before to measure it in that manner. I only know it can hold me. I spread one blanket, so we aren't on the cold wooden boards.

173

"Lie down," I softly command as I set the beer bottles on the platform. Scotia drops down to the blanket and lies back. I settle next to her and tug the second blanket primarily over her. I'm not cold despite the November air. We both gaze upward.

"Wow," she whispers. I tuck my arm behind my head and just stare up at the star-splattered sky. The night air is crisp, and the darkness overhead is filled with pinpricks of light. After a few low breaths, I calm from the past forty-eight hours. Scotia is stock-still next to me, and eventually, I roll my head to look at her. She's still gazing up at the nighttime covering.

"Why are you here?"

"I had something to tell you last night and didn't when I learned about your date." She exhales. There's more she isn't saying, and I should ask what is so important she drove nearly an hour to see me, but instead, I interject with clarification.

"It wasn't a date," I defend, and she twists her neck, so she faces me.

"It was drinks, but as Dewey so eloquently explained, it's all just semantics."

I sigh and turn my attention back to the stars, recalling last evening with Hennessy.

"Fine. She was more than a friend once. She was my first love, but it's old news." When Scotia doesn't respond, I continue. "She stopped by the house a few nights ago, just out of the blue, after all these years."

"How many years?" she asks softly. The weight of her gaze presses on the side of my face, but I don't look at her yet.

"Twenty-one. Twenty-one long years and she stood at my front door like it was yesterday." I'm quiet again, recalling how she looked last night. Her makeup a little heavier than I remembered. Her eyes hesitant when I asked her about her husband's death. She admitted again she had children —two boys aged nine and six.

"What happened?" Scotia questions. On the one hand, I want to tell her she probably doesn't want to hear my tale. I'm not certain I want to share it with someone like Scotia, who might judge me for my history, but then I consider what she told me about her husband and how I'm the only one she's ever told.

"When I met Hennessy, she was seventeen, and I was twenty. I was working in a gas station, and I pumped her gas. She didn't want to get her pretty dress dirty, and I wanted a closer look at her shiny red sports car. Our eyes met, drifted apart, and then met again. She smiled at me, and I was a goner, but I knew better. Hennessy Miller was out of my league. I was raised in the system."

"System?" Scotia questions.

"I was a foster kid." Like the boys I now foster, only my life was nothing like theirs. "I didn't have nice things like my boys, though." I don't want to go into detail about trailer parks and small apartments. Fists and insults. People working the system only for a check. There are bad people in the foster industry. Then again, there are also angels, like Maura Hawes.

Scotia doesn't respond, so I continue. "Later that night, Henny returned to the service station and bought a soda. She lingered in the store, and we chatted." I exhale hard, recalling how Henny flirted with me, and how I gave it right back to her. "I was everything her silver-spoon, rebellious spirit needed to piss off her daddy, and she was just everything to me." Everything I longed to have. The woman. The family. The home.

"I wasn't good enough for her," I state, staring up at the sky but no longer seeing the constellations. The dots of light blur together.

"That can't be," Scotia whispers, and I close my eyes.

"She went off to college after we had a summer fling, and I worked my ass off to learn everything about running a gas station. Fast-forward five years, and the owner died, leaving me everything." Frank Sepco didn't have any family. He left me that old service station and a nest of money.

"Kid, I see something in you," he muttered around a burning cigarette and a haze of smoke. "You can ride, but don't you die for anyone else but yourself." He didn't want me mixed up with some of the local motorcycle clubs within the surrounding valleys and manning his service station kept me out of trouble.

"You remind me of myself, but I want you to be bigger than all this." He waved his cigarette around the garage attached to the shop, and I held my breath, hoping the ashes didn't hit a gas spill.

"What an incredible gift," Scotia says, and I finally turn to her.

"I turned that one station into two and then acquired a third. By the time Henny graduated and returned to Knoxville, I had a plan for another. I didn't have much to offer her when she went off to college, but I promised her I'd make something of myself."

"I'll wait for you," she'd promised me in return. Lies. Everything had been a lie.

"You certainly have," Scotia mutters, and my stomach sours. Is she another woman only interested in status and finances? She was certainly curious about me when she knew me as only Chester Chesterfield. But she knows more about me now than most women ever have. We've discussed my net worth, but the other night, she told me she wasn't interested in my money. The *way* she said she wasn't interested led me to believe she was telling the truth. Could she want something else from me? Something more meaningful?

"It wasn't enough." I pause, taking a second to collect my thoughts before speaking again. "I'd never had a home, so I built her a house. I wanted to marry her. Instead, she got engaged to someone else and married him."

"Jeffrey Heiner asked me to marry him." I remember staring at Henny in disbelief.

"But I want to marry you. I've built you a home." We were sitting in the driveway of the house. Me in the driver's seat. Her in the passenger side. She didn't even ask to see inside the mountainside mansion I'd constructed over the previous year for her.

"I never asked for this," she replied.

"You said you'd wait for me," I reminded her.

She didn't answer me.

"What are you doing with me, then?" I'd snapped at her, wondering *why she was even sitting in my car if she didn't want the house or my heart. She shrugged and then gave me a sheepish grin.*

She wanted a part of me, which was all too willing to please her.

"How could she do that to you?" Scotia sighs, interrupting my memory with displeasure in her tone.

I turn back to her. "She wanted his money, his name, and his status." The bitterly spoken words hit the mark, and Scotia flinches. She shifts to peer back at the sky, and I take in her profile. Her midnight hair nearly blends with the night sky, but that white stripe is like a beacon shining out at me. Her eyes glow despite the darkness around us. She chews at her lip.

"I guess you have a habit of attracting shallow women."

Do I? Is it that I attract those wanting something from me? Or am I attracted to them for some sick reason? Am I the one trying to prove I'm good enough for them?

I definitely have my concerns that Scotia would eventually walk away from me. I'm keeping her at arm's length because of those doubts. She'll grow bored of various parts of my life, realizing I'm not three slivers but one man. A man trying to do right by three boys and build them a future.

I blame Henny for the triggers inside me—the doubt and the fear that I'll never be enough for someone.

"So how did your date go?" Scotia's voice turns edgy, and I don't bother to correct her for the hundredth time.

I nervously sat at the bar, downing a whiskey before Henny arrived at the Knoxville pub where we agreed to meet. She entered, and I expected my heart to beat right out of my chest. I was so anxious. Why now? *This question riddled me over and over again. Why was Henny knocking on my door now? Was it the death of her husband? Was it her two fatherless children? Was it her move to a cabin in the woods?*

Nothing made sense to me.

"It's so strange that you found me again, Hen. After all this time."

"Is it strange? We were always meant to be," she stated, and that's when I needed another whiskey. She was playing with me, just as she'd done all those years ago.

"If we were meant to be, we would have been," I stated, not wanting to hurt her but protecting myself.

"We can be again," she said, her voice lowering as her lids dipped. Once upon a time, a simple smile from her would have brought me to my knees. I would have done her bidding and her pleasuring. Now, I wasn't so eager to kneel.

"Life is more complicated now," I told her, and she snorted.

"You have no idea," she muttered under her breath, then rapidly finished the drink before her.

What I did know was the pattering in my heart was not an attraction to her. Her forehead was too smooth, and her lips were too big. She *did* look plastic like Hunter said. Then there was the hesitation in her voice when she told me about her husband's death. She hardly mentioned her children, only stating her oldest was a handful.

With Henny's list of woes, I'd wondered if she needed money. She seemed aware of my continued success, but I wasn't offering a handout. I told her I could give her a job, asking if she possessed any skills. With narrowed eyes, she told me she'd never worked a day in her life, relying on her husband for everything. He ran her father's company.

"She propositioned me." I finally answer Scotia's question, finding the admission strangely similar to how I met Scotia. Was Scotia another woman to prove myself to? Was I worthy of her?

"Bless her heart," Scotia mutters beside me, and I continue to stare at her as she closes her eyes and swallows.

Is she jealous again?

"I turned her down."

"You did?" Scotia's voice squeaks as she returns her focus to me. Her quiet question echoes softly around us. Those gray eyes of hers sparkle with their own set of pinpricks, softening at my confession.

Henny laid a hand on my forearm, giving me a look that would have worked in another lifetime, but did nothing for me now. When her blue eyes met mine, I realized they weren't the right color. I wanted silver eyes gazing up at me—like the ones sparkling in the dark beside me now. Henny's blonde hair was a little too golden, and I found myself thinking again the coloring was wrong. I preferred midnight ink with a streak of white. That undefined stripe was like an undefined part of the woman looking at me.

"I've kind of had someone else on my mind lately," I admit.

"You have?" She rolls to her side, angling toward me. Her lips slowly curl into a smile while her eyes sparkle. I shift my head from the arm it was on and reach out for her.

"I'm not interested in Henny . . . or Savannah," I clarify. We still haven't discussed what happened the other night—why she pushed me away when Savannah caught us kissing.

"You were embarrassed to be kissing me," Scotia whispers.

"Not embarrassed. Just shocked by the interruption." We'd been in our own little bubble as Scotia opened up about her late-husband, and Savannah's disruption brought me back to where we were—in Maura's office kissing.

"You said I was no one to you."

"I never said that, darlin'. Don't put words in my mouth." And for that fact, let's not talk anymore. "Come here."

Scotia scoots closer to me. I tuck my arm under her, pulling her into my shoulder and pressing a kiss to her forehead, lingering a moment in the quiet of the cold night. Being here like this, under the stars, breathing in the scent of this woman beside me, calms me a bit. I hadn't realized how unnerved I'd been with Henny's return or how unsettled I was that Scotia thought drinks was something other than *just* drinks.

Somehow telling her about my past with Henny and what happened last night has me rethinking Scotia rushing off. *Might she stick?* I'm afraid to admit how much I like her snuggled into me. If it weren't so cold, I'd be angling to have my hands on her skin. Touching her brings me comfort, like connecting skin-to-skin assures me she's real, she wants me, and she isn't going anywhere. She's anchoring me when I hadn't realized how adrift I've been.

I don't know what it would take to keep a woman like Scotia in my life. I'd already tried to give everything to someone else who rejected all I offered. If Scotia doesn't need my money, and she doesn't want my status, why would she be with a guy like me?

CHAPTER 21

MOONLIGHT BUS TRIPS

[Scotia]

I've kind of had someone else on my mind lately.

Could he mean it? Has he been thinking of me as much as I've been thinking of him?

In the dark of night and the quiet that surrounds us, the world around me just feels so big. The air is cold, but snuggled into Chet, I'm warm. Touching him calms me, like he doesn't want to let me go and he won't give up on me without a fight. He hasn't lost faith in me and being with him makes me want to be better, *do* better. I've been lonelier than I'd like to admit, and I've been admitting some hard truths to myself lately. I'm achingly empty inside and longing for my heart to be filled.

I shiver.

With Karl gone and Darlene off saving the world, plus my sisters all falling in love, I've never felt more alone. It's one reason I took the volunteer work at Harper House. I wanted to feel connected to others, even if they were children.

Slowly, I connect the dots of Chet's story. If Harper House is really

Chet's home, and he built a house for the woman of his dreams, that means . . . the house was intended to be theirs—his and the woman he went on a date with.

Oh, Chet. From what he's told me, he worked hard to better his circumstances, be a self-made man, and earn what he has, and that woman squandered his devotion for someone else.

I can't imagine it.

Then I realize I can.

At seventeen, I might have done the same thing. I married Karl and was pregnant within a year. With his last name came money and status, family and security. Then again, if a man had loved me with the passion Chet displayed to his former lover, my decisions might have been different.

Money or love? The answer should seem simple, but not when you've come from nothing.

Chet suddenly shifts, and I assume cuddle time is over. We've each been quietly in our own thoughts for a while.

"Everything alright?" I ask.

He sits upward next to me and reaches forward for the beers. He cracks one and offers it to me. I sit up as well, keeping the blanket over my legs. It isn't cold so much as crisp with a definite chill in the air. I'm warm enough in most places, minus my cheeks and hands.

Chet opens the second beer and taps the neck of it against my bottle. He chuckles to himself, as if a funny thought occurred to him, and then lifts the brew to his lips. I watch as he swallows, taking a long pull. I take a small, quick drink of mine. I'm not necessarily a fan of the stuff, but this one has a fruiter taste to it, like a hard cider, not a bitter beer.

"Tell me three things," he states, and I'm reminded of our first encounter.

"I understand what you mean about a poor upbringing."

"Darlin'," he groans, turning his gaze to me. He sits with one leg stretched forward and one bent. One arm leans to support him while the other rests on his raised knee, hand holding his beer. "Don't mock me."

"I'm not. My upbringing was with very strict parents. The church, according to Willard and Winifred Winters."

His brows lift as if I'm kidding him.

"I grew up in Cedar Gap. People just assume I'm from Green Valley. I was bussed into the valley for high school."

"Cedar Gap?" The question in his voice asks everything. It's a small community no longer on a map.

"My parents wanted a place where they could practice the righteousness of their beliefs. Where else to begin the work of God than in a mountain-top armpit?" I'm not mocking my parents' work. "For my entire upbringing, I believed in their idea of God and my place in His plan."

You are special, my father would say to me, and I truly believed him. Extraordinary in more ways than all others because of my hair. When kids taunted me that I wore the mark of the devil, my father assured me I'd been touched by an angel.

The weight of Chet's gaze presses against my cheek as though I'm some religious nut. In the name of faith in a higher being, I should turn the other cheek to his glare. Instead, I face him.

"When you're raised with a sense of entitlement, like you truly are better than others, you tend to believe it, and I did. I drank the proverbial Kool-Aid." My parents were not whacks. It wasn't a cult. They just had a strong belief system which included themselves at the center and their purpose as the right course in life—the hand of God in their interpretation.

"Their opinions of others included a sense of being better than average."

"So . . . hypocritical," Chet interjects

"Hypocritical?" I question. I don't care for the censure in his tone.

"Imitating some god doesn't include casting out others. Putting others down. It draws a line between right and wrong." I ponder his comment, knowing in my heart he isn't wrong. Anyone who believes that a supreme being made all things equal should treat all things as equals. I have never lived by that rule, and I swallow the confession.

Instead, I defend myself. "There *is* a right and wrong."

"Then it's wrong of you to think you're better than others," he states like he's laying down a new commandment. *Thou shall not believe in one's self.*

Suddenly, I'm not certain how telling him about my upbringing has turned into a sermon on my behavior. I stay quiet and glance up at the stars again.

If there's a heaven, God must exist, right?

And that God will judge who enters.

Will you enter, Scotia? Have you always done right by others? It sounds like something my daddy would have asked. The dichotomy is real —being raised that you're one of the chosen ones, and then being damned for acting like one. I might have misinterpreted Daddy's lessons.

"I've sidetracked us," Chet mutters. "Tell me more."

This certainly isn't the romantic three things perhaps he thought I'd mention. I shrug, not certain I should continue, but I do. "We didn't have much, but we believed we had more than most. As I grew older, I saw it wasn't true. I noticed more of what was out there . . ." I wave a hand to the invisible *there*. "And I wanted it. I didn't want to be the poor girl bussed into the valley but the queen of the mountain." My voice rises in false triumph and then dies back.

"I met Karl while he was in college. It's a simple tale . . . we fell in love. Well, our kind of love. We got married so I could follow him to medical school. Then I learned the truth."

The painful moment of walking in on my husband kissing another man during what was supposed to be a study session will forever be burned into my brain. Was the hurt that he was kissing someone of his same sex? After years of coming to terms with Karl's sexual orientation, I'd realized it was the betrayal of my heart. Karl had embodied everything I'd ever dreamed of having—the man, the money, the home, the future—but I would never have his heart.

"Why did you stay with him?"

"He begged, and I wanted to be needed. Leaving him would ruin him, and I didn't have any other options. I wasn't college-educated. I'd taken classes but didn't have a formal degree." I crane my neck to give him a frustrated glance. "Karl really was one of my best friends, one of my only true friends, so we just worked it out."

I sigh because working it out hadn't turned out how I'd hoped. There'd been moments of great difficulty—pretending all was well while I was shattering inside—and the best way to mask my own unhappiness was to tear down the happiness of others. If she was prettier than me, I found fault. If she had more wealth, I found error. At every turn, I tried to make others feel beneath me because I felt so low myself. And by rejecting others first, I didn't risk being hurt by their rejection.

"I could make a million excuses for myself," I begin. "Everyone wants to be needed. Everyone wants to be loved. Even those professing they don't need love. And everyone wants to feel important to someone else. My best defense is I had ambition and whether you agree with my end goals or not, nothing is wrong with being determined. You've lived the same life."

Chet's quiet for a moment.

"We've done the same thing, Chet Chester Chesterfield Big Poppy. Maybe for different external purposes, but there's no difference in the internal drive between us."

"There's every bit of difference, darlin'. I did it for love. You did it for some misconception of status."

"Didn't you have the same misconception? If you had money, if you had status, if you were worldly, you'd get the girl?" Punching him in the stomach with the reality of his actions and thoughts does not make me feel good. "I did it for love. A different kind of love."

While unrequited in a romantic sense, I stuck to my marriage out of loyalty and commitment. I stand by the fact that as difficult as it was to play house, and pretend I was a happy wife with a good life, I did it for friendship . . . and our daughter.

I could never admit to our child who her father was. He was a god in her eyes. She knew nothing of his affairs until his death, and even then, she did not know it was with a man. Her father was simply killed coming out of a random hotel littered with condoms, proof of sexual exploits with someone other than his wife.

Chet finishes the rest of his beer while I simply hold mine in my hand.

"Why all the names?" I ask. It's something I've been curious about.

"I'm Chester Popielarski Chesterfield. My middle name was my mother's maiden name. Davis found out and started calling me Big Poppy. When I bought The Fugitive, the nickname felt strangely appropriate and separated me from my other businesses. Only special people call me Chet."

I look at him as he explains his various layers. "You let me call you Chet."

"You're one of the special ones." My insides flip-flop at his response. After a long pause, he asks, "What did you mean when you said you wanted someone to belong to you?"

I swallow around revealing another hard truth. Unable to face him, I squint off in the distance as I answer. "I never had Karl. He was my friend and partner, but he didn't belong to me. He didn't want me like I want to be wanted. I had half of him, but I want a whole man, a whole heart."

Chet's gaze is on me, but I can't bring myself to look at him. Even in the dark, I feel like he can see every inch of me inside and out. I told him near Halloween I wanted a second chance at making a first impression on him. I have no idea if he's impressed or continues to be appalled by me.

"Going to drink that?" I glance down at the beer in my hand and shake my head. He takes the bottle from me and sets it on the corner of the platform along with his empty one. His seated position shifts so he's leaning toward me, and he grabs the white strip in my hair, twirling the strands around his finger. He spirals his finger down to the edge and starts again. The show of affection is strange, yet I find the touch soothing.

After doing it a second time, he tucks his fingers into my scarf, working his hand to cup my neck. His touch is soft for a big man. I've never felt the way I feel when his hands are on me. Not even in those early days with Karl when I thought I loved him did it feel like this. Probably because our relationship had always been a façade.

"Every time I think I have you figured out? I don't," Chet says. For some reason, I smile at how mysterious that makes me sound.

"I'm really an open book," I state.

"You are many things, Scotia Simmons, and not one of them is what I first thought."

"Oh yeah? And what did you think when you met me? Tell me three things," I tease. *Am I flirting?* Is this how it's supposed to happen?

"I thought, 'She's drunk.'."

My mouth falls open, and then I burst out laughing, shaking my head. "I was, wasn't I?"

"But I also thought, 'She's so beautiful . . . and sad.' There was something about the way you looked at me, like you really wanted me. 'You. Me. A bed.'. Never been propositioned quite like that before."

"Worst come-on ever," I mock of myself.

"I liked your directness, but a vulnerability existed underneath your proposition. Of course, by the time we got to your room, I learned that look in your eye was the need to vomit."

"Oh, God." I lower my head. "Not one of my finer moments."

"You asked me to stay. That would be my third thing."

"I did?" My head pops up, and I search for his eyes, which are hard to distinguish against the dark night. *Is he teasing me?* I don't recall asking this of him.

"You gave me the saddest look I'd ever seen," he whispers in the quiet.

"So you stayed because you felt sorry for me." I'm disgusted with myself, and my tone expresses it.

"You were real, Scotia, and I couldn't walk out." His deep voice softens.

"You held me that night," I remind him, recalling how I woke with his arm over me.

"I could say a hundred things like I didn't want you to choke on your own vomit or die in your sleep, but the truth is, I held you, because you seemed like you needed to be held. You needed a hug."

Butter on biscuits, that was sweet.

"I need to return the favor sometime," I admit as I've found myself in too many compromising positions with this man. After what he's told me about his past, I ask, "Who holds you when you need it?"

He doesn't move. His hand stills on the side of my neck. I'm not certain he's breathing, and the truth hits me. *No one.* He's done everything on his own over the years to either prove something or take responsibility. Building the house. Taking on the boys. Opening his home to others. He's done none of it for him, and that's the difference between us.

He needs a hug as well.

"Let me be the one to hold you, Chet." The plea in my voice sounds almost as pathetic as that of the woman who suggested he stay with her. There's so much honesty in my asking. I want to be needed by him. I want him to belong to me, but I want to belong to him.

I scoot forward and slip my arms around his neck, cradling him to me. One set of fingers comb through his hair while my other hand slides down to his broad shoulder blade, tucking him against me as best I can. I press a kiss to his thick hair and breathe him in.

Is it too late to want love like this in life? I certainly hope not.

Warm lips touch my throat after a minute. Soft suction and the wet tip of his tongue brush along my neck. He loosens my scarf, and I tip my head back to allow him better access to my skin. My arms still circle him as best they can, but he's reclaiming control. His mouth opens, and he nibbles at my jaw. He bites my chin, and I gasp. The drop of my jaw offers him an invitation, and his lips cover mine. His tongue thrusts forward. The kiss is equal parts hesitation and hunger.

Our bodies shift, pressing closer as our mouths speak of missed desires and ancient hurts. The moment feels so sad that my closed eyes prickle with tears, but I can't bring myself to stop kissing him. It seems wrong to give him my kisses in the depths of our unrequited memories, but I don't know what else to offer him.

Then the kiss alters. It's no longer an attempt to put a bandage on the past but an acceptance of the present. This is not one-sided. This is equal, eager, and desperate. He wants me as much as I want him.

His hands slowly roam, outlining my body but not straying outside some invisible line. He doesn't cross to the achy swell of my breasts or dip to the thumping pulse between my thighs. He coasts his thick palm over my hip and around my waist, along my back and into my hair. He holds me close as though I'm precious while his mouth never leaves mine.

With the same exploration, my fingers comb through his hair and curl around his nape. One hand slides to his chest and feels his heart racing even through layers of clothing. His mouth against mine speaks a thousand words, none of which I can interpret other than this is real. He wants me for now. We aren't going any farther than where we are—making out under the stars—and fully dressed, I'd never felt more naked and raw in my entire life.

* * *

188

I don't know how long we've kissed, but eventually, I shiver, and it isn't from the passion of kissing this incredible kisser. It's getting cold.

"Let's head inside," Chet offers as his lips slowly pull back from mine. I nod, accepting his invitation. I hadn't really intended to stay the night, although I'm grateful for the hint I might. I don't know why I felt the need to see him, which is a lie I tell myself. I could have called him. Driving nearly an hour down a treacherous road in the dark was not one of my smartest decisions, but I just wanted to be near him.

Chet tosses the blankets over his shoulder and climbs down the ladder, guiding me to follow him. Once I near the end of the ladder, he grips my hips and lowers me. He takes my hand and leads me inside the much warmer bus. The hum of electricity surrounds us, but Chet turns off most of the lights once we enter, leaving on only the soft-glowing lamp over his stove. We stare at one another a second, and my shivers return. I'm still cold in my clothing cooled by the night air, but his gaze on me causes my skin to heat.

"Take off your clothes, darlin'."

I stare at him, dumbfounded by the directness, and don't move.

"We aren't talking anymore tonight," he adds. In many ways, I'm relieved. I'm talked out. I don't want to keep offering confessions of my past. I've let so much of it go, and it needs to stay where it belongs —behind me.

"You can strip, or I'll strip you. What's your choice?" That gleam in his eyes turns devilish but not devious.

My hands shake as I reach for the buttons on my coat and slowly unbutton them. He does the same with his leather jacket.

As I bend to unzip my boots, he mirrors my position to remove his own. Tugging them off, he exposes a sock with his big toe through the end. I'd laugh at the hole if I wasn't so turned on by our matching striptease act and the building anticipation of being naked with him.

Next removed is my sweater. His thick fingers unbutton a few of the buttons on his flannel before he tugs it over his head by the back of the collar, revealing his broad chest and the mass of curls across it. My fingers twitch to run through that coarse hair. He eyes me, a brow arching, hinting at continuing our clothing-for-clothing disrobing.

189

Tit for tat.

Tits come next as I unclasp my bra, revealing my breasts, and his lips crook up in the corner. We stand facing each other, bare chest to bare chest, but we aren't finished. I pop the button on my jeans and work them down my legs. Our eyes lock as he does the same with his pants. I need to sit in order to get the skinny fit over my ankles, so I collapse on the bench seat at his dining table. I watch him as he takes off his socks, and I do the same with mine.

A girlish giggle tickles my throat. I've never been so wound up watching a man take it all off.

"Best striptease ever," he mutters as if reading my thoughts. Only one article of clothing remains on each of us. My skin pebbles, but his nearly naked body has me hot and bothered.

"One more piece, darlin'. Then sit on the edge of my bed."

I've been naked before this man before, but this night feels different. I slip my fingers into the sides of my fancy lace panties.

"I love how you love pretty things." He exhales before biting his lip as he watches my thong descend my legs. Once the thin fabric reaches my knees, I wiggle my legs to drop the lace further. I step out of the thin material and stand facing him as naked as one can be. My heart feels just as exposed. He's going to ruin me.

"Bed," he growls, leaving his boxer briefs on. I take the short steps backward until my thighs hit the top of his bed. The raised mattress is almost level with my backside, so I need to hike myself upward. Chet stalks toward me—a man on a mission. He clasps my knees, drops to his, and lowers his face between my thighs. Without preamble, he's devouring me, tongue wild.

The sounds. The wetness. I grip the edge of the mattress as my body vibrates. I move to fall backward, but one strong hand catches me at the small of my back.

"Stay like this," he demands. He hardly breaks his attention from his actions. The hand on my lower back remains in place, keeping me in a seated position, while his other hand joins his tongue. One finger forages forward, dipping into me before pulling out and a second joins the first. My knees spread wider, and if I thought I was exposed on the rooftop or standing bare before him, it's nothing compared to what he's doing to me right now.

And I'm loving every second of it.

Quickly, my body responds. My legs quiver. My feet dance beyond my control. I'm outside myself as both hands clutch at his hair, holding his head between my thighs. My mouth falls open as I come undone against his tongue. He's relentless until I beg him to stop. I need a breather, but he doesn't halt. He continues his feast, adding a second finger and nipping at me in a new way. The second release crashes into the first, and I cry out his name, unfamiliar with my own voice.

He abruptly pulls away from me and rubs his moistened lips against my inner thigh. Standing, he startles me, which is absurd, but I fall back on the bed.

His boxers slip down his hips, and he's at my entrance.

"I have an IUD now," I blurt, not knowing why I'm announcing it quite the way I am or why I'm so loud.

"Thank fuck," he states. "You need to feel this. For once, you need it real and raw. You need to feel all of me inside you." Without further ado, he slips into me, fast and hard. My feet kick at the walls on the edge of his bed. My fingers fist into the sheets under me. I feel *all* of him. The length. The depth. The fullness. I feel him down to my toes and at the ends of my hair. He's filling my soul and my heart beats in a way that matches the rhythmic thrusts of him.

I've. Never. Felt. Anything. This. Incredible.

I don't allow my thoughts to dip into my memories. The most important moment is now. Him. Me. Nothing will ever compare to this sensation. He moves, and the friction, the tension, the rush of skin against skin . . . I'm outside myself again.

He takes his time to work me. In and out. Back and forth. I'm upside down and turned around. He lifts my leg to rest my ankle at his shoulder and he nips at me there. I'm so grateful for yoga, but this isn't what I'd ever had in mind with my classes. I'm open to him in a new way. He grunts and growls, words incomprehensible as his hand coasts down my shin.

My hips move. My pelvis thrusts. I place my free foot on the edge of the mattress for leverage and I let myself loose. I meet this man surge for surge. With his hands gripping my hips, squeezing hard, I'm certain there will be marks, and I want to wear them. I want the evidence he lost control over me like I continually lose control over him. He lifts me by said hips. My backside clearly off the bed, and then he stills within my depths. Every jolt, every pulse, every everything happens within me, and my heart hammers in my chest.

I'll never be the same after this.

Him. Me. And this moment.

CHAPTER 22

COFFEE RUN

[Chet]

In the morning, a part of me has risen with the sunshine and cannot be denied. With Scotia's backside pressing against my front, I want to hike her leg over my thigh, opening her up to my exploration. But I have a question first.

I perch up on an elbow and kiss her shoulder. "Explain the IUD to me," I say, wondering when that happened.

"Well, after what happened at Winston Auto . . ." Her voice drifts, not needing to clarify further. "I went to the doctor. I just couldn't bear that happening again and so publicly. The doctor recommended an IUD to help . . . you know . . . and I just thought you should know." She rolls to bury her face in the pillow and mumbles something else.

My hand gently pulls at her shoulder, guiding her back to a position where I can hear her.

"So what exactly does this mean?" Last night, she didn't stop me from doing what we did. For once, she didn't ask for a condom, either.

"It means, although it's typically a form of protection, which it still is, in my case, it's also there for another purpose."

The only word I needed to hear is protection. "You okay, darlin'? Should we have done what we did last night or waited?" I pause a second, pondering. "And when did you have this done?"

"At the beginning of the week."

"That why you didn't come to Harper House?"

"It was. I just wanted a day to rest after the procedure, but I'm okay. We can do . . . things." Her eyes close, clearly embarrassed by the openness of this conversation. My hand strokes up and down her arm.

"You should have told me. I could have taken you to the appointment or something."

Her face pinkens. "That wasn't necessary, but you're sweet."

I lean forward, kissing her mouth as best I can in this position. Quickly, we gain momentum, and I'm fully ready to enter her. Rolling her back to her side, I skim my hand over her belly to tug our bodies flush and lower my fingers between her legs, finding her willing and ready for me. I hitch her leg over my thigh and wedge myself between her spread ones.

"Like this?" She gulps.

"Just like this, darlin'." We remain on our sides—her back to my front —as I slide into her. Her breath hitches, so I keep it slow as the angle is different. She guides me into her body, fitting over me so well. I cup her shoulder and press her forward a bit, bending her a little while my other hand still works her pleasure point. My dick glides in and out of her.

"Chet," she whispers, her voice catching on my name.

"Get there, darlin'. It's gonna be quick for me." I want to take my time with her, but my body is too revved up. With this new freedom to be bare, I'm coming out of my skin inside her. I want to chase this woman into morning ecstasy.

"I don't know . . ." Her voice drifts, but she's responding to me. Her leg slips off my thigh, tightening her hold on me, and I'm ready to blow. I hiss as her thighs clench. Her ass presses back, meeting me thrust for thrust. My fingers play her like a fiddle, working the strings in a racing tempo, urging her to get where I'm going.

I can't hold out. I still, firing off into her. She just feels so good. Then she lets loose, and her release prolongs everything. Silvery stars flash before me as she milks me dry.

"Sweet Jesus," I curse, leaning back a bit when she finishes. I'm still attached to her, and my hand rests on her hip. "Are you okay?"

I hate to ask. I don't want to wonder if she enjoyed it like I did. She pulls free of me and twists to look at me over her shoulder.

"I'm good." Not the rave review a man wants to hear, so I lift my head to face her better.

"Good morning, darlin'."

A smile crosses her lips. "Mornin', Chet." She leans toward me, and we kiss again for a long minute. This is the way to start a day.

Once we slowly rise and dress, a funny feeling fills my belly. I can't define it exactly, but it feels like dressing rewinds who we were in that bed.

Suddenly, I'm awkward. "I don't have coffee here. Usually take it in the bar." I nervously scratch under my chin.

"Are you open this early?" she asks, her expression showing her disapproval. My heart skips a beat. I don't like the fact she might be judging me . . . or maybe I'm jumping to conclusions.

"Actually, no. But Todd and I hang out in there handling business. I work remotely on most days and take care of things from the empty space during the morning hours."

She nods as though she understands. We stand in my kitchen area, as much as you can consider this section of my bus a kitchen, with its booth seats and galley strip of mini-sized appliances.

"You said you had something to tell me last night. Was that it?" I nod toward the bed, meaning this new freedom to be bare. I'm not complaining about this information after last night and this morning, but it doesn't seem like news worth driving almost an hour to tell me.

"No." She blushes a bit. "It's going to sound silly now, but the other day when I went to have my nails done, I saw a woman in the salon with a little boy who looked just like Malik. They looked eerily similar to each other," she adds for emphasis while I try to dismiss the fact she said, *had her nails done.*

How am I standing before another woman who can't paint her own damn nails?

195

"Did you ask her about him?" I question as a pressure builds on my sternum. We still haven't been any closer to getting Malik to open up or to find someone searching for him as a missing person.

"I didn't. I was too stunned by the boy. I even thought it was Malik at first and called him such." She finishes flipping her hair and tugs at her sweater. Her movements are fidgety.

"What happened?"

"He stared at me with eyes like Malik's. I can't shake the look he was giving me as if maybe . . . I don't know . . . he knew Malik, once I mentioned him."

Propped casually against the countertop with my hands cupping the edge and my ankles crossed, my gaze doesn't stray from her. I'm hyper focused. "Do you think that's true?"

"I don't know." Her voice drops as her eyes shift. This woman certainly has a soft spot for that kid.

"Did the woman speak to you? Did she call the boy by a name?"

"She didn't." Scotia tilts her head. "She was very careful *not* to call him by name. She reminded the boy he shouldn't speak to strangers. She also said they were new to the area, renting a cabin in the woods."

This has my full attention, and I don't like the thoughts running through my head.

"Do you remember anything about the woman? What she looked like?" I'm afraid to ask.

"Her hair color was all wrong for her, and I doubt Tabatha did the dye job. She has a much better eye and would never have colored that woman's hair in such a brassy blonde. The shade didn't compliment her skin tone, especially as her face looked like it had some work done. Her skin was pulled too tight on her forehead. And those lips. Botox."

I chuckle without humor because, for once, it might be beneficial Scotia is so observant of someone's flaws. *Good to see our chat about right and wrong, and judging others hasn't changed her.* But I can't ignore Scotia's descriptions. I don't want to believe I might know who she describes. The coincidence would be uncanny.

"Blonde, you said?" I feel uneasy thinking what I'm thinking.

"Brassy blonde," Scotia clarifies.

"Ah." I nod once, my head filling.

After her explanation, we walk to the bar, and I offer her a coffee in a to-go cup. I worry the sendoff hints at a brush off, but she tells me her day is full anyway.

"So, I guess I'll see you . . ." Her voice drifts as I stand beside her SUV, facing her. Her thumb plays with the lid on her coffee. This is the part where I'm not good. I'm a successful businessman. I run a home for boys. I have excellent friends, but I'm shit at women. Especially as I don't have them spend the night in my bus, so I'm out of my league here. Without thought, I reach for the white strip in Scotia's hair and twirl the strands around my finger, rippling down to the ends. She slowly grins at me, and I think she likes the new habit I'm forming.

I should ask her out on a date, but the thing is, I don't date. I'm more a *hang out* guy. Hang out at the bar. Hang out in my bus. Hang out with the boys. I don't do fancy dinners and movie nights. Chester Chesterfield hates putting on airs and pretending to be polished, which is one reason he does it so rarely. Big Poppy and Chet? We despise that kind of formality.

"Yeah, I guess I'll see you . . . soon," I respond, sounding noncommittal and lame even to me. Yet I don't move from leaning against the driver door, preventing her from entering her SUV, and I start the hair-twirling thing once again.

"I'm hosting a pickle party on Sunday at Genie's Country Western Bar in Green Valley. Are you familiar with the place?" She told me National Pickle Day is November fourteenth. I still want to know about her husband's phallic phobia and how it equates to her profession, but I don't ask this morning. "Maybe you and the boys would like to stop by. If you come earlier in the evening, the crowd will be more families."

My eyes follow the trail of my finger spiraled in her hair.

"Okay, darlin'," I say, and the smile on her face explodes into a brightness the likes of which I haven't seen in a long time on a woman.

"Okay." She places a hand on my chest and pats it twice. With her hand over my racing heart, I realize I'm in deep with this woman.

"Kiss me, Scotia."

She glances around, noting the broad daylight. There's only a bike or two in the lot. It's early. And this is my territory. I'm not hiding out on my own property.

When she looks up at me, I cup her jaw and bring my mouth to hers, marking her for anyone to see.

I'm not fucking keeping her a secret.

* * *

No longer touching her skin or playing with her hair, I'm suddenly rethinking things. As I watch Scotia drive away after turning that kiss into a mini-make-out scene against the side of her car, I realize deep with Scotia might be *too* deep. I've opened up to her more than I have any other person in years, and I don't know why she brings stuff out in me.

I stare into the empty opening of The Tail after her car disappeared and questioned again what the hell I am doing with this woman because she's going to leave me. At some point, she's going to wise up and be gone for good.

By the time I re-enter the bar, Todd is present, and I've grown grumpy. A knowing expression fills his face. He looks so much like his brother, Nathan, but Todd's face is edgier while Nathan's is more playfully mischievous. Todd worked hard to keep his brother out of trouble and felt he failed his younger sibling all those years ago. Of course, the world has been restored to rights as Nathan has returned, found the love of his life, and lives on the straight and narrow now.

"I should fire your ass for that move last night," I bark at him, still a little befuddled by how Scotia left this morning.

"She didn't rock your world last night?" Todd teases, arching a brow, and heat rushes my cheeks.

"I didn't say that," I mutter.

"But there's trouble in pickle paradise?" he jokes, topping off my coffee as I take a seat at my normal table in the empty bar. I like the quiet of the place. I've never been good at sitting in an office, underneath fluorescent lights and the watchful eye of others. I guess you can take the man out of the service station, but you can't take the service station out of the man. I need to be outside the norm. Thus, the tiny house bus and the oversized home on the hill filled with kids, none of whom are my own.

"I don't know what I'm doing with that woman," I say, voicing my sudden doubts.

"What do you mean?" he questions.

"I don't know if it's smart to be with someone like her." The words are the opposite of how I feel, though, and a sudden sourness fills my stomach after I speak. I lift my steamy mug to my lips and burn my tongue on the hot liquid. *How's that for karma?*

"What's wrong with her?" He chuckles, wiggling his brows like a teen. Honestly, I can't think of much other than her being a little opinionated. I like her hair. I like her smile when she aims it at me. I like how she looks at me, like she wants something from me, and it isn't marked by dollar bills. I take too long to offer Todd an explanation, so he asks another question.

"Is this because of Henny?" Todd remains standing next to the table with the coffee pot in his hand. He can act like a busy body, sticking his nose into my business. Then again, I'm the one who told him my first love has returned. I figured if any man understood the confusion of the situation, it would be him. Todd lowers into a chair, settling in for this conversation.

"I'm not attracted to Henny. It's more the idea of her. What she represented."

"What did she represent? Besides crazy sex in your twenties that we can't quite replicate as we near fifty." He laughs at his own assessment.

"Speak for yourself," I mock, and his brow arches again with another knowing glance about my night with Scotia. I won't be sharing details, but he doesn't doubt that I've had sex with the illustrious Scotia. *Good sex.* "Anyway, Henny stands for that drive and determination I had to prove I could be something greater than my beginnings."

"And you have done great things. Your businesses. Your boys."

I nod to agree, but I still feel like I'm missing something.

"You know you don't need to prove anything to anyone else. Didn't then. Don't now. It's your life, man. As long as you're living it to your fullest, by your definition, what does anything else matter?"

"I am living my life to the fullest," I defend, but the words lie flat. Something is still absent, and I hate to admit the one thing I don't have.

Love. A partner. An equal. The idea I could offer something—myself actually—to someone else and I know I'd be good to her.

I want someone to belong to me.

"If I could add one bit of advice." *Here we go.* "If a woman came for me down that road in the dark of night . . ." Todd points off toward The Tail outside the bar. "And she looked as fine as Scotia, plus she made me smile—"

"What the—"

"Et." He holds up a finger. "Let me finish . . . because you're still smiling like a fool this morning despite a grumpy disposition. I don't think I'd be considering it a *bad* idea to keep her. In fact, I'd think it pretty fucking special that a woman wants me bad enough to risk things for me."

My head slowly lowers, feeling all kinds of guilty. The Tail is unforgiving, and it takes some courage to drive it, especially at night. Scotia did come here when she could have simply called me. Wasn't she hell-bent on jealousy, though? She thought I'd gone on a date with Henny when it was only drinks. On second thought, it's kind of nice she might be jealous. It means she wants me.

"She spent the night in your crappy bus," Todd adds, interrupting my thought process.

"My bus is not crappy," I defend, lifting my head back up.

Todd chuckles. "Okay, you're right, it's awesome, but she must see past things I know you're harboring as a barrier to letting her all the way in. Are you really gonna finish things before they start? Don't blow her off because of some unfair comparison."

"I'm not comparing her to anyone," I snap.

"Aren't you?" Todd questions. "Haven't you measured every woman against one?"

Todd holds up a finger. "She's a socialite."

He raises a second digit. "She's rough around the edges."

Another finger. "She obviously has a reckless streak."

Another finger. "She's opinionated."

I chuckle softly. He doesn't know the half of it.

"Buuut," he exaggerates. "She's good in bed, right?" He lowers a finger, and I glare at him. We both know that isn't everything.

"She's been volunteering with your boys and adores them. She's good with them." He retracts another finger.

"She's independently wealthy and runs her own business, so she doesn't need any of that from your sorry ass," he teases, lowering one more finger, leaving one remaining.

"And she's crazy about you," he lowers the last finger.

"How do you know?"

"Man, I saw the hurt on her face when you walked away from her on Halloween. She wants you bad, and I don't think the bus-rocking is the only thing she wants."

I stare at my friend, whose hand is now a fist. "You've got nothing to lose," he says, lowering his tone, bumping his fist once to remind me he has no fingers in the air, no strikes against her.

Of course, there's my heart, which I never wanted to open again to a woman.

"Henny's the one you need to let go of, my friend. Not Scotia." With that advice, he stands, taking the coffee pot with him, and I stare at my coffee mug, wondering when Todd Ryder got so wise.

CHAPTER 23

PICKLE PARTY

[Scotia]

The day of the pickle party is a blustery day. I already fear that no one will show up at Genie's, despite the bar's popularity. During the quarrel Genie Lee and I had when we first pitched the idea to her, she didn't hesitate to tell me that a party with my name on it might not draw the public. I had to remind her that In A Pickle would be the name of the *business* hosting a party in her fine Green Valley establishment.

"Never in your life would you associate with the likes of me or the company I keep," she had snarled. *Now I wanted something from her.* She didn't say it. She didn't have to. Genie was no dummy when it came to business, and she recognized I did want something from her, mainly *her name* to draw patrons.

Quick to note the underlying tension between us, Gideon interceded during that proposal meeting as the party had been his idea. He thought we should celebrate, and I didn't disagree. My business *was* an accomplishment, and one I was proud of despite it being one more thing I'd done on my own. While owning a small business wasn't solitary, I didn't have a lot of family rooting for me when I opened. My sisters and I were estranged then. Darlene was off in medical school. My best friend, Diane, had disappeared, and of course, Karl was gone. My desire for something in my life provoked this turn of events, which I really did want to celebrate.

"It's a good thing you've got Jennifer Winston on your side," Genie tsked as we were setting up for the party, and I wanted to question what she meant, but Gideon had already slipped an arm around Genie to guide her away from me.

The country western bar was an explosion of pickles. Gideon had secured pickle-shaped helium balloons along with plastic tumblers and T-shirts as prizes. He'd even convinced Genie's staff to wear a green-colored T-shirt with Genie's name and logo on the front while the back said, "Pickles please" with our logo underneath.

Gideon and I already had a conversation about greeting patrons.

"Don't frighten the children," he warned. "Or the adults. We're here to pass out samples, share the swag, and offer a few games for T-shirt prizes."

Swag? Who came up with that word?

While I'd never worked a day in my life as waitstaff, I donned a shirt like the rest of them but remained in my pencil skirt and heels. I wouldn't be serving food exactly, just greeting people and passing out some samples. I'd had plenty of practice serving guests in my home for medical staff parties over the years, so I figured it couldn't be that hard.

It wasn't that hard.

It was excruciatingly difficult.

First, my feet ached from my high heels and the hardwood flooring of Genie's.

Then there was the fact I was constantly in the way of Willa Monroe, Genie's niece, and Patty Lee, Genie's daughter, who waited on tables like professionals, which they are. In our tumblers, they served beer to adults and sodas to anyone who ordered one.

Eventually, I relegated myself to cleanup duty as a way to question what people thought of the samples and then offered to rinse out cups for customers to take home once they completed their meal. This meant I actually had to speak with people.

Gideon's reasoning was that word of mouth spreads positivity the most.

If the locals loved my product, they'd purchase it, share it, and request it. *Reputation was everything*, he told me, and that's when I worried my personal repute might be a hindrance to my professional success. I'd never been concerned that people didn't like me. It didn't matter what their opinion of me was. In matters of business, though, In A Pickle *was* me. My personal opinions needed to step aside, and a new Scotia needed to step up.

Like when I served Beau Winston, who owns Winston's Auto Shop, and his girl Shelly Sullivan. Shelly witnessed my female mishap about a month back and I owed her a semblance of gratitude. With an In A Pickle tumbler filled with beer in each hand, I approach their table.

"Beau. Shelly. Thanks for attending the party. A beer, on the house."

"We aren't at the party," Beau clarifies, watching me set the green tumblers on the wooden table. "Just looking for a quick bite at Genie's."

"Well, the fried pickles are on special tonight. Willa will be around with a sample in a minute." Both Beau and Shelly stare at me, and I take a deep breath. "And thank you, Shelly, for your assistance a while back at the garage."

Beau's red-haired head swivels to Shelly as she continues to look up at me with that blank face she can have. She hadn't actually helped me during that god-awful incident in their garage, but the situation was jarring, and while mortifying to me, I feel the need to apologize to her as she'd been present.

"I just wanted to say, I am very sorry, Shelly. I know I can be . . . I can have a real sandpaper personality sometimes."

Beau's face drops into one of confusion while Shelly's expression remains inscrutable and intense.

"I know what that's like," she says, giving me a slight nod. "No apology necessary."

I still can't read her, but as I'm learning, not everyone can be taken at surface level. Perhaps, Shelly and I have more in common than I thought. We've both been misunderstood in the past.

"Anywho, enjoy your beer." I point between the cups. "And your night." I excuse myself, trembling with the effort to remain polite, positive and professional. Perhaps Shelly had not shared with Beau what happened to me in their shop as a small show of female solidarity.

Thank goodness for small miracles.

I stalk toward Gideon when I see Maura enter with all six boys in tow. My breath catches in excitement. I'm so happy she took me up on the invitation. I promised I'd cover their entire meal. I wanted to treat them all. Then I do a double take when Chet enters at the tail of the crew.

He came.

I can hardly admit to myself how happy I am that he's here.

He nods at me once he stands within the doors.

After a hug to greet Maura and smiles for all the boys, I watch as Patty pushes two tables together to seat the larger group.

"Order whatever you'd like," I say, excitement flowing from my lips once the boys take seats. "Whatever you want, it's all on me."

My hands clasp in front of my chest and my heart hammers as I'm pickle-pleased by their presence.

"You're spoiling them, darlin'," Chet says behind me, and I turn to face him. My cheeks heat.

"A child can never be too spoiled," I state. "And I'm so thrilled you're here."

"It looks like someone vomited pickles in here." He turns his head, taking in all the green pickle balloons. "In a good way, of course." His deep eyes return to me, a spark in them as our first meeting comes to both our minds.

"I'd like to cover your dinner as well." I hold out a hand, pointing at a seat for him.

"I can cover my own, darlin'." While I know he can—he could easily purchase Genie's outright and stay stocked in pickles for the rest of his life —I still want to do this for him.

"When was the last time you ate?"

The questions surprise me, and I count back the hours. "I had coffee this morning." I've been a bundle of nerves the entire day, and my stomach hasn't considered food an option.

"Then eat with us, and I'll let you take the tab."

I smile. "I'm working."

"Want me to speak to your boss? I might have an in with her." My insides flutter when his lip slowly crooks in the corner. I'm certain I'm blushing like a schoolgirl, although I don't recall ever feeling like this as a teenager.

"An *in*, huh?" I tease. "If you ask her nicely, will she let you do anything you ask?"

"I don't know. Will she?" The flirtatious standoff has my face heating further and my knees trembling. I want to launch myself at this man despite the public place.

"Let me just speak with Gideon."

When I point out the table of boys and mention having dinner with the group, my assistant eyes me suspiciously.

"Isn't that the man who barged into the office a while back, demanding to see you?"

"Is it? Did he demand to see me?" I glance across the room at Chet.

"That man was on a mission." Gideon's head swivels from Chet to me and back. Then he hums, tapping his finger on his lower lip. "Is he the one not attracted to your mean streak?"

My mouth gapes, remembering the conversation with my assistant, but I quickly clamp my lips shut.

"Don't you worry. Your secrets are safe with me. But just so you know, I don't think he's *un*-attracted to you." Gideon lowers his voice and winks while nodding to the table. I turn to find Chet watching us. "That man's savoring you like he's never had a fried pickle in his life, and he's discovered that salty snap and crispy fried go together surprisingly well."

I stare at my young apprentice and laugh. "Gideon." *What the heck is he saying?*

"Go. Shoo. I've got this. It's your company, but everyone knows I'm running the show." He winks again, and I hold back a retort. He wishes he was in charge, but I'm the queen. Or at least, the princess.

"Thank you," I whisper, excusing myself and taking a seat between Malik and Chet.

Dinner with the boys is a chaotic mess of laughter and jokes and one spilled soda. Hugh tells me about his studies. Dewey informs me of his latest building efforts in the Harper House great room, and Louie and Hunter want to know when I'll be back to read. Campbell tells me more about their MMA lessons. Malik remains quiet at my side although I

L.B. DUNBAR

catch Chet watching him from time to time, his eyes narrowing in question.

Has he considered what I'd told him? Does he have a way to investigate with the information I'd shared? Maybe my suspicions amount to nothing other than being wound up after Malik ran away?

"So, phallic symbols?" Chet quietly mutters next to me, interrupting my thoughts as he leans closer. "Ever going to explain this one?"

"Karl was freaked out by anything remotely phallus in nature. Fire hydrants, eggplants, pickles. You get the point."

"A bit ironic, don't you think?" Chet keeps his voice lowered, his eyes shifting to a display of pickle-shaped balloons.

I chuckle softly, understanding his meaning. "The issue was, he worried expressing an interest in any of these types of items would give him away, so the opposite occurred. He overreacted to anything that could be misconstrued or interpreted as penis-shaped." I worry I might have spoken too loudly and clear my throat, side-eyeing the table of young boys.

I also notice how close Chet and I sit, leaning toward one another as if we're telling secrets. His eyes drift to the white strip of hair near my face and I want him to reach for the strands. I want him to twirl his finger through the stripe, making a statement to everyone present.

Chet chuckles, his gaze shifting to mine. "Mushrooms?"

"Yes." I bite my lip. His eyes lower there.

"Bananas?"

"I suppose." I struggle with a grin.

"A corn silo?"

"Possibly." I pause as his voice rises, laughter filling the air around us. I cross my arms, nipples peaked inside my bra for some reason. "Are you done yet?"

"One more." He lifts a thick finger close to my face. "The Washington Monument?"

"Okay, fine. Yes." My arms slip apart, and I can't help the huge grin on my face.

Chet's chuckle turns into full-on guffawing. "Well, it's like a penis-imposter explosion in here tonight. And eggplants? Really?"

My gaze drifts to his lap and then leaps back up to his face. "I suppose that one would hurt, but so might a fire hydrant."

Chet leans back, smacks the table, and laughs harder. The sound bellows out of his chest and vibrates around us. The deep echo warms my insides even if it's at the expense of my deceased husband. I want to bottle that laughter . . . in a phallus-shaped cylinder.

Eventually, I help the boys gather their things before leaving the restaurant until I feel a tug at my arm.

"What do you need, precious?" I ask as I lower to Malik. He looks around the room and then dips his head in embarrassment, crossing his legs on his seat.

"Oh. *Oh.* Do you need to use the restroom?" I push back my chair and hold out a hand. "I'll show you where it is."

I pause when he takes my hand. "Anyone else need the potty before you head home?"

"The potty?" Chet snorts while Hugh groans.

"We aren't babies," the teenager mutters.

"Well, you're all humans and drank too much soda. Anyone else need the restroom?" I tease, clarifying for Hugh. He chuckles, and Campbell raises his hand. He's ten, but I hadn't considered how to handle boys and a bathroom until I near them.

"Uhm . . ." It didn't seem right to take two young boys into the women's room, especially as they weren't kin, and I was considered a volunteer to the home.

"Campbell, I need you to be the young man I know you are and stick with Malik."

I hate the thought of sending two young boys unattended inside. Suddenly, a hand touches my shoulder.

"I was gonna let you sweat it out, but need some help?" Chet chuckles beside me.

"We have it all under control." I turn to Malik and offer his shoulder a squeeze.

"Sure, you do, darlin'," Chet mutters, propping open the door to the men's room and leading his young charges inside.

He thought he was so smug. I snicker to myself as they disappear into the bathroom, and I wait outside. When they return, we walk as a group back to the table, only I stop short. My hand moves to Chet's wrist. Malik bumps into me from the back, but I don't move. I hold my position, taking a protective stance in front of the child for some reason.

"Chet," I whisper. "That's the woman." I can't take my eyes off her. Her brassy hair glistens in the dim house lights of the bar. Without glancing at Chet, I sense his head lift and neck crane, scanning the lively space.

"Where?"

"There." I nod without pointing. "She's standing near the bar but facing the table where the boys sit."

"The petite blonde?" Chet's voice croaks, and the sound twists my neck in his direction. My brows press to a sharp crease.

"Do you know her?" The stare he's giving the woman writes his recognition of her all over his bearded cheeks. My hand slowly slips from his wrist, but the release is more than letting go of his arm. The distance between us becomes miles.

"It can't be her. That's Henny," he quietly offers, and I turn my attention back to the woman standing near the bar. She's the same woman from The Beauty Mark, but I see her now in a different light. She was the love of Chet's life. The woman who said she'd wait for him and didn't. The one he'd built a home for and raised his millions for. He'd wanted to marry her, and she'd rejected him. I hate her for breaking his heart. What did she want with him now? The things she'd thrown away before? I didn't put it past her, even without knowing her.

I speak without thinking. "She's a gold digger."

"She is not," Chet defends with a clipped tone.

"She is," I retort, facing him.

"Because it takes one to know one," he bites, narrowing his eyes at me, and the insult stings. The vibration of his comment echoes around me, and I quiver at the thought he believes I'm only interested in money.

"Perhaps. Or maybe I'm not too foolish to recognize a lonely woman without means."

Chet's head turns, his brow furrowing. "She has means." He speaks more to himself than to me.

"Well, how *fortunate* for her then that she's here now and available to you." I pause, then add, "But it's her. I'm positive. That bad dye job and Botoxed lip is unforgiving, and unbecoming on her."

"Who cares about her hair or her lips? You're just being your condescending self, Scotia. I don't like you like this." The combination of *our line* and his defense of her is really irritating me. Did he invite her here this evening?

"Chet, seriously. Forget her dye job and bulbous mouth. Enjoy her as she is, then." I need to return the boys to the table and return to my evening. Gideon is correct. I'm the boss, and I'm running this pickle show. I glance over my shoulder and then spin, placing my back to the dining area.

"Where's Malik?" My eyes search the space near the restrooms. I spin again and notice the swing of the kitchen entrance door. Without a word, I walk away from Chet, leaving him to his woman, who gave him all kinds of past rejections.

Pushing my way into the kitchen, I almost knock into Patty Lee who is exiting it with a tray full of dinners.

"Watch it," she grumbles, and I step back.

"Scotia Simmons, you need to get out of this kitchen. We're too busy for you in here," Genie herself calls out to me, but I ignore her warning.

"Where is he?" I whisper as if I don't want anyone to hear me, but I need Genie to listen.

"Where's who?" she looks exasperated.

"The boy? Did he come in here?" I'm frantic as I scan the kitchen, walking around the ovens without permission, and glancing under an island as if he's as small as a ketchup bottle and hiding beneath the counter.

"Scotia, just what the—"

"One of the boys from that big table . . . I think he came in here." My eyes plead with her to understand. Woman to woman. Mother to mother. "He's only a child." My voice cracks. I don't have a good feeling about him disappearing again. The caseworker has already come to investigate the first time he went missing, as the authorities had to be notified. While Maura is held in the highest esteem with the Department of Child Services, they still had to question how he could slip away.

"Is that him?" Genie speaks behind me, and I twist to face her. Her eyes soften for a second, looking past me at something, and then she points at a mop bucket, nodding her head at me with a tired frown on her face. The frustrated expression is directed at me, not the boy. I follow where she aims her finger to see a dark head tucked between little knees, as if the position disguises him.

"Malik," I whisper-hiss in relief and step to the corner. I drop to a lady-like squat, my skirt keeping my knees together.

"Is he okay?" Genie asks, her voice notably softer with worry for the boy.

"Malik, precious," I try again to gain his attention.

"Scotia, just what are you doing?" Genie grouses behind me, as if she thinks I'm the one who frightened the child, but I ignore her. My focus is solely on the scared boy behind a mop bucket.

"What is it, honey? You can tell me."

Malik's little head slowly lifts, and watery dark eyes look at me. Fear fills those glassy orbs.

"Let me help you." My voice shakes as I ask a question I know could be leading. "Is it the woman? The blonde in the restaurant?"

Malik kicks the pail on wheels. The force of it shifts the bucket toward me, and water splatters onto my skirt. I startle and fall back on my heels, slipping a bit and catching myself with a hand on the tile floor before my backside hits the ground.

"Hey, kid," Genie says, and I crane my neck to look up at her from my position. Her eyes soften once again for him, while her forehead furrows with unease. She glances back at me, and that compassionate gaze turns stern once more, but I don't have time to deal with Genie.

"Malik," I cry a little louder as he stands, pressing his back into the corner as if the crease could open and swallow him inward.

"Tell me. Tell me something so I can help you."

He shakes his head, eyes still wide, and I know I'm not wrong. That woman has something to do with Malik's fear. The other thing I know is I'm not taking him anywhere near her. Within minutes, Maura enters the kitchen.

"What's going on here?"

"There are too many cooks in my kitchen," Genie mutters, throwing up a hand.

"Malik, honey, it's time to go," Maura states, holding out a hand after suspiciously looking from me to him.

"He's scared." I whisper as if a caged animal stands before us. The frightened expression on the boy's face worries me. *What happened to him?*

"What is it?" Maura asks me.

"That blonde woman near the bar. I think he knows her." I don't take my eyes from Malik as I speak about him. If only *he'd* speak. We need him to tell us something so we can help him.

Maura continues to watch Malik as well, lifting a hand forward for his. "Malik, you need to come with Maura, honey. Remember, we talked about what could happen if you run away again?"

She speaks of herself in the third person, reminding him of a conversation I assume they had about the investigation and the possibility of placement with another family. The caseworker thinks it might be time to move Malik into a single-family home despite not knowing who his real family is. The standard belief behind the decision is a set of parents will give him undivided attention and service him better than a group setting. Maura and I already spoke about this and how I disagreed.

"I can't help what the system decides," Maura stated. She wasn't being cold-hearted. She understands it's a process, but I don't like the recommended solution.

"What does Chet think?"

"Chet will follow the rules. He won't risk the boys."

I recall thinking at the time, *Did she mean collectively all the boys or only his nephews?* He's hardly a selfish man, though. He's done right by the boys as a whole.

I step over to the swinging doors and peer out into the dining room.

"You can't take Malik out there with her," I whisper.

"What do you suggest?" Maura suspiciously glares at me.

"I'll drive him to the house." It's the craziest thought. Actually, I'd like to suggest I take him to my home. He can have his own space in one of the guest rooms. I can keep him safe, protect him.

"Scotia, you've done generous things by these boys, but I don't know about this suggestion." Her eyes question mine. Her expression is a combination of emotions. I don't want her to do anything to jeopardize her position at Harper House or as a foster parent, but I want her to trust me.

Her shoulders sag. "Fine."

My eyes widen in surprise.

"But you bring him right to the house," she warns. "I'll distract Chet. Get him to move the woman away from the boys so I can get them out to the van."

"Did Chet arrive with you? How will he get home?"

"He's a big boy. I'll let him worry about that," Maura huffs, and I don't like that answer. Because there's a real possibility Chet could go home with his former lover.

CHAPTER 24

DOUBTFUL

[Chet]

Scotia has placed doubt in my head, and I don't like it. With Malik slipping away from us, though, I fear I can't dismiss that something is amiss between Hennessy and the boy. Maybe he's her eldest son—the one giving her trouble—which means he needs to be returned to his mother. The boy is her problem, and I'm not saying that to be hard-hearted. I'm thinking of Henny. How frightened must she be that her child has disappeared, if he is in fact her child?

With the initial misgivings planted the other day by Scotia's description of a woman similar to Henny, I had some serious questions about the woman I once loved. There could be tons of women with brassy blonde hair in the Green Valley area, especially ones renting a cabin. But I cannot let go of the suspicion that a second child, looking like our lost Malik, was with her. After Scotia told me what she saw, I called the authorities with the weak lead of information.

I should not have snapped at Scotia as I had. Implying she was a gold digger isn't fair, especially in light of all she'd told me about her relationship with her husband. I didn't really believe Scotia was such a thing, but that woman can push my buttons, and when push comes to shove, I push back. I'm starting to understand what she meant about putting others down before they can hurt her. My protective instincts kicked in when she started insulting Henny. Not that I'm sensitive to Henny, but I don't like when Scotia goes into mean-*woman* mode.

My eyes shifted to Maura when I neared the table, and I tipped my head toward the kitchen, hinting her assistance was needed in there.

As I approach Hennessy, something warns me not to be too forthright.

"Hey, Henny, what are you doing here?" I attempt to keep my tone level while her eyes widen when she sees me.

"Chester." Her voice squeaks. "My boys like the fried chicken fingers from here, and I thought I'd bring some home for dinner." She scans the room. "What are you doing here?"

"It's a pickle party," I mock, turning my head toward all the damn balloons. I'd be worried about my manhood, too, if I saw this many phallic symbols floating around a room, but I can't think about what Scotia has told me.

"Do you have time for a drink?" I offer, pointing at the bar. I can't leave the boys unattended yet, but I'd like to stall Henny and ask her some questions. Her face brightens with the offer.

"I'd love to stay, but I need to get right back home. Maybe another night?" Her hopeful suggestion does not dissuade me from confronting her on a few more things.

"To the cabin you're renting." I try to clarify her reference of home.

"Yes." The sharpness of the singular word sends a prickle down my spine.

"And where is that again? Maybe I know the place."

"Oh, you wouldn't. It's a family place." Her fingers come together, clutching and unclutching in a nervous habit.

"You're renting from family, then?" I inquire, finding it odd she'd have to pay family to stay in a cabin, not to mention I'd never known Henny to have family in the valley. *They must be from her husband's side*, I tell myself because I don't want to believe otherwise. I want to prove Henny has no connection to Malik.

Damn Scotia.

"Did I say renting? I meant staying. We're staying in a cabin owned by family, which they rent to people outside the family when family isn't staying there." Her rambling would be cute if it didn't sound so suspicious.

"So fried chicken tonight for your boys. Are they at the cabin?"

"Yes." Again, the singular-syllabled word does nothing to reassure me.

"You never told me, what are your boys' names?"

"Timothy and Brandon," she states without a blink. I'm about to ask another question when I sense someone approaching. Genie holds a to-go bag in her hand and nods to Henny. On the bar owner's heels is Scotia.

"Here's your order, ma'am."

"Chet," Scotia speaks behind Genie. "I was wondering if you could accompany me home this evening."

The directness of her request startles me but apparently not as much as the bar owner who almost drops the bag of fried chicken. "Loose morals, my ass," the woman mutters.

"I . . ." I falter.

"You!" Henny groans.

My attention shifts from Scotia to Hennessy. "Do you know one another?" I ask my ex-girlfriend of years past.

"We haven't been formally introduced, but we've met. At The Beauty Mark, remember?" Scotia clarifies, holding out a hand and speaking in a sugary-sweet tone. "I'm Scotia Simmons."

"Hennessy Heiner," Henny states, returning the introduction while holding her hand in a manner that expresses Scotia's touch is unwelcome. Once releasing Scotia's fingers, Henny reaches for the bag dangling from Genie's hand. "Thank you. If I could just pay, please. I need to get home." Henny's eyes come up to mine, and it feels like a warning of some type.

Genie levels a scornful look at Scotia before leading Henny to the front of the bar, and I turn on Scotia. "What are you playing at, darlin'?" My voice drips with its own sugar, but it's not sweet.

"I'm saving you from yourself."

I don't have time to question what Scotia means. "Where's Malik?"

"In the kitchen with Maura. I was going to drive him home, but seeing as that woman is scurrying off, Malik can return to Harper House with the other boys as he should."

"What does that mean?"

"It means, Maura told me if Malik runs away again, he might be placed in another home. His caseworker is worried about his mental stability, and so am I. That woman clearly triggers him, and you need to do something about it." Scotia folds her arms and stomps her foot, emphasizing her words. It'd all be comical if my irritation wasn't building. I don't like her accusations about Henny, but I have a funny feeling her suggestions regarding Malik and Henny aren't wrong. I want to tell myself Scotia is just riled up with petty jealousy, but this thing—Malik and Henny—is bigger than a lover's squabble.

"I have Malik's best interest at heart," I defend.

"Do you? Are you sure you aren't getting sucked into something else?" Her head tips toward the door where Henny has exited, and I don't appreciate her insinuation that I'm foolish when it comes to Henny.

"Hennessy is not your concern." The words are sharp because my head is spinning. Henny just confirmed the names of her boys, plus the fact they are both at her home—the rental, or the family place, or the rented family cabin—wherever it is she's staying. Her boys are waiting on her, as she said. Malik cannot be her son, but something won't let me dismiss the thought so easily. Henny *is* acting rather strange.

Shaking the thought, I address the boys' housemother as she re-enters the main dining room holding Malik's hand. "Maura, it's time to go." She nods, giving Scotia a sympathetic look before minutes of chaos ensue as the boys slip into coats, grab tumblers, and collect pickle T-shirts from the table. Scotia gives them each a balloon, and I've never been so eager to pop something in my life.

I don't want to see the phallic symbol. I don't want to consider Scotia's suspicions. And I definitely don't want to doubt Hennessy, because if I do, it means Henny lied to me. Again.

And if Henny is somehow connected to Malik? I don't want to consider those thoughts.

I'm following the boys and Maura to the exit when Jedd Flemming enters the bar with his fiancée, Beverly.

"Big Poppy," he cheerfully calls out upon seeing me. Jedd's hard of hearing in one ear, and it causes him to be louder than necessary. "What are you doing here?" Many are surprised to find me in Green Valley as I spend most of my time at The Fugitive in North Carolina. However, lately, I find myself more and more in this damn valley.

"Here with the boys." I nod to the gaggle following Maura to the mini-van. Beverly stands next to Jedd, and her head turns to follow the trail of children.

"You have kids?" she questions, looking back at me. Beverly has eyes that match her sister's—gray and piercing—but they've softened over the time I've known her. She's aware of a few secrets between Jedd and me, so she should know I don't have children. However, she might not know about the boys' home as I try to keep them separate from connections with my business affairs.

"I run a foster home of sorts," I tell her, sensing I can trust Beverly. Her brows lift with the information, and then her face softens, breaking into a wide grin.

"That's mighty generous of you, Big Poppy. You're a good man." Jesus, that nearly rips out my heart for some reason.

"Jedd, I've been meaning to call you." For all of five minutes. I need some help investigating someone, and as much as I hate to admit it, it needs to be done. I want to keep this on the down low before I turn this into a legitimate investigation, and I know Jedd used a guy to try to help him find his younger brother about a year ago.

I don't want to stir up trouble before there's a need. Henny doesn't need it. She's already lost her husband, or so she says, and I hate that I'm doubting that as well. What do I really know about this new version of her other than her eagerness for us to get together again? A warning in Scotia's voice goes off in my head. Why did the pickle vixen need to ruin tonight? The evening had been fun with the boys. Trouble just seems to follow that woman.

Or maybe it's that trouble likes to find me.

"Have a drink with us," Jedd invites, and Beverly smiles to encourage the offer.

"I hate to intrude on date night," I tease.

"Naomi and Nathan are joining us. We're here to support Scotia," Beverly adds.

Dammit. I'm here myself for the same reason. If I want her to respect all my businesses, I decided I needed to show her I believe in hers. Plus, the boys begged to attend the celebration. Scotia should be proud of all she's accomplished in the past five years. I'd been thinking about what she said and how similar we might be given that we both started our own businesses and worked to better ourselves. We'd also both thought money would improve our lives, our status, and it's proven the opposite. In addition, we'd both hoped for love in our first relationships, which fell flat and left us disappointed.

"I should really help Maura get the boys home," I say, hesitating as I'd like to stay.

"Maura?" Beverly questions while Jedd shakes his head.

"Man, I cannot keep up with your harem," he teases, which causes Beverly to look over at him. Her face falls as she turns back to me, and I wonder what she's thinking. More importantly, what does she know? Has Scotia talked about me? Does her sister know a thing or two about us?

"No harem. Just a house full of boys." Somehow, that sounded wrong, and I chuckle as I scratch under my chin. I see the reverse lights of the van through the window and excuse myself from Jedd and Beverly. As I enter the parking lot, Maura stops the minivan and I step up to the driver's side.

"What's going on?" She knows me well enough to question my expression.

"I don't know exactly, but would you mind if I stayed?" The great thing about Maura is I don't always need to explain myself to her. She gives me a knowing look and sets the van back in reverse. I tap the side of the vehicle, waving at the boys before returning inside Genie's.

Scotia gives me a surprised look upon my re-entry but doesn't say anything to me as I cross the bar and take a seat with Jedd and Beverly at a table. We both need time to cool off—her with her accusations and me with my sudden doubts. I haven't known Jedd for long, but I trusted him instantly upon meeting him. We have a business agreement.

"Tell me how horse training is going." I know nothing about horses, but I listen as Jedd explains the types of horses on his property and how he's working them, training bucking broncs for the rodeo. He's also taking on students with the hope of entering his prospects in the local circuits next spring, and he offers horseback-riding lessons.

"Always need to start somewhere," he states positively, and that's what I like about him.

"I should bring the boys over."

"You know you're welcome anytime."

Shortly after our conversation, Nathan Ryder arrives with his wife, Naomi. I've known Nathan for a long time through his brother and became better acquainted with him once he returned to Green Valley a few years back. He's more jovial than his sibling but still intense at times. His wife seems to be the opposite of him, but they look at one another as if they were a match made in heaven. Fate brought them back together, Nathan would say. The first time Nathan explained their relationship, I was actually a little nauseated by the cuteness of it. And to think it all started at The Fugitive.

"Hey Jedd, come get another round with me." I've asked awkwardly, but I need to speak to him privately. When we step over to the bar, I explain my need for an investigation of something off the record, and Jedd gives me a name.

"Ever hear of Cletus Winston?"

"I use his shop for my car." Besides my motorcycle and truck, I take my 2019 Dodge Challenger to him for maintenance.

"If you want to know the who's who in the area and their history, he's the man."

I nod, acknowledging I understand.

"Use my name." Jedd pats me on the shoulder and turns back toward the table. I feel sick at the thought of investigating Henny, but I need answers. I'll have to turn her over to the authorities if I find something, and God, I hope I don't learn anything that will force me to do that.

Once back at the table, we laugh and drink, and I listen to the couples picking on one another, wondering what it would feel like to be a part of a group like them. If Scotia and I were something more lasting than some hit-or-miss nights in the sheets, could we do things like this? Hang out with friends? From what I heard secondhand, she hasn't been close to her sisters, but the impression I have is they are working on mending a long-standing, broken relationship.

Sitting here among friends has calmed my irritation from earlier. I wasn't actually upset with Scotia as much as the possibility she's right. Something is amiss with Malik disappearing tonight upon Henny's arrival. It reminds me he went missing the same night Henny showed up at the house. With this revelation, I look up to see Scotia wandering over to the table.

"Well, y'all sound like you're having a good time," she says, but there's an undercurrent in that tone and a forced grin on her face. Is that displeasure? Exclusion? Does she sense she's missing out? Everything in me wants to reach out and tug her onto my lap to make her a part of this circle. Like I'd thought the other morning, I'm not hiding her, but we're on her ground here.

"Join us," Beverly suggests, a hint of hope in her tone.

"Come sit, Sissy," Naomi says next.

"Some of us have to work," Scotia remarks, sharper than she should, and I wonder what she thinks her sisters do. Naomi's a librarian. Beverly runs a soap-making business and a farm with Jedd.

"We're here to support you," Beverly states, and Scotia's mouth opens, then quickly shuts. She has something to say in response to her sister, but I see her biting her cheek.

"Thank you for coming," the eldest sibling grits out, fisting her fingers and then excusing herself. As she stalks back to her associate, I watch her fine ass sway in her dark, tight skirt. I don't know what it is about her body, but it calls to mine. So does her attitude.

"I'll be right back," I mutter, excusing myself and standing. I follow Scotia, grip her upper arm, and tug her near the bathrooms. Once we enter the small hallway, I spin Scotia, who looks ready to spit nails.

"What is the problem?" I snap when I intended to stay calm. Her aggravation with me is something I can handle, but her rude behavior toward her sisters, who are here for her, is another thing.

"Nothing," she lies, staring up at me, eyes searching mine a minute. "I-I'm sorry for earlier." Her apology completely stumps me and derails my new ire.

"For what exactly?"

"Henny." She swallows around the name. "Malik is in your care. I just don't want anything to hurt him." Her eyes lower, and her shoulders fall. The tension inside me releases a bit as well. I don't want to fight with her tonight. This was her night. This was her party.

"I'm proud of you," I say, reaching out for those white strands of hair that soothe me.

"You . . . what?" Her voice lowers as she swallows around the question.

"You had something to say to your sister, and judging by the way you were gnawing the inside of your cheek, I suspect it wasn't pleasant. So, I'm proud of you for holding back and not saying something to hurt Beverly." I've met that sister on more than one occasion, and I have a soft spot for her.

Scotia stares at me, and her arms cross. Her hip juts to one side, and then she turns her face away from me. I've stumped her.

"Now, tell me what you were going to say."

Her attention snaps back to my face. "What?"

"It's still bothering you, so get it off your chest by telling me instead of taking it out on your sister."

Scotia's hands fall to her sides as she considers her thoughts for a second. Eventually, she huffs. "Fine. While I appreciate Beverly saying they are here for me, where were they when I started this company?" As soon as the words leave her mouth, her expression falters.

"Where were they?" I repeat back to her and her head tilts again.

"What do you mean?"

"What was going on in their lives when you started your business?"

Scotia hesitates before speaking. "Beverly was still recovering, wallowing in her self-imposed reclusiveness, and Naomi and I just weren't close as she was letting guilt and the goddess rule her life."

I don't exactly understand the goddess statement, but I give Scotia a hard glare.

"So what you're saying is they were busy with troubles in their own lives. And were you there for them?"

"I—"

"Et." I hold up a hand.

"But—"

I shake my head.

Her shoulders fall. "No." Her eyes close. Her head lowers. At least she admitted the truth, if to no one else but me. A pinch of pride fills my chest. I can't help myself. I step forward and pull her into me. With her forehead pressing into my sternum, I place a kiss on the top of her head.

"I'm a really awful person," she mutters against me.

"You're a work in progress. That doesn't make you awful. It means you're tryin'. There's a difference."

Her head pops up as she remains leaning into me. "Do you really think there's hope for me?"

"I already told you I did, darlin'."

"I appreciate your faith in me," she whispers. "Not many people have believed in me in the past."

I don't know what she means because she seems to have enough faith in herself to weather any storm, but there's that sweet and vulnerable side she gives to me. I understand that it's nice to have support from others. It's nice to have others believe in you, be proud of you. Maura's been there for me, and Todd, too. Hell, I even count Savannah and Nathan and Jedd. Who was there for Scotia when she was holding up that farce of a marriage? Who was there when she started her business venture? Scotia asked who holds me, and I recall that look she had when we met. Who held her? Would she let me be the one to always be there for her?

"Okay, boss lady. Get back to work selling deep-fried phallus."

She laughs lightly in my arms, and I lean down, giving her a quick kiss. The action surprises both of us, and she slowly smiles afterward. As I release her, a thought strikes me.

"That's why you do it, isn't it?"

"Do what?" she asks, slowly disengaging herself from my embrace.

"You're symbolically deep frying his dick, aren't you?"

Scotia chuckles nervously. "I don't know what you're talking about."

"And it has nothing to do with his sexual orientation," I continue. "You're boiling his tiny pecker in hot oil because of his unfaithfulness. *Peter Piper picked a peck of pickled peckers.*" He screwed around but she didn't.

"It's peppers," she corrects me.

"His pecker?" I question, returning to the subject at hand and arching a brow.

"I have no idea what you mean," she says, smoothing her hands down her skirt and walking away from me. Then she cranes her neck to look at me over her shoulder and winks.

Someone remind me never to get on Scotia Simmons's bad side.

CHAPTER 25

THREE THINGS

[Scotia]

The Pickle Day-slash-anniversary party was a big success, and I'm pleased as a pickle with the turnout. Between the high of the celebration and a shot or two in my honor, I might have been a teeny bit tipsy by the end of the night. Even Genie gave me a weak smile, disregarding all the questions in her head about Malik hiding out behind a mop bucket in her kitchen.

"Thank you again," I say to Patty and Willa who worked their tails off with the patrons, and the extra service required to share the fried pickle samples. Gideon tipped them each generously for their efforts. I'm exhausted yet exhilarated. My siblings and their significant others are long gone, but Chet stayed the remainder of the night. I had to remind myself to call him Big Poppy in front of the others, although I'm certain they all know his real name, and this isn't his biker bar.

"What a good night," I say to Gideon as I walk him to the front door, surprising him with my cheerful tone.

"See you in the morning," he tells me in a tired voice.

"Let's start at noon tomorrow." His brows lift, but he doesn't question me as he looks over my shoulder at the burly man sitting at the bar waiting on me.

"Have a good night, boss."

"You worked hard tonight, Gideon. Thank you." I've stumped him a second, and he simply smiles before speaking.

"I knew you could do it. See, a genuine compliment wasn't so bad, right?" He tips up a brow. Perhaps the boss has been schooled by her assistant.

I softly chuckle. "Get out of here," I tease and then watch him walk to his car with a handful of pickle-shaped helium balloons.

After Gideon leaves, I cross the bar for Chet, and he reaches for my hip, tugging me between his spread thighs as he sits on a barstool.

"Tell me three things," he says, a grin gracing his lips.

"My feet hurt. I could use a drink. I'm exhausted," I jest, placing my hands on his chest.

"Interpreted as massage, wine, and sex. Got it."

I let out a sharp laugh which he captures, melding his lips to mine as we linger in the nearly vacant bar. The kiss is tender, hesitant, and soft. He takes his time to work over my mouth, drawing out the suction of my bottom lip before covering both once more. My knees buckle, and I fall into him, leaning against his firm body. His hand holds my hip, and the other slides to my lower back.

"We're closed," Genie hollers, dinging on a bell from the kitchen. "Get your groove on somewhere else."

I twist to face her, feeling her watching me, and she gives me a look like she's never seen me before, like I'm someone new to her, and she nods towards the door. I'm hoping after tonight—between the party and the situation in her kitchen—she does see me differently. Not that I really care what others think of me . . . but I do, a little bit. *Okay, maybe more than a little.*

I look back at Chet, flushed at being caught kissing a man in public, but I want people to know he's with me. He's mine.

"Are you mad about Henny?" My fingers play with the collar of his shirt while he rubs his hand up and down my back.

"Not mad," he clarifies. "But that green-eyed jealousy blends well with your pickles."

I smile weakly, ready to retort I'm not jealous, but I realize I am. Of course, I deny it. "I have nothing to be jealous of," I state, defending my own honor, but Chet surprises me.

"That's right. You don't, darlin'." The softening of his rough voice does something to my insides. Is he telling me he isn't interested in his first love? Does he believe my suspicions? Does this mean we're exclusive?

"I don't like fighting with you, so can we drop Henny, please?" he asks.

"Okay," I whisper, not wanting to fight with him about her either, especially with him holding me like he is. He feels so warm against me. He smells like beer, lemons, and man.

"So my place or my place?" The hour is late, *and yeah,* I'm propositioning him. It has been a good night as I told Gideon, but I know what would make it better.

"Sometimes, I like how you think," Chet whispers.

"Sometimes, I just like you," I tease him back before I take him home with me.

* * *

"Oh, Chet," I groan as he clutches at my backside, tugging at my cheeks while he hammers into me repeatedly. My arms wrap around his broad back as our chests press together. We might be in the missionary position, but this is anything but vanilla. This is chocolaty heaven and sinfully delicious rolled into one.

"Come on, darlin'," he gasps as his body moves, sliding back and forth. I can't possibly have another in me. He's already given me two orgasms that curled my toes and made my knees weak. With a thin layer of sweat, our bodies slip against each other.

"I can't," I whimper.

"You can," he grunts. "Give. It. To. Me." He's demanding, and I love it. I also want to please him without being selfish, but he's determined I release once more before he gives himself relief. I think he likes the sense of accomplishment.

My legs slide off his back, propping my feet on the bed. I use the position to leverage myself, and Chet growls. He's a sensual man, turning me upside down and inside out with his experienced touching and kissing. Sex with him is on a level I've never had, so I'm empowered by the gleam in his eyes and the desperation in his clutching hands. He wants us as close to one another as we can get.

"Darlin'," he groans. Then he shifts, lifting himself in a way so that each drag of his length rubs my clit, and I see stars. I scream, despite having never been a screamer during sex. I've never been this enthusiastic about it either, or let a man do all the things Chet's done to me. Tongue. Lips. Fingers.

Not to mention, when his amazing appendage fills me, it brings me to a peak so high I can't catch my breath.

My fingernails dig into his firm backside, holding him to me, but he resists. My body rattles under him as he pumps faster, harder, deeper and then . . . he stills. His head tips back. His neck strains. It's the most beautiful thing I've ever seen. *He's* the most beautiful man I've ever known.

He collapses over me and shifts a bit to my side, so he isn't squishing me. He breathes heavily against my neck, and I close my eyes, tightening my arms around him. I'm overcome with emotion and a tear leaks from my eye. Then another. And another.

His lips press against my jaw, and he lifts his head.

"What's this, darlin'?" His typically rough tone softens as the thick pad of his thumb brushes my cheek.

"I don't know," I whisper, so uncertain of myself. I feel bare, laid open to him in a way I've never been exposed to anyone before, and I don't know what to do with the emotional overload.

"What are we doing with each other?" I question, keeping my voice quiet. Chet's eyes search my face as he brushes back hair stuck to the edges.

"I don't know, darlin'."

For some reason, I want him to ask me what I want us to be, and I want him to agree with my opinion. *I want us to be together.* I want someone to belong to me. I want him to be exclusive, only us, only him and me. Yet it's not something I feel comfortable asking of him. I'm demanding and domineering in all things but asking this man to be only mine feels daunting. I'm afraid he'll say no, and the rejection would crush me.

I shake my head, chewing at my lip while my eyes look everywhere but directly at him. Another tear slowly seeps out of the edge of my eye and rolls down my face toward my ear. I hate that I'm crying in front of him, but I'm so overwhelmed between the robust sex and the tenderness afterward. Every time he calls me darlin', I should demand he correct the slang and add a "g," but I don't. I like it as is. After years of being called *dear*, like a patronizing slur, I like how Chet's voice shifts when he speaks an endearment toward me.

He slips out of me and stands from the bed. "Be right back," he tells me, stepping toward the bathroom attached to my bedroom. I was a little nervous about bringing him here, to this room, the same place I'd spent more than two decades sleeping next to a man who wasn't fully mine. In one night, another man has obliterated all those memories with his vigorous sexual energy.

When he returns to the bed with a small towel in his hands, I take it and excuse myself. I need just a minute of separation to gather my wits because I'm all over the place. My body still vibrates with what we'd done, even though we've been together a few times already. It's my heart that can't seem to settle and accept this for what it is.

I don't know.

Are there three worse words? I can think of three better ones, but we aren't at that point. Do I love him? Could I love him? I'm not certain I know exactly what love should look like, feel like, sound like, but I also realize it comes in different forms. I have yet to experience it on the level I've longed for most.

I stare at my reflection in the mirror. Hair askew. Makeup melting near my eyes. Lipstick completely removed. I'm a mess. I look ravished, and my body feels amazing. After swiping my fingers through my hair, I grab a robe off the back of the bathroom door and return to the bedroom. Chet sits on the side of the bed, his pants back in place.

"Are you leaving?" My heart hammers in a different pattern.

"Do you want me to leave?" His head slowly lifts, and those deep, dark eyes question mine.

"Only if you want to leave," I reply, wondering why I'm not asking him outright to stay. That invisible mask is itching to be pulled upward and protect me.

"You're doing that thing," Chet warns, lifting his hand and pointing toward my face.

"I don't know what you mean." But this man reads me so well, he isn't missing the hidden effort.

"That thing where you start to lock up on me." He pauses, observing my expression, which makes me anxious. He sees all of me. I purse my lips, twisting them this way and that as if I can change what he sees.

"It's a bit of a habit, I guess," I say, lowering my lids, relaxing my face, and brushing my hair over my ear. I look at my toes. His feet are bare, and I'm relieved to see them. It means he isn't rushing to escape me.

"Is it so hard to be open with me?"

"Are you always open with me?" I question. I didn't intend to be defensive, but as we're trying to be *open,* I'm curious about him.

He softly chuckles and swipes a hand through his hair. "I guess not." He shifts his gaze from me, looking at my nightstand, which is now devoid of a photo of Karl and me I once had perched there. Darlene no longer lives at home and Karl's been gone for long enough, so I've removed most of his pictures throughout our home to make this house more my own.

"I'm honest when I say I like you a certain way."

My attention is drawn to his face. "There are times you don't like me, though." I recall his response when I argued Henny was a gold digger or even when I snapped at my sisters. I'm still a work in progress.

"Times you don't like me either, darlin'." His face softens under his beard, which grows unruly and then is trimmed back to his jaw with no pattern of consistency. "Thing is, we're gonna fight and disagree, but as long as we come back to each other, as long as we have times like this." He nods at the bed. "Then I'm going to like you all the time, darlin'."

My answer is quick and eager. "I like you all the time."

"What about Big Poppy and the bus?" A bushy brow arches.

"Yes."

"And we've already established Chester Chesterfield is a hit with you," he teases.

I chuckle softly and then cup his cheeks with my hands. "I think I prefer Chet, the man somewhere between the two. The man with the heart to take in three boys not his own and give up his home for them. The man taking on other children along with those boys. The man who owns a million-dollar corporation and a motorcycle bar and motel because he's full of drive and determination but not uptight in those traits. The man who sees me. Has faith in me. Won't give up on me. Not yet at least." Hesitantly, my eyes search his as he stares up at me. His soften.

"Darlin', if I hadn't just had you for like an hour straight, I'd take you on my lap again." His hands move to my hips, and he drags me closer to him, pressing his head into my belly. My fingers comb through his hair, pausing on the back of his neck.

"Tell me you want me to stay," he mutters to my cotton robe.

"I want you to stay," I whisper.

His head lifts, and soulful eyes look up at me. "Was that so difficult?" He slowly smiles and I'm reminded of what Gideon said earlier about being genuine.

"It wasn't that difficult." I grin. Being honest with Chet wasn't so hard because if anyone understood me, it was him. With his relationship history, he'd know how nerve-wracking asking someone to stay can be. And he wasn't going to leave.

Reaching up for the back of my head, he pulls me down to him, attaching our lips and winding us up once again.

* * *

The light of day brings new perspective and awkwardness once more. The morning after is usually our hot time, but today, I wake to see Chet dressing at the end of my bed. The scene reminds me of our first morning when we remained quiet after the craziness of two strangers discovering one another. He dressed in silence then. I watched him move.

I do the same now.

The buttoning of his pants. The buckling of his belt. The tug of his T-shirt over his head. Him dressing feels like a curtain call. The show is over, and the audience is stunned for a moment before the applause. He watches his own fingers as he buttons his shirt.

"We should probably go on a proper date one of these days." He smirks, and I suppose it is funny we haven't been out to dinner or to a movie or whatever people do nowadays for a date.

"We don't need to do that," I say, dismissing the implied invitation as if I don't care when, in reality, I'd really like that.

"Still don't want to be seen in public with me," he teases, but the tightness of his tone suggests he isn't joking.

"We were in public last night, even if I want to keep you all to myself." Thinking I'm being coy, something in his expression tells me I'm not. I swallow around the intensity of his gaze.

"Like a dirty secret," he quietly retorts. "I've already been one of those." He roughly tucks his shirt into his pants.

"That's not fair," I defend. I'm nothing like the woman who has caused him to keep his walls up over the years. His words cause me to pull the sheet tighter around my breasts. I'm not one to sleep in the nude, but whenever I'm with him, I do, loving the feel of his warm skin against mine.

"What's not fair is being a secret."

"I'm not keeping you a secret. I want everyone to know we're together." I feel vulnerable and raw with the admission, but if I expect him to read into what I've said, I'm wrong.

He huffs, turning his back to me to reach for his socks on the floor. He sits on the end of the bed.

I hate how he's hinted at Henny, bringing her into this bedroom and between us. He's the one who said he didn't want to fight about her. And as much as I think he should handle her, I can't seem to let this unnerving feeling about her go. "What do you plan to do about that woman?"

Chet freezes. His back straightens. His hands still as his sock only covers his toes. "What do you mean, what do I plan to do?"

"She's obviously connected to Malik somehow. What are you going to do about her?"

Tilting his head over his shoulder, he doesn't directly look at me. "I'm not going to *do* anything about her."

Anxiously, I swipe fingers through my messy hair. "What do you mean? You have to do something. For Malik."

"Look, there's nothing that says he and Henny have a link. He got spooked coming out of the bathroom. And she's . . ." His pause raises the fine hairs on my skin.

"She's what?" I question, growing more defensive. Does he know more about her than he's letting on? Has he seen her other than just the night when he had drinks with her? Why is he protecting her?

"She's just in a fragile state right now."

"What does that mean?" Our entire conversation feels defensive and vague. Our opposing positions is reminiscent of so many disagreements with Karl.

"It means I'll handle Henny."

"How?" The question is quick and sharp, like an arrow spiraling toward a target. What will he do with her? What will he say?

"Darlin', as I told you last night, she is not your concern, and I don't want to fight about her." His use of the endearment reminds me of Karl calling me dear. *Yes, dear, I called so-and-so. No, dear, I did not take out the trash yet. Yes, dear, I'm going out again.*

"I disagree. I'm very concerned because of Malik." That poor child needs some answers, and he needs reassurance. He's more than spooked. It's *her*. I just know it. "And that Botox Barbie-wannabe was something to him."

Chet abruptly stands, turning to face me, no longer concerned about the sock covering just his toes.

"Scotia, I don't need your assumptions, especially when it comes to Hennessy. I do not like you like this."

"Why? Are you still in love with her?"

The silence that follows could be cut with a knife. The air is as thick as a cake layered with his anger.

"I will not dignify that question with an answer." His eyes roam down the bed, taking in the sheet-covered length of me.

"Then tell me what you're going to do with her." My voice cracks. *Tears of frustration will not fall.* Other than last night, I'm a master at controlling them. The daylight restores my willpower. *Mask back in place, Scotia.*

"I'm not discussing her with you." His tone brooks no argument on the subject, but I won't let it go.

"There's an open investigation into Malik's background. If you have the slightest suspicion about her, you have to report it." I watch his face for a hint he's considered my concerns, but he's also a master of disguise.

"Why didn't you report it, then?" he snaps. "When you first saw her?"

"I did. I told the man in charge of Malik's care and well-being. *You.*"

The comment stills him. I don't think he's even breathing, but his face colors a touch. Chet stares back at me, and then he bends to grab his other sock and his shoes. He straightens and turns to the door, and my heart drops to the pit of my stomach. Clutching at the sheet, I hold it tighter to my chest.

I take a risk and softly say, "Chet, tell me three things." I need reassurance from him that we're okay, but his broad back says all I need to hear.

"I'll call you," he grumbles without a glance back and exits my bedroom with a sock still half on.

Those are not the three words I wanted to hear.

CHAPTER 26

INVESTIGATIVE AFFRONTS

[Chet]

Scotia can be the most frustrating woman. I hate to admit it, but the seed of doubt has been strongly planted against Hennessy. Her storyline isn't adding up for me. When I think about Malik and his silence, I hate to consider what Henny might be to him. Is he her child? Did he run away from her? If so, why? And why hasn't she mentioned it?

Even though I reported my inconclusive information to Deputy Boone, I decide to do a little sleuthing myself.

"Whatcha doing?" Todd asks me as I sit in the bar later that same morning. I decided against calling Cletus Winston for investigative assistance, instead giving in to the urge to search the internet on my own. People pry into my life, as Scotia admitted she'd done with the *Fortune 500* tribute. Henny is clearly aware of my current corporate status as well. But it doesn't make me comfortable to look into other's lives. Still, I need answers on Hennessy, and the internet seems like the first place to start although less than half of what's found might be true. I know I should call the authorities again, but I'm still spiraling a bit with my doubts and want to do this search on the off chance I'll find something to exonerate Henny immediately.

"I'm researching someone." There's no point in hiding what I'm doing from my best friend.

"Scotia Simmons," he teases, finding my new obsession with the Green Valley socialite rather interesting. I'm perplexed by my attraction myself until I consider how well our bodies move together. Scotia lets me do what I want with her, eager to experiment. The way I slide into her heat. The way she holds me in her depths. The way she doesn't want me to leave her body. Her responses to our experiences are unparalleled for me. A cold sweat breaks out on my body.

I also consider how vulnerable she is. The softness in her voice when she asked me to stay last night. The tenderness in her touch as she held my face and told me Chet was who she liked best—the man between two others who actually embodies all my parts. Her honesty when she's genuine and real.

Damn, that woman is under my skin.

"No, actually. I'm looking up Hennessy Miller."

"Why?" Todd groans. "I thought you weren't seeing her again."

"I'm not, but I ran into her last night at Genie's in Green Valley, and things aren't adding up. That kid Malik I told you about had a strange reaction to her, and I'm just curious . . ."

What exactly am I curious about?

I'm staring blankly at the screen before me as if it will provide immediate answers.

"Move," Todd demands, reaching across me for my laptop and taking a seat in the chair next to mine. With some quick work of his fingers, he reads what he finds.

"Hennessy Miller marries Nashville royalty Jeffrey Heiner."

"Information already known."

Todd keeps clicking away. "Two children. Timothy and Brandon." He's muttering as he reads something before he clicks hard on the keyboard.

His eyes drift over the laptop. "Her husband died." This confirms what I already know. "So did her children."

"What?" I shift on the seat, pulling the laptop to face both of us. Todd clicks a link to a news report.

"Prominent businessman and CEO of Miller Energy, Jeffrey Heiner, died in an automobile accident late Friday evening. Heading southbound on US 72 near Green Valley, Tennessee, Heiner collided with an oncoming semi tractor-trailer on the winding mountain highway under less than favorable conditions near eleven p.m. Icy roads and poor visibility caused the semitruck to lose control and crash into Heiner's SUV. Pronounced dead on the scene, Heiner's two sons, aged five and eight, were also present in the vehicle. One child died on the scene shortly after emergency assistance arrived while the second son was taken by helicopter to Knoxville, where he died two days later.

Heiner was the son-in-law of Arthur Miller, having taken over the CEO position when his wife's father died of a heart attack seven years ago. Under Heiner's rule, the company was rumored to be up for sale in a major takeover by Overseas Electric. Since its inception, Miller Energy's focus was the use of the Little Tennessee River for hydroelectricity. The Chinese buyers completed the transaction shortly after Heiner's death in a controversial buyout."

I stare at the video as it ends. An arrow spins, waiting on the next story to begin, but Todd hits pause.

"Her children," I whisper.

"Poor Henny," states Todd without knowing her.

My own company's headquarters wasn't far from her father's, hoping to encroach on his excessive property along the riverfront. I wanted to be neighbors so he could look out his window and see my building. I wanted Arthur Miller to glance across that river and know that I'd made something of myself. I never needed him to be proud of me. I wanted to rub it in his face that I was damn proud of myself.

"Want me to keep digging?"

I nod without speaking as my brain tosses around what I've learned.

Henny's children died.

Her children could not be at a cabin in the woods.

Henny didn't—couldn't, shouldn't—have any children with her.

Why would she lie to me?

239

"Pull up images. Maybe something will show a picture of the family."
Todd ignores my terse tone, and his fingers fly over the keyboard.

An image appears of Jeffrey Heiner, polished and trim with his beautiful wife beside him, blonde and perfected. Two children stand before them. Both blonde. Both blue-eyed. They look like Henny. Their formal attire suggests the family was at a fundraising function or business event.

Two boys aged five and eight. Timothy and Brandon.

Scotia saw Henny at the beauty salon with a child, though. A child who looked similar to Malik, and neither of these boys pictured with Henny look like him. *So whose child does she have?*

"Can you search the rentals in the area? Anything under Heiner or Miller? Anything . . ." I don't even know what I'm looking for. More lies perhaps, or am I grappling for some honesty? Had Henny moved back to the Knoxville area when her husband took over her father's company? She hadn't mentioned that. She said they lived in Nashville. She said her children were alive.

They'd be a year older if they lived. Six and nine.

My stomach pitches.

"And additional family," I mutter, thoughts spewing out as they come to me.

Todd types away for minutes without speaking and then fires off fact after fact.

"In-laws living in Florida. Both her parents are deceased." I never thought Henny's mother was a bad person, despite Arthur's disapproval of me. For a moment, I'm sorry that Henny has no one in her life, finding sympathy as I'd lost my only family in Harper and Davis. But I still have their three children.

"I'm not finding anything about a rental under Miller or Heiner, especially because many of them are managed by a management company and not listed by owner." Todd's brows crease, and I sense the search could take a while.

"Forget it, man," I mutter, my heart sinking as I know what I need to do. My suspicion runs deep. Even though I haven't seen her with kids, I can't dismiss the sickening feeling in my belly from the things Henny told me. And there's no doubt her children do not match Malik's appearance.

Maybe she isn't right in the head over the loss of her babies. Maybe she's still not processing what's happened to them. Maybe it's post-traumatic stress disorder.

As much as I want to reason with myself and diagnose excuses for Henny's behavior, I can't deny she was at the bar last night, telling more lies and ordering enough food for a small army, or at least, a small family.

Oh, Henny, what have you done?

I reach for my phone. I have another call I need to make.

* * *

When I call Maura to tell her what I've done and check on Malik, she tells me he's more withdrawn than ever. I hate to admit Scotia might be our secret weapon with him. It'd be so much easier if he spoke to us, explained what happened to him, and told us why he freaked out over seeing Hennessy in the bar last night.

I decide to head to Harper House later that afternoon and find Scotia and Maura discussing Malik.

"You can't allow him to be removed," Scotia interjects.

"We might not have a choice," Maura counters, and I pause inside the door of Maura's office where the two women are in a standoff with one another. I don't want the boy to go, either, but without answers, I'm nervous that his caginess might mean it's time for alternative placement. We can't have him around the other boys if he's a risk.

Maura tips her head at me in greeting, causing Scotia to turn and face me.

"Chet, tell me it isn't true? He can't be taken away from here without answers."

"That's how the system works. If he's any sort of threat to himself or the others, he needs to be in a place where there is more individualized attention like a home with no other children, not our group setting."

Scotia turns away from my clinical answer. "Is he a threat to the other boys?" she questions of Maura. "He'd never hurt anyone." Her statement is said with confidence, yet I don't think Scotia is qualified to assess him.

"We don't know for certain that he won't," I state, and Scotia rounds back to me.

"You can't say for certain he will," she defends.

"His erratic behavior might say otherwise." I huff. "Scotia, I keep telling—"

She stops me by holding up a hand. "It's not my concern," she mocks but continues. "If you thought he was a threat, why did he remain here in the first place? He's been here since July."

"The social services department asked us to keep him," Maura clarifies. I'm certain Scotia already knows this fact.

"So you did, and he's been fine, until . . ." Scotia glares at me, not mentioning she-who-shall-not-be-named.

"I'm handling it," I tell her.

"How?" Scotia snaps just as she did this morning in her bedroom.

"I'm having dinner with Henny." The statement falls in the room like a hammer on an anvil. After calling Deputy Boone, I called Hennessy, prepared to ask her out to dinner. It isn't that I didn't trust Boone to do his job, but I had my own plan. I had to do something as Scotia suggested. I'd hoped Henny would invite me to her cabin, and I'd see for myself if she had a child in her presence. A child that was not hers. I still can't wrap my head around the thought.

But Henny hadn't answered her phone, and I have to let the authorities handle things for the moment.

"You what?!" Scotia barks, snapping me out of my thoughts. She blinks at me, lids fluttering in disbelief.

"You need to trust me," I say in response, not ready to give her the details of my plan.

"Trust you? How can I trust you? One minute, you're fucking me, and the next, you're going out to dinner with that . . . that . . ."

Maura gasps behind Scotia, but I ignore her and instead focus on Scotia's rising temper and my growing anger.

"Don't hold back, Scotia. Give it to me," I taunt, wiggling my fingers at her.

"That potential kidnapper!" Her voice cracks. I flinch. The words are like a slap, even though they've been lingering in my head all day.

"We don't know that," I state, crossing my arms and glaring at Scotia.

"Why do you keep defending her?" Scotia questions. While her voice climbs an octave, her shoulders slump, but she isn't defeated. This woman has a lot of fight in her.

"Because she's had a difficult life." Her husband died. *Her children* are dead.

"We've all had difficult lives in some way," Scotia snaps, twisting a bit and stepping back when she remembers Maura's standing behind her. "Tell him." She tosses out a hand, hoping Maura will support her.

"When I mentioned dating, Hennessy was not who I had in mind," my friend states. "And this . . .," Maura says, pointing at Scotia, then me. "I did not see this coming."

"Yeah, well, neither did I," Scotia states, crossing her arms and tipping up her nose.

"Just what does that mean?" I question.

"What happened to opening up to each other?" Scotia asks, forgetting Maura again and dismissing my question.

"It doesn't mean we are accountable to each other for everything."

"Oh Chet," Maura mutters, shaking her head side to side.

"I see." Scotia's voice falters. The shutters slam shut on those silvery eyes, which are now dark steel. Her crossed arms hold her tight, and the invisible armor swings around her body.

"You're doing that thing, darlin'."

Scotia holds up her head. "You know, Mr. Chesterfield, you might think I'm a cold-hearted witch at times, but I do have feelings. That boy *is* my concern. I care about him just as I care about each and every other boy in this house. I want what's best for all of them, but right now, Malik especially, because he needs it the most. And there might be another child out there who needs help as well." Scotia means the child she saw with Henny.

"I—"

"It seems the only boy I was fool enough to care about in this home was you."

Silence falls around us, and Scotia steps forward, coming into my space.

"I willingly gave myself to you because I thought you saw me differently, but I can see now you don't. And while you're a good man at heart . . .for these boys, for your businesses, and for Hennessy Miller, you aren't good for me."

My head starts to shake, brimstone and flames brewing on my tongue, ready to lash back at her.

"I opened up to you, giving you my body and my heart, and it's not enough, is it? You'll always want her. But what you were searching for from that woman, you won't ever find. Not in her. Not even in me. The only person you need to prove something to is yourself, and all you've proven to me is I'm not worth anything to you but good sex. And even that is questionable."

What the . . .? "I told you, I'm handling it."

"I suppose sex is one way to get Henny to open up to you, too."

Scotia's mark is hit. "You're out of line."

"No, I'm out of *here*." Scotia turns to Maura. "I'll check back tomorrow about that thing we were discussing."

"What thing?" I interject, anger vibrating off my large body in waves strong enough to knock both women over.

"It's not your concern," Scotia sneers, turning back to me and tossing my own words in my face. She steps around me, careful to keep her distance, and disappears behind me. My eyes meet Maura's.

"What have you done?" Maura whispers.

"I didn't mean for you to hear all that," I mutter, lowering my head.

"You were blocking the exit, so I had no choice but to be a witness to that train wreck. And you have bigger issues than me hearing a few words." Her exasperated tone tells me she's disappointed in more than being forced to stand here during my argument with Scotia.

"I've made another grave mistake where a woman was concerned." My voice lowers, my head hangs. I'm not asking a question; I'm pointing out facts.

"With Hennessy Miller?"

"With Scotia Simmons."

Maura's eyes narrow, anger flaring in them. "That woman would do more good than harm to you."

"Don't you mean more harm than good?"

"No, I mean exactly what I said. You have a big heart, Chet, and you need a woman who matches it. Her convictions might be loud where yours are quiet, but you need her in your life."

"I don't need anyone," I quickly retort, realizing it isn't exactly true. I've needed Maura and the boys.

"Good luck going it on your own, then, Chet." Maura pats my chest as she storms around me the same way Scotia did.

I don't know what she means, and I don't get a chance to ask, leaving me as puzzled as I always am with women.

When I told Scotia I was having dinner with Henny, it wasn't completely true. Hennessy hadn't agreed to a date yet. She hadn't returned the call I'd made to her after I'd learned the information about her history. For some unexplained reason, I wanted to help her because she needed help. She needed to face her most recent past. I knew how dangerous it was to live there, and she had to move forward.

After Scotia stormed out of Harper House, and Maura put me in my place, I decided on something I swore I'd never do. I chased Scotia.

"Good luck going it alone," Maura had said. I'd been alone for so long I was comfortable by myself, but I didn't want to be. I'd like to think Scotia's reaction is just classic Scotia. She's salty off the cuff and vinegar in her venom. She'd shut down but perhaps that shield of armor was because she was hurt . . . by me.

"She would do more good than harm." I tried to see things from Scotia's perspective. She was looking out for Malik. And it would have stung me if she told me she was going out with another man, no matter what the reasoning. I needed her to trust me, but I hadn't been open enough with her. I hadn't shared my plan with her.

I didn't miss what she said this morning. *I want everyone to know we are together.* I want us together, too. I just need her to see that.

Hoping I can entice Scotia into letting me make dinner for her so we can talk, I'm in the Piggly Wiggly picking up steaks. I'm at the meat counter waiting on my order when I see Henny out of the corner of my eye.

"Hennessy?" I say, turning fully to face her. I don't miss the possessive motion of her arm sweeping around the shoulders of a little boy and tucking said child behind her. My eyes lower to him, but Henny quickly draws my attention.

"Chester. It's so great to see you." The strain in her voice tells me our surprise meeting is anything but pleasant. "I didn't realize you spent so much time in this valley." There's an unasked question, considering I told Henny when we met for drinks that I live in North Carolina. I hadn't mentioned The Fugitive for some reason, just that I had a place over the border and made the trek to Knoxville a few times a week. She only knows Chester Chesterfield, owner of Chesterfield Oil, the parent company for Stop-and-Pump, is headquartered across from her father's hydroelectric company. I was a poor man from the valley who wanted a mountain ridge home. I wanted her, once upon a time, no matter the cost.

I'm not that man anymore, though.

"Where should I be?" I tilt my head, eyes drifting to the boy she's keeping pressed to the back of her leg, shielding him as she speaks with me. I don't wait for an answer.

"Who's this?" I question instead, lowering to a squat, not missing how Henny draws him farther behind her, shielding him between her body and the meat counter at her back.

"This is my son, Timmy. He's terribly shy." I look up at her from my lowered position, searching her face for the lie. I'm on fragile ground here, like an unstable layer of ice on a lake before it cracks. I don't want to do anything to spook Henny. I certainly can't just reach for the child, so I need to stall. I need to see if she'll open up to me.

"And your other boy? Brandon was his name, correct? Where is he?" While I ask the question, I see the child at her legs struggle. I smile as gently as I can, considering the tension suddenly pressing at my chest. I pretend to play a sort of peekaboo with the boy by swinging my head from one side of Henny's hips to the other. Henny fights to keep the child hidden behind her each time he shifts. Her hands reach down and stop him from peeking around her thighs.

"He isn't with us this evening. He's at home."

"Alone?" My head pops up as I slowly lift my body, meeting Henny in the eye. "He's a little young to be left alone. Eight, you said?" I pause, waiting for confirmation.

"He's nine now." Her terse answer is spoken through clenched teeth.

"Hen, I—"

"Well, my, my, isn't this cozy?" The saccharine-sweet but completely false tenor of Scotia's voice interrupts me. I close my eyes, wishing this moment wasn't happening, but it is. I'm this close to getting Henny to speak to me. I know her lie, and she's in grave danger if she doesn't come clean. I don't need Scotia to ruin things.

However, Scotia brings herself close to my side, stopping just inches from touching me. She looks from Henny to me and back to Henny. Scotia's lips curl deeper, her cheeks lifting higher on her face as she mockingly stares at my former love.

"Family outing?" Scotia asks bitterly, and I hate that she's slipping into that mode where she's ready to insult. I have to remind myself she's not interpreting this situation correctly, and she's jumping to a conclusion I can't rectify at the moment.

"Yes," I state, stepping closer to Henny, placing my back to the meat counter. "Scotia, you remember Henny from the other evening? We planned to have drinks together, but instead, she's invited me to her place to meet her boys." I gaze down at the child.

"And you decided to go grocery shopping together? Isn't that precious?" Scotia looks from the child to me, her expression hardening. An almost visible film of protection covers her face as she reaches for a string of pearls at her throat.

"I'll be meeting her other son," I say, hoping Scotia understands my meaning. Deep down, I'm hoping not to find another child at Henny's home. I'm suddenly only concerned about the one before me. It's evident this boy isn't hers. He looks nothing like her, and from what I remember of Jeffrey, the child doesn't match him either. Not to mention the cold truth I discovered online—her children are dead.

"Actually, tonight isn't a good night," Henny interjects. "My son is sick," she says to Scotia, a detail she hadn't mentioned to me. "And it probably wouldn't be a good idea to bring a stranger into the house to meet him."

"I'm not a stranger, Hen." I turn on her, placing a hand on her shoulder in what I hope is a comforting manner. It's obvious she's in trouble, and I'm willing to help her, but the only way I can do that is to get closer. For the sake of the child at her legs, I don't want to tip her off. "Let me come meet the boy. We can purchase soup for him."

Henny peers up at me, eyes narrowing a bit. "Another night." Her teeth clench again as she speaks. "I should really get going. We've been gone too long." Turning for her cart, she puts her hands on the child's shoulders and guides him between the cart and her body. Pressing him forward, she awkwardly steers him down the aisle tucked protectively in front of her body. He tries to take one last look around her hip, but Henny's hand cups his face, forcing his eyes forward.

"Well, this was certainly—"

I hold up a hand to stop Scotia. "You need to trust me, darlin'." Without losing sight of Henny, I follow her retreat, keeping a short distance between us. Only, the tap-tap of heels follows me.

"I think we need to talk," Scotia says, keeping her voice low but loud enough that I hear her irritation. "Now."

"Scotia," I grit, trying to keep calm and my attention on Henny as I pick up the pace, hoping not to appear obvious. "Trust me."

"If you want that brassy-haired hussy, I'm not going to stop you," she says, chasing after me, her heels continuing to make a racket as she struggles with my longer stride. "But I can't keep sleeping with you if you're sleeping with someone else."

Her voice rises enough that both the checkout counter clerk and Henny turn in our direction. I can't have this kind of conversation with Scotia in the Piggly Wiggly, let alone when I'm in pursuit of a woman I don't want to believe may have committed a crime, when everything inside me tells me she did.

Turning on Scotia, I pin her against to the shelves with my big body, lifting my arm above her head and covering her mouth with my hand.

"Would you shush?" I hiss. "You need to trust me, darlin'. Please."

With widened eyes and raised brows, Scotia mutters something under my palm. We stare at one another for a long minute until I hear the swoosh of the store door open. Slowly, I release my hand.

"Don't speak," I snap, and for the first time probably ever, Scotia obeys.

CHAPTER 27

CLEANUP IN AISLE FIVE

[Scotia]

He did not just shush me!

That was my first thought, but the urgency in his plea warranted no argument from me. However, he almost pulls my arm out of the socket when he grabs my hand and drags me forward. I'm stumbling in my heels, click-clacking behind him, making a racket on the tile floor. As we near the end of the aisle, I see Henny has left the building, and Sarah Stokes, the nighttime cashier, stares at me. Her face is a mixture of concern and question.

"He's my boyfriend," I blurt, without thinking of any other explanation for a man tugging me out of the Piggly Wiggly. Chet snorts as we round the checkout station.

"You Winters Sisters have all the luck in here," she mutters loud enough I hear her. I have no idea what she means. "Where'd you find him?" she questions as we pass the counter and near the front door. I twist in Chet's hold, walking backward only a foot before I answer.

"In the meat department."

Sara just shakes her head before turning her attention toward the back of the store.

"My car is over there," I say to Chet, who still hasn't spoken, but he ignores me, pulling us quickly to his truck. He opens the passenger door, grabs my hips, and lifts me into the seat.

"Well," I huff with his haste.

"Buckle up," he warns as he slams the door in my face. I do as he asks while he jogs around the front of the truck and hops in. He presses the ignition and jolts us into reverse.

"You have some explaining to do, mister," I growl at him as his attention focuses on the taillights of a sporty car exiting the parking lot.

Chet speeds up and presses the wireless headset service on the truck.

"Officer Boone," the deep tenor of a masculine voice fills the cab.

"Boone, Chet here. I'm in pursuit of that possible lead I told you about in Malik's case. I just saw her at the Piggly Wiggly with a little boy, claiming he was her son. I already explained to you how he can't be, though."

My head swivels, and I stare at him as his focus remains out the front window.

"Chet, you're not an officer of the law, and this isn't the *Dukes of Hazard*. We can't have you frightening a suspect by chasing her."

What the heck?

"I'm heading east out of the Piggly Wiggly parking lot. I didn't think it would be sensible to grab the kid, but it's definitely not her child."

Not her child. The words echo in my head.

"It's not sensible to be following her either," the rough male voice iterates. "We haven't gotten a location on her yet,"

"That's why I'm following her." Chet's voice is full of frustration, and I'm slow to realize what we are doing. We—collectively—are chasing after Hennessy Miller. Does this mean . . . he believes me? Is he suspicious of that woman?

"I'm not letting her go," Chet says into the phone as he returns his eyes to the road. "She's turning onto Green Valley Road."

"Don't do this, Chet. I'm sending someone now."

"I'll keep you posted." Chet ends the call before Boone can respond.

"Does this mean you believe me?" I finally get to ask my question.

"Her husband died. She had two children. Two boys." His expression falls from edgy concentration to sympathy. "They both died with their dad in a car accident."

"Oh, Chet." My hand covers my mouth as I turn back to the road ahead as though I'll see said accident before me. I don't like the woman, but I don't wish her enough ill-will that she'd lose her family in such a horrific manner.

"So the boy with her—" Chet begins.

"Isn't hers," I finish for him.

"But she told me he was her son, and she was just explaining to me how her other son was at the cabin she rented." He pauses, allowing me to make my own conclusions, which clearly caused trouble a few minutes ago in the grocery store.

"And I interrupted your plan," I quietly state. I misread the situation. *Think before you react*, Gideon once said to me. "Do you think she was going to tell you the truth?"

Chet's face hardens, and his hand tightens on the steering wheel. "I don't think the truth exists for Henny. I think she intended to keep up the ruse, but I intended to find out why she lied to me."

My heart breaks a little for this man who can't see the woman he once loved still is and always will be who she was—conniving, manipulative, a user of others.

Some people change. Some people don't.

I do not want to be considered like her.

"And you were right. The boy looks exactly like Malik."

"I know, right?" I say, a bit too enthusiastic over the comparison. Then I consider that Malik and his potential brother might be separated, and somehow, Hennessy has committed a crime against them.

"Go ahead. Gloat. Tell me I told you so," Chet mocks.

"I wasn't going to say that."

"But you want to, don't you?"

Well. "No. No, I do not want to say that. I want us to find her and save that boy. I want him returned to his brother." Poor Malik. My precious boy.

"Do you think she hurt him?" I whisper as horrible thoughts fill my head. I'm afraid to ask, but also afraid of Chet's reaction. He doesn't want to see the potential for malice in this woman although he's speaking words of doubt and anger.

"Let's not go there quite yet." He swallows after he speaks, his mind going to a similar place.

"We cannot lose her, Chet," I state, staring out the windshield at the taillights ahead of us. Chet is keeping a healthy distance. As the road curves and wraps, there's a ditch on either side of us. Caution on these switchbacks is a must, which means there's no place for Henny to escape us and hide.

"I'm not losing her." The conviction with which he makes the statement turns my stomach a bit. I hope he means we won't lose her because she's a criminal, not that he doesn't want to lose her because of his heart.

"Why didn't you say anything?"

"I had a plan," he says, and I recall our fight earlier in the day. *He was handling it. Henny was not my concern.*

"She's turning," he says, interrupting my thoughts, and we slow as she does. She's pulling up to a gate, and Chet breezes past the drive. I twist in my seat, turning back to watch if she retreats or enters the community. There's only one along this road with a series of houses, both privately owned and open for renters.

"She went in," I say, and Chet hisses beside me. He brakes hard, and I hold my breath, hoping we don't tumble into the ditches, as he does a skilled three-point turn. When he's pointed back in the direction of the gate, he drives closer to it before cutting the lights. He keeps the engine running and hits the call button on his wireless phone again.

"Boone," the officer growls into the phone.

"She pulled into a gated community off Green Valley Road."

"I know where that is. We're on it. Chet, stay put."

"Not going anywhere," he says.

"That's what I'm afraid of," Boone mutters and disconnects the call.

We sit in silence for a second. I don't know what to say to him and keep my hands folded in my lap.

"So I'm your boyfriend, huh?" His voice teases while still tense.

"I didn't know how else to explain a madman dragging me out of the Piggly Wiggly."

Chet softly chuckles, rubbing his hand over his mouth and down his throat. The scratchy sound of his beard fills the cab while he stares out the windshield, not giving up sight on that gate.

"What were you doing in the Piggly Wiggly anyway?" He'd been at my home this morning and Harper House this afternoon. The man certainly travels around.

He shifts in his seat, dangling his wrist over the steering wheel and turning toward me.

"I was there buying steaks for you. For us."

My brows pinch as I stare at him in the dark truck.

"I was hoping to come over and surprise you by making dinner. Thought we could talk."

"You wanted to make me dinner?" My voice lowers. That's so . . . *sweet.* "What did you want to talk about?" I swallow after the question as my mind races with all kinds of thoughts. *Maybe he doesn't want to be my boyfriend. I mean, he is a man. Then again, he said he wanted to make me dinner. That's kind of like a date. So, it can't be that he doesn't want to see me again.* I'm all over the place.

Chet sighs, and I turn my head, staring back out the front window. Now isn't the time to talk, I surmise. We're in hot pursuit of a kidnapper.

"This is not how I wanted to do this," Chet mutters. "But here it is . . ."

I crane my neck back to him, holding my breath.

"I like you, Scotia. A lot. And I hate fighting with you. I've felt sick all day about how things went this morning. I just want one night and one morning that we get through without something coming between us."

"Nothing's between us," I whisper.

"Earlier, you said the sex between us wasn't good."

"I did not say that!" I practically shriek. That is a bald-faced lie if there ever was one. "I said I wasn't good enough for you."

"Here's the thing, darlin'. You're too good for me, and I'm racking my brain every day, wondering when you're going to wise up and leave me. Why are you hanging out with me, having sex with me, chasing me over this mountain and spending nights in my bus with me?"

"Because I like you," I state, startled by all the questions he has. "You're good for me."

"Earlier you said I wasn't."

"I was . . . reactive." I swallow as I think back on what I said and how I didn't mean it. "I can be like that." I'm shocked he hasn't left me considering how often he's mentioned my shortcomings.

"How am I good for you, then?" he questions as if he's truly puzzled by my interest.

"You listen to me. You let me speak. You call me out when I've been wrong but support me when I'm right."

Chet stares at me, his mouth slightly agape.

"I've never had that," I say, lowering my voice. "And I think sex with you is out-of-this-world amazing."

His mouth snaps shut, and he huffs. His thick hand swipes down his face as he turns to glance out the windshield and then quickly looks back at me.

"Do you have any idea how much I want you naked and straddling me right now?"

It's my turn for my mouth to fall open. "We're in the midst of pursuing a kidnapper, and you want to have sex with me?" I choke.

"I always want to have sex with you, darlin'."

"You do?" My voice squeaks.

"Like I said this morning, as long as we come back together after disagreeing, I'm here for you." He pauses, staring at me. "Get over here, darlin', and just kiss me for now."

I unbuckle my seat belt so fast it clangs against the passenger door. I scoot over to where his arm is outstretched, ready to draw me in. My arms circle his neck, and our mouths crash together. His beard scratches my chin, and his mustache tickles, and I savor every second of kissing this man. We aren't soft. This kiss is hard, full of frustration over fighting and fear over losing one another. It's hunger for more of this, and more openness, and more time together.

But a siren is heard off in the distance, and blue and red lights flare in the night. I pull back from Chet but not without one long look into those soulful eyes—the same eyes that drew me to him on that first night. He saw me differently, just as I thought he might, and I see him for who he is.

A man with a gigantic heart.

CHAPTER 28

PURSUING IS HOT

[Scotia]

"Hang on," Chet says. Reaching over me, he hands me the middle seat belt buckle, keeping me next to him in the truck. Even though I'm quickly secure, his arm crosses over my chest as he guns the accelerator, and the truck practically hops on the road. Chet wastes no time following the two sheriff cars that have access to the gate.

"How will we know which one is hers?" I ask, but too soon, the cars before us slow. One pulls into a deeply sloped drive while the other blocks the end of it.

"This is it," Chet says, putting the truck in park and shutting off the engine. "Stay here."

He pops open the driver's door, but I'm unbuckling my seat belt.

"Darlin', please." He pauses once he slips free of the driver's side and turns back to me. "I don't know what's going to happen in there, and I don't want you hurt."

"I can take care of myself," I tell him, toughening my voice.

"I know you can, darlin'. But do this for me? I can't be worrying about you while I'm trying to save the kid."

"Okay." I easily acquiesce when he puts it like that. He'll worry about me, and he needs to save the child. I give him a weak smile, promising to stay still as he leans in for a too-quick kiss and then closes the door. He clicks the locks as though he'll be keeping me in, and I give him my best smile as he rounds the truck.

Because there's no way I'm staying put.

I watch him head down the drive and speak to an officer. It looks like an argument, but I can't hear the men from inside my gilded cage.

"Scotia Simmons will not be contained," I mutter aloud, waiting out Chet's actions. He follows an officer, and then I see the front door of the cabin open. It's hard to make out the structure from here. There are only two lights on—one glowing through the front room, beaming out onto the covered porch, and a single light coming through a window near the back of the home.

I watch as a woman throws herself at Chet and he presses her into the home, holding her at his chest.

"Oh, no. Not on my watch," I snap, scooting back to the passenger door and fiddling with the lock. Since it's automatic, it takes me a second to realize he locked me in from the driver's side, and then I unlatch myself from that side of the truck. As quiet as I can, I close the door.

My shoes crunch on the gravel drive, and I worry about the damage the small pebbles are doing to my heels.

"These are my Jimmy Choo Lavish Pumps," I grumble to myself, imagining the wear on the soft leather, but I continue to walk the drive. The November night is cold and crisp. The stars fill the sky, and it would be beautiful if my heart wasn't racing with anxiety.

Where is the boy? I wonder as I walk.

The driveway runs the length of the cabin. I can't see inside the living room where the windows face forward, but from the dining room window on the side, I see Chet's head as he sits on a couch, and Henny presses into his side.

Red isn't the color I see. It's maroon and purple and black, and I want to scream, but a thumping noise to my side distracts me. I continue the length of the house to the soft glow coming from a back window. It's a door, leading off a kitchen. Feet from this exit is a shed with its back to the drive.

More thumping ensues, echoing in the silent night.

The noise could be a raccoon, a skunk, or worse, a bear, but my gut tells me otherwise.

I pause, listening for the sound another second. The night falls quiet. The summer insects are long gone and sleeping. An owl hoots off in the distance, and I tip my head back to look up at the sky once more.

"Give me strength," I say to the moon. If my sister's goddess exists, I'll need her guidance as well.

The aggressive rattling begins again.

I stare at the corner of the shed. A decorative path leads around the side, and without thought, I follow the large, flat stones. The door happens to be opposite the drive. It's dark, spooky, and impossible to ignore the hammering against the wood and the muffled sound coming from within the shed.

Pound-pound-pound and *umph-umph-umph* form a rhythm.

"Hello?" My voice squeaks at first, and I swallow before forcing it louder. "Hello?"

The thumping sound stops, and I hold my breath. My heart races, filling my ears with the rush of my own blood.

"Scotia, you are imagining things," I tell myself aloud and turn away from the shed. Something cracks under my foot, and I nearly come out of my skin. I stifle the scream, covering my mouth. I bend to see what I might have stepped on, and the thumping pounds begins again, more frantic, more insistent.

The muffled mutters grow louder.

Without a second doubt, I turn back, holding my hand along the side of the shed as a guide.

"Hello. Can you hear me?" I'm not certain why I ask such a thing, but the rattling grows louder as I near the opposite corner of the structure. I round the edge and see the door rapidly jiggling back and forth. Quickly stepping forward, I find a lock on the closure holding it in place. My hands cup the cold metal as I speak to the door.

"Who's in there?"

The door moves, rustling on its hinges but unable to open completely because of the lock.

"It's locked. I can't help you."

I yank at the metal, willing it to pop open. *Why does this always look so easy in the movies?* I'm not a sleuth. I don't have a hairpin to pick it, and I wouldn't know how to do that anyway.

I tug and tug until I realize it's only hooked through the latch but not clasped in place.

Thank you, Moon Goddess. I'll never doubt Naomi again.

With shaky fingers, I hurriedly slip the hook from the eye, and the door swings outward. I step back, and something small falls at my feet, cowering. Tiny hands cover the back of a head, and I realize it's a child whimpering.

Sweet baby Jesus.

"It's okay, my darling. I'm not here to hurt you. I'm here with the sheriff. We're here to help you." I bend at the waist, hesitantly reaching for his back. His body is small. His clothing thin.

The small form moves and dark eyes I can hardly see look up at me. He's dressed in only a T-shirt and shorts despite the November temperature, and I squat to help him stand. My hand cups his elbow reassuringly.

"Come here, my darling," I whisper, and he slowly rises, keeping his face turned to mine. Once he's reached his full height, he's eye level with me in my crouched position. I remove my jacket and wrap it around him.

"Are you cold? Are you hurt?"

He stares at me.

"Do you know someone named Malik?"

His eyes dip to the pearl necklace at my throat.

"I know where he is, and he's safe. He misses you." I sound as if I'm luring him into more treachery, but I don't know how else to encourage his trust in me other than to continue speaking about the other boy.

"Is Malik your brother?"

The child's eyes open even wider. "I'm not allowed to talk about him."

I almost burst into tears, and my eyes prickle with them, but I need to stay strong for this little man.

"That's okay, my boy. He misses you. You don't have to tell me more. I'm a stranger, right? We shouldn't talk to them. We shouldn't trust them, but in this case, I hope you believe me. I know Malik, who loves *Artemis Fowl*, Pokémon, and Legos. He wants to see you, and the deputy is here to take you to him."

His eyes remain on the pearl necklace at my collar, and I notice his bare feet. They must be freezing on the uneven rocks. With my too-large coat wrapped around him like a blanket, it's not enough for his small toes.

"I'm going to carry you, okay? I don't want you to cut your feet on these cold, rough stones," I tell him, worrying for only half a second that he'll try to run from me. My tone remains calm, soothing even, as if I'm speaking to a frightened child, which is exactly who stands before me.

"Do you want to hold my necklace? Would that help?"

He doesn't speak but curls his little fist over the pearls at my neck.

"It's time to go home, baby," I tell him, reassuring him as I pick him up, and he wraps his arms and legs around me. We walk like this—me stumbling in my heels, and his frail body clutching mine—until we near the house. I turn toward the porch, and the boy tightens his grasp.

"It's okay, darling boy. The sheriff is inside. He's here to take you to Malik." My eyes well again at the thought. After stepping onto the low porch, I reach for the screen door, swinging it open, and catching it with my hip. I push the front door to open it, and several officers shift their positions as I enter. One even lowers his hand to his gun holster.

My eyes latch on to the woman pressing her head into Chet's chest as they sit on the couch. Her cheek rests near his heart while a hand rests on his body. Her eyes catch mine.

"My, what a fun game of hide-and-seek you had going on. This child was locked in the shed at the end of your drive."

"What are you doing, holding my child?" Henny growls out, pushing off Chet and standing. She sounds like a feral animal, a mother lion unleashed, but this isn't her child. As she steps forward, Chet now standing behind her, catches her around the waist. A deputy steps toward me, and I lower the boy on my hip to his feet and then squat next to him.

Our eyes meet, and it's as if Malik is staring back at me. "Your name isn't Timmy, is it?"

The child toys with the pearl necklace at my collar again.

"It's okay, darling," I say.

At the same time, Henny yells at the child, "I told you to stay in your room."

"Is his room the shed?" I snap back at the woman struggling in Chet's arms. Deputy Boone clears his throat.

"Get the child out of here," he barks at the second officer. He gestures toward me. "Her too."

Then he turns on Henny. "Mrs. Heiner, would you like to start over with your story?"

Henny lets out a horrific scream, and I instinctively pull the child into me. An officer approaches us, but I'm not handing over the boy.

"I'll go with you," I say to the second officer and turn back for one more glance at a broken woman. My eyes find Chet, but his are dazed while he struggles with the woman in his arms. His face is etched in pain and confusion. He wants to know how he could have misread her all those years ago.

"She didn't deserve those children," Henny whisper-groans, and my heart drops at the start of her confession. I don't hear the rest as I carry the child in my arms out to the sheriff's car.

CHAPTER 29

DANCE PARTIES HAVE SOUL

[Chet]

I watch as Scotia disappears out the front door with a miniature Malik in her arms, the boy clutching at her pearl necklace. I'd give anything to follow her, but in my arms is a broken woman, crumpling to pieces.

"Mrs. Heiner, would you like to start over?" Boone asks her, and Henny falls into body-shuddering sobs. She's lost so much. Her husband. Her children. Her father's company. But it isn't going to change my heart. She was an entitled child looking for wealth and prestige, and she has had no boundaries as an adult.

My eyes stay trained on the door. Another officer takes over holding Henny, cuffing her as her Miranda rights are read, but I don't hear them. I'm released to exit the cabin. The car with Scotia and the child has already left the premises.

I need to call Maura and the caseworker, Veronica Mason, but I want to know how Scotia found the child.

And for once, I might be glad Scotia didn't listen to me.

That damn woman, I softly chuckle to myself, surprised to accept that her meddling helped in this situation.

I wait until Henny is escorted to the second vehicle, and then I climb into my truck and blindly follow the sheriff's car to the department. By the time I get there, Veronica Mason is present, and Scotia has been sent home. Maura appears shortly after I arrive at the station.

"Scotia offered to go to the house and sit with the boys," Maura tells me, and I nod, accepting it's going to be a long night.

* * *

Hours later, we return to Harper House with a sleepy boy in summer pjs and a blanket wrapped around him. Until we can further identify him, Veronica Mason, his new caseworker, has asked Maura to keep the boy overnight, especially given he's told us Malik is his older brother. Omari Evans is six years old, according to him, and his brother is nine. Veronica doesn't press for more details about his life as he's young, and a specialized investigator needs to be present to properly question him. That person can't get to us until tomorrow. Until then, we've been sent off with strict instructions not to ask him about his experience. We don't want to accidentally influence his answers. Veronica is the final car in our caravan back to the house where Scotia has been waiting with the sleeping boys.

Only when we arrive, well into the wee hours of the morning, the house is lit like a beacon in the dark. I pick up a sleeping Omari from Veronica's back seat. As we near the house, music hits our ears, and we open the front door to thumping bass and someone calling out movements. As I enter the great room, I find the boys in various states of nightwear from sweats and T-shirts to dinosaur pajamas, and in the middle of the group is a barefoot Scotia in her slim skirt, blouse untucked, hair up, doing the Macarena.

I watch for a full minute as she moves her arms in a complicated series of motions before jumping to her side, and the boys follow along with the music. Veronica stands beside me equally flabbergasted by the scene before us, but Maura walks to the couch, retrieves a remote, and mutes the music.

A chorus of confusion echoes in the room as the boys look around and notice the three adults at the edge of the room.

"Oh," Scotia says, slightly out of breath. She swipes at a loose lock near her face, and she's never looked so beautiful to me. *Is that a K'Nex piece holding up the rest of her hair?* I want to rush her, tug her into my arms and kiss the daylights out of her in front of everyone. Instead, I take a deep breath, taking in the flushed faces of the boys all frozen in various forms of chagrin and concern when only moments ago, they were laughing and calling out the directions of the song.

"What's going on here?" Maura interjects, eyeing each boy as they slowly lower their heads. Scotia looks just as guilty but straightens hers.

"We were dancing."

"I can see that," Maura retorts. "But do you have any idea what time it is?"

"It's party time," Louie deadpans, and Hunter chuckles beside him. Hugh grabs the back of his little brother's neck like I've done to him a hundred times, and Louie winces.

"Technically, we were not having a party," Dewey clarifies. "It was a dance."

Scotia bites her lip, and the urge to kiss her returns.

"Mrs. Pickle started it," Hunter tattletales.

"I did no such thing," she chuffs, and Hugh shakes his head as though he's exasperated. They might have already had this discussion.

"Technically, Dewey started it," Campbell clarifies. "He challenged Mrs. Pickle to the Cha Cha Slide."

"It's a part of the dance lessons in physical education," Dewey explains.

"Why aren't they teaching you how to play basketball?" I question, my face scrunching.

"Because of the new common core. Actually, Physical Education isn't one of the core classes regulated by the state standards, but it's required we learn a variety of kinetic outlets, dance being one of them."

"What happened to square dancing?" I ask, still stumped that the boys are learning something like the Cha Cha Slide in school.

"How do squares dance?" Hunter asks, and then he yawns.

"Never mind. You hooligans need to be in bed," Maura directs, waving her arm as if sweeping the gaggle up the stairs.

The only one who doesn't move or speak is Malik. Tears pour down his face as he stares at the sleeping form in my arms.

"Chet," Scotia says, her voice quiet, and I step forward. None of the boys move much other than to give Malik some space as he remains next to Scotia.

"Hey, little man. Do you know this guy?" I squat, slipping Omari's sleepy body between my bent knees.

"Malik!" the little boy shrieks, squirming to get out of my arms until I set him free to run to his brother. Malik pulls him into a tight hug, swiping at his own face repeatedly, but the tears don't stop. I glance up to find Scotia struggling just as much. Her hand lifts to the back of Malik's head and she pulls him to her while he still embraces his brother.

"I told you he was a good man," she repeats over and over, swiping her fingers through his hair. She bends over him to kiss his head.

I slowly right myself to standing.

Veronica steps forward and addresses Malik. "I take it you recognize this boy." Her voice is calm and controlled. Malik nods, his head still lowered toward his younger brother, who hasn't let go of him. Hugh claps a hand on Malik's shoulder, and Louie steps forward to pat the back of the younger brother. Campbell squeezes in to hug the siblings, and then Dewey opens his arms around the collection as best he can. Only Hunter stands to the side, staring at the group of them.

"Why is everyone crying?" he asks, and Scotia starts to chuckle, swiping at her cheeks.

"Because we're so happy," she says, looking at him with the grace of a mother, and I realize at that moment, I'm in love with her. I love Scotia Simmons. For all her harsh words and strong opinions, Scotia has a huge heart, and she's taken to loving the most important part of my life—these boys.

The thought hits me hard, and I rub at my chest. The urge to step up to the group and just kiss her senseless returns, but I hold back, vibrating with the need to touch her skin. She anchors me, and until this moment, I didn't realize how untethered I've been.

"Y'all are strange. You laugh when you're happy, not cry. And I still want to know how squares dance." This causes Scotia to actually laugh a little bit more, and I love the sound. I want this entire room to reverberate with it. For a second, I have a vision of Scotia standing in this room every day, just as she is—shirt untucked, hair pinned up with a construction toy, laughing as she loves these boys.

Maura walks over to the hugging heap.

"Alright, all my fine gentlemen, time for bed. Malik, we'll put Omari with you." The boys slowly break apart, and Maura leads the crew toward the front hallway.

"I should help her," I state, and Scotia nods.

"I'll be going," Veronica Mason says when neither Scotia nor I move from looking at one another.

"Thank you," I finally say, pulling my attention back to the caseworker for a second. She holds out her hand to shake.

"I'll see you in a few hours." She softly chuckles, as morning is growing closer. "And I'll see myself out." As Scotia and I haven't really moved, Veronica offers one final smile and exits.

"I'm sorry. I didn't realize how late it was," Scotia says as soon as Veronica leaves the room.

I wave a hand to dismiss her. "Looked like fun, darlin'."

Slowly, she smiles. "It was fun. Dewey woke up and started questioning me, and the discussion was only meant to be a distraction. I guess things got out of hand a bit." Her face still glows from the tears she shed, and her makeup is smeared a bit from it. With her hair up and her feet bare, she looks casual and comfortable standing in this big room with all the lights on and the paused music video on the television over the fireplace.

"How are you?" she asks, and the current situation slams into me. Henny at the sheriff's department. Omari and Malik reunited. Two small boys still without their family.

"We'll know more in the morning, I suspect. A social worker will come to further assess Omari and Malik, and then the sheriff's department will want to speak with them. It's all a process until we can find out where they are from and then find their parents."

I take a deep breath, stepping closer to her. "Darlin', just what the hell

269

were you thinking?" I ask, trying to keep my voice even but recalling her wandering around Henny's cabin and finding that boy.

"I was just trying to help."

"How did you know he was out there?" I've been wondering this all night.

"I didn't. I just heard a noise when I left the truck."

"The truck I told you to stay in," I admonish, but my tone has no bite.

She shrugs. "I have difficulty being told what to do." She smiles, but I'm still wound up at the thought of her wandering around Henny's place.

"What if something had happened to you?" I brush back the hair near her face, curling it over her ear. Her eyes widen, focusing on mine.

"I hadn't really thought about it."

"Well, I have," I admit, taking another deep breath because if something had happened to her, I'd never forgive myself, and I'm not certain how I'd live without this woman in my life. I lower my forehead to hers, and her hand cups my cheek, fingernails softly scratching my beard.

"But how are *you*?"

I blow out a breath, pulling back to look at her. "I'm exhausted," I admit, feeling emotionally drained, A crash after the adrenaline rush of the last few hours settles in. I exhale once more before admitting, "I need you."

"Anything," she whispers, and I reach for the white strip of her hair, curling the strands around my thick finger.

"Stay with me tonight. Stay here with us."

"Would that be appropriate?" she questions, looking off toward the entry and the staircase leading up.

"Nothing we do is appropriate, darlin', yet I can't think of anyone I want to be more inappropriate with than you."

She softly chuckles. "I look a mess," she says, reaching up for the toy in her hair.

"You look beautiful, darlin'. You look like you belong here," I add, letting emotions ripple out of me in my exhaustion. My finger releases her white hair and starts the process over again.

"Should we help Maura put the boys to bed?" she questions.

"Probably," I mutter but don't move to lead her upstairs. Instead, I whisper, "Put *me* to bed, darlin'."

"Where?"

I slip my hand down to hers and lead her through the dining room, across the kitchen, and into a room kept for me. It isn't large or flashy— just a bed with a nightstand and a small lamp. I don't need anything else in here, but I need this woman.

"This isn't just sex," I say to her, reaching for her blouse and fumbling with the tiny buttons in my thick fingers.

"Okay," she replies, watching me undo her shirt.

"I need you in my bed. Not just occasionally, but all the time, Scotia. Do you understand what I'm saying, darlin'?"

She looks up at me with those silvery eyes. "You want us to be together?"

"On the regular," I clarify. "Dates. Dinner. Sleepovers. Preferably nightly."

Scotia softly laughs as I brush back her shirt, revealing a pretty peach-colored bra. My woman loves pretty things. "I *really* like you like this," she says.

"I *really* like you," I say and then lower my mouth to hers, tired of talking and thinking and other *-ing* thing. The only thing I want is to be with this woman.

CHAPTER 30

PILLOW TALK

[Scotia]

After spending the night at Harper House, I woke early, leaving a sleeping Chet in his bed to have a long talk with Maura. I'd already planted a seed with her a few weeks back, and finding Omari solidified my plan. The boys were going to be moved to an alternative placement until a family member could be contacted, and emotional evaluations given. It broke my heart to learn they were leaving Harper House, but the house was only licensed for six, and Omari made number seven. No one wanted to separate the brothers now that they'd found each other again, so they left together. However, I was confident I'd see them soon.

Within two days, the *Green Valley Ledger* highlighted the news of a woman found in the valley who kidnapped two boys. Their identities will remain protected until they are reunited with their family. *If there is family,* I consider. Hennessy Miller's life was splashed across the pages, along with the sad history of her husband and sons perishing in the automobile accident near the valley. The article explains how she will be charged with two counts of child abduction, again without mentioning the boys' names, but it did include their ages—nine and six.

I climb the stairs to my room and slip out of my clothes after the second day of restlessness. I've had trouble concentrating on work and spent hours on the phone. I pull on a favorite nightie and slide into my bed. I miss Chet, but he's had so much on his mind as well. He's working with authorities to figure out how Malik and Omari were abducted. He's leaving the emotional welfare of the boys up to Maura and Veronica, and it's just as well because I don't want him to know my plans until they are solidified.

I quickly drift off to sleep but toss and turn, restless and anxious for some reason. I've never felt so out of control. Malik and Omari. Chet. Harper House.

At some point, I wake with a start, sensing the presence of someone in the room.

"Karl?" I call out although it's a silly reaction. Not only has he been dead all these years, but I've also never felt haunted by him.

"How is it you're always calling out his name in my presence, darlin'?"

I shift at the too-familiar male voice and glance toward the door. A large, able-bodied man stands inside the frame, leaning casually against the jamb with his arms and ankles crossed. I smile in spite of myself.

"How did you get in here?" I ask, thinking I'm dreaming the beautiful, solid man taking up space in my bedroom doorframe.

"Picked the lock," he teases.

"Do I even want to know?" I chuckle, turning completely on the bed to face him.

"My past isn't roses, darlin'," he says, his voice turning serious. He's told me about Davis and Harper, his foster home upbringings, and Hennessy Miller and the heartbreak of loving her. There can't be too much else to shock me.

"You're a good man, Mr. Chesterfield," I say, tucking my hands under my cheek as I stare at the outline of him.

"What about the other guys?" he questions.

"I think Chet has a heart of gold, and Big Poppy . . ." I shrug. "He has a nice tiny house."

Chet hangs his head and laughs. I reach out a hand, dangling my arm off the bed.

"How come you're so far away?" I ask, keeping my voice low. He presses off the jamb with the question and crosses to the edge of the bed. I roll to my back, keeping my eyes on him as he kicks off his shoes and untucks his shirt. He pulls it over his head by the back of the collar, and I hold my breath when I see the expanse of hair and the breadth of his pecs. He's such a beautiful man. Solid in every way. Physique and heart.

He crawls over me but tumbles onto his back next to me, and I rotate to face him. He has something on his mind, and I wait for him to speak.

"Henny's been charged with two counts of child abduction."

I sigh. "I read that in the paper."

"She confessed to taking the boys off a school lot. They were sitting outside after hours. They lived in the same neighborhood. Her boys didn't go to the public school, but Malik and Omari had heard of them."

My heart patters in my chest. It's frightful to consider.

"Their parents are dead. Killed in a small aircraft accident. Their closest relative was a great aunt on the mother's side, so the state asked her to take them in. She's in her eighties and did it for the money. She'd forgotten them at school."

"Sweet Jesus," I whisper. How do you forget two small children? My heart hammers harder, upset on their behalf.

"Henny admitted she offered the boys a ride when she saw them on the school steps. It's how she got them in the car."

Goodness.

"Malik didn't want to take the ride, but Omari was sick. It was raining, and he didn't want to walk home in the rain."

Though frightening, it's an honest mistake. If the boys thought she was someone's trusted mother, well . . .

"Did Malik confess these things?" I ask, surprised by what I'm learning but equally surprised Malik spoke.

"He wrote it out on paper. He's being assessed for speech although the social worker believes he can talk. He's just traumatized. His parents' death. Living with an elderly aunt. Kidnapping. Running away. Losing his brother." Chet exhales. It certainly is a lot for a little person. For any person.

"How did he get away from Henny? Why did he leave?"

"The deputy and forensic investigator have made up a scenario. They both think he saw an opportunity to escape and hoped to get help. Maybe got lost and wandered up the mountain until the boys found him. He didn't know where he'd come from or how to get back to his brother. Chances are, he thought all hope of finding his brother was lost."

"Poor precious," I whisper, and Chet turns his head to face me.

"He's going to need a lot of psychological help, which we can't offer at Harper House."

I understand. I do. Maura has explained.

"I don't like it," I say, keeping my voice quiet as I swallow the lump in my throat. The boys are being moved again, and with Chet revealing the great aunt, I panic. "Will they be returned to their aunt?"

"No. One strike against her is her age. She already lost them once, proving she had difficulty caring for them, and then, she never reported it. It's pretty clear she's not capable of parenting two small boys. Chances are they'll remain in the foster system, preferably together. Hopefully, they'll get adopted, but these cases are hard, and they'll have intense emotional scars to battle."

"They weren't physically harmed?" I question, suddenly feeling sick to my stomach.

"Not that we know of. Yet. Let's hope for the best there, darlin'." Chet shifts on the bed and mirrors my position. I'm lying on my right side, but he wiggles his finger into my hair and curls the strands he likes best around his finger, finding comfort in the movement, I suspect.

"A group home isn't ideal for every kid," he says by way of explanation. "A single-family home is considered the best setup. But even then, I know the system can be rough." He's speaking of his personal experiences growing up. While he's playing with my hair, I reach for his jaw, stroking over his beard with my fingertips. It's almost time for a trim, though there seems to be no rhyme or reason for how or when he'll do it. It doesn't matter to me. I'll take him either way—burly or bare—although I can't imagine him without facial hair.

"Can I ask you something?"

One brow arches encouraging me to ask.

"Why don't you live with the boys all the time? Especially Davis's sons."

"Darlin', I should not be in charge of children." He chuckles with the dismissive statement, but I disagree.

"You're amazing with those boys, and they need a strong male role model. You've shown them compassion, sacrifice, devotion, determination, and love."

Chet stares at me a few seconds before turning to face the ceiling and blowing out a breath.

"You know, Scotia, you're the first woman to know anything about those boys other than Maura." He rolls his head to face me once more. "First woman to connect with them outside of her and Savannah."

I smile slowly, proud that I'm included on the list.

"Remember when you said you didn't want to share me with anyone and keep me all to yourself? That's how I felt about them. I didn't want to share them because I didn't want anyone to hurt them. I couldn't bring a woman into their life if she didn't love them."

"I love them," I blurt, enthusiasm filling my voice.

Chet chuckles. "I know you do, darlin', but let me finish. I couldn't risk their hearts after losing their parents, and honestly, I didn't trust a woman to love them like I do. I mean, Maura does and Savannah, too, but I mean someone along with me. Someone like a partner in life."

A partner in life. The words whisper through my head, but I stumble on the thought. I was Karl's partner—we were equals, friends, comrades in our secret—but I wanted passion. I wanted purpose. I wanted love.

"I see," I whisper, and Chet rolls to face me.

"Do you? Do you understand that it's a risk to bring someone into their life? If that person leaves me, she leaves them, too, because I'm a package deal. You can't have me without having them."

I stare at him, completely puzzled. "I don't understand." What is he saying to me? Is he breaking up with me? I just told him I love the boys. I understand he comes with them, and they come with him.

"What I'm trying to say, and apparently not doing a good job of, is . . . I love you. I love that you love them. And they love you, and I'm hoping you might—"

I cut him off with my mouth plastered to his. I rise up, partially covering his body and kiss him, over and over again. I turn my head to angle better, taking his lips with mine and sucking at him. My heart races. My mind blown.

Then he chuckles against my mouth. "Darlin'?"

I don't let up. I need to kiss him. I need to feel him. My hands cup his face and stroke down his neck. My body is on the move, straddling him. My fingers find his chest and rake through the hairs on his firm pecs.

"Baby," he mutters, changing up the endearment, and I stop.

"Say it again," I whisper.

"Baby?"

"The other thing."

"I love you?" He softly chuckles, and my body vibrates over his. My hands cup both of his cheeks, and I lower my mouth toward his lips but stop just short of kissing him.

"Say you belong to me," I whisper to his lips.

"I belong to you, darlin'. And you belong to me."

Tears threaten my eyes. "I love you, too," I whisper with a soft breath, and he lifts his head, capturing my mouth and taking over control. I'm flipped to my back, and his hands wander up my sides, pushing up the nightie.

"I love how you love pretty things, darlin'." He returns to my mouth as his hand lifts the silky material until I'm naked. "But you're the prettiest thing I like to look at."

He's too much, and I can't get enough. His mouth lowers to a breast, sucking at me, swirling his tongue around the nipple and then giving me a nip. I arch into him.

"Again," I groan, and he repeats the action on my other breast. While his mouth works my upper body, his fingers lower. Tender fingertips find sensitive skin, and he easily slips into me. I'm on sensory overload as he laves one part of me and teases the other.

"Chet," I groan, tugging at his hair. He smiles against my breast, rubbing his rough chin hair between the valley of them.

"Gonna take my time tonight, darlin'. Gonna discover every part of you."

"You already know every part," I tell him. My head tips to the side and I sigh at the movement of his fingers at my core. *Oh God, that feels nice.*

"I want *every* part of you, Scotia. Body. Heart."

I turn my head back to him, meeting his eyes. "You have my heart, Chet." I purr after he twists his fingers in a way I don't recognize but appreciate. I have *so* much appreciation for his touch.

"I like you like this," he says, keeping his eyes on me while he lowers his mouth to a breast again.

"I love you like this," I admit. Chet moves down my body with those words, pressing open-mouth kisses along my skin until he gets to my center.

"I—" I choke on whatever I intended to say to him as his tongue flattens, and he licks me. He's tasted me before but not like this. Not by taking his time with me, torturing me, drawing out the deliciousness of his tongue over folds so sensitive and ready for him.

"You're wearing too many clothes," I whimper.

He laughs against me, and the vibration adds to the building tension. His tongue returns, and all thoughts are lost. I break apart, my body melting into the bed with the bliss of this man pleasuring me. Slowly, he lifts his body, holding himself up with one hand and undoing his pants with the other. He shoves them down only so far, and I hook my feet into the waistband, forcing them farther down his thighs.

He holds himself outside of me, toying with me, dragging himself through a place ready to accept him.

"You gonna be good to me, Chet Chester Chesterfield Big Poppy?" I flirt.

"So good, darlin'. You just wait and see."

He slides into me with those words, filling me like he does, and I marvel that each and every time seems better than the last. It makes no sense. Then again, neither do we—the biker-bar-and-motel-owning oil man with a past and the socialite pickle princess—but we're going to make it work.

Because I'm Scotia Simmons, and I always get what I want.

* * *

The next morning, I wake to the smell of bacon. Slipping a sweater over my nightie, I slide on thick socks and traipse down to the kitchen. Before me stands Chet clad in his jeans from the night before and a T-shirt. His backside is so fine in those pants, and the pull of his back muscles makes me want to curl into him. I hesitate only a second before walking up behind him and slipping my arms around his waist.

Standing in my kitchen, I press a kiss to his broad back, and he stills under my lips. Our position feels intimate in a new way. We've had sex. We've cuddled. And now, we've shared tender moments and precious words. A big hand covers my forearms, and he rubs his warm palm down my skin.

"Mornin', darlin'."

"Good morning. How are you today?"

"Feeling grateful," he states, and he spins in my arms. "Which reminds me, Thanksgiving is in a few days. What are you doing for it?"

"Oh, I . . . um . . . I didn't really have plans. My Darlene is going to visit her new man's family, and I don't want to intrude on my sisters. This is their first year with their men." Naomi and Nathan married last Christmas while Beverly and Jedd got engaged in the spring. They need time to continue basking in the glow of new love, and I don't want to encroach, even though I know they'd both include me if I asked to attend dinner.

"Come to dinner with me at the House, and then let me take you some-where." He isn't asking as much as telling me, but I don't mind.

"Where?" I ask coyly, leaning into his chest.

"Just something I do every Thanksgiving." His head lowers, and he twists his lips from side to side as though he's anxious about his invitation. I cup his jaw, lifting his heavy chin as best I can.

"Whatever it is, I'm going to love it."

"I love you," he says, his voice quiet, and I recall how I went into over-drive when I heard those words last night. Karl and I said them, but it was in more a casual, best friend manner. *Love you, Scotia. Love you, too.* The full phrase did not exist. There was no depth of meaning behind the words.

"I love you," I say, confident and louder than him. I tip up on my toes and press a kiss to him. Quickly, it heats, and as I try to pull back, he catches the back of my head to hold me to him.

Suddenly, I'm being lifted by the backs of my thighs. A yelp escapes me as Chet takes two steps and sets me on the island across from the stove. His mouth comes close to mine, but he doesn't kiss me.

"I like how you kiss me," he mutters.

"And how's that?" I question, breathing him in.

"Like you can't get enough of me."

"Hmm, that's what I was thinking."

A crooked smile tips the corner of his mouth, and he closes the distance. Our mouths meld together, slowly savoring one another in a lazy morning connection. I'll take these kinds of kisses any time of the day. My thighs spread, and he steps between my open legs. With my hands circling his neck, he slips his hands to my backside and tugs me to the edge of the counter. My heat meets his excitement, straining behind his zipper.

"Ever fuck on a countertop?" he questions, his mouth curling into a smile against mine.

"And if I have?" I counter, feeling a challenge coming on.

"I won't believe you," he teases, leaning me back with the press of his body. "I like what you're wearing, darlin'." His eyes roam my sweater over the silk nightie and my thick socks. He reaches behind him and turns off the stove. "But it's time to take it all off."

Oh, my.

CHAPTER 31

GRATITUDE

[Chet]

"Happy Thanksgiving, my darlings," Scotia cries out as the boys swarm her on Thanksgiving Day. I'm filled with more gratitude than I think I have a right to because the woman I love loves the people I love most in this world.

Maura scheduled dinner for one o'clock as she knows I have secondary plans later this evening. She understands.

Several times throughout the day, I'm caught staring at Scotia, and each time, she's looking back at me. Casual touches happen between us without thought, and Hugh finally side-eyes me.

"Uncle Chet, should we be having 'the talk'?" He lifts a teasing brow.

I grab his neck as I do and give him a gentle shove. "What do you know about 'the talk'?" I tease. We've had a talk about sex, but Maura handled more of the particulars. Davis would kill me if I let his son do the things we did at fourteen and that includes messing with girls. I take that back. Harper would be the one to hurt me. She wanted her sons to be gentlemen, and as I watch Scotia interact with them, I'm certain they will get some schooling in etiquette. Either way, Hugh's going to be a heart-breaker whether he's careful or not.

"Guess you upped your game." He winks at me, and I squeeze the nape of his neck.

"Yeah, I upped it." I can't help the smile on my lips, and I take another peek at Scotia, who wears a questioning expression when she gazes back at me. Sheepishly, she smiles and then looks back at Louie when he demands her attention.

Scotia was only melancholy a few times during the day, missing Malik as much as the boys did.

"We'll make it right somehow," I say to reassure her although I'm not certain what will happen next for him and his brother.

The meal and day pass too quickly, and I'm seeking out Scotia as we need to get a move on to the next activity when I hear her and Maura speaking in Maura's office.

"And you think this is the best way to proceed?" Scotia questions.

"Yes. You already offered legal guardianship. The great aunt accepted. That makes it so much easier for the state to place them with you, but it all depends on how quickly you complete the training and home visits. If you hustle, it shouldn't take more than three months."

"Three months? That seems like a lifetime," Scotia scoffs, and I'm trying to figure out what they're discussing.

"If you want to adopt them, you better get used to having some patience, Scotia."

What the fuck? "Excuse me," I stammer, stepping into the room and staring at my date. Scotia looks at Maura, and Maura lowers her head.

"I told you. You should have told him," Maura mutters.

Scotia sighs and holds her head higher. Turning it in that manner where she looks regal and refined, she glances up at me.

"I'm hoping to adopt Malik and Omari."

"Have you lost your ever-loving mind? Do you have any idea what it takes to raise kids like them?"

She stares at me, and it takes me a second to recall she has raised a child. A *girl* child. Who doesn't have half the issues Malik and his brother will have.

"Thank you for questioning my abilities as a mother," she dryly states.

"Do not give me the heiress attitude, darlin'. You know what I mean. Malik and Omari will need extensive support for their intense emotional needs."

"I accept that and plan to do all I can to help them." Her voice remains haughty and slightly aloof. But this isn't putting a bandage on a cut. These boys went through some serious shit.

"Maura thinks I have a good case," Scotia adds, and my attention turns on my partner.

"Did you know about this?" I direct at her.

"I . . . did." She folds her hands before her and lowers her head once again. I stare at my friend, wondering how she could allow this. How she could give Scotia hope.

"I've already raised a child, who is now a successful doctor. These are points in my favor. I'm financially sound, own my own home, and I'm not too old."

I stare at her, and her eyes slowly narrow.

"Do not give me a look like that. Forty-eight is not too old to adopt. Diane Keaton did it at fifty."

"We are not discussing Diane Keaton," I state, raising my voice.

"Plenty of foster parents are older, wanting to give back and help children. The system isn't perfect. You told me that yourself, but you're also proof that there are good places for those in need. I want to be one of those places."

"You don't know what you're getting into," I say, flabbergast by her decision, not to mention she hadn't told me *and* Maura knew.

"Actually, I do. From the moment I connected with Malik, I began researching the process to foster and foster-to-adopt specifically. Ms. Mason is aware of my desire. When it seemed Henny was in question, I reminded Maura what I wanted, should there be a need. Ms. Mason is thrilled that I'm offering to take Malik and Omari, as it is harder to adopt older children. But they are adoptable, and the goal is to get them out of the system when you have willing placement. I'm a willing placement. Plus, I already know Malik, and we have a connection. This helps my case for guardianship. Once I have that, the ball gets rolling."

I swipe a hand into my hair and stare at her, still thinking she's lost her damn mind.

"This could take a year," I state.

"I have time." Her eyes hold mine, and I sense a challenge in them. *Will I still be present in her life in a year?* I damn well better be.

"Fine," I mutter, and Scotia's shoulders relax. Maura's mouth falls open.

"Fine, as in you'll support my decision?" Scotia asks.

"Do you need my support?" I question.

"No." Scotia hesitates. "But I'd like it all the same." The first signs of chagrin cross her face, and I can't help myself. I reach for her, tugging her to me.

"If this is what you really want . . ."

"This is what I really want," she says, a smile in her voice.

God, help me with this woman. "Okay, darlin'. We'll figure it out."

Her head pops off my chest, and she peers up at me. "We?"

"Together."

* * *

"You're still mad," Scotia says from the passenger seat.

"I'm not mad," I state. I'm just trying to understand and process all the things. The woman I love wants to adopt two children who might have some intense needs. I've been reconsidering some things in my life, and I just don't see how this is all going to work, even though I promised we'd figure it out. I just want some time with her since all this is new between us. New to me.

"Fine. But, will you tell me where we're going?" she questions next. We're traveling The Tail, and it's growing dark quickly. I wanted to get us to our destination before sunset.

"I host Thanksgiving at The Fugitive. It's for the guys on the road. Riders who are alone. We don't know who will show, but we have a handful of regulars who know we're open and have been coming for years. I don't like to think of people out there alone on a holiday. Davis and I never wanted anyone to feel left out. He started the tradition, and I continue to honor it. I promised to always offer a spot at my table—a table at The Fugitive."

"Your heart just gets bigger and bigger," she whispers, and I risk a quick glance at her.

"I don't know what that means."

"The boys. These men. You are generous, *Big Poppy*." There's a smile in her voice, and that's what I need to hear because taking her to this dinner is a risk. She could hate what she hears, hate what she sees, and I need her to love all the parts of me.

"It might be an evening of rowdy motorcycle enthusiasts, drinking beer, and playing pool," I warn.

"I think I'm up for it," she states, confident in her answer.

"Yeah," I tease. "Might want to put away your pearls because the rest of this night could be rough." I wink at her. "And don't be flirty with any of the men in my bar."

She chuckles. "And if they flirt with me?"

"I'll be making it known you're my woman."

"Your woman? How very Neanderthal of you." She laughs harder.

"We've already established I like to carry you out of the bar over my shoulder."

"It was piggyback," she corrects with another laugh.

"Regardless, I have my ways. They all know you're mine," I state, and I sneak another quick glance to find her smiling.

"I might like you all caveman like this," she teases.

"I definitely like you as my woman."

When we arrive at The Fugitive, Scotia literally removes her pearls and unbuttons an additional button or two on her blouse.

"Whatcha doing, darlin'?"

"I'm getting as close to motorcycle mama as I can."

Not an inch of this woman from her high heels to her formfitting skirt and the uptight, starched shirt says, 'ready to ride', but after opening a couple of extra buttons and removing the pins from her hair, I'd say she's as close as she's ever going to get to being motorcycle material.

"You unbutton any more, darlin', and we aren't leaving this truck."

"Promises, promises," she sasses me before opening her own door and hopping out into the cold November night. I round the truck and reach for her hand, helping her over the icy lot. A light snow is falling, signaling winter's approach. When we enter the bar, we see Todd has the place set up with a banquet table set off to the side to hold all the potluck fixings and the turkey he cooked. Several tables are pushed together so no one sits alone.

News of our meal spreads by word of mouth. A set time is given so people know when dinner will be ready. The few stragglers who arrived early have been put to work.

"What can I do?" Scotia asks. "I've served hundreds of doctor dinners." The reminder of her late-husband irritates me, but I'm fully aware that Scotia is a socialite with etiquette training.

"Don't be expecting formal manners here, darlin'. This is a man's man kind of feast."

Scotia blinks up at me, and I want to press her against the bar and kiss her silly.

"A man's man," she chuffs. "Don't be turning sexist on me, Chet."

"Big Poppy," I remind her, stepping up to her and running my fingers down the length of the white stripe in her hair.

"Can I have a nickname?" she teases.

"Darlin', if we call you Mrs. Pickle here, there's going to be all kinds of razzing and inappropriate comments, not to mention unseemly gestures."

Scotia's lips slowly curl into a smile. "Maybe I'll like it."

"Maybe, you'll behave yourself. I don't want other men lusting after my woman," I growl as I lean forward to give her a quick kiss.

"Hey, pass that loving around," someone hollers, and Scotia stiffens.

"Saving all my kisses for this one. Sorry, Herbie." I tease the old man at the bar who doesn't need to be here tonight. He has a wife at home, but he comes here on the regular. I slip an arm around Scotia's back and tug her to me.

"Well, she sure does brighten up the place," Herbie comments, eyeing Scotia before he winks at her. "Though I don't know what a woman like her is doing with the likes of you."

"I ask myself the same thing," I mutter. Scotia places a hand on my belly.

"I'm giving all my kisses to this one," she calls out to the man on the barstool, and he laughs so hard he almost falls off.

Damn, she might fit in better than I thought.

The night proceeds with vulgar gestures and uncouth manners, and Scotia takes it all with a grain of salt, adding her own spice to the mix. She's attentive to everyone at the table, asking questions and sensing when there won't be an answer. She's not being intrusive but trying to get each man to speak while giving them her undivided attention for a few minutes. I hold my breath a time or two, thinking she's taken offense by what's said or on the verge of asking too much, but each man takes her in stride, knowing she's curious while generous with her interest.

I'm not much for small talk myself, but I watch and observe as Scotia seems to have this role down to a science. She knows just what to ask, how long to speak, and when to move on. Her socialite ways are showing, but I'm not upset.

When desserts are provided by the two girls who work for me, Scotia turns to me, placing a hand on my forearm.

"I wish I had known. I should have brought something to contribute," she says to me, but Striker answers from the other side of her.

"Just you being here is a contribution," he flirts.

"Am I gonna have a problem with you?" I challenge, and the fireman laughs.

"Not me, man. But I can't help how tempting she is."

I push back my seat, a physical warning to shut it. "*Ch*—Big Poppy, honey," Scotia says, turning her body toward mine and setting her hand on my thigh. My eyes meet hers, and they spark. She has this same look when I'm entering her. She's freaking turned on by this display of male dominance and show of aggression over her.

I lower my voice for only her. "You like me fighting for you, don't you?"

"No one's ever fought for me." Her eyes hold mine, but it's her quiet tone that raises the hairs on my neck.

"Here goes nothing then, darlin'. Ready?" Before she can answer, my hand is on her jaw, and I'm leaning in for her. She must sense what I'm about to do because she meets me in the middle, and our lips crash together, giving the entire table a sight as I kiss the stuffing out of her. Her hand comes to my cheek and her head tilts, giving me better access to her mouth and a swipe of tongue. She's leaning toward me, and she's going to be in my lap any second if I don't dial us down.

"Damn, that's something to be thankful for," Todd says, and Scotia pulls back, her eyes still on my face as she smiles sheepishly.

And I realize, I am most thankful for her.

* * *

The night runs late.

"Want to stay in a room?" The motel isn't full, and we could stay in a regular room if she wishes.

"Is something wrong with the bus?"

One brow shoots upward. "Besides the fact you don't like my bus?"

"I like your bus," she says, leaning toward me again, her gaze dipping to my lips. "But it's actually a tiny house. There's a difference."

Oh, boy. I laugh as I give Todd a wave. Scotia and I have already helped with cleanup. When she tried to reorganize our small kitchen, Todd had enough and kicked her out.

"We're efficient enough," he muttered.

I lead Scotia out the back door and then scoop her up in my arms, cradling her to my chest. She lets out a squeak, wrapping her arms around my neck as I make a path to my *tiny house.* Snow has continued to fall and piled up enough that she'd break her ankle in her heels.

"There's the caveman," she teases.

"I've been acting like a caveman all night over you," I retort. This moment shouldn't be anything new.

"Actually, this is romantic," she says, leaning her head on my shoulder.

"Oh, darlin', I do not do romance."

Scotia laughs in response.

When we reach the door, she uses her foot to press it inward, opening it enough so I can set her on a step, and she makes the climb into the bus herself. Once inside, I flip on the generator.

"It's going to take a bit to warm up but not too long," I say, rubbing my hands together as Scotia wraps her arms around her middle. Suddenly, I'm anxious about being on the old bus in the cold. "Maybe we should stay in a room."

Scotia steps up to me. "You could warm me up," she says seductively, curling her fingers into the edges of my jacket.

I stare at her for a second, taking in her silver eyes and midnight hair. The pure snow stripe along her face. My fingers pinch the strands, then twirl them over my finger, giving it a tug.

"That's the plan," I say.

"What else is the plan?" she questions, her voice dropping.

"What do you mean?" I ask, focusing on that strip of hair I love.

She shakes her head, dismissing her own question. Her fingers curl deeper into my jacket.

"Tell me three things," she whispers.

"You. Me. A bed." I tease, and she smiles up at me, fully accepting of my suggestion. I drag my finger down the fine white hair and think of three other things. "I love you."

"Chet," she whispers. I lean toward her mouth and wrap my arm around her back, lifting her off her feet enough so I can walk her backward and set her on the edge of my raised bed. She pulls back when her backside hits the mattress, and her hands reach for my scruffy cheeks.

"I love you," she says. "Thank you for today." She leans forward and kisses me. "And yesterday." She kisses me again. "And tomorrow."

"Darlin'." My throat clogs.

"Thank you for every day, Chet."

Jesus, do I love her.

"Thank you, darlin', for giving us a chance." My mouth lowers to hers, and I plan to show her how very grateful I am to have a chance to love her.

CHAPTER 32

GRATITUDE PART TWO

[Scotia]

I wake to dim light and excessive heat. Chet is wrapped around me, and I notice the darkening shades have been pulled around the bed area. It's very quiet, and for a moment, I feel as if I can hear the sound of peace. I take my time to recall the night before. The things Chet did to me. Bent over this bed. Straddling him on his giant chair.

He's a very sexual man and a generous lover. In everything we do, he considers me before doing it, and there isn't anything I'd deny him.

A kiss presses against the back of my neck. "Morning, darlin'," he grumbles in a sexy, deep voice. I twist in his arms and press a kiss to his nose.

"Good morning, honey." I bite my lip, thinking again of all we did last night and ignoring the tingle down low that wants a repeat of everything.

"I think it snowed all night," Chet says.

Filled with excitement at the prospect, I sit up and lift the edge of the darkening shade. "It's a winter wonderland out there."

A finger drags lazily up and down my naked spine. "You're a wonder-land," he states, his voice still rough from sleep. I smile to myself, gazing out the window. I sense him shift behind me, sitting up and pressing against my back.

"Let me see," he states. Chet lifts the shade higher and takes in the view.

"It's gorgeous," I say, unable to remember the last time I really looked at the beauty of nature around me. The world is covered in white with a light dusting still falling softly over the trees around us.

"You're gorgeous," Chet says at my back, and I turn to him as he leans against me.

"Who says you aren't romantic?" I kiss him, soft and tender, delicate and deep like the snow outside the window.

"Might need to call today a snow day," he says when we finally part, turning his sight out the window once more.

"What would that mean?" I ask, keeping my eyes focused on his profile. The strong features of his nose. The edge to his cheeks. The thick scruff on his jaw.

He glances back at me, his face close. "It means a day in bed and a repeat of all the things."

"*All* the things?" I teasingly question.

"All the things," he confirms. "But I need some coffee and a shower. Unfortunately, mine does not have room for two people."

Showering together?

"We could step over to the motel and use a room there." Chet hesitates, reminding me of his suggestion last night.

"I think I'm okay to stay right where we are," I flirt, leaning in for a kiss. He kisses me back but pulls away before I'm finished with his luscious mouth.

"Are you, darlin'? Are you okay with where we are?"

My stomach drops. Isn't he? I thought we were in a good place. "Aren't you?"

"I'm thinking." A thick palm swipes down his face. "What if I did move in with the boys permanently?"

I stare at him, uncertain what to say, but the pit in my belly has turned to flutters of excitement. He'd be so much closer to me if he lived in Green Valley.

"I think that would be wonderful. The boys would love to have you around all the time." I hesitate. "But what about here? The Fugitive and your bus?"

"I've been thinking about all that as well. I work remotely, mainly from the bar, so why can't I work at the house? Especially once the boys are at school." He looks around the space. "I love the bus, but it doesn't have a two-person shower or a decent kitchen. I still owe you a steak dinner." He's teasing me about the dinner we never shared on the night of Henny's arrest. We've had plenty of other dinners since that night.

"What will Maura do?" It isn't that I'd mind if Maura and Chet lived together. I'm confident in their relationship being one of strong friendship, not too dissimilar from Karl and me. There's no romantic interest, just a platonic business arrangement between them.

"You know, I snapped up Maura when she wanted to leave foster care. Something happened that isn't my story to share, but she agreed to be what amounts to a round-the-clock nanny. When Hunter came along, Maura fell in love with him, and the foster home was born. She'd had so many troubled teens, and she just wanted to start at the bottom for once. Adopting an infant really helped her. I know she loves my boys, but I think in her heart, she's ready to have her own home with a little less chaos in her life."

I nod, thinking Chet knows her best.

"So you'd live in the house with the boys full-time."

"Yep." He slowly smiles. "This way, you could come to visit. It's a helluva lot less driving and a less risky drive at that." Navigating down The Tail of the Dragon in the winter wasn't exactly something I wanted to do, but I'd take the risk to see him.

"I'll help Maura get set up somewhere and give Savannah some other options for employment."

"What about cooking?" I lift a brow.

"I'll just have to practice. Been a bachelor most of my life, so I have a few skills." He wiggles his brows, and I snort, then cover my mouth at how unattractive it sounded. Chet removes my hand and kisses me, melting away my embarrassment. Then he pulls away again too quickly.

"So what do you think?"

"I love the idea," I say because I do. I want him to be closer to me. I want the boys to have him all the time, and I think it would be good for him to live with them. He can do this. He just hasn't given himself enough credit.

"I'm probably going to mess them up," he says, pressing a kiss to my bare shoulder.

"Parenting isn't a perfect job."

"I'm not their parents." His voice drops, and I hear the sorrow at the loss of his friends.

Reaching for his jaw, I press his face upward. "Chet, you're the parent they have now. You aren't replacing what they lost, but they're gaining you. You've always been there for them, and that's all they need to know. They can't have their parents back, but they can have you. That's all that matters."

He stares at me for a second.

"You're going to be great for Malik and Omari," he says, his voice quiet.

"Yeah?" I whisper.

"Yeah. It's going to be a lot to take on, especially at first. I hope you still have room for me and the boys in all the chaos."

"Chet," I whisper. "I'm not going anywhere. And if I have any say about it, neither are you. You're going to fit right where you are. In my heart. In my bed. I'll need you."

He gazes at me while I speak and slowly nods. I don't like the doubt in him, but time will prove I want to be with him. I want to be with all my men—him and the Maverik boys, and Malik and Omari.

"They're going to be so lucky to have you."

"I'm going to be lucky to have them." I press a kiss to him. "And I'm lucky to have you."

"Now, who's being all romantic?" he teases.

"I really like you like this," I flirt.

"I really love you," he says, leaning in for another kiss.

"Mmm," I purr as our mouths meet. "That too." Then I kiss him back, and this time, I don't let him pull away so quickly. We tumble back to the bed, deciding neither of us needs a shower or coffee yet. Snow day in bed it is.

CHAPTER 33

ADOPTING A NEW PERSPECTIVE

[Scotia]

December

I've never spent the day in bed exploring a man and talking with him, but Chet and I do just that. The rest of the weekend's a blur.

On Monday, I continue the process to seek legal guardianship.

"You are persistent, Mrs. Simmons," Ms. Mason, the caseworker, states.

"You haven't seen anything yet, honey. I want those boys sooner rather than later." Every day apart feels like a day we lose on building our own relationship. Thankfully, Ms. Mason agrees on supervised visitation with the boys in their alternative placement. This gives me peace of mind and gives her time to observe our interactions together.

After hours of phone calls and internet searches, I place my elbows on my desk, my head in my hands, and close my eyes for a second.

A cup of coffee is placed before me.

"Gideon?" I stare up at my assistant.

"I just want you to know I think you're doing a good thing."

I sit straighter in my chair, leaning back and peering up at my assistant, who's standing on the other side of my desk.

"What do you mean?"

"Adopting those boys." Gideon sniffs. "I just think it's wonderful."

"Gideon, do you have nothing better to do than listen in on my phone calls?" I glare at him. We're working on getting our pickle nuggets to each vendor before the next holiday, especially New Year's since appetizers are plentiful in places hosting parties. I should be working on such things, but instead, I've spent most of this day organizing.

"Don't you sass me, Mrs. Simmons. Not when I'm trying to compliment you," he snips, and I should scold him for insubordination, but I don't have the energy. Plus, I like him. He's a hard worker, and that's credit I don't often give to others.

"What have you heard?" I sigh, knowing even though his desk is outside my office, the door has been open all day.

"You're going to adopt those poor babies kidnapped by that crazy woman."

"She wasn't crazy," I state, surprised at myself for defending her. To me, Henny Heiner was a sad, pathetic woman who never accepted what she had was enough until it was too late, and even then, she still felt entitled to more. If she loved her children, I can't say I blame her for losing her mind a little bit over the loss of them. Hennessy will spend eighteen months per conviction in prison, which was two counts of child abduction. She'll be up for parole before those three years are served if she displays good behavior. Either way, she'll need heavy psychiatric support. Mental illness was a part of her plea, including post-traumatic stress disorder. As she had no prior convictions of any sort, she's receiving a minimal sentence.

Chet and I eventually discussed *why* Henny came back to him. He didn't have any answers, only assumptions. He'd learned that Henny's husband was leaving her which is how he was on that mountain road the night of the accident. Jeffrey Heiner sold off Henny's father's company in order to free himself of his wife. Henny had lost so much—her children, her husband, her wealth—and she was grappling to restore the past with new children, a reclaimed lover, and a man with money at that. It's the best answer we could think of to explain her actions and intentions. Eventually, we decided we didn't need to know Henny's motives. *She* was in the past for Chet.

"Well, either way, adopting two little boys . . . it's just so noble."

"I don't feel noble." I pause, looking up at him. "Am I doing the right thing? Would they be better with a young couple instead? Am I thinking too big?"

Gideon slowly lowers himself to the chair opposite the desk. "Can one think too big when it comes to children? Could you love them unconditionally?"

I stare at him a second, knowing what he means and forming my answer, but he speaks before me.

"What I mean is, can you accept that they had parents they lost and know that you can't replace them? You'll need to love without immediate gratification, at least until they learn you're a good woman when you want to be."

I said something very similar to Chet.

"Is that a backhanded compliment?" I question, taking his meaning. If I put my mind to doing right, I know the difference from wrong.

"It's a comment. If you're doing this for the right reasons . . . because those boys need someone stable to love them . . . then yes, you're doing a good thing."

"Am I too old?" I question, speaking out loud doubts I hadn't felt when I first decided to take on Malik, and then Omari. "I'm forty-eight. Is it too late to be raising children, especially ones who aren't mine yet?" The question of *yet* leaves me longing for them even more.

"Age is relative, as they say. You aren't spry, but that doesn't mean you can't spring. You have the energy of a twentysomething with the temper of a two-year-old and the tongue of someone eighty. I think you can handle two little boys who aren't toddlers and not quite teens."

"Thank you, Gideon. I think." My hands slide along the edge of my desk. My gaze lowers to my fingers, noting the veins sticking out on the back of my hands. *It's time for this desk to be replaced*, I decide on a whim.

"People are going to talk. Some will judge me. Some will say I did this for nefarious reasons. Others will disagree with my decision."

"With all due respect, Scotia, when have you ever given a fig what other people think of you?"

Honestly, I've worried what others thought of me all my life. Lashing out at others first was to protect myself from judgement and rejection. *Mask in place, Scotia.* It's been a lonely life living with Karl's secret, constantly working at keeping it, constantly worrying others would find out.

"In some ways, I've always given a *fig*," I state, using his word. "But then again, I normally do what I want, don't I?"

"You sure do," he says, laughter filling his voice. "And that isn't always a bad thing. Look at this business." Gideon tips back and looks around the room with samples of our wares and designs over the years along with that phallus-like trophy and a few other plaques awarding my fried pickles.

"You know, if I take on a second family, I'm going to need you to pull more weight around here, young man," I say to my assistant, who sits up in his chair, stiffening his back. "You're going to have to stop eavesdropping and actually do some work."

Gideon's eyes widen, but a slow grin curls his lips, and my own follows his lead.

"You're a better woman than people give you credit for," Gideon says, leaning forward and whispering as if conspiring with me.

"Let's keep that between us. I have a reputation to protect." I wink.

"Think it's going to be shot to hell when people start seeing you around town with tall, dark, and dreamy."

I laugh. "Who's that?"

"Don't you play coy with me, missy. I know what you almost did on this desk with that lumberjack wannabe."

"Gideon! I don't know what you're talking about."

"Uh-huh." He stands. "Your secrets are safe with me." With that, my assistant dismisses himself but turns back to me at the door. "I'm proud of you, Mrs. Simmons."

He exits before I can express my gratitude, but I say it all the same to the empty office. "Thank you."

* * *

"You're going to *what*?" Beverly stares at me over the table at Daisy's Nut House. Naomi has remained speechless during my explanation.

"I'm going to be a foster parent to two young boys," I repeat. I've just informed them of my relationship with Chet, volunteering at Harper House, and how I met Malik, and eventually, his brother, Omari.

"Why?" Beverly asks. This is the question I'm expecting to answer over and over again, even though I just explained myself to my sisters. When I met Malik Evans, there was just something about his quiet reserve that told me a lot was going on in his mind. He was either going to shut himself inside or lash out at the world as I had. His silence frightened me on his behalf. He needed to know someone cared and had his best interests at heart. Without knowing what happened to him, I made that person be me.

"Because I want to," I state, frustrated as I've already explained myself. Naomi's mouth falls open with my explanation while Beverly stares at me. Exasperated, I ask, "What do you think the reason should be?"

"To give love. To help others. To be a teacher and a listener and a provider. To inspire and to comfort. To—"

"To be all the things you want to be," Naomi interjects, holding her gaze on me. "You want to adopt them to give them all the things you can give to others." Naomi's voice softens as if she really understands my reasons.

"I just want these boys," I say.

"Because Darlene is gone? Is this some empty-nester thing?" Beverly's daughter, Hannah, is on the verge of leaving their home.

"I'm not looking to replace Darlene."

"What does she think of this?" Naomi asks. My own daughter is old enough to be a mother to children the ages of Malik and Omari.

"She doesn't know yet." She's busy living her life as she should, but I want to keep living mine, and this is what I want to do with it. I want to take on these two children. I want to do things my way this time.

"What about Big Poppy?" Beverly questions, lowering her voice, and I almost chuckle at his biker name coming from her.

"Chet is equal parts hopeful and hesitant. He's worried about the boys and me, but he also accepts that we need each other." And I need him and his boys.

"Is it so wrong to want this?" I lean back in the booth, staring out the window at the lightly falling snow. It's the beginning of December, and Christmas will be here soon. The coming holiday season has an air of excitement I haven't felt in years.

"There's nothing wrong with what you're doing if you're doing it for the right reasons," Naomi says, and my head swivels back to my sisters sitting across from me in the booth.

"I'm not saying you shouldn't do it. I'm just trying to understand," Beverly adds.

Does she need to understand? Does anyone? It's my decision. It's my life.

"I hope you'll both be involved aunts." The statement shocks them. Hannah and Darlene are not close despite being first cousins. We kept our lives relatively separate from each other when they were children. I don't want that to happen again.

"Of course, we will," Naomi says for the two of them, lifting her clasped hands under her chin as a slow smile brightens her face. She now has two stepdaughters with Nathan, the youngest is near Malik's age and has a crush on Dewey Maverik.

"We're here for whatever you need," Beverly says, reaching across the table for my hand. I hesitate before I take it but gratefully accept the offering.

"Why do I feel like we're having a *Steel Magnolias* moment?"

"Because you act like Shirley MacLaine's character, Ouiser," Beverly retorts.

"Who would that make you?" I ask.

"I'm more like M'Lynn hovering over her daughter, I guess," Beverly admits, a smile crossing her lips.

"That makes me that one who didn't know anything about sex," Naomi adds. "But I do now," she proudly states, and Beverly and I can't help but laugh.

She has no idea how much I can relate to that.

CHAPTER 34

A NEW YEAR

[Scotia]

January

It took six weeks to obtain legal guardianship and have the boys awarded to me for residential living. I called Ms. Mason every day until she was so sick of me that she rushed through my requests. It also helped that I was willing to be a kinship placement—with the legal guardianship status—while we waited for my official foster parent license to come in. My criminal background checks and references had been processed quickly thanks to my volunteer work at Harper House, so all we were waiting on was a few training classes to be completed. I wasn't interested in the money the state would provide me for support, so it worked out best for all of us.

While it might have seemed soon, I moved in with Chet after Christmas to give Malik and Omari familiarity with a place they'd already been. Chet is already licensed to foster, and I've almost got mine, plus I have guardianship of the boys, so there isn't much of a 'legal' issue with all of us living together. I also just wanted to live with him. We wanted to be together as much as we could with our newly hectic lives.

Maura and I had a long talk and she told me some horror stories and heartbreak of being a foster parent, although not all tales were such. Her heart is so large but she's also only human, and she could only take so much. Her last 'child' had been a teen and his history nearly broke her. When Chet asked her for help, and eventually Hunter arrived on their doorstep, she took it as a sign. Not only that her time as a foster mother wasn't done, but a chance to become a mother to her own child had arrived.

She was ready for a family that belonged only to her.

"You're our family as well," Chet reminded her, telling her our door was always open to the Hawes family.

With Campbell and Hunter, she moved into my house. "Take it as a gift," Chet told her as he handed her the keys and Maura sobbed, assuring us it wasn't tears of regret that she was leaving the house on the mountain but gratitude at Chet being her friend. I'm glad she considers me a friend as well.

Savannah was offered a position at The Fugitive, but she declined.

When Malik and Omari finally arrive, there's a bit of excitement. We have gifts and a party, celebrating as if it's a birthday. A new day. A new start. It's eventually overwhelming for the new boys, and I see Malik shutting down. That's when I ask him and Omari to follow me.

We climb the stairs of the large home, which has four bedrooms on the upper level. Hugh has his own room now. Dewey and Louie share. Chet and I have a room, and there's a final space.

"This is your bedroom," I say, opening the door to reveal a set of twin beds and a newly decorated room in a variety of blues with a splash of red. Originally one of the guest rooms, now it is permanently theirs.

Omari is more verbal and enthusiastic, and he rushes for a bed, bouncing on it. Malik remains quiet, slowly taking in the space around him.

"Do you like it?" I whisper, lowering to a squat next to him. "We can change it if you don't."

Malik turns to look at me, his eyes wide and cautious. We have a ways to go to get him to fully open up, and I accept this permanent move to Harper House as one more change for him. But this is the final stop on the craziness of his life over the past year.

If there's one thing I sense with Malik, it's that he trusts me, and it's made such a difference to me. His blind faith that I'm here for him speaks volumes even when he's quiet.

I point at the bookshelf. "I've bought a few things, but we can go to the bookstore for more. I have a library card, so we can go to the library and get as many books as you'd like. My sister Naomi works there, remember? She can't wait to see you again."

Malik and Omari were introduced to my sisters in stages so as not to overwhelm them. Naomi was an instant hit with her quirky style and *Harry Potter* knowledge. Malik hadn't read the books yet and we are working through them together. Naomi assured him he'd love the library as its newly reconstructed and improved with multiple departments. The children's section is still a hit.

Beverly and Jedd met Malik and Omari together. Despite Jedd's loud voice, he has a way of soothing souls, like his horses, and Omari took an instant interest in the mechanics of Jedd's 'bionic' arm as he calls his prosthetic. Beverly recognizes the closed off demeanor of Malik, and she tells me it might take time for him to open up, but he'll get there. She eventually let people back into her life. She's promised both boys Jedd will teach them how to ride horses. When she offered to teach them how to make soap, Omari worried he'd have to bathe more often.

"We can design one specifically called Omari Odor and make it smell like dirt," Beverly told him. He might have instantly fallen in love with her.

Omari has moved off the bed he's been jumping on and rustles around in a bin of Legos.

"Feel free to build whatever you'd like. A tower to the moon or a bridge between beds," I tell him. He doesn't look up at me, but Malik slips his hand to my shoulder. His hesitant touch startles me, and I turn back to him.

"You're going to be safe here, Malik. We'll get through this. All of it. Together." I place my hand on his lower back. I've been told not to expect affection from the children and to be cautious with my own. I'd ignored the rules already—offering my hand at will and allowing him to lean into me —long before this moment. So when he leans against my arm, the position doesn't surprise me. What does is, he slips his arm around my shoulders, and I gently tug him to my side.

"I'm so glad you're here, my precious boy. We belong to each other now." I bite my lip when a tear trickles from his eye.

We're going to be okay. All of us.

EPILOGUE

TENNESSEE ENTREPRENEUR CONVENTION

[Chet]

March

We've just entered the bar when I hear Scotia speak.

"Oh no, she didn't," she mutters and releases my arm, making a beeline for a group of women. They could be the same women from last year she told me about . . . or not. I have no idea, as my sight was only set on one woman a year ago. And now, she is the same woman on my arm.

We're back at the Omni Hotel for the annual entrepreneurial conference. Scotia Simmons was nominated once again for her female-led small business. She didn't win *again*, but she politely cheered on the winner.

"I've already won everything I need to win," she'd said earlier when I turned to her, trying to gauge her reaction.

That's my girl.

I slowly follow her rapid steps to the gathered group of women.

"I wonder who he'll go home with tonight," mutters one of the three ladies seated at a low table.

"He does look fine in a tuxedo, but something's different about him this year. I can't place my finger on it," a second woman states.

"Hi, y'all," Scotia drawls in her sugar-sweet killer voice. *Uh-oh.*

"Oh, Scotia, honey. I hadn't seen you there. We were just discussing Mr. Chesterfield. Too bad you're out of the running this year as I heard you had him last year," the last remarks.

What the fuck?

"*Had* him?" Scotia defends, tsking as she shakes her head from side to side. Her eyes meet mine as I stand close enough to hear this interaction but just out of sight of two ladies. The other looks up to face me.

"I'm not interested in *sharing* him, ladies. That's the issue. That's my man you're speaking about." Her smile grows, and I softly chuckle.

Well, look at my Scotia, being all cavewoman.

"And yes, he does look fine in a tuxedo. He looks even finer out of it, but y'all will never know that detail." Her smile ratchets up to something so forced it must hurt her cheeks, but she's defending me, so I let it go that she just told these ladies how *fine* I look naked. "And the difference in him is he's in love. With me." She points at herself, and I see her chest rise. If I didn't know any better, I'd think she's ready to throwdown with these women right in the middle of their seats. But I know my girl, and she'd never physically hurt someone. Verbally, maybe, but not with her hands. Her hands are reserved for tender touches and teasing caresses, which reminds me I want to get upstairs instead of working this bar.

With five boys between us, we hardly have alone time. Our lives are filled with chaotic activity. MMA classes and horse-riding lessons. School-work and discipline. Hugh and his girlfriends, and Dewey and his science projects. And the only thing I'd change, if I could, is my best friend seeing his boys thrive.

"Darlin'," I say, tipping my head to the door, and Scotia gives a finger wave to the women.

"See ya'll next year," she states. "You ladies have a good night." She circles the group and slips her arm back into mine. I chuckle as she does.

"Well, I certainly didn't expect that," I state.

"I'm just defending what's mine," she says, and a wave of pride rolls over me. *I'm hers.*

"Might have been a bit much, especially that part about me looking fine without my tux."

"I'm just being honest," she flirts, leaning into my arm. We've talked about her *honesty*, and she admits she's been trying to rein it in, especially when it comes to less than positive remarks about others. She's definitely been a work in progress, and I hope the job is never complete.

"I was one breath away from telling them how good you are in bed, but I thought that would be a bit much."

"You can show me how good I am once we get to the room," I growl, pulling her into the elevator. We're returning to the scene of our first night. Only this time, Scotia won't be spending a portion in the bathroom. Not unless it involves both of us in the shower or me taking her against the sink. Either sounds like a fine option.

We enter the room and tumble onto the bed.

"Tell me three things," she whispers under me.

"You. Me. Love," I whisper, and her eyes turn dreamy. There's no more sadness hidden behind those silver orbs. No more shutters or shield to protect her heart.

"I love you, too, honey." Her voice is a breathy whisper when she says them back to me as though each word has its own deeper meaning. She. Loves. Me. I lower for one more kiss before I say what's been on my mind lately.

"I have three other words for you," I state and rush out the rest. "Let's get married."

"What?" Scotia whispers, pulling back from me a bit. It's not exactly the reaction I was expecting from her, but then again, I didn't know what she'd think. We already live together but I want something that marks us as permanent in every way. She belongs with me, and I belong to her.

"I'd like to marry you, Scotia." Her fingers cover my lips, as if she can trace the words from my mouth and imprint them on her fingertips. Quickly, her mouth follows, meeting mine. The kiss is abrupt. She pulls back, and I wonder if we should forget the past few minutes and what I said. She's going to refuse me.

"I'd like to marry you, too." Her eyes shimmer.

My shoulders relax, and I exhale a breath I didn't realize I was holding. "You don't think it's too soon?" However, everything with his woman has been fast. Our first morning. Our second chance together. Our falling in love.

"Are you trying to talk me out of it less than five seconds after asking me?" She chides, stroking her fingertips against the scruff on my jaw.

"No, darlin'. I want you to belong to me."

"I do belong to you," she whispers. "And if you'll have me, I'd love to marry you, Chet Chester Chesterfield Big Poppy."

"You know I'm really only one man."

"I might have a crush on all three, though." Her mouth slowly curls into a smile.

"Which one do you like best?" I tease, lowering to rub my nose against hers, and she gently pushes my face back to meet my eyes.

"This one," she says, holding my gaze. "I like this one best. The one who looks at me like you do. The one who holds my hand and my heart. The one giving me new perspective and taming my tongue."

"I like that tongue."

Her smile grows, splitting her face into a large grin. "I like best the man who loves me, and I love him." She pauses a beat. "I relish him." A small giggle escapes her.

"Did you just make a pickle pun when I'm trying to propose to you?" I laugh as well while I partially blanket her body, and she swings a leg over my hips.

"That I did. Now show me your pickle."

"Darlin', you know it's more than a pickle down there."

"Eggplant?" She scrunches up her nose, recalling our discussion once about phallic symbols.

"I thought you said that'd hurt," I tease.

"The only shape I want is the shape of you and your giant . . . heart." She breaks into laughter at her teasing, and that's my cue to kiss her senseless. Because if there's one thing I know about Scotia Simmons, it's that she loves to kiss me and she easily comes undone under me.

"I love you like this," she says against my mouth as I work my hands under her skirt.

"I love you," I remind her. "Sweet *and vinegar.*"

"Mmm," she purrs when my hand drags up her inner thigh and I reach her sweet spot. "I like to hear that." Her breath hitches as my fingers brush aside the pretty panties she loves to wear and enter her. "And I love you too, honey. *All* of you.

That she does. She loves each part of me, and I love each part of her, even when she gets a little mouthy. As she continues kissing me, I realize her mouth might be one of my favorite parts about her.

ACKNOWLEDGMENTS

(L)ittle (B)its of Gratitude
And a few bits of explanation.

This book is a work of fiction, and in such, I've taken liberty with The Tail of the Dragon, a beautiful and dangerous stretch of road linking Tennessee and North Carolina in the Smoky Mountains. As an eleven-mile portion of US129 with 318 curves, it's quite a destination, especially for motorcycle enthusiasts, and I drove it in March 2019 in my Jeep. I'm afraid of heights, and let me tell you, I was shaking by the time I finished. White knuckled. Sweaty armpits. Heart thumping. The drive taught me that this road is no joke and takes a lot longer to travel than I've portrayed in this book.

Please remember, this is fiction.

What isn't fictional—and I tried my best to have correct—is the foster care system. I have great respect for those willing to take on children in need. Parenting anyone is never easy. Parenting children with special circumstances can seem daunting, but people do it. People like the Maura Haweses in the world. People like M. E. Carter, author and friend, who helped me extensively with information about foster parenting: the roles, the rules, the process, and the emotions. I am so very, very grateful for her extra eyes on this work, and if fault is found with anything, I take full responsibility.

This work, along with *Love in Due Time* and *Love in Deed*, concludes the Winters Sisters chronicles, the lives of three sisters created by the wonderfully talented and generous author Penny Reid. It has been an extreme honor to take her characters, make them my own, and give them a story. It was a bit challenging to take on Scotia Simmons, a character readers love to hate. Giving Scotia a reason for her meanness, I'm hopeful she has a second chance in Reiders' hearts. I adore her (now). Remember: we never know the silent sufferings of others. Be kind. Penny Reid and her Smartypants Romance imprint embodies this philosophy.

On that note, I want to thank the other authors in the Smartypants Romance sisterhood. The collection of talented, sensitive, and creative writers in the group is incredible, and again, I'm so honored to be among them on this journey.

Thank you to Brooke Nowiski and Fiona Fischer for administration at SPRU, and your time and energy in corralling us authors. And additional gratitude to SPRU editors Judy and especially Rebecca who made me rethink much of the story.

And for those in the know: Shabnam, Erica, Stacey, Lois, Shannon, and Anne Marie – thank you for your generosity to do yet another read when panic set in and I freaked out. Your quick responses and attention to detail where a huge help.

Thank you, generous reader (or Reider), for allowing me to enter Green Valley, help build the world of a beloved fictional community, and make my own small mark among book-family and book-friends we love dearly.

On my individual writing team, I want to thank Melissa Shank for her endless support and patience, and Jenny Simms for edits (She edited 13 books of mine in 2020!). Thank you to Karen Fischer for her finishing-touch proofreading skills.

To all the readers in Loving L.B., who enjoy a shared love of things sexy and silver and over 40, thank you for taking this detour into Green Valley with me. It takes a village – or rather a valley – and you are my people, who keep me grounded, laughing and sane.

And finally, gratitude to my family: Mr. Dunbar, MD, MK, JR and A, for indulging Mom's fantasy and allowing me to make my dreams come true as a wife, a mother . . . and a writer.

ABOUT THE AUTHOR

Love Notes
www.lbdunbar.com

L.B. Dunbar has an over-active imagination. To her benefit, such creativity has led to over thirty romance novels, including those offering a second chance at love over 40. Her signature works include the #sexysilverfoxes collection of mature males and feisty vixens ready for romance in their prime years. She's also written stories of small-town romance (Heart Collection), rock star mayhem (The Legendary Rock Stars Series), and a twist on intrigue and redemption (Redemption Island Duet). She's had several alter egos including elda lore, a writer of romantic magical realism through mythological retellings (Modern Descendants). In another life, she wanted to be an anthropologist and journalist. Instead, she was a middle school language arts teacher. The greatest story in her life is with the one and only, and their four grown children. Learn more about L.B. Dunbar by joining her reader group on Facebook (Loving L.B.) or subscribing to her newsletter (Love Notes).

* * *

Keep in touch with L.B. Dunbar
www.lbdunbar.com
Stalk Me: https://www.facebook.com/lbdunbarauthor
Instagram Me: @lbdunbarwrites
Read Me:
https://www.goodreads.com/author/show/8195738.L_B_Dunbar

Follow Me: https://www.bookbub.com/profile/l-b-dunbar
Tweet Me: https://twitter.com/lbdunbarwrites
Pin Me: http://www.pinterest.com/lbdunbar/
Get News Here: https://app.mailerlite.com/webforms/landing/j7j2s0
AND more things here
Hang with us: Loving L.B. (reader group): https://www.facebook.com/groups/LovingLB/

Find Smartypants Romance online:
Website: www.smartypantsromance.com
Facebook: www.facebook.com/smartypantsromance/
Goodreads: www.goodreads.com/smartypantsromance
Twitter: @smartypantsrom
Instagram: @smartypantsromance

ALSO BY L.B. DUNBAR

<u>Lakeside Cottage</u>

Living at 40

Loving at 40

Learning at 40

<u>Silver Fox Former Rock Stars</u>

After Care

Midlife Crisis

Restored Dreams

Second Chance

Wine&Dine

<u>The Silver Foxes of Blue Ridge</u>

Silver Brewer

Silver Player

Silver Mayor

Silver Biker

<u>Collision novellas</u>

Collide

<u>Smartypants Romance (an imprint of Penny Reid)</u>

Love in Due Time

Love in Deed

Love in a Pickle

The World of True North (an imprint of Sarina Bowen)

Cowboy

Studfinder

Rom-com for the over 40

The Sex Education of M.E.

The Heart Collection

Speak from the Heart

Read with your Heart

Look with your Heart

Fight from the Heart

View with your Heart

A Heart Collection Spin-off

The Heart Remembers

THE EARLY YEARS

The Legendary Rock Star Series

The Legend of Arturo King

The Story of Lansing Lotte

The Quest of Perkins Vale

The Truth of Tristan Lyons

The Trials of Guinevere DeGrance

Paradise Stories

Abel

Cain

The Island Duet

Redemption Island

Return to the Island

<u>Modern Descendants – writing as elda lore</u>

Hades

Solis

Heph

ALSO BY SMARTYPANTS ROMANCE

Green Valley Chronicles

The Love at First Sight Series

Baking Me Crazy by Karla Sorensen (#1)

Batter of Wits by Karla Sorensen (#2)

Steal My Magnolia by Karla Sorensen(#3)

Fighting For Love Series

Stud Muffin by Jiffy Kate (#1)

Beef Cake by Jiffy Kate (#2)

Eye Candy by Jiffy Kate (#3)

The Donner Bakery Series

No Whisk, No Reward by Ellie Kay (#1)

The Green Valley Library Series

Love in Due Time by L.B. Dunbar (#1)

Crime and Periodicals by Nora Everly (#2)

Prose Before Bros by Cathy Yardley (#3)

Shelf Awareness by Katie Ashley (#4)

Carpentry and Cocktails by Nora Everly (#5)

Love in Deed by L.B. Dunbar (#6)

Dewey Belong Together by Ann Whynot (#7)

Hotshot and Hospitality by Nora Everly (#8)

Love in a Pickle by L.B. Dunbar (#9)

Scorned Women's Society Series

Common Threads Series

Mad About Ewe by Susannah Nix (#1)

Give Love a Chai by Nanxi Wen (#2)

Key Change by Heidi Hutchinson (#3)

Educated Romance

Work For It Series

Street Smart by Aly Stiles (#1)

Heart Smart by Emma Lee Jayne (#2)

Lessons Learned Series

Under Pressure by Allie Winters (#1)

CPSIA information can be obtained
at www.ICGtesting.com
Printed in the USA
BVHW072342031021
618069BV00003B/160

9 781949 202762